See

A native of Dundee, Marion Todd studied music with the Open University and worked for many years as a piano teacher and jobbing accompanist. A spell as a hotel lounge pianist provided rich fodder for her writing and she began experimenting with a variety of genres. Early success saw her winning first prize in the *Family Circle Magazine* short story for children national competition and she followed this up by writing short stories and articles for her local newspaper.

Life (and children) intervened and, for a few years, Marion's writing was put on hold. During this time, she worked as a college lecturer, plantswoman and candle-maker. But, as a keen reader of crime fiction, the lure of the genre was strong, and she began writing her debut crime novel. Now a full-time writer, Marion lives in North-east Fife, overlooking the River Tay. She can often be found working out plots for her novels while tussling with her jungle-like garden and walking her daughter's unruly but lovable dog.

Also by Marion Todd

Detective Clare Mackay

In Plain Sight
Lies to Tell
What They Knew
Next in Line
Old Bones Lie

MARION TODD

See them run

San Diego, California

Canelo US
An imprint of Printers Row Publishing Group
9717 Pacific Heights Blvd, San Diego, CA 92121
www.canelobooksus.com

Printers Row Publishing Group is a division of Readerlink Distribution
Services, LLC. Canelo US is a registered trademark of Readerlink
Distribution Services, LLC.

This edition originally published in the United Kingdom in 2020 by
Canelo.

Published in partnership with Canelo.

Correspondence regarding the content of this book should be sent to Canelo
US, Editorial Department, at the above address. Author inquiries should be
sent to Canelo, Unit 9, 5th Floor, Cargo Works, 1–2 Hatfields, London SE1
9PG, United Kingdom, www.canelo.co.

Publisher: Peter Norton • Associate Publisher: Ana Parker
Art Director: Charles McStravick
Senior Developmental Editor: April Graham
Editor: Traci Douglas

Production Team: Beno Chan, Julie Greene

Design: Brianna Lewis

Library of Congress Control Number: 2022941725

ISBN: 978-1-6672-0382-9

Printed in India

27 26 25 24 23   1 2 3 4 5

For my mum and dad,

Catherine and Jack

Chapter 1

Saturday, 18th May

'And if the bride and groom would like to lead the way… let's have you all up on the floor for the Orcadian Strip the Willow.'

Couples began streaming onto the dance floor. 'Strip the Willow' was popular enough, but the Orcadian version was a floor-filler and the highlight of any Scottish wedding reception. From within his sporran, Andy's phone began to buzz. He fished it out. A text message from a number he didn't recognise.

HEY YOU. LIKE THE KILT!

Andy looked at the message. No name at the end. He ran through a few options in his head then typed back:

GLAD YOU LIKE IT.

The dancers were lining up now. Andy watched as his wife, Angela, rose unsteadily from her seat across the table. She pulled off the gold, sparkly shrug she had worn to keep her arms warm and let it fall to the floor. A whiff of stale sweat reached his nostrils and he hoped she wouldn't try to persuade him to partner her. He slid his phone off

I

the table and back into his sporran, but he needn't have worried. She tottered over to one of the ushers seated at the next table and hauled him up to dance. Always the same. She never could hold her drink. His sporran buzzed again.

SO, R U A REAL SCOTSMAN? WOTS UNDER THE KILT?

What indeed! He felt a familiar stirring and leaned back in his seat, stretching his legs out under the table. The dance floor was busy now, but the alcohol had been flowing all day and the dancers were taking some sorting out. Angela stepped out of her shoes and fired them across the floor in Andy's direction. A few others followed suit. Andy reckoned there'd be some bruised and broken toes by the end of the dance. He had to admire the smart ones who had brought trainers in a poly bag. But that wasn't Angela's style. Always done up to the nines: hair, nails, shoes – the full works. Only she didn't look so glamorous now, after nine – or was it ten – vodkas.

Fergus, the accordionist, his eyes almost obscured by his thick, dark hair, ran his fingers up and down the keyboard. Impatiently. He looked, Andy thought, as if he'd had enough for one night. Who could blame him for that? Weddings were one long hang-about. Andy studied the band. He could see why Hammy was the front man and not Fergus. Tall and sinewy, as fair as Fergus was dark, Hammy had the patter and the twinkle in his eye to match. Andy thought he might be a good lad to have a pint with, judging by the beer he'd swilled over the course of the evening. Probably knew his way round the ladies as well. Anyone who could sink pints and tease those reels and jigs out of his violin, while winking at the dancers had to be worth getting to know.

Hammy tried again. 'Two long lines, ladies over this side, gents over here. Bride and groom at the top. Where are you, Sandra and Davie? Ah, here they come.'

Fergus gave a quick trill of 'The Wedding March' to cheers from the guests. Hammy gave him a look that told him to quit it, and he turned back to the dancers. 'If the bottom half could move down a bit... from the man in the sexy trews...'

There was a laugh at this, and the tartan-clad man acknowledged it with a flourish and a bow, before leading his partner further down the room.

Andy took his phone out again. So, she was wondering what was under his kilt, was she? He typed back a reply.

WOULDN'T YOU LIKE TO KNOW

The bride was shouting to the guests still in their seats to get up and dance. A few of the elderly rellies declined with a wave. Andy looked for Angela and saw she was near the top of the hall, thrusting her hips towards the usher who was responding in kind. Hammy began to explain the dance with the bride and groom demonstrating. The phone buzzed again.

I WOULD AS IT HAPPENS.

Andy scraped his chair back until it was almost touching the wall. He glanced left and right then tapped back:

WE'LL HAVE TO SEE ABOUT THAT THEN

3

There was a flourish from the accordion; Hammy picked up his bow and the drummer began beating out a rhythm. Andy watched as Sandra and Davie started to whirl each other round and he smiled as Sandra slipped and slid across the floor on her back, colliding with two men further down the line. His phone buzzed again.

HOW ABOUT NOW?

Andy looked round. Was the mystery texter someone in the room? The bride was back on her feet now, hauled up by the men she had almost bowled over. She re-joined the dance and began whirling again, from arm to arm, working her way down the line of dancers. The second top couple began turning each other as the band belted out 'The Atholl Highlanders' jig. As the dance progressed it was harder to see across the room. Most of those sitting down were older couples. Certainly not anyone who looked like she might be the mystery texter.

WHERE R U? he texted back.

He watched the screen, impatiently but the reply didn't come immediately. The music switched to another jig as more and more couples joined in the dance. One over-enthusiastic young lad, all arms and legs crashed into the chair next to Andy and carried on as if he hadn't noticed. Andy rose and began walking to the door at the back of the hall. It would be quieter outside the ballroom. As he walked the phone buzzed again.

BOTTOM OF DRIVE. COME NOW!

He glanced back at the dancers. Angela wouldn't even miss him. He pushed open the ballroom door and walked

4

out into the reception area. A slim man in a suit looked up from behind the mahogany desk, his smile fixed but pleasant. Andy gave him a nod and carried on to the front entrance, forcing the heavy brass revolving door into life.

He emerged into the cool evening air and stopped for a second as the odour of cigarette smoke reached his nostrils. From the sound of it, the smokers had gathered at the side door and he was briefly tempted to join them. Time enough for a fag *after*, he told himself and picked his way softly across the gravel to avoid being heard. A burst of laughter from the smokers confirmed he had nothing to worry about and he quickened his pace.

The front garden was illuminated by fairy lights, strung along the drive which curved gently towards the main road, lined on one side by a high beech hedge. As he walked, he wondered about the mystery texter. Who the fuck was it? He had an idea. A couple of ideas, actually.

He took out his phone and looked at the text message again. Real Scotsman? He'd show her what was under his kilt all right. He glanced round to make sure he wasn't being observed, then stopped and pulled his boxers down. His sporran was already stuffed with a handful of crumpled tenners, so he screwed up the boxers and hid them in the hedge. Easy enough to retrieve them on his way back.

As he walked further down the drive, the hotel vanished from view and the drive narrowed. The hedge gave way to high sandstone walls on both sides, the aged stonework picked out by the headlights from an unseen car. *It must just be round the bend.* He quickened his pace, feeling the stirring beneath his kilt turn to a full-blown hard on.

And then he saw it; or, rather, he saw the headlights. Dazzled by the full beam, he stood for a minute, then lifted his kilt to give her a flash of the Real Scotsman.

The car revved in response.

Oh, she was ready for it, all right.

The car revved again and lurched forward.

Calm the fuck down. I'm coming!

But the car didn't stop. Looked like it was speeding up.

No escape on either side. He turned and started to run back to where the path was wider.

Stupid fuckin—

There was no bang. No crash. Just the crunching of tyres on gravel. No time to cry out. The ground came up to meet him and the pain shot through his legs. Instinctively he tucked his head into his chest, pushing down into the gravel. And then it was over.

It was over, and he was still alive.

He lifted his head and tried to focus. He saw the car ahead of him, picked out in the fairy lights. Saw the tail lights and the square number plate. Looked like an old Land Rover. *Bastard!* He forced himself to look. To remember. He'd get the bitch. He clawed at the ground, trying to raise himself up and away from the car. But the pain was indescribable. Oddly, not in his legs now but up his back and into his brain.

He blinked as the brake lights came on. He waited for the door to open. For her to jump down mobile to her ear as she dialled 999. But the door didn't open. He heard the idling of the engine then saw the white reverse lights. Panic seized him and he gasped for air. Someone must come, surely someone? He gasped again and tried to cry out as the white lights came nearer. He tried to roll over

6

towards the wall but his limbs wouldn't obey. The white-hot pain in his head was overwhelming. His phone buzzed again, a message he would never see, and the blackness overtook him.

Chapter 2

Sunday, 19th May

It was just after midnight when Clare heard the phone. Years of shift work and late-night emergencies at Glasgow's busy Maryhill Road station had trained her to snap out of even the deepest sleep. After two rings, she was sitting up in bed. 'DI Mackay.'

'Sorry to wake you, Clare. We need you out.'

'What's up, Jim?'

'Hit-and-run. Looks deliberate.'

She put the phone on speaker and climbed out of bed, carrying on the conversation. 'Locus?'

'Kenlybank Hotel. Off the A917.'

'A917...'

'The coast road out of St Andrews. Head for the swimming pool and bear left. You'll see the cars...'

Clare had been to the East Sands Leisure Centre a few times since arriving in St Andrews a couple of months ago. It was a fun pool for families really, but better than nothing when she was short of time. 'I know the road,' she told her sergeant. 'Give me fifteen minutes. Twenty, tops.'

'Cheers.'

'Oh Jim...?'

'Aye?'

'Give Chris a bell. SOCO too. And some uniforms to secure the scene.'

'All done.'

You had to hand it to Jim, Clare thought. He was no ball of fire but he got the job done. Young Chris could do with taking a leaf out of his book.

Clare thanked Jim and hung up. She took a pair of work trousers from the wardrobe and stepped into them. A plain grey sweater hung over the back of a tub chair and she pulled this on. She drew back the bedroom curtain and glanced out into the darkness. No rain on the window pane at least. She brushed her dark hair quickly, scraping it back with an elasticated tie and ran downstairs. In the kitchen, Clare filled a water bottle from the tap and grabbed a Danish pastry from the bread bin. Her eye fell on a long cream envelope propped up on the kitchen table, still unopened, and a familiar knot began to form in her stomach. A knot that took her away from St Andrews, back to Glasgow. To Glasgow. To Tom and the past she had left behind.

Later, she told herself. *Later. Or tomorrow maybe…*

Forcing the memories to the back of her mind, she pulled on her coat, picked up her work bag, and headed out into the night, hoping it would be a straightforward one.

–

The journey from Clare's house just off the centre of St Andrews, to the Kenlybank Hotel, a mile or so south of the town, took her just ten minutes. Ignoring Jim's directions, she had taken a shortcut along Lamond Drive, easing her Renault Clio over the speed bumps. A few cars were parked awkwardly, and she cursed at an ominous clunk from the underside of the car as it passed over one of the bumps, lopsided. Maybe Jim had a point.

At the Y-junction she left St Andrews behind and travelled along the coastal A917 for a mile or so. To the east of the road lay the North Sea and, glancing across, she could see a tiny speck of light. A ship, presumably, heading out to fish. As she drove on, the night sky, an inky carpet of stars, was lit up by flashing lights from the distant emergency vehicles. As the road veered to the right, she saw a row of police cars and an ambulance bumped up on the verge at what she presumed was the hotel entrance. The hotel itself was screened from the road by a high beech hedge but Clare saw the brown AA sign pointing towards the entrance and she pulled in behind the row of vehicles.

She bit into the Danish pastry and jumped out of the car, taking a crime scene suit from the boot. Jim met her at the gate and led her past the cordon which took up most of the gravel drive. Beyond the tape, two white-suited scene of crime officers were bent over a body while another was carrying out a fingertip examination of the area around it.

'Can I just?' Clare began.

One of the SOCOs looked up and shook her head. 'Ten minutes, Inspector.'

Clare nodded and turned back to Jim. 'Chris?'

'Up at the front door. Speaking to the guests.'

'It's a wedding?'

Jim nodded. 'Yep. Rotten ending to their big day.'

'Thanks, Jim,' Clare said. 'You get back to the gate. I'll find Chris.'

She walked briskly up the drive and, as she rounded it, a large, Victorian edifice came into view. Probably a country house at one time, Clare thought, taking in the long, casement windows and ornate front entrance. The recessed revolving door had been added later, she decided, but the honey-coloured stone pediment over the door looked original. It reminded her of a stately home she and Tom had visited.

She carried on up the drive, taking in the scene before her. Guests were milling about in their finery, some smoking, others huddled in groups. A child of three or maybe four in a white flower-girl dress clutched her father's leg, a soft toy of some sort tucked under her arm.

Clare hesitated for a moment, suddenly conscious that eyes were turning towards her. Even without a uniform, her wiry five-foot-eight frame carried an air of authority. Years of running major enquiries had given her that. But this wasn't Glasgow, with its busy Major Investigations Teams to hand, Glasgow where experienced detectives were ten a penny. This was St Andrews – a small seaside town known for being the home of golf, its population swollen by the students who studied at its centuries-old university. As the most senior officer stationed in the town, Clare was in sole charge of what was happening around her. And, two months after moving from bustling Glasgow, it felt like a lonely place to be.

She looked round, scanning the drive for Chris, her DS. He noticed her and began walking over. She waited for him, keen for an update out of earshot of the guests. Over his shoulder, Clare could see a woman in full bridal regalia, sitting on a wooden garden bench near the front entrance to the hotel, rocking and howling. She cut an incongruous figure, Clare thought, enveloped in layers of gleaming white taffeta, at odds, somehow with the ugly wailing. A couple of wedding guests were fussing round her while a kilted man stood awkwardly at her side, taking furtive slugs from a small silver hip flask.

Clare nodded towards the woman as Chris approached. 'That the wife?'

He shook his head. 'Victim's sister. Wife's over there.' He indicated a woman in an orange dress. She sat, perched on the edge of a stone trough smoking a cigarette, her face devoid of expression. Clare wondered if the woman was in shock. Or was there another reason for her lack of reaction?

'Are we sure it's her husband?'

Chris nodded at the hip flask man. 'Groom identified the tartan, what's left of it. He was the only one at the wedding wearing that pattern.'

'Okay.' Clare nodded. 'Name?'

'Victim's Andy Robb. Wife's Angela. And there's something else you should see.'

Clare scrutinised her DS. Even in the dark, with only the fairy lights, she could see his eyes looked pink and there was the unmistakable odour of whisky on his breath. 'You've been drinking.'

Chris ran a hand through his hair and avoided her gaze. 'Saturday night, boss...'

'And you're on call.'

'Aye, but—'

'Aye but nothing. You think if you throw on a three-piece suit, no one's going to notice?'

Chris shifted uneasily on his feet. 'Sorry, boss.'

'It's not the first time, Chris, is it?'

There was no response to this. Clare fished in her pocket and pulled out a pack of extra-strong mints. 'Here,' she said, 'crunch a couple of these and, for God's sake, keep as far back from witnesses as possible. Oh, and Detective Sergeant...'

'Boss?'

'If you insist on wearing a waistcoat, don't do up the bottom button. It's naff.'

'Yes, boss.'

'So, you said there was something else I should see?'

'Yeah, over here.'

Chris led her to a gap in the beech hedge where some clothing had been stashed. 'Looks like a pair of boxers.'

'You think they're our victim's?'

'Probably. Poor bastard's kilt's ridden up. Caught in the car wheel, maybe. It's not a pretty sight but he certainly wasn't wearing anything under the kilt.'

Clare glanced at the hedge and the crumpled clothing. 'Get them bagged. I'll see how the wife is. If we can get her to look at them...' She looked across to the cordon. The SOCOs were standing now and she walked back over.

'Anything?' she asked.

'Nothing out of the ordinary,' one of them said. 'I'll be surprised if he wasn't killed by the impact. Head's at an odd angle. He was probably running to get away from the car. Maybe looking back when it caught him.'

'Could it have been an accident?' Clare asked. 'Driver lost control?'

The SOCO shook her head. 'Doubt it.' She indicated the stone walls. 'No damage here – or on the other side.

13

I'd say the driver came up here, drove at our man – or rather *over* our man, then reversed back out again.'

Clare looked at the body and down the drive, imagining the victim's terror as he tried to escape the car. The drive was narrow at this point. He'd have had no chance. His last moments must have been desperate ones. A wave of nausea swept over her and she began to regret the Danish pastry. She cleared her throat, then said, 'Right over?'

'Afraid so. Both sets of wheels, I think. And then back over as the car reversed away. See how the body's been forced into the ground?'

Clare forced herself to look at the mangled body. The victim's white shirt was marked with what looked like tyre tracks. 'Think you can get something from that shirt?' she asked. 'If we can narrow down the tyre…'

The SOCO nodded. 'Should do. And if the shirt's no good, there's a pretty good mark where the gravel's been scraped away. Might be able to cast it.'

Clare turned to Chris. 'Any marks out on the road?'

Chris shook his head. 'Skid marks, mainly. Obviously a quick getaway.'

'There's something else, Inspector,' the SOCO interrupted. 'Chris has seen this already, but you really should take a look.'

Clare raised an eyebrow.

'It's an odd one.'

'How so?'

The SOCO reached down and lifted an evidence bag. 'Found this on the victim's chest. Pinned to what was left of his shirt.'

Clare peered at the bag. It appeared to contain a white card, about the size of a postcard with a number five written on it, probably with a broad-nibbed marker pen. She turned back to Chris. 'What's it for?'

'No idea.'

'Party game, maybe?'

'I don't think so,' Chris said. 'I've already asked the groom. There wasn't anything like that.'

'Table number?'

Chris shook his head. 'Tables were named after tartans. McPherson, McLeod... that sort of thing.'

Clare frowned, turning it over in her mind. Maybe the wife could shed some light on it. She looked back up the drive at Angela Robb who was grinding the end of her cigarette into the path with an orange and cream sandal. Clare walked towards her and flashed her badge as she approached. The woman looked up, her expression still blank.

'Mrs Robb? I'm Detective Inspector Clare Mackay. I'm so sorry to trouble you at a time like this.'

Angela didn't meet her gaze but continued pushing the gravel back and forward with her foot. 'S'all right. Got your job to do. Suppose he really is dead?'

'We're waiting for the doctor but, yes, I'm afraid there's no doubt.'

'Hit-and-run then?'

'He was struck by a car, yes.' Clare hesitated then pressed on. 'Have you any idea what he was doing out here? Down the drive I mean? It's a bit far for a smoke.'

Angela gave up on the gravel and lifted her gaze to meet Clare's. 'If I know Andy, he was probably after a quickie in the bushes. Wouldn't be the first time. He disappeared while I was up dancing. I sent a text asking where the fuck he was, but he never replied.'

'We've discovered a pair of boxers in a hedge, near where your husband was found. Would you feel up to identifying them?'

Angela nodded and made to move but Clare put a hand on her arm. The body hadn't been moved yet and she didn't want to upset Angela unnecessarily. 'You stay put. I'll ask the hotel to let us have a room and we'll show you there. Away from the other guests. Is there someone who can keep you company while we sort it out?'

'Francine. My friend. She's the bridesmaid – over there.' Angela indicated a tall woman in a long red dress. Clare motioned to her to come over. 'If you could just stay with Mrs Robb for a few minutes?'

Francine nodded and moved to put an arm round Angela.

Clare walked back to where Chris was hovering, awaiting instructions. She noted with some relief that his breath now smelled mostly of mints. 'We'll need a couple of rooms to interview guests, Chris. You and I will take Mrs Robb and the immediate family. Jim and the rest of the uniformed cops can make a start on the other guests. Get contact details for them all plus the usual stuff – where they were, what they saw, did they hear anything. Particularly any smokers who were outside at the time. Staff too. Was there a band or a disco?'

'Band. They're all packed up and waiting to go.'

'Then they'll just have to keep waiting. Immediate family first, then staff.'

'Band were on a kind of raised bit at one end of the ballroom. They'd have had a good view of anything going on.'

Clare considered this. 'Okay, then let's do them after the family. And prioritise the bride, for God's sake. She'll wake up every dog in the town with that racket.'

They crossed the gravel and pushed through the revolving door that led to the hotel reception. A neatly dressed man in his late twenties was hovering by the desk. His badge said *Pawel Nowicki – Duty Manager*. Clare explained their requirements and he led them to a side room, opening the door and flicking on the light. The room wasn't large but had a table and six chairs. Clare ran her eye round it and nodded to the man. 'Perfect. Is there another one like this?'

He motioned to them to follow him and he opened another door, revealing an identical room. 'We use these for clients who have business meetings.'

'Thanks, Pawel. These will be fine.'

He smiled and left them to it.

'Right,' Clare said. 'Jim and the uniformed guys can have this room. You and I will take the main players next door. We'll start with the wife.'

Clare thought Angela Robb might be in her early forties. Her blonde hair owed more to her hairdresser's attentions than to nature, and her fake tan was almost as orange as her dress. But, despite the tan, she looked pale and drawn and seemed numbed rather than distressed by her husband's violent death. Clare was concerned enough to offer a doctor.

'I'm fine,' was all she said. 'Francine'll see me home.'

'We'll run you back, don't worry about that,' said Clare.

Angela identified the boxers as belonging to her husband and was quite clear that she didn't want them back. She answered their other questions mechanically. No, she didn't know why Andy was outside but, yes, it was probably to meet another woman. Yes, he was in the habit of having affairs and she was well used to it by now. Yes, she'd had affairs of her own and, yes, she did currently have a boyfriend.

'Billy Dodds,' she told them. 'Lives in Cupar.'

Clare glanced briefly at Chris.

'Small market town,' he said, his voice low. 'About ten miles west of St Andrews.'

Clare smiled her thanks and pressed Angela further on Billy Dodds.

Yes, she went on. She could give them Billy's address and mobile number, but she very much doubted he cared enough to run Andy over. No, she didn't know who would, but Andy had probably upset enough husbands in his time. No, she had no idea who all his women were. She didn't care. No, she couldn't think of anyone he'd fallen out with. Maybe his sister could tell them, if she stopped fucking howling long enough.

Clare then brought up the question of the number five card found on his body.

At this, Angela registered genuine surprise. The first real sign of a reaction. 'What, like a figure five?' she asked.

Clare sent Chris to fetch the numbered card and when he returned with it, safely stowed in the clear, evidence bag, she placed it on the table in front of Angela.

Angela gaped at it. 'And this was pinned to his shirt?'

Clare nodded.

Angela looked at a loss. 'Honestly? Not a clue. He must have had it on him when he went outside. Sorry, I've no idea.'

Outside, the police doctor had arrived and, having pronounced life extinct, spent a few minutes with Angela, at Clare's request. He gave a sleeping tablet to Francine with instructions not to give it to Angela until she was safely inside her house. Clare arranged a car to take the pair to Angela's home in Scooniehill Road and promised to call in on Sunday morning.

The bride, now Mrs Sandra McDade, had exhausted her supply of tears and was nursing a large vodka and lemonade. Her face was tear-streaked and one of her false eyelashes was starting to come loose.

'I'm so sorry to trouble you Mrs McDade,' said Clare. 'Just a few questions and we'll let you go.'

Between sniffs, Sandra confirmed that she had been inside dancing and only came out when one of the smokers said there had been an accident. At this, she began to cry again.

Clare waited while she composed herself then pressed on. 'Did your brother have any enemies? Anyone that might have upset him?'

Sandra's eyes widened, and the eyelash slipped a little more. She tried to press it back into place. 'Enemies? But it was a hit-and-run, wasn't it? Somebody knocked him over and drove off?'

'At this stage we can't be certain. We have to investigate all possibilities. So, is there anyone he might have upset?'

Sandra shook her head. 'Everyone loved Andy. He was a great lad. Great brother.'

The eyelash was coming loose again and this time Sandra gently eased it off. She cut a comic-tragic figure now with just the one thick eyelash.

'Was his marriage a happy one?'

Her face hardened. 'What do you think? You've seen *her*. Bloody nightmare to live with.'

'Did he have other girlfriends?'

'A few. I think he and Angela stayed together for convenience. Separate bedrooms for years now. But neither of them would leave. They both mucked about with other folk, though.'

'Would you know any of your brother's girlfriends?'

'The lads at his work might. And I think he went out on Thursdays to some club. Not sure where, though. But *she* might know.'

Clare noted the name of Andy's workplace, and after a few more questions she let Sandra go. Her new husband, Davie, could add little more, other than confirming that Andy was a bit of a lad. He thought he was *doing a line* with a lassie in the town but not sure if it was still going on or not. Clare asked him for Andy's mobile number then let him escape to his bride and her one good eyelash.

Interviews of the remaining bridesmaids, ushers, parents and friends all yielded much the same story. Andy was known for having a few women, Angela knew about it and didn't seem to care much but no one thought he was the kind of guy to get himself killed. A few of the smokers had seen him striding down the drive but not paid much attention. One said he thought he heard a car pulling away and assumed Andy had jumped in and gone off somewhere with the driver. Two of the band members, the accordionist and the drummer, had seen him tapping on his phone before walking down the hall and out of the door.

'We need his phone records as soon as,' Clare said to Chris. 'Can you get onto it?'

'No problem. I'll do it now. Anything else?'

'Traffic cams. Any round here?' It was said more in hope than in expectation.

'I doubt it. In the town, yeah, if the driver went that way. But there are so many back roads here.'

'Well, we have to try. At least we have a pretty accurate time of death. The roads must have been quiet at that time of night. Let them know we need footage for an hour before and an hour after. If SOCO can give us an indication of the vehicle we can look at the footage.'

Clare looked at her watch. It had gone three in the morning and most of the guests had either retired to their rooms or left in a succession of taxis. The main drive had been taped off and a white tent erected over the spot where Andy had died. An ambulance had borne his body off to the mortuary in Dundee for a post-mortem, although the cause of death wasn't much in doubt. SOCO were packing up for the night and there seemed little left to do until they had forensic information. She looked back up to the front of the hotel, lights still burning in most of the windows. It really was a lovely old building. She wondered what the restaurant was like, and then reminded herself she had no one to dine out with. Suddenly she was tired and longing for her bed.

'I think we'll call it a night, Chris.' She stationed a couple of cops on duty at the site and climbed wearily back into her car. So much for straightforward.

Chapter 3

At just after eleven on Sunday morning Clare and Chris drew up outside Angela Robb's semi-detached bungalow on Scooniehill Road.

Clare had slept fitfully, and it seemed that she had only just dropped off when the alarm sounded. Peering in the bedroom mirror, she saw dark circles beneath her hazel eyes, the product of a few sleepless nights lately, and wondered if her sister had been right when she'd suggested a short course of sleeping pills.

Fortified by strong coffee and the desire to prove to her new colleagues that *the girl from Glasgow* was up to the job, she hoped she sounded brighter than she felt. Stopping outside the address Angela had given them, she killed the engine and glanced at Chris. 'You look better than last night, at least.'

Chris began fiddling with his mobile phone. 'Yeah, sorry about that, Clare. Just a slip up. You know how it is.'

Clare's face softened. 'Chris, you'll get over it. Emily, I mean. There are plenty of lovely girls who'd be much better for you.'

He tried to smile, his lips thin. 'You mean plenty of lovely girls who wouldn't carry on behind my back; with my ex-boss.'

Clare squeezed his arm. 'Forget Tony McAvettie. He's a Class A bastard.'

'Correction. He's a Class A bastard and a DCI who could very well be brought into this case if we don't wrap it up quickly.'

'Then we'd better get it done,' Clare said. 'I phoned ahead,' she added, 'so she'll be expecting us.'

Chris looked out of the car window at the house. The blinds were still closed. 'How did she sound?'

'Matter-of-fact, I'd say. Maybe still in shock.'

'Or glad to be rid of him?' Chris suggested.

Clare unclipped her seatbelt. 'Could be. Come on – let's find out.'

The sun was breaking through the clouds, and the pavements were full of children buzzing to and fro on bikes and scooters. A boy in a red football strip came to a halt on his bike and sat, watching Clare and Chris as they emerged from the car. Across the road two little girls were drawing pictures on the pavement with coloured chalks, and somewhere someone was using a strimmer, its nasal whine cutting through the Sunday morning birdsong. It all seemed so perfectly ordinary to Clare and a million miles from the horror of Andy Robb's death twelve hours before.

They mounted the stone steps, bordered on one side by a square patch of grass and on the other by a few straggly heathers. As they approached, the door was opened by Francine, still wearing the long, red dress from the night before. She had pulled on a navy sweater for warmth but her feet were bare, the silver sandals kicked to the side of the door. She stood back to admit them.

'Saw you from the upstairs window,' she said. 'Keeping the blinds closed for now. Neighbours and all that.'

Clare nodded and asked about Angela.

Francine considered. 'Quiet. Not like herself. But then it's a lot to take in.'

She led them into Angela Robb's front room. It was, Clare thought, not unlike her own rented house, a mile or so across town. Modern, boxy, 1960s-built; identical to the neighbouring properties. The sitting room was square with a picture window looking out to the street, the cream lateral blinds pulled closed. The room was dominated by a large television screen and, looking round, Clare noticed a collection of pottery angels arranged on wall shelves. Angela was sitting on a cream leather sofa, her feet tucked under her, cradling a mug of coffee. She was watching a cookery programme and, as they entered, she looked round for the remote control. Francine passed it to her, and she sat up, slipping her feet into a pair of furry slippers.

'Suppose you'll be wanting a cup of something,' she said.

'You stay put,' Francine said. 'I'll get it. Coffee okay?'

'That would be lovely. Chris knows how I take it.' Clare inclined her head in the direction of the door. He took the hint and followed Francine. Clare turned to Angela who gave her a wintry smile.

'Funny, ye know,' she began. 'He could be a right bastard. Women, practically from the start. But he was *my* bastard. I didn't think I'd miss him but…' She dabbed at her eyes.

'It's a lot to take in, Mrs Robb.'

'Angela. Just Angela.'

Clare smiled at her. 'Sleep much?'

'I did, actually. God knows how but I slept a good eight hours.'

'Those doctors know their stuff.'

Angela nodded. 'My GP phoned. Coming in later, he said.'

'That's good. Now, Angela, I'm going to give you my card. If you're worried about anything – anything at all – or if something occurs to you about Andy, give me a call. Day or night. Okay?'

Angela took the card. She blew her nose and smiled again, her eyes bright. 'So, you gonnae catch him? The hit-and-run guy?'

Clare squeezed her hand. 'Oh yes. But we'll need your help. We want to get a picture of Andy. Who he was, what he was like. Where he went, who he saw. Friends, work colleagues, that sort of thing. And, if there are any computers or laptops in the house, we'll have to take them away. You'll get them back of course.'

Angela nodded. 'I'll fetch them. His phone… Oh, he must have had it on him.'

'Sadly, it didn't survive the accident,' Clare was choosing her words carefully, 'but we'll get his call records from the phone company.'

Angela went to fetch the laptop and Clare took the opportunity to look round the room. The pottery angels were everywhere. Angela must collect them. But there was little evidence of Andy, as far as she could see. No photographs of the couple, no discarded sweaters or jackets, slippers even. And the DVD collection was mostly chick flicks. She wondered if they had separate sitting rooms, but the house didn't seem large enough. Maybe he…

Angela burst in on her thoughts, carrying a laptop bag with a cable trailing behind. She put it down beside Clare. 'That's Andy's laptop. You've got his mobile number?'

'Yes, thanks.'

Angela sat down, tucking her feet under her legs again. She picked up her coffee cup and put it to her lips then pulled a face. The coffee had gone cold. She set the cup down and picked up a cushion instead, clasping it across her front.

Clare smiled her thanks. 'We'll get the laptop back to you as soon as we can.'

'No rush. I don't use it. The iPad does me fine.'

Clare pressed on. 'How long were you married?'

'Sixteen years.'

'Long time.'

'Too long for Andy. Should have called time really, but it's convenient. It *was* convenient.'

Clare sat forward. 'I'm so sorry to ask, Angela – I know you said last night you didn't know who the other women were, but if you could remember any of them it would be such a help.'

Angela waved the apology away. 'Don't worry – I'm under no illusions about Andy. But I can't help you. I don't know who they were. Didn't want to know, to be honest. He lived his life and I lived mine.'

Clare tried another tack. 'Could any of them be work colleagues? Or might his friends know?'

Angela shifted and clutched the cushion again. 'Sorry, Inspector. I don't even know who he was pally with these days. We shared a house, but that was about it.'

'I believe Andy worked for a taxi company?'

'Yes, that's right. Swilcan Taxis.'

'Swilcan – it's unusual. Is that the name of the owner?'

Angela laughed. 'You're not from St Andrews, are you Inspector?'

'Glasgow,' Clare said. 'And I thought I was getting the hang of this town.'

Angela reached forward and picked up her cigarettes from the coffee table. She fished one out and offered the pack to Clare who looked at it with something approaching regret.

'Better not. Been stopped five years.'

Angela lit her cigarette, drew deeply on it then exhaled. 'The Swilcan Bridge is a wee stone bridge over a burn on the Old Course. You know what that is, right?'

'The golf course by the hotel, yeah. The famous one.'

Angela nodded. 'That's it. So the bridge is a bit of a tourist attraction. And on Sundays, when you can walk on the golf course, it's full of tourists having their photos taken on the bridge. Christ knows why.'

'But Swilcan Taxis?'

Angela shook her head. 'They've pinched the name; probably 'cause it's well known. Tourists can say they saw the bridge then took a ride in a Swilcan cab.'

'Ah okay. So where's the office?'

Angela took another drag. 'Up North Street. Albany Place, to be exact.' She saw Clare's confusion. 'It's a short section of North Street. Down from the pictures. You can't miss the sign.'

Clare noted this down then said, 'Had he been there long?'

Angela considered. 'About five years, I think. He was on the rigs before that but got fed up with it.'

'If you could jot down the number in Albany Place – phone number too.'

'Sure.'

Clare paused to let Angela write on a Post-it, then continued. 'Sandra said something about Andy going out on Thursday nights. You wouldn't know where he went, would you?'

'Sorry, no. I never asked. He did go out on Thursdays, though. Most weeks.'

'Dressed up?'

Angela thought about this. 'Not jeans, but not a suit either. A bit in between, probably.'

Chris opened the door and Francine followed him in, carrying a tray of mugs and a plate of chocolate biscuits. She handed out mugs then sat down next to Angela.

'I'm goin' home in a bit, if that's okay, hun,' she said. 'Need a change of clothes 'n' that, but I'll be back.'

Angela waved this away. 'I'm fine. I'll phone work and let them know I'll be off for a day or two.'

'Will you hell! I'll phone them. And, when the doctor comes in, we'll get him to give you a line.'

'We can arrange for a constable to be here, if it would help,' said Clare.

Angela shook her head. 'I just need some peace. Sort myself out, ye know?'

Chris cleared his throat. 'Do you have an up-to-date photo of Andy we could have? On your phone, maybe.'

Angela snorted. 'Like I'd have him on my phone pictures.'

'Facebook, maybe?' Chris suggested. 'Or Instagram?'

Angela picked up her phone and began tapping and swiping. She handed the phone to Chris. 'That do?'

Chris smiled. 'Perfect. If you could just forward it to this number...' He held out a card and Angela copied it into her phone. Seconds later there was a ping from Chris's mobile. He swiped to check then said, 'Thanks, Angela. Got it now.'

Clare went on. 'Did Andy have a car? His own car, I mean? Or did he bring the taxi home?'

'His own car. Parked outside. Red Mégane. Keys are on the hall table. Help yourself.'

'We'll take the keys if you don't mind and send round a forensic team to look it over. There might just be something that will help us find the person responsible.'

'Sure. Whatever.'

Clare picked up her mug. They had stayed long enough. 'We'll drink this and then maybe we could have a look round the house? Where Andy slept, any other rooms he used.'

When they had finished their drinks, Angela led them upstairs to a small bedroom. 'He slept here,' she said then turned. 'Across the hall is his study. He sat there if he was at home, watching telly, gaming, that sort of thing.'

Clare thanked her and said they would be as quick as possible. Left alone in Andy's bedroom, she and Chris pulled on latex gloves. She moved to the door and listened for the sound of Angela going back downstairs, then she spoke in a low voice. 'Get anything out of Francine?'

'Not much, other than she thought he was seeing a young blonde.'

'Name?'

Chris scanned his notebook. 'Vicky Gallagher. Works in a restaurant on South Street. Jensen's Diner.'

'Get her address?'

'No, Francine thought she lived up by the swimming pool, but she wasn't sure.'

'No problem. We'll get her at work. If she's not there they can give us her address.' Clare surveyed the room. 'Okay. We'll take any paperwork, anything that might give us a clue to what he got up to outside the house. Keep an eye out for anything that might indicate he was *using*.'

They began their search, working mostly in silence. It wasn't a large room. Clare thought Angela had probably bagged the biggest bedroom for herself, relegating Andy to this smaller one. It was simply furnished – single bed with a small table to the side, radio, wardrobe and a chest of drawers. There were no ornaments or mementos, except for a framed photo of Andy smiling on a beach. A navy polo shirt bearing the logo of Swilcan Taxis lay on the bed and there was a small pile of clothes – dirty washing, she guessed – on the floor. 'Yours,' she nodded to Chris and he sighed as he moved to search through the clothing.

There were a few paperbacks on top of the chest of drawers and some receipts from petrol stations but very little else. This clearly wasn't a room where Andy spent a great deal of time. There was no evidence of drug use and the search was concluded within half an hour. Bedroom done, they moved across the hall to the small room Andy had used as his study. Here, there was more evidence of the man. A reclining chair was positioned in front of a large television screen and a games console. A collection of empty beer cans and an overflowing ashtray suggested this was where Andy came to relax.

'Pretty violent stuff,' Chris commented, leafing through a selection of Xbox games, 'but mostly shoot-em-ups. Nothing too dodgy.' He cast an eye round a shelf of DVDs. 'A few porno films here, boss.'

'Check inside the cases to see if any of them are home movies. Otherwise, just leave them.'

There was nothing much more of interest, so they moved on to the bathroom where the only things that seemed to belong to Andy were a contact lens cleaning kit and a toothbrush. Everything else appeared to be Angela's.

Chris worked his way through the medicine cabinet. 'She takes a lot of pills.'

Clare was about to answer when she heard the door-bell. She moved quickly to the hall in time to see Francine admitting a tall man with close-cropped blond hair, dressed in jeans and a light blue T-shirt. He stepped into the hall as soon as Francine opened the door, without waiting to be asked. Clare noticed that he fiddled with his car keys as Francine shut the door behind him.

'Aw Billy, good you've come,' they heard Francine say as she led him into the sitting room.

'Billy Dodds,' Clare surmised. 'You carry on here and join me as soon as you're done.'

Clare slipped quickly down the stairs. Francine had closed the sitting room door behind Billy.

'Maybe just give them a minute, eh?' she suggested.

Clare gave her what she hoped looked like an apologetic smile then tapped gently on the door and went in. Billy stood in the middle of the room, his arms round Angela, holding her in a tight embrace. She thought she heard Billy whisper *free now*, but she couldn't be sure. She cleared her throat and they broke apart.

'DI Clare Mackay. Maybe we could have a word, sir?'

Clare led Billy out to the back garden where there was a white, painted bench. Chris, having completed his examination of Andy's clothes and possessions, came downstairs and went out to join them. Francine was watching from the kitchen window. Clare knew Angela would be close behind.

She turned to Billy. 'You'll be aware by now that Angela's husband died in a hit-and-run accident last night.'

Billy stroked his chin. 'Aye, awfa business. Terrible for Angela, even though they weren't—'

'We have reason to believe Mr Robb was targeted. That his death was deliberate.'

'Deliberate?' He shook his head. 'Like some'dy meant it? Fucksake. I mean, dinnae get me wrong, he was a right one for the lassies. Never done chasing them. But that's no reason to run the bastard over.' He shook his head again.

Chris took up the questioning. 'How did you and Mrs Robb meet?'

'We both work up at the hospital. She's a receptionist and I'm a delivery driver. She caught my eye. Good-looking woman, Angela. I was delivering one day, and she was just leaving for her break, so I said come and get a coffee over the road.'

Clare raised an eyebrow. 'Somewhere nice?'

'Just the supermarket. Has a cafe, ye ken. We hit it off straight away, and the rest is history.'

'Did you meet Mr Robb at all?'

'Naw. Kept out of his way. I only came over here on Thursdays, when he went out. Mostly we went to my place or out to the pictures and that.'

Clare took out her notebook. 'Where is your place, Mr Dodds?'

'Cupar. Wee bungalow, just off the Ceres Road. Does me fine.'

'Just you?'

'Me and the dog.'

Chris saw his opportunity. 'I've a wee dog myself. Just got him. Border Terrier.'

Billy smiled. 'Cracking wee dogs but they bark a helluva lot.'

'Tell me about it. What have you got?'

'German Shepherd. Had him three years. Great company.'

Billy was sitting back now, one ankle crossed over his knee. He seemed set to continue chatting to Chris about dogs. Clare took her chance.

'Obviously we have to ask everyone, Mr Dodds,' she said, 'but can you tell us where you were on Saturday evening?'

The corners of his mouth kinked into a smile. He looked Clare straight in the eye. 'Frankly, Inspector, I didnae care enough to risk damaging ma car.'

'What do you drive, Mr Dodds?'

'Qashqai. It's outside if you want a look.'

'And last night?'

He took a moment before answering. 'At home all night. Me and Caesar.'

Chris's tone was light. 'Doing anything particular?'

'Telly mainly. Can't remember what else. Ordered a curry from Spice Palace. Came about half eight.'

Chris frowned. 'Spice Palace in St Andrews?'

'Aye.'

33

'Not Cupar? There's a couple of curry houses there you could have ordered from, surely?'

Billy smiled. 'I know the lads at Spice. Good bunch. They always throw in a bit extra, ye ken. Makes it worth paying the delivery.'

Chris nodded and went on, his tone light. 'Sounds good. I missed *Match of the Day* myself. See anything of the Spurs match?'

A ghost of a smile played on his lips again. 'You need to keep up, son. *Match of the Day* wasnae on last night. The league finished a week ago. Last night was that Eurovision shite.'

Chris had the grace to blush. 'Who won?'

Billy met his eye for a few seconds. 'The Netherlands. The Netherlands won. Okay? Satisfied?'

Chris smiled but said nothing.

Clare rose to her feet. 'If you don't mind, Mr Dodds, we'll take a look at your car then be on our way. I'll send someone round to see Mrs Robb later on and we will of course keep her fully informed.'

Billy followed them back into the house. 'I'll see she's all right. Don't you worry.'

As they walked towards the car, Clare said, 'He was certainly ready with his answers – about that Eurovision thing.'

'Wasn't he just.'

'Too ready?'

Chris shrugged. 'Maybe.'

They walked past Andy's red Mégane and approached the dark grey Qashqai. As they looked at it, Clare said, 'I think I'll pay Spice Palace a visit. Find out if they did deliver to Billy last night. And, more importantly, what time.'

Chris began walking round the Qashqai parked outside Angela's gate.

'Nothing visible,' he said. 'No obvious mud on the tyres.'

'He could have put it through a carwash,' Clare said. 'Take a photo of the tyres, would you? See if you can get the number on the rim. Front and rear. Tread, too.'

Chris took out his mobile and photographed the front of the car and each of the tyres.

Clare stared at the car. 'It's certainly big enough to run someone over. Let's get back to the station and see what SOCO have turned up from those tyre tracks.'

Clare handed him the keys. 'I'll let you drive back. For a special treat.'

They climbed into the car and Chris started the engine. As he pulled away, Clare said, 'Like you could look after a dog!'

Chapter 4

The police station in Pipeland Road was a long, low, red-brick building, with parking to the side. The street was usually a quiet one but today, in the May sunshine, the gardening brigade were out in force. As Clare and Chris stepped out of the car the aroma of barbequed meat reached their nostrils.

'I could murder a burger,' Chris said, as the automatic door slid open.

Inside, Jim was manning the public enquiry desk. 'Phone records are back,' he said.

Clare shrugged off her jacket and hung it on a coat stand behind the desk. 'Great, Jim. Can you and Chris get together and compare notes on his contacts? Calls and texts from yesterday, in particular.'

Jim nodded then the phone rang. He answered it and began scribbling notes. Clare waited until he had finished. He put down the phone and ripped off the note, handing it to her.

'Bit of luck with the tyre tracks,' he said. 'It's a big tyre – 7.5 Latitude Cross, they said. Need to check with a tyre seller but they reckon we're looking for a 4x4 or another kind of off-roader.'

'Good. Now we're getting somewhere.' Clare looked round the station and her eye fell on one of the younger, uniformed officers. 'Sara, can you phone round tyre centres, please? If we can narrow down the vehicle it'll save a huge amount of time, trawling through ANPR footage.'

Sara smiled. 'Will do.' She rose and Clare noticed Chris's eye following her as she moved to a desk to begin making calls. Sara had a new haircut, a neat dark bob that swung softly as she moved. It suited her and this hadn't escape Chris's notice.

'Oy, Romeo,' Clare called after him, 'phone records!'

Chris sauntered over and looked at the note Jim had given Clare. 'Could be a stolen car, boss,' he said.

'Good point. Okay, you get on with the phone records. Jim, can you check for stolen cars in the past two weeks? Any large vehicles – I want to know. If there's nothing within two weeks go back another two. In fact, go back three months. There can't be that many of them. Cross-reference with the ANPR footage. And see if Sara can help narrow down the type of vehicle.'

Chris's expression told Clare he'd far rather be chasing up stolen 4x4s than the tedious job of trawling through phone records.

'Just Fife?' Jim asked.

Clare considered this. 'Might as well take in Tayside and Lothian too. The car could easily have come from another county.'

'Could be a lot of cars, if we have to check them all out.'

'Needs must, Jim. But if Sara turns up the vehicle type, that'll cut the work down.'

She smiled at them. 'Right, that's it. Let's get to work.'

Clare went through to the staff area and into the small kitchen where she made herself a quick coffee in her travel mug. Calling to the team to radio if they turned anything up, she headed out taking the keys to one of the pool cars with her. The sun was fully out now, and Clare regretted leaving her sunglasses at home. Still unsure of the back roads, she drove out onto the main Largo Road towards the historic West Port, the gateway that led to bustling South Street. It was Clare's favourite part of the town, running all the way from the West Port to the ancient St Rule's Tower, the site of a medieval cathedral. The pavements were broad and the street strung with quirky, individual shops and cafes with student flats above. The students, often seen wearing their traditional red gowns, were conspicuous by their absence today and Clare wondered if it could be exam time. She slowed to a halt as a gaggle of tourists stepped out onto one of the many pedestrian crossings. As she waited for them to cross, she admired a neo-Jacobean school building set back from the street. Just beyond the crossing she saw Jensen's Diner. She scanned the street, left and right for a parking space then saw the white reversing lights on a car just ahead. She hit the brakes and flashed the driver out, driving quickly into the space before anyone else could take it. As she emerged from the car she heard the strains of bagpipes playing the ubiquitous 'Highland Cathedral'. Having worked the centre of Glasgow on many a busy Saturday, Clare would happily go to her grave never hearing a piper play that particular air again.

She picked her way through the dawdling tourists and headed for Jensen's. It was an American-themed restaurant, with a vintage Harley-Davidson on a raised platform. The Beach Boys were playing from faux-retro speakers and the restaurant was buzzing.

A waitress in a 1950s style uniform approached with a smile. 'For one?'

Clare took out her badge and asked for Vicky. The waitress looked around.

'I think she must be on a break. I'll check.'

The aroma from the kitchen was irresistible and, although she had eaten breakfast, Clare wondered if she might have time for a quick snack. She glanced at the menu to see if they did takeaway food, but the waitress returned before she had finished perusing it.

'Vicky's in the back,' she said. 'I'll take you through.'

Clare followed her, through the swing doors that led to the kitchen, out another door at the back and into a small staffroom. The waitress made to leave.

'If you could give me five or ten minutes with Vicky then come back?'

The waitress closed the door softly behind her. Vicky had been eating a hot dog and reading a magazine. She looked up when Clare entered and wiped a smear of ketchup from her lips. Clare was surprised by how young she was compared to Angela. She wondered why it was that men of a certain age felt the need to discard their wives in favour of younger models. But she could see easily why Andy Robb had fallen for this young waitress. Vicky's uniform hugged and accentuated her figure and she was blessed with the kind of clear skin found on airbrushed models in magazines. Clare introduced herself and explained the reason for her visit. Vicky's shocked expression told Clare that she either knew nothing about Andy's death or that she was a damn good actress.

'Andy's dead? Are you sure?'

'I'm afraid so, Vicky. And I'm sorry to tell you we believe his death wasn't an accident.'

'But, what...? Why would...?' Her blue eyes filled with tears and she felt in her pocket for a tissue. 'I'm sorry.'

Clare gave her a few moments to compose herself then spoke gently. 'Vicky, we need to find out as much as possible about Andy. Where he went, who he saw. That sort of thing. We've spoken to his wife, but she didn't really know who he was friendly with. If there's anything you can tell us, it might help.'

At the mention of Angela, Vicky scowled. 'Oh her. She probably did it. She hated him. Always having a go.'

Clare thought back to Angela, self-possessed, even in grief. She doubted very much if Angela had been troubled enough by Andy's love life to have him run over. She had formed the impression that, whatever their marital arrangements, conflict didn't play a large part. More likely Andy was angling for sympathy from Vicky.

She diverted the conversation away from Angela. 'Can you tell me how long you've known Andy?'

'Six months on Wednesday. Or it would have been...'

'And were you in a relationship before that?'

'Not for a couple of months.'

'No ex-boyfriends pestering you? Anything like that?'

'No,' Vicky said. 'My last boyfriend went off to join the Army. We agreed a long-distance relationship wouldn't work but we've stayed friends.'

Another dead end. Clare noted down the ex-boyfriend's details but doubted it would prove relevant. 'Did your parents know about Andy?'

'Oh yes. I mean I didn't tell them he still lived with *her*. Just that he was married but separated. My dad wasn't too happy to start with, but he came round.'

Clare wrote down Vicky's parents' names and address then turned the conversation to Andy's interests. 'Did the two of you go out much?'

'Now and then. Neither of us earned very much so we'd quite often watch telly. Pub sometimes.'

'Name?'

'The Thistle. Down from my house. I live up by the swimming pool.'

Clare knew the pub. She tried to keep her tone light for the next question. 'What about Thursdays? Did you see Andy then?'

'Not on Thursdays. Saturdays, usually, maybe Tuesday or Wednesday through the week but Andy went to a club on Thursdays.'

'Which club?'

'Oh, I don't know. He never said. We didn't really talk about it.'

'Okay, not to worry. Anyone he'd fallen out with recently?'

She shook her head. 'Everyone loved Andy.'

And the tears began to flow again.

Clare moved to the door and found the waitress hovering. 'I think Vicky might need to go home. She's had some bad news and is a bit shaken.'

The waitress gave Vicky a sympathetic smile and scooped her up. 'C'mon, Vic. We'll get your coat.'

Clare sat on in the staff room for a few minutes after Vicky left. She couldn't see the girl being involved in Andy's death. Even if her father hadn't approved of Andy, it would be stretching things a bit to run him over. And then there was that number five card — what did that mean? Or was it nothing to do with his death? She shook her head. Maybe the staff at The Thistle would be able to help.

Out on South Street the piper had changed to a rousing rendition of 'Scotland the Brave'. Further along the street, a small crowd had gathered to listen to a Hellfire and Damnation preacher and Clare could hear some good-natured heckling. She reversed out of the space and drove on, turning right at the end in the direction of the swimming pool. Half a mile along the road she saw The Thistle and drew into the side, just beyond the entrance.

The pub had been an old, stone-built cottage at one time and was now extended and modernised. It was light and airy inside and as busy as Jensen's had been. At one side of the bar there were tables filled with customers eating Sunday lunch. A plump waitress breezed past, carrying two plates of roast beef, and said she'd be there in a minute. Suddenly tired from her broken night's sleep, Clare looked round for a vacant chair but couldn't see one, so she leaned against a wall, taking the weight off her feet. As she waited, she took in the clientele, mainly couples in their thirties and forties. Not exactly the kind of pub she imagined Vicky Gallagher being drawn to, but Andy was probably right at home. And it was handy for Vicky's flat.

'Hi,' the waitress said. 'Bit of a wait for a table, I'm afraid.'

Clare showed her warrant card. 'I'm not after a table but I'm hoping you can help me.'

'I'll try.'

Clare took out her phone and showed the waitress Andy's photo. 'Do you recognise this man?'

The waitress nodded. 'That's Andy. He comes in with his girlfriend. Vicky, I think she's called.'

'Does he always come in with Vicky?'

The waitress looked doubtful. 'I'd have to ask the other staff. I don't think I've seen him with anyone else. Not for a few months, anyway.'

Another two plates loaded with roast beef appeared through a hatch to the kitchen and the waitress eyed them. 'I'd better get these to the customers. But if you can hang on for a bit, I'll ask the manager to come out.'

'Thanks.'

Len, the manager was as spare as the waitress was plump. His trousers, shiny with wear, hung loosely while his shirt gaped at the neck. He tapped his fingers together unconsciously and his eye kept straying round the restaurant. He followed Clare with some reluctance to a quiet corner where a table had just become vacant and sat, perched on the edge of a chair. He remembered Andy well and looked shocked when Clare told him Andy had died.

'Good lad, Andy,' he said, shaking his head. 'Hard to take it in. Heart attack, was it?'

Clare ignored the question. 'Do you know his girlfriend?'

'Aye, Vicky. Nice kid. A bit young for him, I'd say, but he has an eye for the young ones, I reckon.'

'Any reason you think that?'

He hesitated and shifted in his seat. 'I'm not sure, really...'

'It is important.'

He stared. 'Was it not a heart attack, then?'

He was fishing for information, but Clare wasn't biting. 'If you could just tell me.'

'He had a couple of girlfriends before Vicky. Both young. Early twenties, I'd say.'

'Names?'

He rubbed his chin. 'Oh, now you're asking…'

Clare waited and at length he spoke again. 'Before Vicky, he was knocking about with a Polish girl. Marta, I think she was called. An au pair, or something like that.'

'Would you know where she lives? Or anything else that might help us find her?'

'Sorry, no. I think she went back to Poland. Something to do with her mother.'

'And before Marta?'

The hesitation was enough to alert Clare. 'We're treating Mr Robb's death as suspicious. Anything you can remember would be most helpful.'

He sighed. 'One of our barmaids. Nice lass called Kayleigh. She was pretty upset when he dumped her for the Polish girl.'

'Does she still work here?'

He nodded. 'She'll be in for the evening shift if you want to speak to her.'

Clare thanked him and said she would return later to speak to Kayleigh. 'Oh,' she added, 'I'd be grateful if you wouldn't tell Kayleigh about Mr Robb's death. I'd like to break the news to her myself.'

The manager raised an eyebrow but said nothing and Clare took her leave. The car was in full sun now and stiflingly hot. For a few seconds, she leaned back on the headrest, tempted by the thought of a quick nap. And then a picture of Andy Robb's mangled body flashed across her mind and she was back in the moment. There was work to do. Time to check on Swilcan Taxis.

North Street, with fewer shops and cafes, wasn't as busy as South Street and Clare managed to find a parking space close to Albany Place. Swilcan's office was in the lower half of a house with a narrow lane to one side, just wide enough for a car to pass through. Wandering up the lane, Clare saw it led to a yard, surrounded on all sides by high stone walls. Faint markings on the concrete indicated five or six parking spaces, three of which were occupied by cars. She went back round to the front and pushed open the shop door which *dinged*. The receptionist, a dark-haired woman in her late forties looked up as Clare entered but she continued speaking into a headset microphone as she dealt with a succession of calls.

While she waited, Clare looked round the office. Its faux-pine walls were redolent of 1970s décor and the cork pinboard covered with business cards did little to elevate the interior. It was clean enough but in serious need of updating. Clare turned her attention to the receptionist whose badge said *Jakki* and decided she probably wasn't one of Andy's conquests. She was too near his own age for starters. She was not unlike Angela to look at, although her hair was darker. She had the same detached manner and seemed unperturbed by the length of time she was keeping Clare waiting. When, at last, she looked up, Clare showed her warrant card and asked Jakki to turn the phone to silent for a few minutes.

Jakki frowned. 'The boss won't like it.'

'He will when I explain I'm investigating the murder of one of your drivers.'

Jakki's mouth fell open. 'Who?'

'Andy Robb. So I'll need to speak to everyone who works here. And I'd like to see the vehicles too.'

Jakki said there were three drivers on duty. One was outside having a smoke and the other two should be back soon, if Clare could hold on. Clare went back out to the yard to examine the taxis while she waited. Two saloon cars and one seven-seater. She had a good look at all three but, judging by puddles on the concrete, they had been washed that morning. She took out her phone and photographed the tyre rims and tread on the seven-seater to check against the information SOCO had gleaned, but it was probably a long shot.

Ten minutes later the three drivers, all men, had gathered in a small staff room. Two of them, Harry and Robert, were around fifty, she thought, while Gil, the young lad, looked to be in his mid-twenties. They all wore polo shirts like the one she had seen in Andy's bedroom but, other than that, they were an ill-matched trio.

Harry was what Clare called hefty. His polo shirt was tucked into his trousers, under protest, if the rolls of fat spilling over the waistband were anything to go by. He was perspiring visibly, mopping his brow with his hand before wiping it on his grimy trousers. On his knuckles were faded blue tattoos and his fingernails were grubby.

Robert, by contrast, was as neat as a pin. His hair was turning to silver but was neatly trimmed, as was his small moustache. He smiled at Clare and seemed as eager to help as Harry was reluctant.

Gil appeared ill at ease and avoided Clare's eye. She wondered about him. He wasn't your typical taxi driver. A quiet lad, possibly still living at home with his mother.

She pondered whether he might have a girlfriend. Or a boyfriend. He struck her as someone who struggled with social situations, making taxi driving an odd choice of career.

Harry looked at his watch. 'We've fares to pick up, Inspector, so if you could hurry it along...'

Clare decided she didn't much like Harry. Had he and Andy been friends, or had they clashed? She delivered the news of Andy's death carefully, watching their reactions.

'Fucksake,' Harry said. Then, 'What – really? Andy's dead?'

Clare nodded. Robert, she thought, looked shocked while Gil continued to stare at the floor. She let this sink in then went on.

'And I have to tell you, gents, that we believe Andy's death to be suspicious.'

Again, it was Harry who found his voice. 'Suspicious? Like what? Some'dy had a go at him?'

Clare didn't answer this directly. Instead, she asked, 'Would that be unusual? Was Andy the kind of man who upset people?'

Harry shrugged at this but said nothing.

Robert shook his head. 'Not really, Inspector. He was a bit of a lad, you know, but everyone liked him.' He looked round at the others for confirmation. Harry looked noncommittal and Gil said nothing.

'Did everyone here get on okay with him?' Clare asked.

'Yeah, fine,' Harry said. 'We all get on. Besta pals.'

Robert met Harry's eye then glanced over at Gil but said nothing.

Clare wasn't convinced but she let it go. 'Anyone know where Andy socialised? Any of you go out with him? Pubs, clubs, that sort of thing.'

They shook their heads.

'Not even Thursday nights?'

They looked genuinely surprised at this.

'Why Thursday?' Robert asked.

'We believe Andy went out regularly on Thursdays, but we don't know where he went.'

'Somewhere he could pick up lassies,' Harry said.

Clare looked at the three of them. They weren't giving much away. Was that because they didn't know much about Andy, or were they hiding something? Young Gil certainly was.

She asked a few more questions but learned little that she didn't already know. Yes, Andy was a ladies' man but, as far as they knew, he hadn't upset anyone. He was a good driver who generally got on well with customers.

It didn't look as if any more was forthcoming, so she took names, addresses and vehicle registration numbers, then let them drift off. When they had gone she spoke quietly to Jakki. 'Could you ask that young lad to come outside for a minute, please? Discreetly.'

Jakki nodded and Clare went out into the street. A few minutes later the door opened. She saw Gil hesitate, then come out, closing the door behind him. She motioned to him to come further up the road, out of sight of the office.

'It's Gil, isn't it?' she said, perching on a wall.

The lad hesitated, then sat beside her, unwilling to meet her eye. 'Yeah.'

'Well, Gil, I've been in this game a few years now and you get good at spotting when someone's being evasive.'

Gil stared straight ahead. Clare thought she saw his lips thin. He glanced at her quickly then glanced away again.

'You didn't like Andy Robb, did you?'

He shrugged.

'Any special reason?'

There was a silence. He swallowed and seemed to be considering what to say. 'Guys like him...'

'Yes?'

'Think they own the place, don't they? Think they're God's gift.'

'With women, you mean?'

'Yeah.'

Clare was starting to understand. 'Do you have a girlfriend, Gil?'

Gil began to worry a loose paving slab with the toe of his shoe. 'Used to.'

'Something to do with Andy?'

Another silence. 'He didn't even want her. Just wanted to prove he could.'

'Who was she?'

'Marta. Marta Mieszko. She was Polish.'

'Was she a student? Or did she work in the town?'

'She was an au pair. For one of the university professors. I think she's back in Poland now, though. At least that's what I heard.'

'Do you know the name of her employer? The professor?'

'Yeah. Professor Slater. House in Wardlaw Gardens.'

Clare noted this down then looked back at Gil. He was twisting his hands.

'Gil, where were you on Saturday night?'

'Here. Working.'

'Which car?'

'The seven-seater. It's all recorded.'

'What time did you finish?'

The slab was quite loose now, and he rocked it back and forth with his foot. ''Bout two.'

'Two o'clock on Sunday morning?'

'Yeah.'

'Can you remember where you were about midnight, Gil?'

'Uh-huh. Driving a couple back to a farmhouse. Just off the A915.'

It took all Clare's self-control not to react. The A915, she now knew, ran parallel to the A917. A short detour across a side road would have taken Gil right to the Kenlybank Hotel. And a taxi driver would know this too.

Gil turned to meet her eye for the first time. 'I know how it looks,' he said, 'Andy told us he was going to a hotel out that end of town. His sister's wedding, he said. But I didn't go near the place and I didn't kill him. I might have wanted to, but the truth is I don't have the guts.'

Clare looked at him. He was the picture of misery.

'I didn't kill him,' he said again.

Gil was near to tears now. Clare wondered how many more lives Andy Robb's womanising had ruined. 'Okay, Gil,' she said, giving his arm a pat. 'We'll leave it there for now.'

She lingered on the wall, lost in thought after Gil had gone back into the office. A minute or two later Jakki came out, looking for her.

'I know what you're thinking,' she began, 'but that lad wouldn't hurt a fly. Andy was rotten to him, with his girlfriend and all that, but the lad wouldn't do something like that.'

Clare smiled. 'Noted.'

Jakki hesitated. 'There's something else, though. About Andy. The boss, Martin… well, he's not here today. But they had words. Last week. I heard them arguing.'

'Any idea what it was about?'

She shook her head. 'Sorry. I started to listen then the phone went.'

'Did they often fall out?'

'Andy could cause a row in an empty house. And not just with Martin either. Martin's a good boss but Andy – well, he could be difficult.'

'Is Martin at home today?'

'No, but he'll be back tonight. I'll give you his mobile number.'

Clare took the card with Martin's name and number and tucked it into her pocket. 'One more thing – did Andy ever work on a Thursday night?'

'Oh no. I can tell you that for sure. He would only ever do a day shift on a Thursday.'

Clare thanked her and headed back to the station. The list of people Andy had upset was growing. She'd have to pull Jim and Sara in to help with the interviews and maybe some of the others, too. As she started the engine and pulled away she wondered where the hell Andy had gone on Thursday evenings and whether it had any bearing on his murder.

Chapter 5

Back at the station, Clare called Chris, Jim, Sara and a handful of uniformed cops into the incident room to pool information.

'Right,' she said. 'We have Andy at the Kenlybank Hotel as a wedding guest last night and for some reason he heads off down the drive around midnight. Any update on his phone records, Chris?'

'Yep. We have his contacts and we're working our way through them. Checked his calls too. No calls on Saturday but he receives a text at 11:50 p.m. from an unidentified number. Probably pay-as-you-go. He replies, and a bit of flirting goes on between them. Looks like the texter was inviting him outside for a liaison.'

'Can you get a printout of the conversation, Chris?'

Chris nodded. 'There's a final message, about twenty minutes later from Mrs Robb, asking where the fuck he is.'

'That it?' Clare asked.

'Yep.'

'So, let's assume the texter is our driver – the murderer. Now, Andy's known for shagging around. The driver sends suggestive texts to entice him out and, when he's far enough down the drive, runs him over.'

'How did the driver get Andy's number?'

'Good point, Chris. Is it someone who knows him? Does Andy have his number visible on Facebook? Could it be one of his existing contacts, using a different phone?'

Clare turned to the whiteboard and wrote *11:50 p.m. – text exchange between victim and murderer.*

'Any chance it could have been an accident, Clare? Hit-and-run – driver panicked and drove off?' Jim asked.

'Doubtful. The car drove right over him then backed over him again on the way out. If it had been an accident the driver would probably have hit the brakes as soon as he collided with Andy.'

'It could have been a taxi arriving to take someone home?' Jim persisted.

'Fair point. Check with local taxi companies to see if they took a call for a pick-up around midnight. Don't forget the hotel staff, either. Someone might have asked them to phone for a cab.'

Chris raised his hand. 'What about that numbered card, boss?'

'What indeed. Any theories, guys?'

Heads shook and Clare pressed on.

'Tyre tracks – Sara, any progress?'

'Yep. Spoke to a couple of tyre fitters and both said the same thing. These tyres are generally fitted only to Land Rovers or Range Rovers.'

'Couldn't be a Qashqai?'

'Definitely not.'

'Any news on stolen cars, Jim?'

'Narrowing it down. Forty-plus in total over the three counties, but I'll see how many are Land Rovers or Range Rovers and let you know.'

Clare looked round the room. 'Who's going through the ANPR footage?'

A uniformed cop raised her hand. 'Me, boss.'

'Okay, Gillian, I want the reg numbers for any Land Rovers or Range Rovers picked up between eleven p.m. and one in the morning. Time, direction, owners, stolen or not.'

Gillian scribbled in her notebook and Clare carried on.

'Now that we have the make narrowed down we need to speak to owners of Land Rovers and Range Rovers – not just the stolen ones. Let's start with a ten-mile radius of St Andrews and see what that throws up. If the owners are close by, interview them in person, otherwise, by phone. Jim, can you get onto that?'

Jim nodded.

Clare continued. 'Chris, I'd like you to concentrate on stolen cars, in case it was joy-riders. I suspect not, but we have to check.'

She looked round at them. 'There's a fair few folk need interviewing. Martin Simms, the owner of Swilcan Taxis. Prioritise him. He and Andy had a difficult relationship. Then Andy's current girlfriend, Vicky – we need her parents spoken to. Did the dad have a problem with his daughter seeing a married man? Billy Dodds' background needs checking too. He's Angela's boyfriend. Delivery driver for the hospital. Drives a Qashqai which doesn't have the right tyres but we can't rule him out yet. I've a couple of ex-girlfriends to check which I'll do shortly. Chris and Jim, when you're done with cars and phone contacts, can you look into Billy, please? Plus Andy's phone records for calls received in the last month.' She looked around. 'Anything else?'

Chris raised his hand again. 'Thursday nights. Should we be looking into where he went?'

'Good call. You carry on as planned and I'll do that. Let's put in a couple more hours, then call it a night. Back here for eight tomorrow morning.'

Clare found Professor Slater's phone number with little difficulty and sat down to call him. He confirmed that Marta Mieszko was their au pair and that, to the best of his knowledge, she had returned to Poland almost a year ago.

'My wife drove her to Edinburgh airport to catch her flight.'

'And have you heard from Marta since then? Is she still in Poland?'

'I believe my wife's still in touch with her. On Facebook, I think. I can ask her if you like.'

'Thanks.'

Clare put down the phone and drew a line through Marta's name in her notebook. It was worth checking if she had boarded a flight to Poland a year or so ago but it was almost certainly a dead end. Time to see if Kayleigh the barmaid could throw any light on Andy's murder.

–

The Thistle was quieter than at lunchtime. A young, dark-haired girl with lips the colour of claret was polishing glasses behind the bar. Clare flashed her warrant card and asked for Kayleigh.

'I'm Kayleigh,' the girl said. 'Len told me to expect you.'

Clare thought Kayleigh looked more curious than upset. It looked as if Len hadn't been tempted to tell

55

her about Andy. 'Maybe we could sit down for a few minutes?' she said.

Kayleigh led Clare to a table at a window, one eye on the bar. 'You were asking about Andy?'

'You were his girlfriend, I gather?'

'That's right. For a while anyway, till he met that au pair girl.' She looked tearful. 'He said he loved me. But he didn't really. Just wanted... well, you know.'

'You mean sex? He was just after sex? Sorry to be so direct, Kayleigh, but I'm trying to build up a picture of Andy.'

Kayleigh nodded. 'Yes, that's about it. Once he'd got what he wanted – well, he lost interest.'

Clare gave what she hoped was a sympathetic smile then went on. 'Kayleigh, can you tell me where you were last night?'

Kayleigh's eyes widened. 'Here. Working. Why? Has Andy done something?'

'I'm afraid Andy met with an accident last night and we're asking anyone who knew him to tell us where they were.'

'Is he all right? Is he in hospital?'

'I'm afraid he died.'

Kayleigh said nothing, for a minute. Her eyes were bright but Clare could see she was making an effort to remain composed. 'He *died*?' Her voice was a whisper.

'Yes.'

'And you think I had something to do with it?'

Clare looked at the girl. A more unlikely murderer it would be difficult to imagine. But she knew from experience not to make assumptions. 'We need to check everyone who had a connection with Andy. That's all. So, last night?'

'As I said, I was here. Behind the bar. Ask Len. He'll tell you.'

'What time did you finish?'

'Midnight, officially, but Len opened a bottle and we all had a drink after closing. I left about quarter to one.'

Clare noted this down and hoped Len would confirm Kayleigh's story. The more she learned about Andy the less she wanted any of these young girls to have been involved. He'd caused enough heartache already.

Kayleigh's eyes strayed to the bar. A customer was standing, wallet in hand. 'I'll have to serve this customer. Was there anything else?'

'Only if you can think of anyone who might have wanted to harm Andy.'

'Harm him?' Kayleigh said. 'Oh no, Inspector. He treated me badly, but I wouldn't go that far. He's not worth it.'

She went off to serve the customer and Clare pressed a bell on the end of the bar. Len, the manager, appeared from the kitchen. When he saw Clare, his face fell momentarily then he forced a smile. 'Inspector. I hope Kayleigh's okay? Not upset too much?'

'She'll be fine. Just one more question, if you don't mind. What time did your staff leave last night?'

He hesitated. 'I hope you don't think I've been serving after hours.'

Clare shook her head. 'Not at all. I just need to know.'

'The last few punters left shortly after midnight. I said to the girls to leave the clearing up for the morning and

I opened a bottle. It was a long day and I thought they deserved a drink on the house.'

'How long did they stay?'

He considered this. 'Probably till about quarter to one, something like that.'

This chimed with Kayleigh's story. Either they were in it together or they were telling the truth. Somehow, she couldn't see them as co-conspirators in the murder of Andy Robb, particularly so long after he had dumped Kayleigh. She thanked Len for his time and returned to the station to help with the phone calls.

—

It was almost eleven when Clare shut up shop and headed home. They now had names and addresses for three people who had reported either a Range Rover or a Land Rover stolen in the St Andrews area. Martin Simms had been interviewed by Chris and Jim, as had Vicky's parents and the consensus was, while they weren't Andy's biggest fans, they probably didn't dislike him enough to run him over. Clare's research into Thursday night clubs had been equally unsuccessful. She had tried gyms and sports clubs, pubs with quiz nights, cinema clubs, even bridge clubs. None of them had Andy as a member. She could ask Sara to trawl through traffic cam footage on Thursday nights to check for Andy's car but, at present, she didn't have the manpower. That was something else. She'd have to request a Major Investigation Team to help and they'd probably send a DCI. She sent up a silent prayer that it wouldn't be Tony McAvettie. No one who had been there just before Easter could forget the day that Chris, a newly promoted DS, discovered Tony had been sleeping with his girlfriend.

Chris had almost broken Tony's nose. It was only thanks to them all closing ranks and insisting Tony had slipped and fallen that Chris had escaped the consequences. But Tony wouldn't have forgotten.

Clare yawned. It had been a long day and the prospect of going home to make food didn't appeal. She decided to drive home via Spice Palace. It would give her the chance to check Billy Dodds' takeaway on Saturday night. The shop on Market Street was quiet and, having given her order, she sat down on a plastic chair to wait. And then she remembered Billy Dodds. Struggling to her feet, she asked the girl at the counter to check their records. And sure enough, a delivery had been made to a Mr Dodds in Cupar on Saturday night.

'Oh that's Billy,' the girl said, 'I remember now. About eight thirty it was. Supposed to be eight but we were busy.'

'You know him?'

'Yeah, he's a regular. Gets on well with Arjun, the owner.'

Clare thanked her, paid for her order, and took the bag containing her lamb bhuna out to the car. Market Street was one-way, and she drove over the cobbles until she saw Cromars, where she and Chris had stopped for chips one night after a late shift. She turned left, past the university's Buchanan Building then left again into North Street. She passed the gothic St Salvator's Chapel with its arched entrance to the university quadrangle. The street was deserted now and, despite her weariness, Clare slowed the car and sat for some moments taking in the ancient building, quiet now in the absence of tourists and red-gowned students. She glanced at the clock on the dashboard, saw it would soon be midnight and pulled away again, past the small cinema advertising the Elton John biopic, *Rocketman*.

Tom liked Elton John. He would want to see the film.

And, not for the first time, Clare wondered if she had done the right thing, ending her relationship with Tom and moving to St Andrews. Away from the comfort blanket that had been her life in Glasgow. Tears pricked her eyes as she turned onto City Road towards the house which was beginning to feel less and less like home.

Chapter 6

Clare sat perusing Andy's bank statements. There was a clear pattern. Every Thursday night he withdrew one hundred pounds at a cashpoint, usually in St Andrews town centre. But then he would frequently withdraw more money on Fridays or Saturdays. He was going somewhere on Thursday nights and spending a hundred quid. Casinos? Clare scribbled this down and turned to her computer to search online for the nearest casinos. Betting shops too. Better check them. The worst-case scenario was a private gambling arrangement. They'd never find that.

Chris popped his head round her office door. 'Funny thing, boss...'

'Yeah?'

'One of the stolen vehicles, a Land Rover, was reported stolen by one of the band from Saturday's wedding.'

'What?'

'Yep. Fergus Bain. Plays the accordion. Reported stolen just over a month ago.'

'Well, we can certainly rule him out. A hundred guests danced to his playing while Andy was being run over.'

'It's a bit of a coincidence, though.'

'Agreed. Let's pay him a visit and see what he has to say for himself. Is he local?'

'Farm cottage, just outside town, on the road to Strathkinness.'

'Strath what?'

Chris picked up the car keys. 'I'll drive.'

As they reached the top of Largo Road he pointed out the community hospital. 'Where Angela and Billy work.'

The A915 lay ahead but Chris turned right, away from the hospital and into a housing estate. 'This is Bogward.'

Clare nodded. 'I've been here before,' she said. 'Couple of weeks ago. Sudden death in a house, next on the right. So, where's Strathkinness from here?'

'I'm taking the back road,' Chris said. 'It's a small village a few miles west of St Andrews. If I'm right, I reckon our accordionist's cottage will be this side of the village, about a mile along this road.'

Chris drove on as the housing estate gave way to fields, gaudy with yellow oilseed rape. After a few minutes, Chris indicated right and pulled into the side of the road beside two single-storey cottages. They were low, stone-built dwellings with orange pan-tiled roofs. To the side of one was a garage with wooden doors, secured by a bolt which looked as if it had seen better days.

'I think that's our man's,' Chris said, indicating the cottage next to the garage.

There was no answer to their knock, but a woman, dressed in overalls, her hands smeared with oil, appeared round the side of the other cottage.

'He'll be out on the fields,' she told them, wiping her hands on a rag. 'Does a bit of work for the farmer. Busy time of year.'

Clare smiled. 'Any idea when he'll be back?'

The woman glanced at her watch. 'Usually breaks about twelve. But sometimes he has a piece with him and doesn't come back till later. Can I give him a message?'

She was hovering, fishing for titbits.

'We're just looking into his stolen car,' said Clare. 'But we can pop back this evening.'

'Oh, I know. He's quite lost without it. He has a moped but it's not the same. Can't get your shopping on a moped, can you?'

'Do you remember when it was stolen?'

'Must be a couple of weeks ago now. Parked down at the North Haugh car park.'

'That's near North Street, isn't it?' Clare asked.

The neighbour nodded. 'A bit further down, near the roundabout at the Old Course Hotel. It's free parking there, you know and it's always been fine. Near the university buildings so lots of coming and going. I park there myself. Anyway, he went to do a bit of shopping and when he came back it was gone. You can't trust anyone these days.'

The neighbour seemed to be settling in for a long chat, so they made their excuses and escaped to the car.

As Chris pulled away, Clare's mobile rang.

It was Jim. 'Sorry, Clare, you're needed over at Cromarty House.'

'Where?'

'Big house off the A915. Couple of miles after the hospital. You'll see the police car.'

'What's going on?'

'Looks like another hit-and-run.'

Clare closed her eyes. Another hit-and-run. Christ almighty. Surely there wasn't someone driving round, picking victims off with a 4x4? An uneasy knot was forming in her stomach. 'Okay, Jim. Be there in ten.'

They raced back through the Bogward estate, siren blaring, turning onto the A915 at the community hospital. This time there was no crowd to interview. In fact, there was no one around at all except for the postman who had discovered the body.

'I turned into the drive as usual,' he said. 'Normally I drive right up but as soon as I came through the gates I saw it. Him, I mean. I think it's the owner. Only had a quick look. Dog was running around too.'

Clare looked up the drive. She could see the house, a fairly substantial Edwardian dwelling with white rendered walls, but there was no sign of life. 'Did he live alone? The owner?'

'I don't think so. At least he gets mail addressed to Mr and Mrs. See?' He thrust that morning's mail into Clare's hand.

'Mr and Mrs Bruce Gilmartin,' she said to Chris. 'Ring any bells?'

'I've heard of him,' Jim said. 'Owns a brewing business, out towards Cupar.' He looked up the drive. 'Doing well out of it too, judging by the size of the house.'

Clare pulled on overshoes and gloves, and moved towards the body. He was, she thought, in his late forties, casually dressed in chinos and an open-necked shirt. Boat shoes, no socks. He had either been facing the car when he fell or the impact had spun him round. His eyes were still open, but lifeless. Even in death, Clare could see he had been an attractive man. She crouched down beside the body. It was cold and stiff. 'Rigor's well established,' she said. 'I'd guess at late last night.'

'Pathologist's on his way,' Jim said. 'SOCO too so hopefully we'll get that confirmed.'

'Anyone been up to the house?'

Jim nodded. 'No one at home. Not sure where Mrs Gilmartin is but there's no sign of her.'

'Car?'

'Two. Both in garages at the end of the garden. A Range Rover and a sporty Audi. Garages are unlocked. I put the dog in there to keep him away from the body.'

Chris's ears pricked up at the mention of a Range Rover. 'Let's ask SOCO to give it a look.'

'Yeah, good thinking, Chris. Then get onto the brewery and see if you can find out where Mrs Gilmartin is. If he's been here all night, why hasn't she reported him missing?'

'Why indeed.'

The pathologist pulled up in his van, followed a few minutes later by the SOCO team who began setting up their cordon. Clare walked back out onto the road. The house and garden sat on a gentle curve so a car could have been waiting just round the bend and been invisible to the victim. The similarity to Andy Robb's murder couldn't be ignored. She approached the pathologist.

'Morning, Neil. Thanks for coming out so quickly.'

Neil Grant was someone who smiled easily, somehow at odds with the nature of his job. He stopped short of the cordon to don a white suit and overshoes, and affected a groan. 'I'm getting too old for this, Clare,' he said.

'Rubbish! You're in your prime.'

'Five years to retirement. Not that I'm counting.'

'You'll never retire,' she told him. 'You love it.'

Neil smiled. 'Aye, maybe.' He pulled on a pair of forensic gloves then turned to look at the body. 'So, another hit-and-run, is it? Two in a couple of days. Must be a record for St Andrews.'

'Yeah, it's not great. Look, I know you just got here, but I'm keen to know if there's any chance the victim could have been hit out there on the road.'

Neil slipped under the tape and looked all round the body. 'Doubtful,' he said. 'I'm pretty sure he was hit here. Look how he's been pushed down into the gravel. The ground's pretty dry but he's sunk down a good few inches. The weight of the vehicle has pushed the body down. I'll be surprised if there isn't bruising from the gravel right up the legs and back.'

'So it could be deliberate, then? Someone pulled off the road and ran him down?'

Neil Grant looked down the drive. 'I'd guess he was walking out to the road when he saw the car approaching and he backtracked. Maybe thought he had a visitor and walked back into the drive to make way for the car.' Neil stopped for a minute, looked down at the body then back at the drive. 'Then he realises the car's out of control. He needs to get out of the way and quickly. He starts to run and then – see how he's face-up, but his shoulder's turned? I'd guess he was running up the drive and he turned back to look just as it struck him. The car's caught him and spun him round.'

It was a chilling thought. Being chased up his drive by a car, possibly in darkness. A fleeting picture of the man's last seconds passed through her mind, but she set this aside. There was work to be done. Neil was going through the dead man's pockets. He retrieved a set of keys which he dropped into a clear evidence bag then handed to Clare.

'House keys, probably; a bit bent but you might still get in. Phone's wrecked, though. Hold on…' Neil retrieved something carefully from a top pocket in the shirt. 'Here we are.' He showed Clare a piece of card with the figure four written on. 'Same as the other one. You appear to have a joker on your hands.'

Clare glanced at Chris, an uneasy feeling in the pit of her stomach. 'I don't like this, Chris. I don't like it one bit.' She took the card carefully from Neil and put it into a clear evidence bag.

'Better get both cards fingerprinted,' Chris said, 'although I'll be surprised if our driver didn't wear gloves.'

'Yeah, I suppose so. The thing is, if both cards show the same prints, and these two men were murdered by the same person…'

'What's the connection?'

'Exactly. What would a philandering taxi driver like Andy Robb have to do with a wealthy brewery owner?'

Clare headed up the drive to the house with the keys Neil had found. She let the dog, an English Bull Terrier, out of the garage. A metal disc dangled from his tartan collar: *Benjy.*

'Come on, Benjy,' she said, pulling his lead gently.

He trotted after her, stopping only to cock his leg on a lavender bush. A path from the garage led to a side door with a Yale lock. Her hands still gloved, Clare tried one of the Yale keys on the keyring. The door opened to a large, bright kitchen. She scanned the room and saw the dog's bowls on the floor. Benjy sniffed at them, but both were empty. He looked up at Clare, expectantly. Clare picked up one of the bowls and filled it with water. As Benjy drank she opened cupboards until she found a bag of dry dog food. She poured some into the other bowl. Benjy fell on it and Clare took the opportunity to look round the kitchen. She noticed a wall planner pinned up next to the fridge. The word *Amsterdam* was written in red across five days, from the seventeenth to the twenty-first.

'Looks like the wife is away,' she said to Chris when he joined her in the kitchen.

'So, they use a red pen for her and blue for him?' Chris said, rubbing the dog's head.

Clare nodded. 'Think so. Unless he was into Pilates and yoga. Can you get onto Edinburgh airport please, Chris? Find out if they fly to Amsterdam on a Friday. If not Edinburgh, try Glasgow. See if she went.'

'Will do.'

The dog was sitting at their feet now, having emptied his food bowl. 'Not quite sure what we do with you,' Clare said, picking up the end of his lead. 'I'm guessing our victim was out giving the dog a last walk when he was run over.'

'No neighbours nearby. Want me to take him back to the station?'

'If you could. And we'll need some bodies out here to check round the house in case it was an aggravated burglary, although it looks unlikely. We'll also need to get in touch with Mrs Gilmartin and let her know the sad news. Maybe the brewery staff can help. Can you get onto that too, please?'

'Yeah, sure. We are assuming she isn't the one who ran him over?'

Clare's expression hardened. 'Nothing ruled in or out at this stage.'

Outside, SOCO were examining the area around the body for tyre tracks, although the ground was drier than on Saturday night.

'Might get something off his trousers,' one of them told Clare.

'Does it look like the same tread? Land Rover or Range Rover?'

'Impossible to say out here. We'll have a better idea in the lab where we can measure it properly. But it does look to be quite a wide tyre.'

'There's a Range Rover in the garage.'

'We'll check it out before we go,' the SOCO man said.

Clare stood. The two murders were so similar and so close together, there must be a connection. But what? What could the two victims possibly have in common? If there was a link, it would mean she was only looking for one killer but what on earth would the motive be? And there was something about those numbered cards that worried her. First a card with the number five and now an identical card with the number four. Could it be some kind of countdown? What if this was a serial killer? And one that was too clever for them all? Her mouth suddenly was dry and she licked her lips. Who was doing this – and why?

From somewhere, a dim recollection – a film or a book maybe – *You can expect three more of these.*

Chapter 7

When Clare returned to the station, she found that Benjy the Bull Terrier was officially a hit. He was sitting atop the broad front counter being fed titbits and thoroughly admired by staff and callers, including a reporter from the Fife Newsday website who had somehow heard about Bruce Gilmartin's death.

'Any news on what happened to Mr Gilmartin? Prominent businessman and all that. I'm sure our readers will be keen to know.'

Clare smiled sweetly and suggested he contact the press office, giving him the number. He hung about on the pretext of entertaining the dog until Sara gently but firmly led him to the door.

'I'll call back in a wee while,' he said, as Sara closed the door behind him. It was opened again seconds later by a tall man in a dark grey suit and what looked like an old school tie.

'DCI Alastair Gibson,' he announced. 'Inspector Mackay?'

Clare, who had been poring over a printout of Andy Robb's phone contacts, whirled round on hearing her name. She moved forward to meet the visitor. 'I'm Clare Mackay. I take it you're our SIO, sir?'

He didn't immediately respond but raised a single eyebrow. '*Clare* Mackay, did you say?'

Clare met his gaze steadily. Whatever he had heard about her, she was determined not to be intimidated, particularly by someone whose bearing was clearly designed to do just that. 'Yes, sir.'

He looked at her, unsmiling. 'Hmm – your office please, Inspector?'

Clare led him through the security door to the back of the station and into her office. She held the door open and was dismayed to find him stride past her and plant himself in her chair. She was thankful, at least, that they hadn't sent Tony McAvettie. Clare took a seat opposite and waited.

DCI Gibson pressed his hands together and scrutinised Clare. After a few moments he said, 'So I need to know, Inspector, if you're fit for this kind of duty. After that incident in Glasgow. The Ritchie lad – and the gun.'

Below the desk, Clare's hands found the sides of her chair and she gripped them tightly. Was she never going to stop having this same conversation? 'Of course, sir,' she said, her tone as pleasant as she could manage. 'I've been here for two months now.' She avoided his eyes and said, 'Had a few investigations under my belt since Glasgow.' This wasn't strictly true but she wasn't having this jumped up suit from some posh station in Edinburgh thinking she wasn't up to the job.

'You sure? I can easily bring in another inspector for this one. Let you concentrate on the routine stuff. I'm sure we could find plenty for you to do.'

Clare became acutely aware of the pulse beating in her temple. She wondered if the DCI could see it. She felt her cheeks redden and she swallowed a couple of times before finding her voice. 'Thank you, sir, but this is my patch and my investigation.'

He looked at her intently. 'If you say so, Inspector. Now, bring me up to speed, please. What's been happening?'

Clare moved her chair closer to the desk, feeling rather like a visitor in her own office. 'We've had two sudden deaths, both hit-and-runs, both look deliberate. One on Saturday night, one discovered this morning, probably happened on Sunday night.'

'Connection?'

'There is a link, sir, but I can't make sense of it.'

'Explain, please.'

Clare told him about the two numbered cards found on the bodies. 'The first was a five and the second one a four. Forensics have them but from what I could see it looks like the same card, same ink.'

'And you've no idea what it means?'

'Not yet, sir. But we've yet to interview the family of the second one. Employees too. He owns a brewing company near Cupar.'

DCI Gibson sat forward in his chair. 'Not Bruce Gilmartin?'

'Did you know him?'

He winced at her use of the past tense. 'I certainly did. We were at school together. Great chap. I – I can't believe it. Has anyone told Jennifer?'

'Jennifer?'

'Mrs Gilmartin. Surely you've told her?'

'We can't get in touch with her. It looks like she's on a short break in Amsterdam. Our DS is checking with Edinburgh airport. We'll find her, but it'll take time.'

DCI Gibson took out his mobile phone. 'I have her number. I'll give her a call.' He began navigating through his contacts to find it.

Clare frowned. They didn't even know if she was in Amsterdam. Didn't have enough information to rule her out.

She cleared her throat. 'Wouldn't it be better if the news came from an official police source?'

He glared at her. 'Are you suggesting, Inspector, that I am not an official police source?'

'No sir, only that she might react differently to you, being a friend. And – well – we don't know yet that she *is* in Amsterdam. She could even be a suspect.'

'Don't be ridiculous, Inspector. I've known Jennifer for twenty years.'

'I'm just saying I would like to judge her reaction. Hear how she takes the news. Just to satisfy myself.'

'I think you can safely leave that to me, Inspector. I have done this once or twice, you know.'

She made one last effort. 'Can I ask you to put it on speakerphone then, sir, so I can at least hear her voice?'

'Nope.'

He was about to tell her to go when the call was answered. 'Ah, Jennifer, how are you? Al Gibson. Good to hear from you… yes, I can hear that. You're where? Ah yes. Lovely city…'

Clare strained to hear but there was music in the background and it was hard to make out what Jennifer

Gilmartin was saying. The DCI swivelled the chair round, turning his back on Clare.

'I'm afraid it's official police business,' he went on. 'Yes, I fear I have some bad news. It's Bruce. He's met with an accident... No, I'm so sorry, Jen. Bruce died last night.'

There was a pause, then the DCI took up the conversation again. 'When are you flying back?'

Another pause.

'To be honest, Jen, it's probably just as well leaving it until tomorrow now. I'll send a car to meet you at Edinburgh if you let me know the time. I know, it must be such a shock. Yes... Post-mortem... I can't say too much at this stage, but it seems to be a road traffic accident.'

Clare thought that was stretching the truth a little, but she understood his reticence.

'Okay, Jen. Take care now. See you tomorrow.'

He terminated the call and scowled at Clare. She wasn't quite sure why, but her place seemed to be firmly in the wrong.

'How did she take it?' she asked.

'She's devastated of course. Fortunately, she's out there on a girls' weekend so at least she has her friends with her. Flying back tomorrow afternoon. Send someone to the airport to meet her.'

Clare bit her lip. They weren't exactly drowning in manpower. On the other hand, if she sent someone astute like Jim, he could gauge her mood. See if she really was a grieving widow. 'No problem. I've a uniformed sergeant who's good at that sort of thing.'

'I want everything thrown at this, Clare. He's a high-profile businessman and he was a bloody good friend.'

'Of course. Do they have children?'

The DCI shook his head. 'Just the two of them. She'll be on her own now.' He lapsed into silence for a moment then recovered himself. 'What about the other victim?'

'A taxi driver, name of Andy Robb. Lives in the town. He was at a wedding — hotel a mile or so out of town. We believe he received a text message to meet someone outside. He went down the hotel drive and was run over.'

'Not an accident? One of the guests driving over the limit?'

'Normally, that would be my first thought. But we can't ignore those numbered cards.'

'It's odd, certainly,' the DCI agreed. 'Anyone in the frame?'

'Not yet, sir. We're working our way through the contacts for the first victim and gathering information about the second.'

'Fair enough, but I'd like to see some progress. And soon, Inspector.'

Clare's phone began to ring and she snatched it up. SOCO.

'Inspector — we've recovered a USB stick from the first victim's car. Tiny little thing, taped to the underside of the glove box.'

Clare thought this might be the break she needed. 'I'll send someone over for it now.'

She dialled Chris's number and turned to DCI Gibson as she waited. 'Any chance of a few more bodies, sir? We're running two murder enquiries on a shoestring here.'

'Yes, of course. I'll have another three detectives over in the morning. Could do a uniform or two as well if necessary.'

'It's okay. The team here can do overtime for now. And Cupar station will help out. I might come back to you though if we don't make headway.'

Chris's voice said, 'Yes, boss?' in her ear.

'Chris, I need you to get over to SOCO please. They've found a memory stick in Andy Robb's car.'

'Anything on it?'

'That's what we need to find out.'

There was a tap at the door and Sara poked her head in. 'Boss, there's a man here looking for you. Said you were investigating his stolen car? Fergus someone.'

The accordionist from the wedding.

Clare remembered Fergus Bain from Saturday night. He'd had little to say then, other than confirming Andy had headed outside while the other guests were dancing Strip the Willow. His statement had told them nothing they didn't already know, and she'd let him go after a few minutes.

But now there was his Land Rover. Stolen a couple of weeks ago, according to the neighbour. Could it be the vehicle used in the two attacks? If so, he might have information that would help them find it. She looked at him now with renewed interest. He was stocky with a weather-beaten face, doubtless earned through years of outdoor farm work. He seemed uncomfortable in his surroundings, his shoulders hunched, hands plunged deep into his pockets.

'I hear you were askin' about ma car.' His accent, Clare thought, was broader than those she had become used to hearing in St Andrews. More west Fife, perhaps.

'That's right. If you'll follow me...' Clare opened the door to a small interview room. Fergus hesitated then walked into the room. Clare followed and offered him a chair. He sat slowly on the edge of the seat, as if ready to bolt. Clare sat opposite and took out her notebook.

'So, Mr Bain, your car was a...?'

'Land Rover Defender.'

'Ah yes... We have the details on our system. And it was stolen on...?'

'Third o' May.'

'From the North Haugh car park?'

'Yeah. Have you found it?'

'I'm afraid not. But we are looking for a Land Rover or Range Rover in connection with the death at the Kenlybank Hotel on Saturday night. Now I know we spoke to you then, but have you remembered anything else about that night? Anything at all?'

His dark eyes were expressionless. 'Like I said. I was on stage all night, 'cept for a break about ten. But the guy was killed later, wasn't he?'

Clare didn't answer this. 'Going back to the day your car was stolen, can you recall seeing anyone acting suspiciously? Or is there anyone you suspect might have taken it? It is important, Mr Bain.'

He shook his head. 'It wasnae even that new. Cannae think why someb'dy would want it.'

'Can you recall what the tread on the tyres was like?'

'Pretty good. Has to be to get a grip in the fields, like.'

'I don't suppose you have a photo of it?'

'Naw. Not ma style. Cannae be doing with folk always taking photos of stuff. 'Specially cars. Cannae see the point.'

Clare rose. 'Well, thanks for coming in, Mr Bain. I'm sorry we don't have any news of your car yet, but we'll

77

keep in touch. Meanwhile if you do see it or hear anything about it you will let us know, won't you?'

'Aye. No' getting my hopes up though. It'll probably turn up burnt out somewhere. Wee scumbags.'

Clare thought he was probably right and went back to her office to update the DCI.

–

Chris appeared half an hour later with the memory stick in an evidence bag. 'They've gone over it for prints so we're okay to have a look,' he said. 'I can have a go, but it might need to go down to Tech Support in Glenrothes if I can't find anything.'

'Supposing there's something to find,' the DCI said.

'He must have hidden it for a reason,' Clare pointed out. 'See what you can do, Chris. We don't have time for a forty-mile round trip.'

The DCI ignored this. 'Let's have a look at it, then.'

Chris inserted the stick into a computer and waited while the security software scanned it. 'Of course, if it's password protected or the file's encrypted, we'll have to send it to Tech Support.' The drive appeared. 'Our lucky day. No encryption.'

'Now why would someone who went to the trouble of concealing it in the furthest corner of the glove compartment leave the contents unprotected?' the DCI wanted to know.

Chris navigated various empty folders on the drive. 'I would guess because there's bugger all on it. It looks like one Word document and a folder with around sixty megabytes of files.'

'Can you open them?' Clare asked.

He clicked the Word document and immediately was prompted for a password. 'No luck with this,' he said. 'Password protected.'

'You can't bypass the password?'

'Nope. I mean Tech Support probably can. They'll have cracker software. Might take a few days though.' Chris moved to the folder and double-clicked.

'Now we're getting somewhere,' Clare said, as the folder opened to reveal an array of files.

'Sorry, Clare. Afraid not.' Chris jabbed the screen with his finger. 'See the file names? Look at the extensions...'

Clare looked. '.gpg – I've never heard of that. What kind of file is it?'

'Can't tell the type of file. But the extension is the giveaway. They're all encrypted. Gnu Privacy Guard.'

'Which is?' The DCI's tone was becoming testy.

'Encryption software. Free to download. Quite commonly used.'

'So we can't open them?'

Chris shook his head. 'Not without the keys.' He saw Clare's expression. 'Like passwords.'

'But Tech Support have software to crack passwords, you said.'

'Not this kind of password. Even if you had GPG installed you would need whoever encrypted the files to give you the keys to decrypt them. Encryption keys are far harder to crack than normal passwords. It can sometimes be done but it would likely take years.' He looked up at them. 'Sorry.'

Clare stood silent for a few minutes, mulling this over. Then she said, 'Do you suppose it could be anything to do with Andy's Thursday nights out?'

'What's this?' The DCI was becoming impatient.

'The first victim. He went out every Thursday but no one – not his wife, work colleagues, girlfriend – no one knows where he went. He withdrew a hundred pounds from a cashpoint in town every Thursday around teatime then often took out more money over the next few days.'

'Have you checked local casinos?' the DCI asked. 'Best place I know to lose money.'

'It was on my list. Then we took the call about Mr Gilmartin.'

'Get it checked. Pound to a penny that's where he was going.'

Chris was still browsing the contents of the memory stick. 'Tell you what, though,' he said, 'this is interesting.'

'What?' Clare leaned over to look.

'He's installed Tor.'

The DCI frowned. 'What the hell's Tor?'

'It's an internet browser. It lets the user communicate anonymously.'

'You mean send an email and no one knows who it's come from?'

'Kind of. But more often it's used for visiting websites you might not want anyone else to know about. Porn, that sort of thing. Used by criminals, money launderers, drug dealers, as well as more legitimate stuff like journalists protecting sources, whistle-blowers… And some folk just like using it.'

'Get it down to Tech Support,' the DCI said. 'They'll see what he's been up to.'

'With respect, sir, I doubt it. That's why the criminal classes use Tor. It's pretty much impossible to breach.'

'Can you explain, Chris?' Clare was intrigued. Andy's death was starting to look like more than just an aggrieved ex-girlfriend.

'Well, normally when you look up a web page you leave a trail. Anyone examining your computer can see you visited that website. With Tor you can hide your activity because it routes your request to visit a website through a series of other computers. Each computer knows where the request came from and where the next computer in the chain is, but no more than that. So A sends it to B. B knows it came from A and that it's sending it to C. C knows about B but not A. D knows C sent it but...'

'It's like one of those logic puzzles,' Clare muttered. 'How do you know this stuff anyway?'

He looked smug. 'Remember that course you made me go on last month?'

The DCI frowned. 'So, we know that he's up to something on his computer but not what?'

Chris nodded. 'I'll check, but I doubt I'll find the browsing history. Tor deletes it on exit. Cookies are deleted too.'

'What about that document?' Clare jabbed the screen with her finger. 'Can you find out if Andy created it?'

Chris navigated his way to the document properties and shook his head. 'It only says *Created by User* and the date... about six months ago.'

'And there's nothing else?'

'Don't think so. I've had a look and there aren't any hidden files either. Just that document, the encrypted files and the browser.'

'So, he's been browsing the net, probably for something illegal, but we have no way of knowing what?'

'Nope. But...'

'Yeah?'

'The encrypted files – they're quite large.'

'So could be photos?'

'Yeah, or files containing images.'

'I can't help thinking that Thursdays are significant,' Clare said. 'We've spoken to his wife, girlfriend, ex-girlfriend, colleagues – no one knows what he did on Thursdays. I'm guessing, whatever he was up to, he didn't want anyone else knowing.'

'Did the PM show any drugs in his system?' DCI Gibson asked.

Clare took the mouse from Chris and navigated her way to the PM report. 'Lots of alcohol, but then we knew that. No drugs mentioned but we didn't request a full tox report.'

'Better get that done, then,' the DCI advised. 'And let's get someone over to the brewery to see how things are there. Pick up Mr Gilmartin's office computer. And get onto his accountant too. Find out if there were any financial worries. Get bank statements for the business and his personal accounts. And...' he hesitated, 'better check if he did anything on Thursday evenings. I'm not sure I want to know, mind you,' he added.

Clare hesitated. 'We'll have to look round the house, sir.'

He waved this away. 'Yes, of course. And pick up any devices you find in the house, too. Computers, laptops. See if he had this Tor thing installed. Better warn Tech Support. With two murders to investigate, we'll need more than DS West and his computer course.'

Chapter 8

Gilmartin's Brewery sat about a mile outside Cupar, on a large, flat site. It was a modern, unromantic building in grey brick, employing a fair number of staff, if the car park was anything to go by.

'There's money in beer,' Chris observed, as they approached the entrance.

Clare, glancing at him, noticed he had undone the bottom button on his waistcoat. Maybe he did listen sometimes, under that morose exterior.

They pushed open the glass-fronted doors and found themselves in a bright reception area with comfortable seating and fresh flowers. Clare showed her warrant card to the receptionist. A few minutes later, a ruddy-faced man in his late thirties arrived to greet them.

'Sandy Belshaw,' he said, extending his hand, adding, 'general manager. Terrible business.' He shook his head but there was an energy about him that suggested he was tackling his new role as Acting MD with some enthusiasm.

Clare shook his hand. 'DI Clare Mackay and DS Chris West. Thank you for seeing us, Mr Belshaw.' She glanced across at the receptionist who was pretending to shuffle some papers on her desk. 'I wonder if we could talk in Mr Gilmartin's office?'

Sandy Belshaw followed her gaze. 'Of course. I've been working in there this morning myself. It's easier – everything to hand, you know.'

Clare wondered about this. Was the man being a bit hasty, moving into his boss's office... or was he just being practical? She decided to give him the benefit of the doubt. They followed him to Bruce Gilmartin's office. He entered ahead of them and held the door open. Clare entered and looked round the office. A large iMac sat on a substantial oak desk with a leather-upholstered chair behind. Clearly the company was doing well, or wanted it to look that way. Sandy Belshaw indicated some easy chairs arranged round a low coffee table and invited them to sit.

'Business good?' Clare asked.

'Booming. We've just launched a proposal to take over a rival brewery near Dundee.'

'Welcome?'

'Not so far. But they've not seen our offer yet.'

'I'll need details of that. And I'd like access to Mr Gilmartin's email. I'm afraid we'll have to take the iMac too.'

Sandy's face fell. 'Oh, but I've been working here... I mean, do you have a warrant?'

Clare sighed. 'I can get one if necessary, but it will hold up our investigations and I'll have to ask you to stop using this office anyway. We are dealing with a murder investigation, Mr Belshaw.'

Sandy Belshaw stared. 'Murder? But it was an accident, surely.'

Clare watched him carefully. 'I'm afraid not.'

'But – I don't understand. Who would want to kill Bruce? He – he was such a nice man.'

'That's what we're trying to find out. So, in the circumstances, the iMac…'

Sandy Belshaw had the grace to look abashed. 'Well, yes. Of course. I wouldn't want to be obstructive. Is there anything else you need?'

'Can you tell us who will take over Mr Gilmartin's role here?'

'Good question, Inspector. I'll have to call an emergency Board meeting and see what the Board members think. It's up to the shareholders, ultimately, but they usually follow the Board's recommendations. We could put forward someone from within the company or advertise for a new CEO. I really don't know.'

'Would you be a candidate, Mr Belshaw?'

Sandy Belshaw's face reddened slightly. 'Oh, I don't know, Inspector. Is it relevant? I really don't think today's the day to be thinking about it.'

'Sadly, Mr Belshaw, we don't have a choice.'

His hand went to the back of his head, rubbing his hair. 'I'm afraid I've not given it much thought. I mean there's Jennifer too.' Sandy Belshaw's face clouded over at the mention of Jennifer Gilmartin. 'She'll want a say in things, I'm quite sure.'

'Mrs Gilmartin?' Clare said, watching him carefully.

'Yes. She's a shareholder and a director. She and Bruce were the majority shareholders and I'm guessing she'll inherit his shares so…'

'Did she take an active part in the business?' Clare asked.

Sandy hesitated. 'Not as such. But she would attend Board meetings. I – erm – I think Bruce quite often took notice of what she said.'

Clare glanced at Chris. Was there something here? Did Jennifer dominate her husband? Was that what their marriage was like? Jennifer was almost certainly in Amsterdam when her husband was killed but was it possible things weren't entirely rosy between the couple? And, if so, could it have been bad enough for her to have him killed? It seemed far-fetched but someone had killed Bruce Gilmartin. The problem was that same person might also have killed Andy Robb. And, unless they could prove a link between the two men, it didn't seem likely that Jennifer would have had a part in Andy's death.

'Was it a happy marriage?' Clare asked.

'Oh yes, I think so,' Sandy said quickly. 'I mean, as far as any couple is happy these days.'

Clare asked a few more questions about the Gilmartins but Sandy could add little to what he had already said. He edged forward in his seat.

'So, if there is anything else I can help with…'

Clare put thoughts of Jennifer to the back of her mind – for now at least. 'I'll need a full staff list. Names, addresses, phone numbers. And can you give me contact details for your company accountant, please? Or do you have one on the staff?'

'No, we use Osbornes in St Andrews. Jane Leslie handles our business.'

Clare jotted this down. 'I wonder if we could speak to the staff now, please? All together, if possible. Save us some time.'

'Of course. It'll just take me five minutes to round them up.' He made to leave but Clare spoke again.

'Just one more thing – can you tell me about Mr Gilmartin's life outside the office? His social life, I mean. Did he go out regularly?'

'Oh, I'm not sure. He didn't really talk much about it. Maybe Amanda would know. She's his PA. I'll send her in while I round the others up.'

Sandy Belshaw went off to find Amanda.

'Any thoughts, Chris?'

'He certainly seems keen to take over the reins, boss.'

'Too keen?'

Chris looked round the office. A table beside the window held a De'Longhi coffee machine and four small copper cups. There was also an electric kettle and a china tea service. A glossy, black fridge presumably held cold drinks. And, instead of the cream vertical blinds on the reception room windows, there were thick, richly patterned curtains, held back by pleated cords. There was an air of opulence about Bruce Gilmartin.

'I imagine Mr Belshaw's office isn't quite as plush as this one.'

Clare rose from her seat and strolled round the room. The carpet felt thick beneath her feet and she thought there would be no shortage of candidates to replace Bruce Gilmartin. It seemed unlikely any of them would stoop to murder. But sometimes, it happened. She was about to mention Jennifer when there was a soft tap at the door. It opened a little and Amanda Davies appeared. Clare ushered her in and she entered a few steps. Chris held out a chair for her and, after a moment's hesitation, she sat, smoothing her dark red skirt down before clasping

88

her hands together and raising her eyes. Clare appraised her. She certainly looked ill at ease, as though she was preparing to be grilled in the witness box at the high court. Was it the shock of her employer's murder or was there a reason for her nervousness? Clare thought she didn't look the type to have a fling with her boss. But then you never could tell. She was certainly more upset than Sandy Belshaw had seemed.

'It's been such a shock,' she said, her voice shaking. 'He was a lovely man and a good boss. I don't know what'll happen now...'

'Amanda, is there's anything you can tell us... about Mr Gilmartin... I mean before the others come in?'

Her eyes widened. 'Like what?'

'I don't know. Relationships at work, say. Did he get on with everyone?'

'Oh yes. We all liked him.'

Clare went on. 'What about outside work? Was his home life happy?'

Amanda's face clouded. 'As far as I know...'

'No girlfriends? Maybe that his wife didn't know about?'

'Oh no. Mr Gilmartin wasn't like that at all.' Amanda seemed quite shocked at the idea. 'And Mrs Gilmartin – well, she's ever so nice.'

'So, your relationship with him – it was just professional?'

The girl looked shocked at the suggestion and nodded vehemently.

'What about working hours?' Clare went on. 'Did he often work late? Or did he always go home on time?'

'I think mostly he went home about six. I finish at half past five and he usually said he wouldn't be far behind me. Except Thursdays. That was his charity night so he tended to have a microwave meal at his desk.'

Clare was suddenly alert. 'Charity night?'

'Oh yes. He was so generous, you see. Some sort of club he went to on Thursdays. Raising money, that sort of thing.'

'Where was this?'

'I'm not sure. I don't think he ever said. I think he liked to keep it quiet. Not one of those people who want a fuss made when they do something nice.' She nodded to emphasise this, and Clare wondered if she was trying to convince them or herself.

'He sounds like a very kind man. Maybe, if you remember anything about the charity nights, you could let me know?'

'Of course.'

There was another knock at the door and Sandy Belshaw's head appeared.

'I've gathered the staff out in the main office,' he said. 'Too many for in here.'

Clare nodded and, with a reassuring smile at Amanda, they went to meet the staff. There were twenty of them, in all, including Sandy and Amanda, some in smart office clothes, the others in what seemed to be a uniform of cargo trousers and dark blue shirts. Clare looked from one to the next, trying to spot any signs of unease. At length she spoke.

'You have, no doubt, heard that Mr Bruce Gilmartin was found dead this morning.'

One or two of the staff looked tearful at this. Clare continued, watching them carefully. 'You may also have heard that Mr Gilmartin's death was not accidental.'

There was little reaction to this.

'If any of you have noticed anything unusual recently, even if you think it has nothing to do with Mr Gilmartin, I'd like you to let us know about it.' She looked round. 'Anything at all?'

Some of them shook their heads while others looked away. Clare tried another tack.

'I believe Mr Gilmartin was involved in charity work – on Thursday evenings.'

There were nods of agreement, but no one knew exactly what he did. It was, Clare decided, like pulling teeth.

Eventually she gave up. 'I'll leave a note of my phone number at the reception desk. If any of you do remember something that might help – no matter how small – I would ask you to call me as soon as possible.' And, with that, she thanked them for their time and the staff drifted off. Clare took her leave of Sandy Belshaw, giving him her card while Chris carried the iMac and a desk diary to the car. She joined him out in the car park and climbed into the passenger seat.

'Nothing much there, I think,' she said. 'I'll be surprised if any of the staff are involved.'

'I still think that manager's a bit quick to step into the boss's shoes,' Chris said.

'True. But then the company has to carry on, I suppose.'

'What do you reckon to Mrs G?'

'Jennifer? Who knows? Sandy Belshaw didn't seem too keen on her stepping into her husband's shoes.'

'Doesn't mean she killed him, though,' Chris said.

'No, that's true.'

'So, what now?' he asked, his hand on the steering wheel.

'Let's get that iMac down to Tech Support. But, if you could drop me at' – she squinted at her notebook – 'Osborne Accountants. The office is on South Street.'

Chris pulled out into the road. 'Had a call from Jim. While you were talking to the manager.'

'Anything much at the house?' Clare wanted to know.

'Still looking. He says they've taken a laptop, a tablet and a desktop computer. I'll pick them up after I drop you at the accountants and take them down to the tech guys with the iMac.'

'When you're done with that, could you check up on charity organisations? Round Table, Rotary, that sort of thing. Find out if Bruce Gilmartin belonged to any of them and, if so, when they met. See if we can shed any light on his Thursday night charity work.'

'Will do.'

–

Osborne's offices were at the far end of South Street, near the ruined cathedral. They occupied all three storeys of a terraced building, sandwiched between a dry cleaner's and a sushi bar. Jane Leslie's office was on the first floor. She was tall and slim with closely cropped brown hair, flecked with the early signs of grey. She was shocked to hear of Bruce Gilmartin's death. 'Was it sudden?' she asked. 'He hadn't been ill, had he?'

'I'm afraid we're treating it as murder,' Clare told her. 'So, we need to find out as much as possible about him, his business, his finances and so on.'

Jane blinked at this. 'Oh, how dreadful. He was such a lovely man.'

Clare nodded in sympathy. 'I won't keep you long. If you could just give me some background on the business – financially, I mean.'

Jane adjusted the angle of her computer monitor and pulled a keyboard towards her. She wiggled the mouse then began tapping at the keys. 'Here we go,' she said, turning the monitor further so Clare could read it. 'Gilmartin Brewing Company. Healthy enough balance sheet. No cash flow problems. In fact, Bruce told me he was hoping to take over a rival brewery across in Dundee.'

'Could the company afford it?'

'It would have been a push but, yes, I think so. We discussed the offer he planned to make to the shareholders and how he would fund it. But I gather it was regarded with some hostility by the other brewery.'

'How so?'

'I seem to recall Bruce saying the managing director had telephoned him to say it would go ahead over her dead body.'

'Had you made any formal contact with the company?'

'No, but I can give you the details. It's McMillan's. Just outside Dundee, on the Forfar road.'

Clare noted down the company's details then asked if she could see bank records. Again, Jane tapped at the keyboard then highlighted a section of the screen.

'This is a summary of the accounts. If you want to investigate anyone, just click on it.'

'And his personal bank accounts?'

'I don't have access to those. I gather he used the bank along the road, though. They should be able to help you.'

Clare nodded and began trawling through the company's bank accounts. There was nothing remarkable, no large deposits or withdrawals. The company seemed to be in a healthy enough state. At her request, Jane printed off statements for the last six months and Clare took her leave, hoping to catch the bank before it closed.

The branch manager was reluctant to give Clare any information without a warrant. 'I'm afraid my hands are tied, Inspector.'

Clare's lips tightened. She didn't need this. 'I don't have time to wait for a warrant. I've a double murder enquiry to run. Is there no way I can see them?'

The manager spread his hands. 'Unless you can ask Mrs Gilmartin to phone us – but I'm guessing you may not want to trouble her at a time like this.'

Don't bet on it, Clare thought, stepping back out into the street.

She glanced at her watch. Just after four. She took out her phone and dialled the number for McMillan's Brewery. After running a gauntlet of receptionists and personal assistants, she was finally connected with Yvonne McMillan.

'Mrs McMillan? I'm Detective Inspector Clare Mackay. I wonder if I could call in to see you this afternoon please?'

Yvonne McMillan didn't sound keen. 'I am rather busy, Inspector. Can I ask what it's in connection with?'

'I'd rather explain face-to-face. But it is an urgent matter.'

Yvonne McMillan agreed, reluctantly, and gave Clare directions to the brewery.

Clare ended the call and punched the number of the station into her phone. The call was answered by Sara.

'Sara, I'm down at South Street and need a car in a hurry. Can you drive down and meet me please? Just outside the bank.'

Sara declined the offer of a lift back to the station. 'I was heading out on patrol anyway,' she said.

Clare gave her a grateful smile and took the keys. As she set off she punched another number into the phone and switched the phone to speaker. DCI Gibson answered immediately.

'Inspector – any progress?'

'Not as much as I'd like, sir. I need a favour…'

The DCI listened then said, 'So let me get this clear – you want me to telephone Jennifer Gilmartin, just a few hours after she's learned of her husband's death, and ask her to call the bank?'

'Please. The manager won't release his statements without a warrant or permission from Mrs Gilmartin. And I can't wait for a warrant.'

There was a sigh from the other end. 'Leave it with me.' The line went dead.

Chapter 9

It took Clare just over forty minutes to reach McMillan's Brewery. It was set on an elevated section of countryside, looking south towards the city of Dundee. The construction of silvered hardwood, with two pitched sections of roof made it a more interesting building than the rather austere Gilmartin's Brewery. Clare could imagine it had been an attractive prospect for Bruce Gilmartin.

Yvonne McMillan was waiting for her at the front desk and showed Clare to her office. It was sparsely furnished compared to Bruce Gilmartin's but as neat as Yvonne was herself. On the desk was a photo of two gap-toothed girls, grinning broadly. The resemblance to Yvonne was striking.

'Your daughters?' Clare asked.

'Yes. Millie and Joanne. Last summer. Thankfully they have their front teeth now.' She moved to a side table where a coffee machine sat, a considerably cheaper model than the one Bruce Gilmartin had. 'Coffee?'

Clare suddenly realised she had missed lunch. 'I'd love one, if it's no trouble.'

Yvonne poured two mugs and placed one in front of Clare. 'So, Inspector, how can I help? You said it was a matter of some urgency.'

Clare watched her carefully. 'I'm investigating the murder of Bruce Gilmartin.'

There was no doubting Yvonne's reaction. The smile slipped and the colour drained from her face. There was a pause and then she found her voice, huskier than it had been a few seconds before.

'Bruce – is dead?'

'I'm afraid so.'

Yvonne took a moment to compose herself. 'He's been murdered?'

Clare nodded.

'But who on earth would want to kill Bruce?'

'That's what we hope to find out.'

'You surely don't think I can help with that? I mean, you've doubtless heard he was trying to take us over but if you're suggesting I had anything to do with it…'

'Not at all.' Clare smiled. 'I'm just gathering information. Did you know Mr Gilmartin well? See much of him?'

'Probably the last time was at The Brewing Business Awards Dinner, earlier this year. February, I think. I can check if you like.'

Clare shook her head. 'No, don't worry. Does the brewing industry do much in the way of charity work?'

'Oh yes. We sponsor sporting events, apprenticeship schemes, that sort of thing. And Christmas, of course. We always do a charity fundraiser.'

'Are there regular meetings?'

'For the charity events? No. We usually meet a few weeks beforehand for a quick bit of planning. It's done online, mostly.'

'So you wouldn't meet, say, on Thursday evenings?'

Yvonne's eyes widened. 'Why Thursdays?'

Clare decided to change approach. 'Did you ever see Mr Gilmartin socially?'

Yvonne snorted. 'Not likely. We were the competition. I wouldn't have let him in the office, never mind socialise with him. That doesn't mean I'm not sorry he's dead, of course.'

'Of course.' Clare drained her cup and got up. 'Thank you so much, Ms McMillan. If there's anything else we'll be in touch.'

–

It was after six by the time Clare returned to the station. The search of the Gilmartins' house had been completed and Alastair Gibson was preparing to head home. 'Those bank statements you wanted were emailed through ten minutes ago. I think Sara printed them out and left them on your desk.'

'Thanks, sir. Appreciate it.'

'Hmm. I'm not sure Mrs Gilmartin did. Good night, Inspector.'

She watched him go, black leather briefcase in hand. *I bet there's nothing in it*, she thought, and she went through to her office to peruse Bruce Gilmartin's finances. The papers were neatly stacked on the corner of the desk. Clare lifted them and sat down heavily in her own chair. The seat was still warm and she longed to have her office back to herself. The sooner she wrapped up this murder investigation the better.

A brief glance at the printouts told Clare that Bruce Gilmartin certainly didn't have money worries. He had three bank accounts, all with healthy balances. She scanned the withdrawals column and found that, like Andy Robb, he regularly took out cash but that his withdrawals weren't quite as consistent as Andy's. There was also a credit card which he seemed to use frequently, paying it off in full every month.

A loud bark reminded Clare that they still had the dog in the station. She had forgotten about him. She opened her office door and Benjy trotted in, wagging his tail.

'Any volunteers to take Benjy home?' she said, more in hope than expectation.

There was a lot of muttering and coughing.

She looked at Chris who had suddenly become interested in his phone. 'Weren't you talking about getting a dog, DS West? Well now's your chance. Try before you buy.'

Chris rubbed his neck. 'Well, normally I would, boss, but it's a bit tricky this week.'

'Ratbag!'

'That's me.'

Clare looked at Benjy. 'Looks like it's you and me then, kid.' His tail gave a faint wag. 'We'll get some dog food on the way home,' she told him and, picking up the sheaf of papers and his lead, she headed for the door.

–

As Clare opened her front door, stooping to pick up letters from the mat, Benjy rushed in past her legs and began exploring this new place. Having sniffed in the corners and behind the floor-length curtains, he joined Clare in the kitchen where she was hunting through her kitchen cupboards for something to use as a dog bowl. She unearthed a couple of old ice cream tubs from beneath the sink and filled one with water. She set this down and Benjy lapped at it until he heard the sound of the dried food being poured into the other tub. He sat, head turned up, awaiting the food. As she set it down she said, 'Wait...' but it was too late. He fell on it and chomped through the contents of the tub, paying her no heed until it was completely empty and licked clean. Then he trotted back through to the sitting room and settled himself comfortably beneath the long window, basking in the warmth of the late evening sun.

Clare put a lasagne in the microwave to heat and began sorting through that day's post, nibbling on a slice of baguette as she did so. The usual bills and junk mail. She put these on the kitchen table, beside the long, cream envelope, still unopened. There was one other envelope that interested her. Postmarked Glasgow. She took a knife from the drawer and sliced across the top of the envelope. She withdrew the letter and stood, ignoring the beep from the microwave, as she digested its contents. She pulled a kitchen chair out and sat down, her legs suddenly weak, and read it again.

Her flat in Glasgow. Her lovely flat in the west end of the city with its high ceilings and original Edwardian windows now belonged to a young couple from Carlisle. It was signed, sealed and gone from her life. Now there really was no going back. Not for the first time, Clare wondered if she had done the right thing. Had she sleep-walked through the past few months, not really knowing what she was doing?

She went to the wine rack and pulled out a bottle of Chianti. In the warm May evening it was at the perfect temperature and she poured herself a large glass, spooning the lasagne out onto a plate. Benjy, smelling the pasta, trotted up, his nose in the air but he was to be disappointed. Clare sat at the table, poring over the letter and eating mechanically.

When she had finished, she loaded her plate and cutlery into the dishwasher and took the wine glass and bottle into the sitting room. She placed these on a small table and sat down with her feet up on the brown, leather settee. Benjy jumped up and settled down beside her, burrowing into her legs. It was warm and comforting and Clare wondered if she might like to have her own wee dog. Particularly if it was as affectionate as Benjy. The flat was gone now, netting her a tidy profit. Maybe she could make a life for herself here in St Andrews. Buy her own flat – a house, even. There were quite a few estate agents dotted along South Street she could visit. Was it time to think about settling down?

But then she remembered. That couldn't happen, not until she knew about…

An impulse seized her, and she jumped up, making Benjy bark. She went quickly to the kitchen table and picked up the long, cream envelope, weighing it in her hands for a few moments, then carried it back to the settee and carefully peeled back the seal.

She knew what it was before she read it.

And there it was. The news she had expected but also dreaded.

Confirmation that the family of the late Francis Ritchie had applied to the high court to pursue a private prosecution against Clare for his murder.

It was a year ago now. Thirteen months, actually. And she could see it as clearly as if it had happened yesterday.

The screams of the woman in the off licence... screaming for her life? Clare didn't know — no one did — they had no idea what was going on in that shop. Didn't know the guns were replicas. Didn't know the shopkeeper wasn't in any real danger. Not from the guns, at least.

She was an experienced firearms officer and it was a textbook operation. Well rehearsed. They took up positions. The negotiator tried to speak to them on the phone. Then the other lad had ripped the phone off the wall and suddenly it was quiet inside the shop. No sound from the woman. Had they killed her? Produced a knife and stuck it in between her ribs?

And then he came out of the shop. Francis Ritchie. Just fifteen years old but looking older; toting a gun like a seasoned gangster. The gun that wasn't a gun. Only, they didn't know that. And he was pointing it right at Clare. She had a Kevlar vest on but that wouldn't stop him hitting her in the head, or the femoral artery.

Clare's mouth was dry and she reached over for the glass of wine, draining it in one go.

She saw him steady himself. He was going to shoot. She was sure of it. Semi-automatic. How many could he kill? She took the decision and the shot rang out. Clare was good at her job and it only took one shot.

'Killed him outright,' she told Benjy who simply wagged his tail in response. Clare wished she could wag her tail.

Tom had been beside himself. 'You could have been killed,' he said. 'I could have lost you.'

And he had lost her. He had lost her the minute the Ritchie family engaged Tom's employer to represent them.

The Ritchies had chosen well. Jamieson Curr were well known in Glasgow as the champions of lost causes. Tom himself had won many a court case for them, against the odds. He had stepped back from this one, of course. Clare knew that much. Conflict of interest, he said, and she believed him. But the fact remained that every morning he kissed her goodbye and went to work for the enemy. Or that was how Clare saw it.

The Fatal Accident Inquiry drew near. Clare asked Tom to take the week off work. She had hoped he might come with her, sit alongside her in a gesture of solidarity. Show the world where his loyalties lay. But he said he was better being occupied. Better with something to do. She didn't ask him again; and, every day, she went to the Inquiry with only her federation rep for support.

The Ritchies had sat at the front, flanked by two of Tom's partners. Rumour was that the newspapers were paying their fees.

The evenings were tense. Tom was solicitous, cooking stir-fries, pasta bakes, even fillet steaks one night. He set the table while Clare languished in the baths he ran for her. He lit candles, put on music and opened the wine to breathe. They ate. Tom chatted, even daring to ask how the Inquiry was going.

'Fine,' was all Clare would say. 'It's fine.'

After dinner they watched TV, avoiding news reports of the Inquiry, Clare opting for an easy chair, rather than her usual place beside Tom on the settee.

At night, in bed, they lay back-to-back, clinging to their respective sides, pretending to sleep. Tom always fell asleep first. Clare who, by now, was spoiling for a fight, found this hard to forgive. How could he fall asleep when the air was so heavy with tension?

And they went through this same routine every day for a week. It was the most exhausting week of Clare's life.

–

On the final day of the Inquiry the verdict was delivered at lunchtime. She was exonerated of course. Praised for potentially saving lives. There was even a slight nod of respect from one of Tom's colleagues.

Her federation rep wanted to buy her lunch. *Bit of a celebration*, he said. Clare politely declined. Said she just wanted to go home and take a long bath. But she didn't go home. She found a quiet pub and ordered a bottle of red. She sat in the corner, her phone on silent, watching a succession of calls from Tom. He would know the verdict by now. His colleagues would be back at the office and he would know. She finished the bottle then ordered another. The barman looked at her, suggested she go home. Clare had told him to fuck off and left the pub. She found another pub and drank some more. And every time Tom tried calling her she poured another glass.

She left the pub at closing time and the fresh air hit her like a brick. And when she finally fell up the steps to her flat, grazing her knee and chipping a tooth in the process, she found Tom asleep on the settee, and the remains of a shepherd's pie on top of the cooker.

The next morning he had tried to tell her he was glad. Relieved it was over and that she'd been praised for her actions. But Clare didn't want to hear it. She knew then that it was too late. Tom was a Jamiesons' man and she could never forgive him that.

And so she had put her flat on the market and applied for a transfer. *Anywhere*, she had said. *Anywhere away from Glasgow.*

They had all tried. Her parents, friends, her sister Judith and her colleagues. Tried to persuade her to stay. *It's a rough patch*, they had said, *bound to pass. Just give yourself time.* But Clare had been determined. She wasn't one to wait around for things to improve. If they weren't right, it was time to go.

'Would you like me to come with you?' Tom had asked. 'Start again somewhere new.'

But she knew he didn't mean it. Give up his career for her. Especially when he didn't think he'd done anything wrong. If she was being completely honest, Clare didn't think he'd done anything wrong either. But things had changed between them and she could be with him no longer.

And then the post in St Andrews had become vacant and she had grabbed it.

'You sure?' her DCI had asked. 'Maybe give things time to settle down.'

But she had been sure. And here she was now, in this rented house with this borrowed dog, investigating a double murder with an arse for a DCI breathing down her neck.

And the Ritchies were coming for her.

Clare poured herself another glass of wine and began the process of drinking herself into oblivion.

Chapter 10

Tuesday, 21st May

Clare woke early on Tuesday morning. Even with the blackout blinds she could see it was light outside, but she had no idea of the time. Her head felt thick from the wine and she reached for the glass of water at her bedside, draining it in one go.

She checked her phone and was relieved to find no messages or missed calls. Then she heard Benjy, clearly unsettled in his new surroundings. She had made him a bed at the top of the stairs with her spare room duvet, enticing him there with a trail of dog biscuits. But now, thanks to the sun rising just after five, he was awake and looking for attention.

She padded across the floor and opened the door. He rushed in, tail going nineteen to the dozen.

'You know what?' she said to his upturned face, 'I think I'm going to miss you.' She shoved her feet into slippers and went downstairs, the dog at her heels. In the kitchen, she freshened his water and poured some of his dried food into the other ice cream tub. How often did you feed a dog? She hadn't a clue. Still, he would be reunited with Jennifer Gilmartin this afternoon, once Jim brought her back from the airport. Jennifer's flight was due in just after two o'clock so hopefully Jim would have her in St Andrews by four. In a bizarre coincidence, DCI Gibson had booked her a room at the Kenlybank Hotel, where Andy Robb had met his fate on Saturday night. But it was no longer a crime scene and only a few miles from her home, so it made sense.

'Get to the airport a bit early, please, Jim,' Clare had said, when the DCI was out of earshot. 'I want to make absolutely sure that she did go to Amsterdam and that she's only flying back today. Not a word to anyone else, mind?'

The dog food disappeared almost as quickly as Clare had put it out. She squinted at the instructions on the pack and reckoned she'd probably underfed him, so she poured some more into the tub. Again, he devoured it as if he hadn't seen food for days. She opened the back door to let Benjy out and he scampered off to find somewhere to pee. The phone rang. Clare's heart sank. But then she saw it was her sister and made an effort to brighten.

'Jude. Great to hear from you.' Her voice was husky from the wine and she cleared her throat. 'Are you all okay? It's a bit early for a chat.' Clare could hear whimpering in the background. 'How's my nephew?'

'Teething, which is why I'm up at stupid o'clock. Again.'

'Oh God. Remind me not to have kids.'

'Listen, Clare, Mum rang me. Tom was round—'

Clare's heart sank. 'Don't tell me. He told her about the private prosecution.'

'Yes. You never mentioned it. When did you find out?'

'The letter came a few days ago. Just haven't had time to open it.'

'Ten days ago, Tom told Mum. Look, Clare, she's worried about you. Dad too. We all are.'

Clare sighed. 'Jude, there's nothing I can do about it. It's gone to the Lord Advocate for a decision. If he thinks there's sufficient evidence to proceed against me it'll go to court. If not, it won't.'

'But Tom said—'

'Tom is irrelevant.'

Benjy started to scratch at the back door, but Clare was too distracted to notice.

'Oh Clare, come on. That's not true. He still loves you. You know he does.'

Clare was dying for a coffee. She put the phone on speaker and filled the kettle.

'You could come back to Glasgow, you know,' Jude went on. 'Tom said he'd heard they were missing you. I think he misses you too...'

'Tom...' Clare began, then she didn't know what else to say.

'Clare, he knows how difficult it was for you. I think he genuinely regrets not being more of a support. Maybe if you met you could...'

'Jude, I can't talk to you about Tom. He's part of that time in Glasgow. I had to leave it behind. And now this prosecution might happen, well – until I know – I can't think about Tom, or anyone else.'

'Tom says...'

There was a muffled *wuff* from outside, and then another, but Clare was too busy fending off her sister.

'What Tom says doesn't matter any more, Jude. I wanted him with me. At the Inquiry. I wanted him there and he wouldn't come.'

'Yes I know, Clare. But think how difficult it was for him, with Jamiesons representing the Ritchies. He was in a tricky position.'

'Oh yeah,' Clare said, her voice harder than she had meant. 'He was having a *really* hard time!'

Benjy was barking now. The kettle came to the boil with a rush of steam. Clare spooned coffee into the cafetière as her sister continued to plead Tom's case.

'But he *was* there for you, wasn't he? Oh maybe not at the Inquiry but – Clare, is that a *dog* I can hear?'

Clare opened the door to let an excited Benjy back in. He wagged his tail at her. She raised her eyebrows at him, indicating the phone.

'It's a long story,' Clare said. 'I'll fill you in later but I've a double murder on the go just now.'

'Phone me when you can then, yeah?'

'I will. And tell Mum and Dad to stop worrying. Tom did message me to recommend a shit-hot criminal advocate so, if it comes to it, I'll be well represented. And the federation will pay the fees. Now I really must go, Jude. Kiss James for me.'

Clare put down her phone and watched Benjy. He was chasing his tail round and round in her sitting room and had already knocked the TV remote control to the floor. 'Looks like someone could do with a walk.'

–

Clare arrived at the station just before eight, feeling as if she'd done half a day's work already. Was it always this tiring, having a dog? Benjy, now fed and exercised, resumed his position on the front office counter from where he kept a beady eye on the morning's events. At half past eight, DCI Gibson called a briefing.

'Before we start, we're joined by three detectives from Edinburgh. Connor, Steve and Phil – appreciate your help, lads. Make them welcome, please, everyone.'

The three newcomers sat perched on desks in near-identical sharp suits. One was looking round the room without enthusiasm. The others nodded their thanks and the DCI carried on.

'So, Inspector, what do we know about the brewery?'

Clare moved to where she could see everyone clearly. 'Bruce Gilmartin was a popular boss, staff mostly upset, although the general manager seems over keen to step into his boss's shoes. Otherwise, the business appears healthy – they're planning a takeover of rivals near Dundee. McMillan's.'

'Which we know is unwelcome.'

'Yes. I spoke to the MD yesterday but don't think there's anything there to interest us. They weren't friends but she seemed genuinely shocked by Mr Gilmartin's death.'

'Okay,' the DCI said. 'Anything else?'

'His PA said he did charity work on Thursday nights. Chris is looking into local charities to find out if he had any links with them.'

'Any luck?' The DCI looked over at Chris.

'Sorry, sir,' Chris said. 'Nothing so far.'

'I can help with that,' Jim offered, and Chris nodded his thanks.

The DCI turned back to Clare. 'What about his bank statements? You took them home last night, Inspector.'

'Sorry, sir – after feeding the dog, then myself, I fell asleep.'

'Make that a priority this morning, then.'

Clare nodded. Jim raised a hand.

'Sergeant?' The DCI looked faintly nettled by the interruption.

'I brought back a file of papers from the house. I think there are some credit card statements there.'

'Let me have them, Jim, and I'll go through them too,' Clare said.

The phone rang and Chris went to answer it.

'Now, we hope to hear back from Tech Support this morning,' the DCI said. 'With luck, they'll pick something up from the computers DS West took down last night. Whoever takes that call: I want to be informed immediately.'

A few cops nodded at this and he continued.

'Anyone been round the pubs and hotels to ask about Thursday nights?'

'Not yet, boss, but it's on the list.' Clare told him.

'Let's get that done today, then. Photos of both victims please.'

Clare looked at the Edinburgh lads. 'Sara will help you with a list of likely places and the locations.'

They nodded but said nothing. One of them, Phil, looked Sara up and down then gave her a wink. She returned his gaze, her face stony.

Chris returned. 'SOCO,' he told them.

DCI Gibson raised an eyebrow. 'And?'

'They managed to cast part of a tyre track at the Gilmartins' house. It's not a great imprint, so they can't be absolutely sure, but it does look like the same kind of tyre that ran over Andy Robb. On balance, they reckon it's probably a match. Definitely not the Gilmartins' Range Rover, though.'

'And the numbered cards?' Clare asked.

He shook his head. 'Clear prints on both, but not the same person and neither set of prints on the system.'

'What sort of murderer leaves a card on a body covered with his prints?' Phil asked.

'It's a fair point,' Clare said. 'I'm guessing, as the prints aren't on our system, they didn't see it as a problem. Not everyone's that way minded.'

Phil shrugged at this.

'So, it might not be the same vehicle,' DCI Gibson said.

'No. But it's a bit of a stretch having two near-identical cars running folk over,' Chris said.

'I agree,' said Clare. 'There's the similarity in MO plus the similarity in the tyre tracks.'

'But there's something else,' Chris went on. 'The first card – the one with the number five on it – doesn't have a full set of prints.'

'That's not particularly unusual, though,' Clare said. 'Criminals aren't always so obliging.'

'No, I don't mean that. They said it was like the middle finger wasn't long enough to make a proper print.'

'Eh?'

Chris held up his notepad to demonstrate. 'See my notepad? The way I'm holding it means there would be a thumb print on one side and fingers on the other. That's the normal way someone would hold a piece of paper or card.'

'But?'

'But we have three clear fingerprints and one smudge where the middle finger would normally be. Like there was a finger there, but the tip was missing.'

'Covered with a plaster or something?'

'Not according to SOCO. A dressing on the finger would have made it longer and the print, or smudge, would have been further up. This was lower down than the other prints and they think it's almost certainly been caused by a shorter finger. And not from birth because that would still have had a print. This has been an accident or surgery.'

The DCI was becoming impatient. 'So, let me get this straight. We have two murders, both hit-and-runs. SOCO think it was the same car, but they can't be sure; and we have two sets of fingerprints, one with the tip of a middle finger missing, neither of which we have on the system?'

'That's about it.'

Clare had to admire Chris's deadpan response. He really didn't give a toss what the DCI thought.

DCI Gibson turned to Clare. 'You've a lot to sort out, here, Inspector. I sincerely hope you're up to the job.' He marched off into Clare's office and slammed the door, causing Benjy to bark in alarm.

Clare went to soothe the dog, then set about directing the team. Sara unearthed a large map of the town and began explaining the area to Connor, Steve and Phil. Phil – Clare thought it was Phil at least – seemed more interested in Sara's brown eyes than in the map.

'Everything okay, lads?' she called over to them and Phil focused his attention on the map.

'I don't like him,' Chris muttered, adding, 'sleazy bastard.'

Clare patted him on the shoulder. 'Don't you worry – I'm sure Sara can handle herself.'

Chris muttered something about Sara having to put up with harassment and went off to print out photos of the victims. Having set the printer to work, he phoned Tech Support. Jim was working his way through charitable clubs in the area and everyone else was either interviewing friends of the victims or trawling through ANPR footage. Having satisfied herself that they all knew what they were doing, Clare took Benjy into an interview room and spread out the bank statements and bills on the desk. It was a tedious task. Endless transactions, mostly for less than a hundred pounds. She found herself wondering when she might hear from the Lord Advocate's office. The sensible thing to do would be to phone Tom. He could put some feelers out. Then she dismissed the thought. She wouldn't ask Tom for anything – ever again.

Chris appeared at the door. 'Clare.'

She looked up. 'Tech Support?'

He nodded. 'Nothing on the office iMac, unless you really want to look deeper into the brewery finances. The home PC is also pretty much domestic stuff. But his own laptop…'

'Let me guess – Tor again?'

'Yep.'

'Any similarity to the files we found on Andy Robb's laptop?'

'No, sorry. Nothing like that. I mean he could have a memory stick, like Andy's, but we've not found one so far. A couple of the lads are heading back over to the Gilmartins' house, though, to give it a last look over. I'll get them to look out for memory sticks. Mind you, in a house that size,' he tailed off.

'Tor, though... that's interesting. Another link, albeit a tiny one. Thanks, Chris. Let me know if you and Jim turn up any charities or clubs that meet on a Thursday. Oh, and you'd better let the DCI know about the laptop.'

'Will do.' He closed the door and Clare returned to her pile of bank statements. Having found nothing of note in Bruce Gilmartin's personal bank accounts she turned to his credit card statements. Here, there were larger purchases. Lots of shopping. John Lewis, Harvey Nics – it might be a joint card with his wife. Or perhaps he was that rare breed – a man who liked to shop. After an hour or so of perusing the Gilmartins' finances, Clare gave up and walked out into the main office to stretch her legs.

Jim saw her and came over. 'I need to get away to the airport now, Clare,' he said. 'Just letting you know I've not had any luck with clubs or charities meeting every Thursday. Don't think Chris has found any either.' He looked across to Chris who shook his head.

'And those we have found,' Chris added, 'don't have Mr Gilmartin as a member. Or Andy Robb.'

Clare sighed. Maybe the pubs and restaurants would turn up something. The phone rang. She answered it.

'Inspector Mackay...?' The voice was hesitant. 'It's Angela Robb. There's something I wanted to let you see. Could you come over, please?'

–

The street was quieter than it had been on Sunday. People would be at work, children at school. She parked behind

Billy Dodds' dark grey Qashqai. Clare was glad to see he was there again. She liked Billy and hoped he wouldn't turn out to be involved in Andy Robb's death. Angela Robb deserved some happiness. She rang the bell and Angela answered. She had put some make-up on, and looked brighter than she had on Sunday morning.

'Cup of tea?' she asked Clare.

'I'd love one, if I'm not holding you back.'

'No. Glad of the distraction, to be honest. Go in,' she said, pushing open the sitting room door. 'Billy's here.'

Clare went in and found Billy with his feet up on the settee, watching TV.

'Inspector,' he acknowledged.

'How are you, Mr Dodds?'

'Yeah, doin' away, ye ken. Taken a couple of days off to help Angela and that. She's a bit better, like. Finally starting to see the benefit of that choob being gone.'

Clare wasn't sure how to respond to this, so she changed tack. 'Is she sleeping okay?'

'Oh aye. She's tired out, to be honest. The shock and all the upheaval. Funeral to arrange as well. Had the papers at the door. Soon gave them short shrift, though.'

Clare was alert. 'What did they say?'

'Something about another boy being run over. Out one of the country roads, like. Asking if Angela kent him. Didnae mean anything to us.'

Angela appeared carrying a tray and Billy jumped up to take it from her. 'Billy telling you we had the press at the door?'

Clare nodded.

'Another hit-and-run?'

'I can't really say much about it, Angela. But I did want to ask something.'

'Yeah?'

'We found a memory stick in Andy's car.'

Angela looked blank. 'So?'

'Well, it looked as if he'd hidden it. Didn't want it to be found.'

'What was on it, like?'

'Nothing much. A document we couldn't open and a folder with some encrypted files.'

Angela raised an eyebrow. 'Encrypted? Like you need a password?'

'Something like that,' Clare said. 'Have you any idea what the files might be?'

Angela looked at Billy then back at Clare. 'Sorry, not a clue.'

'Fair enough. There was something else though…'

'Yeah?'

'A bit of software loaded onto the stick. It's used to access parts of the internet without leaving any trace.'

Angela's eyes narrowed. 'What parts of the internet?'

'That's what we don't know. I wondered if you could shed any light on it.'

Angela was clueless. 'I've no idea what Andy got up to.'

'It'll be porn,' Billy told her. 'He was a right one for the women. You ken he was, Angela. Bet it was some of those illegal sites. Donkeys and that.'

Clare thought it best to disregard that last remark. She turned to Angela. 'If anything does come to mind, will you let us know?'

'Yeah, sure.'

Clare hesitated. 'Also, this might seem a bit odd, but I wonder if you could both show me your hands?'

'Hands?' Billy's face was a study. 'What, these?' He held out his hands for Clare to see.

She examined them closely, checked all the fingers. No blemishes, no missing fingertips. She smiled and let his hands go. Angela looked at Clare and held her hands out too. Again, Clare examined them closely. Angela's fingertips were all present and correct.

'Thank you both.'

'Mind if I ask why?' Billy wasn't keen to let it go.

'I'm afraid I can't say at the moment. But I'm grateful for your co-operation.' Clare drained her cup and turned to Angela. 'There was something you wanted to show me?'

'Right.' Angela made for the door. 'Follow me.'

Clare followed her across the hall into a dining room. It wasn't a large room but big enough for a table and six chairs with a small sideboard opposite the door. The dining table was piled high with six or seven laptops. Clare looked at her.

'Andy didn't like getting rid of stuff. These are all broken. I said to him to take them into that shop in Market Street. They wipe them clean so they don't have your bank details or anything like that. But he was suspicious, Andy. Didn't trust folk. So, he hung onto them.'

'How far back do these go?'

'Some of them, I reckon, he's had for nearly ten years. We've been in this house eleven years now and I certainly wouldn't have paid the removal men to bring them from the last place. I'd actually forgotten about them. But I've started clearing out Andy's stuff and these were up in the loft.'

'Would you mind if I took them for our Tech Support guys to have a look at?'

Angela shook her head. 'Keep them. I don't want them back. You'll be doing me a favour. I'll get Billy to help you out to the car with them.'

Clare checked her watch. With luck, Jim would be back with Jennifer Gilmartin soon. Maybe she could send him down to Tech Support with the laptops. She started the engine and headed back to the station.

Chapter 11

Clare just missed Jennifer's arrival.

'She's in your office with the DCI now,' Jim told her.

Clare looked over Jim's shoulder towards her office. The door was closed. 'How was she?'

'Shocked. Almost had a panic attack in the car.'

'Genuine?'

'Yes, I think so.'

'And her flights? Did she go?'

'They confirmed she was on the outgoing flight and didn't check back in at Schiphol until this morning.'

'Suppose we can rule her out then.'

'I think so. She seems genuinely heartbroken.'

'Okay, Jim. Thanks for that. Don't suppose you could do me another favour?'

'Aye?'

'I know you're just back but would you mind running a carload of laptops down to Tech Support? Angela Robb unearthed them from the attic. Andy's old ones. Might be something on them that'll help us.'

Jim went to transfer the laptops from the boot of Clare's car to one of the pool cars.

Sara appeared with Connor and Steve in tow. Clare looked at her hopefully.

'Sorry, boss. Nothing yet. We're back for a quick break. Phil's still out, checking clubs.'

Clare frowned. They weren't having much luck. They really needed a break. She looked at the clock. Just gone four. She was keen to hang about until the DCI and Mrs Gilmartin came out of her office. Pound to a penny, the minute she started doing something else, they would appear. At that, her phone began to ring. She glanced at the display. A withheld number. She clicked to take the call.

'Hello, Clare. I'm glad I caught you. We need to talk.'

Elaine Carter.

Clare sank down in a chair and made an effort to sound bright. 'Elaine. What can I do for you?'

'I think we should meet urgently, Clare. I've just been made aware that Francis Ritchie's family have applied to prosecute you privately.'

'Yes, I know that.'

'You should have come to me about this immediately. Do I need to remind you it is your duty to keep me, as the force welfare officer, fully informed of anything that might impact on your role, to say nothing of your wellbeing?'

Clare sighed. Elaine was like one of those little dogs you couldn't shake off your ankle. She would not let anything go.

'Well, it hasn't happened yet, Elaine. Maybe we should wait to hear what the Lord Advocate thinks first?'

'That's all well and good, Clare, but you have to be prepared in case the application is successful. So, let's see. Mm – I could come up on Thursday?'

Thursday. It sounded like a siren in Clare's head. If Andy Robb and Bruce Gilmartin were attending some sort of function or meeting on Thursday nights, perhaps there would be one this Thursday. Today was Tuesday. Andy and Bruce were dead, but was there a chance she could still find out what happened on Thursday nights?

'Sorry, Elaine, Thursday's out.'

'Friday then?'

Clare's office door opened and Jennifer Gilmartin emerged with DCI Gibson's hand on her shoulder. She cut a striking figure in the office, her shoulder-length hair blonde with a few silver highlights. She was simply dressed in designer jeans, soft grey T-shirt and a pale red jacquard jacket, a Michael Kors handbag dangling from one hand. She was almost as tall as the DCI. Clare thought briefly that they would have made a handsome couple and she wondered if there was any history there.

Benjy trotted at her heels, gazing up at her.

'Inspector,' the DCI began, then seeing she was on the phone, raised an eyebrow.

For once, Clare was glad of the interruption. 'I'll call you soon, Elaine,' she promised and ended the call. She smiled at the DCI. He didn't smile back.

'Elaine?'

'Elaine Carter.'

'Hm. The touchy-feely woman?'

'The welfare officer, yes.'

He rolled his eyes but said no more. 'Perhaps you would be kind enough to take Mrs Gilmartin round to the hotel? Check her in and go up to the room. Make sure everything is in order.'

'Of course. But what about Benjy?'

No one had thought about that.

'Not a clue,' DCI Gibson said. 'Do hotels usually take dogs?'

'A few do but most don't, I think,' Clare said. 'I can phone them to check if you like?'

Jennifer Gilmartin looked troubled. 'I'm not sure how he would be. If he barked…'

'It's okay.' Clare said. 'I've been looking after him since yesterday and he's no trouble at all. Would you like me to take him home again tonight? We should have you back in your own house tomorrow.'

Jennifer's eyes began to fill with tears. 'That would be kind, Inspector. I'd be very grateful.'

Jennifer handed Benjy's lead to the DCI who seemed more than a little uncomfortable with it.

'Don't take all afternoon, Inspector,' he said uncertainly. He looked round and his eye fell on Chris who turned quickly back to his computer. He walked over to Chris's desk and held Benjy's lead out to him. 'Job for you, Sergeant…'

Chris took the lead and stared at the DCI's retreating back. 'So now I'm the station dog-sitter?'

–

Pawel Nowicki was again on the reception desk at the Kenlybank Hotel when Clare and Jennifer Gilmartin arrived. DCI Gibson had made the hotel aware of Jennifer's circumstances and Pawel greeted them with quiet courtesy, assuring her of their prompt attention should she require anything. Clare went with her to the room, which was one of the superior doubles. It was comfortably furnished with a view over fields of yellow and green. She looked anxiously at Jennifer.

'Will this be all right? Just for tonight?'

Jennifer attempted at a smile. 'It's lovely, thank you. And please thank Alastair for me. It was kind of him to arrange it.'

'I will. And, if there's anything else you need, anything at all, don't hesitate to call.'

'Just look after my Benjy, please.'

'I will. He'll be back with you tomorrow.'

As she walked down the broad staircase, feeling the plush carpet beneath her feet, Clare wondered if the DCI would have done the same for Angela Robb if her house had been a crime scene.

Somehow, she doubted it.

–

By the time Clare returned to the station the DCI had gone home for the night. Sara and the Edinburgh lads had also gone. Jim had returned from Tech Support and was catching up on paperwork, and Chris had taken Benjy for a walk. There was a note for Clare from Gillian to say that no Land Rovers or Range Rovers had passed any of the St Andrews ANPR cameras between eleven and one on Saturday night. Clare sighed. Another dead end.

The incident room was blissfully quiet, the extra desks and chairs abandoned, the laptops closed. She sat down to think over what they had learned so far. There was a connection between the two victims. She was convinced of that but didn't yet know what it was, and hoped that good, solid police work would throw up some results for Thursday evenings. She moved to the whiteboard and wrote herself a note to review possible connections between the victims in the morning. There were casinos and betting shops – they still needed checking, and she continued scribbling on the board. Stolen cars – that was a priority – she wrote this up, too. Bruce Gilmartin seemed to have no enemies and his wife was at a loss to make sense of his murder. Even Andy Robb's womanising seemed a thin motive. Chris had said Andy's phone calls and texts were mostly to people they had already checked out. There were a few rogue numbers but they didn't seem hopeful. She added *phone numbers* to the board, just in case. His stash of broken laptops might help, though, and she noted this as well. A bark alerted her to Chris and Benjy's return and she went to meet them.

'Any more news, Chris?'

He shook his head.

'Get off home, then. Back in at eight tomorrow.'

Chris didn't need to be told twice and headed out of the door, leaving Clare and Benjy alone in the incident room. Clare looked down at the dog and decided he was a good excuse for going home. She picked up her jacket and car keys, called good night to Jim and headed out into the car park. She unlocked the car and Benjy jumped up, perching on the passenger seat.

'Strictly speaking,' she told him, 'you should be restrained.'

His only response was to wag his tail. She smiled at him and pulled out of the car park. It was home time.

Mindful that Benjy would wake as soon as it was light, Clare decided to have an early night. Oddly enough, she was glad to have the little dog for company. She settled him down in the makeshift duvet bed at the top of the stairs and went into her bedroom, climbing straight into bed. But, tired as she was, sleep eluded her. Thoughts ran round her head. She needed a distraction from the Ritchies and their private prosecution. Something more than a double murder investigation. Maybe a visit to one of the estate agents to see what they had? This house in the Canongate side of town was fine for now. But it wasn't really her style. Maybe she could find an older property. A project. Something to spend her weekends doing up. She had done a few running repairs to her flat in Glasgow.

And then there was all her stuff from Glasgow. Some of it still in boxes. She resolved to start going through her clothes. There were plenty of things she just didn't wear any more. They could be bagged up and handed in to one of the many charity shops in town. It was time to put down roots and start afresh. Time for a new Clare.

But then fifteen-year-old Francis Ritchie's face loomed up out of the darkness. Would he be her undoing? She started to work out what age she would be when she was released from prison, assuming she was eligible for parole. Would the sentencing judge be lenient? Take into account her exemplary record? Her commendations? She began to think of all the times she had visited prisons. What would it be like to be on the other side of the locked doors? How would her parents cope with the shame?

Clare must have fallen asleep; she was surprised to hear her alarm going off so soon and fiddled with it but couldn't make it go off. Then she realised it wasn't her alarm but her phone ringing. She glanced at the clock, saw that it was just past midnight and her heart sank.

Even before she answered the call, she knew it had happened again. There could be no doubt now. She was hunting a cold-hearted, systematic, serial killer.

Chapter 12

Wednesday, 22nd May

Hepburn Gardens was a leafy, residential street, busy enough by day but pretty much deserted when Clare arrived, save for the emergency vehicles. Their flashing lights flickered off trees and bushes and a lone gull, disorientated by this night-time light, flew languidly overhead. A haar had rolled in from the North Sea making everything damp to the touch.

'He's still alive,' Chris told Clare. 'Looks pretty bad, though. Legs crushed, unconscious, lost a lot of blood. Sara's gone in the ambulance with him. Told her to stick to him like glue.'

Even in the darkness, Clare could see the blood loss on the pavement. She pulled on a pair of overshoes and walked gingerly round to a lamp post, bent over with what looked like a bit of dark green paint.

Chris followed her gaze. 'Yep. It probably saved his life. *If* he lives. He was lying between the post and that bit of collapsed wall. I'm guessing he realised the car was coming for him and he saw the gap behind the lamp post. Thought it would save him. Looks like he didn't quite make it. Legs were crushed.'

Clare looked back at the lamp post and shivered as she pictured the scene. 'Don't suppose there were any witnesses?'

'Actually, yes. She's in there.' Chris indicated a house, two or three doors down from the collapsed stone wall.

'Householder?'

'No. Dog walker. She ran there to get away from the car in case the driver spotted her. Householder was still up, fortunately, and took her and her dog in. She's still in there, but she's pretty shaken. The doctor's with her now.'

'Okay. You secure this and call in Connor, Steve and Phil. Jim on his way?'

'Yes. Should be here any time.'

'DCI Gibson?'

'Phoned. Keeping him informed. Don't think he'll turn out tonight but he's called a briefing for eight in the morning.'

'That's something, at least,' Clare said. 'I'll see if the doctor will let me speak to the witness.'

Sally Knight looked to be in her sixties. She was dressed in grey flannel trousers and a navy body-warmer over a checked shirt. Her face was tear-streaked, pale and drawn, but, in the circumstances, she seemed reasonably calm. The dog, a black Scottish Terrier, straight off a shortbread tin, sat on her lap and she was hugging it close. It gave a low growl as Clare entered and Sally fondled its neck, making reassuring noises. The doctor said Clare could have a brief conversation then he wanted Sally home to bed. Clare thanked him and said they would see her home safely. Having secured a promise from Sally that she would contact her own GP in the morning, he left her in Clare's hands.

Clare sat down and smiled. 'Anything you can tell us, Mrs Knight, anything at all, might help us catch the driver of that car.'

Sally brushed back a strand of hair then resumed her hold on the dog. 'Is he dead? The man he hit?'

'We don't know. He was alive when the ambulance left here.'

Sally put her hands over her eyes. 'It was horrible, so horrible.'

'When did you first see the car?'

'I was quite a bit down the road, doing the last dog walk before bed, you know. I saw the car and noticed it was driving slowly. I was behind it, you see. I had just come out of a side road and saw it up ahead. I don't think the driver knew I was there. Surely, he couldn't have, or he wouldn't...'

'Can you say what kind of car it was?'

'I think it was a Land Rover. One of the old-fashioned kind. Dark green, I think.'

'Not a Range Rover? The more modern ones?'

Sally shook her head. 'No, it was like a farm vehicle.'

Clare noted this down. 'And did you see the man he hit?'

'Yes. He was walking along, quite fast. Hands in his pockets. I was dawdling a bit, the dog was sniffing...'

Clare waited.

'Well, then I noticed the car speeding. I thought the driver must be drunk or had a heart attack, or something. I could see the man, still walking. He was caught in the car headlights. And he looked back, the man, as if he heard the revs and wondered what the car was doing. He must have seen it coming towards him and realised it wasn't going to stop. He started to run, but the driver just kept on going. Then the driver turned the car into the pavement, like he was aiming for the man. He must have caught him because he went down.' Her voice was quivering. 'I just... I'm sorry.'

Clare put a hand on her arm. 'Take all the time you need.'

'I think the car went over his legs. I heard the man cry out. The most awful cry you can imagine.' She shuddered at the memory. 'Then the car reversed, and I thought he would get out to help, or even drive away. But he went for the man again. Hit the lamp post. So hard. And then – then he saw me. I had my phone out to call 999, you know, but he saw me. So, I ran.' Sally started to cry quietly. 'I ran and left that poor man. But I was afraid. I thought he might come after me next.'

The dog began silently to lick Sally's hand and she hugged him closer. Clare held her gaze. 'Sally, you did absolutely the right thing. You saved your own life and you may have saved the man's life too.'

'I hope so. Will you let me know? About the man?'

'We will. Now, can you remember anything else about the car or the driver?'

'I saw a bit of the number plate. It was one of those square ones, with the number on two rows. It was definitely SJ on the top row. I noticed that because of my initials. My middle name's Jane, you see. And a seven on the bottom. That's all I can remember.'

'And the driver?'

'I can't be sure...'

'Yes?'

'Well, when the car drove at the man, and the lamp post, it was side-on to me, so I wasn't dazzled, you see. And the light from the lamp post was shining down on it. I know it sounds odd, but I had the impression it was a woman driving.'

'What made you think that?'

'Just something about the profile and the hair. Sort of an old lady style. But it couldn't be, could it?'

Clare didn't reply directly. Instead, she said, 'That's very helpful, Sally.' She looked intently at the woman. 'I think we should get you home. One of our officers will drive you and make sure you're all right. I'll give you my card and, if anything else occurs to you, you can call me in the morning.'

Jim arrived and was despatched to take Sally and her dog home. 'Check her house is secure before you leave her, Jim.'

He nodded and Clare turned to Chris.

'Can you go through the list of stolen Land Rovers? Better do Range Rovers too but Land Rovers first. Sounds like a Defender. Check the registrations. We're looking for an SJ followed by a seven.'

'Will do. I have the list on my phone. Think there were only three so it'll only take a minute.'

'Good. Do we have a name and address for the victim?'

'Yep. Nat Dryden. Lives in Bogward Road. Jim managed to get his wallet and keys before he was taken to hospital.'

'Right. Once SOCO arrive we'll go to the house. See if there's anyone else at home. If not, we'll start going through it. We'll need a police presence up there too. Can you ask Jim to organise that when he comes back?'

'As soon as I see him.'

'Thanks.' Clare took out her phone and called Sara. 'Any news, Sara?'

'He's critical, boss. In theatre just now. Probably going to lose one leg, if not both. Head injury, too. He's lost a lot of blood. Even if he survives the op he won't be able to talk to us. They're saying he'll be put into an induced coma for a few days to let him recover from the op. Couldn't get much more, but I'll let you know when he comes out.'

Connor and Steve arrived, and Clare thanked them for coming out.

'I need you to get down to Swilcan Taxis,' she said scribbling down the address. 'Knock up the owner if no one's there. I want every vehicle checked for damage to the front. Paint scrape too. Unlikely it's one of theirs so I want them ruled out as soon as we can. Then check all the drivers' own vehicles. Anything dark green but chiefly a Land Rover. Oh, and check all the drivers' hands. We're looking for someone with the tip of the middle finger missing. It could be a woman so make sure office staff are checked too.'

'Right-o, boss,' Steve said, and the pair headed off to Swilcan Taxis' office.

She turned to Chris. 'Any luck on those car registrations?'

'No matches, Clare. Sorry.'

'Right. Maybe it's not stolen then. So, I want Land Rover Defenders checked for the SJ and the seven.'

'What, all of them?'

'All of them. Start with registered owners within a fifty-mile radius of St Andrews. We can widen the scope if that doesn't turn up anything.'

'They could be false plates, boss.'

'Yeah, I know. But we have to check. And get on to all the garages and body shops in the area. I want them on the lookout for anyone bringing in a Land Rover for repair. That lamp post will have left a pretty big dent, even in a Land Rover.' She looked at the dark green paint on the lamp post. 'When SOCO get here ask them to take a scraping of that paint. They might be able to narrow it down to the year it was manufactured.'

Clare's mind was whirling. Had she covered every-thing? She thought so, but she knew Alastair Gibson had his doubts about her fitness to lead the investigation, particularly now that one of the victims was a close friend. She had to prove him wrong. She checked her watch.

'I'm heading up to Mr Dryden's house now, Chris. Can't wait any longer for SOCO. Get Jim to help you with the Land Rovers and join me at the house when you can.'

He nodded. 'On it.'

Clare climbed into her car and drove off. She was at Nat Dryden's house in less than a minute. If only he'd been a bit quicker getting home – but, no. This was a targeted attack, the driver lying in wait; and, unless she was mistaken, the third attack by the same person.

Nat's house was in darkness. Clare had a good look round the outside, then knocked on the door. No answer. She tried the doorbell. A neighbouring bedroom light went on and a few seconds later an elderly man appeared from the house next door. He was tying a dressing gown cord as he stepped out into his garden, pulling his front door closed behind him. His eye went to Clare's car then back to her, viewing her with some suspicion. Clare showed him her warrant card and his demeanour changed. He seemed eager to help.

'He's usually home by now. Works in a pub in South Street.'

'Does Mr Dryden live alone?'

'Oh yes. Just him. I hope there's nothing wrong?'

She ignored this. 'Thanks for your help, sir. I have his keys, so I'll let myself in.' And, with that, the neighbour had to be content.

There was no sign of a burglar alarm on the house so Clare put the key in the door and opened it. She pulled on a pair of gloves and turned on the hall light. There were a few letters on the doormat and she picked these up to examine. One looked like a gas bill and the others circulars. She moved into the sitting room. The furnishings were cheap but serviceable enough. There was a gas fire along one wall, set into a chunky Fifestone surround with a two-seater settee opposite. The only other chair in the room, opposite a large flat-screen TV, was piled high with washing. An archway led to a dining area at the rear of the house and Clare walked through, her eyes everywhere.

And then she saw it. An open laptop on the dining room table. It had a mouse plugged in and Clare jiggled it to bring the laptop to life. Then she took out her phone and dialled.

'Chris? Get over here as quick as you can. And bring an evidence bag with you.'

Chris arrived within a few minutes. Clare was waiting at the door. Neighbours had begun twitching their bedroom curtains so she closed the sitting room blinds to afford them some privacy.

'Laptop?' Chris asked.

'Yes. Tor installed. Gloves on, mind.'

Chris pulled on a pair of thin gloves and began exploring the folders on the laptop.

'Then there's this…' Clare held out a Post-it note with some writing on. 'It was sitting next to the computer. Looks like a weird web address.'

Chris looked at the address. It seemed to be a random series of letters and numbers ending with *.onion*.

'That's a hidden page on the dark web.' He looked at Clare, a smile forming on his lips. 'This just might be the break we need.'

'Why the onion bit at the end?'

'Tor. It's short for The Onion Router. So named, because it encrypts the connection in multiple layers, just like an onion. Each one is decrypted by one of the computers it passes through.'

'I'll take your word for it. So you think this is the web address for a dodgy page?'

'I'd be surprised if it wasn't.'

'But, if it's dodgy, why would he write the address down?'

Chris looked at his surroundings. An empty takeaway container sat on the floor next to a couple of beer cans. A glance into the kitchen revealed a sink full of dirty dishes and there was a film of dust on the TV. 'It doesn't exactly have the feminine touch, does it? I'd say he lives alone. There's no point in using a browser like Tor which covers your tracks if you then add the web pages to favourites. Look at that address. See how complex it is. Would you like to remember it?'

She saw his point. 'What time does Tech Support open?'

'I think it's eight.' Chris glanced at his watch. It was only half-two.

'We need to get this down to them urgently. I'll get it bagged up and I'll head down there for eight.'

'Gaffer's called a briefing at eight,' Chris reminded her.

'Damn. So he has. I'll text him and ask if he'll put it back to nine. This takes priority.'

Clare looked round the room. 'I'm guessing if he's daft enough to leave the laptop logged on and this onion address at the side then he won't have bothered hiding stuff. A quick look through all the rooms should do us.'

'Fair enough,' Chris agreed. 'Want a team in for a look round anyway?'

'Discreetly. No need to give the curtain twitchers any more ammo. All being well, he'll recover and be back home, although God knows when, given his injuries.'

As they left the house and headed for the car, Clare was lost in thought. She put the key in the ignition then stopped.

'What do you suppose he uses that laptop for, Chris?'

'Not sure. Could be anything criminal.'

'With some connection to the first two victims?'

'Yeah, could be. What you thinking?'

'I'm thinking we have three victims of hit-and-runs. Two dead, one nearly. And all three have been using that Tor browser.'

'It's not uncommon.'

'Do you use it?'

Chris shook his head.

'Nor do I. So it's a bit of a coincidence, wouldn't you say?'

'I suppose so.'

'Okay, if I'm right, then Andy Robb, Bruce Gilmartin and Nat Dryden have been using Tor, possibly for something criminal. Could be drugs but doesn't really matter what it is at this stage.'

'So those cards we found on the first two bodies, the five and then the four…'

'Yep. It wouldn't surprise me if SOCO found a number three card at the scene.'

'You think someone has a list of victims?'

Clare nodded. 'It's starting to look that way. If it was random, why leave the numbered cards? It doesn't make any sense. And if our driver *is* targeting these men, they must be into something pretty heavy duty.'

Chris exhaled. 'Could be anything. Drugs, money-laundering, people-trafficking, even. But, I agree. It must be something pretty major for him to attempt three murders.'

'Or her.'

'Seriously? You're thinking it could be a woman?'

'Why not? The victims are all men and it doesn't take brute force to drive a car. And our witness tonight – she thought it might be a woman.'

Chris didn't reply. Clare went on. 'Can you see Bruce Gilmartin as the kind of guy to be involved in organised crime? Successful businessman, pillar of the community?'

Chris shrugged. 'Hard to tell sometimes.'

'Well, whatever it is, we'll have to get to the bottom of it. And if this is some kind of countdown…'

'…there are another two potential victims,' Chris finished.

'Exactly. Chris, we need to find them and warn them they're in danger. And with three attacks in less than a week, time's not exactly on our side.'

'You want to go public?'

Clare started the car. 'I'm not sure. If we do, and we manage to warn the other two, we could save their lives…'

'…but they'll disappear.'

'Precisely. Then we'll never find them; or find out what they've been up to. If they escape our driver, they also escape the law.'

'Nat Dryden might help.'

'You think so?'

'If we offer him a deal.'

'Mm, I'm not sure about that. It won't be soon enough for us, anyway,' Clare said. 'It could be days before he regains consciousness, if he ever does. Even then, he might clam up.'

Chris frowned. 'You want a news blackout?'

'I'm not sure. I'd like to know what's on that laptop, before the attack on Nat hits the presses but…'

'…if we have another murder and you didn't inform the press…'

'…they'll blame us for not alerting the potential victims.'

'So, how do you want to play it?'

Clare looked at her watch. Quarter to three. 'Tech Support opens at eight, you said?'

'Yeah, think so.'

'Right. I'll phone the DCI and get a twelve-hour news blackout. Our murderer picks his victims off late at night.

We'll get a statement to the press by three in the afternoon. That gives Tech Support a few hours to come up with something.'

'It might take longer than that,' Chris said.

Clare sighed. 'I know. But we have to hope not. I can't afford to sit on it much beyond three.' She opened the car door and got out of her seat. 'Can you drive while I phone the boss?'

In Hepburn Gardens SOCO had erected a tent close to the lamp post and they were busy combing the scene for possible evidence when Clare and Chris arrived back. One of the white-suited men looked up. His expression bordered on eager, unlike the SOCO officers Clare had encountered at the last two hit-and-runs. He stood to greet them as they approached.

'Interesting crime scene, Inspector,' he said.

'Sorry to drag you out of your bed, em…'

'Raymond. Raymond Curtice. No problem. I don't mind night-time work. Usually no press or onlookers.'

Clare found it difficult to work out how old Raymond was. He was clean-shaven and, thanks to the forensic suit, she couldn't see his hair. He might be thirty or he might be fifty. She introduced herself and Chris. 'What's interesting about it?'

Raymond stepped back and indicated the damaged lamp post. 'This, for starters,' he said. 'Most collisions with things on the pavement are glancing blows, but I'd say this lamp post was hit head on.'

Clare looked back at the road. It wasn't wide. Raymond followed her gaze.

'See what I mean? You have to sweep out then circle round to get the angle right.'

Raymond bent and pointed towards the lamp post. 'This is the main point of impact. And I'd say,' he looked back towards the other side of the road, 'he's backed up and gone for our man a second time.'

'That fits with what the witness told us. She said the driver turned the car in, towards the lamp post and struck it twice.'

Raymond pointed to some markers on the narrow pavement. 'The cops who were first on the scene marked out where the victim was lying. Looks like he tried to get into the gap behind the lamp post, hoping it would save him. But, see here,' he indicated more marks on the ground, 'there wasn't enough protection and his legs were caught by the car.'

It was a grim prospect and Chris involuntarily put his hand to his mouth.

'Try not to spew on the crime scene, Sergeant,' Clare said. She turned back to Raymond. 'Anything else of note?'

'We've taken a scraping of the paint from the car. Should be able to narrow down the make, hopefully.'

Raymond looked down at the road. 'No tyre tracks, though. Hard surfaces, you know. But we've taken some photos, here and there. The damp has given us a few marks but nothing clear. I wouldn't hold out much hope.'

Raymond was clearly happy to chat away but Clare was conscious time was getting on.

'Just one more question, Raymond.'

'Yes?'

'I don't suppose you found a white card, by any chance?'

Raymond's face lit up. 'How did you know that? It was on the pavement near to where he fell. I wasn't sure if it was connected but I popped it in an evidence bag anyway. I'm afraid it's pretty soggy though. The drizzle. How on earth did you know?' he asked again.

'You weren't at the last two, then?'

'I'm just back from holiday. But the others said you'd had another couple of hit-and-runs.' He walked across to their van and retrieved a clear, evidence bag. The ink had run on the card but Clare could still make out the number three. That confirmed her uneasy suspicions. If they didn't catch this one soon, they'd be dealing with another two victims.

'Could you have it checked for prints, please? It's a long shot, I know, but all the same…'

'Will do.' And he returned to his examination of the scene.

'Likes his work,' Chris muttered, his hand still at his mouth.

Clare ignored this. She needed to think. Jim and Chris waited. 'First off,' she said, 'I think we should all get some sleep. It's going to be a long day tomorrow. We need a list of local farms so we can check their vehicles. There can't be too many folk living in the town who drive Land Rover Defenders.'

'You'd be surprised,' said Jim. 'They've become quite trendy these days. Prices have shot up.'

'All the same, if you two could pitch up about seven and make a start working through owners within fifty miles – and get me a list of farms too. Let's say within twenty miles. We can look at it once I'm back. It'll also give us something to tell the boss when he comes in. I'll stand the Edinburgh lads down. They can come in for ten, once the briefing's over. I'll fill them in. Now get home, both of you.'

Confident she had done everything possible at the scene, Clare bid Raymond and the SOCO team good night and drove home. It was after three by the time she closed her front door. She was met by an enthusiastic Benjy, excited at this unexpected night-time activity.

'No,' she said sternly to his upturned face. 'I'm looking at three hours' sleep if I'm lucky.'

She climbed wearily into bed and switched out the light.

Chapter 13

Clare set off for the Tech Support office just after seven in the morning with Benjy perched on the front seat. The office was in a business park on the outskirts of Glenrothes, a post-war new town, twenty miles south of St Andrews. She wanted to be there when it opened to explain the urgency. With luck, someone would be in early and make a head start. The roads were wet from the previous night's drizzle, but the clouds were being blown away by a breeze and the sun was glinting on the wet road surface. Clare reached the office at twenty to eight.

She pulled into the car park in front of the building and killed the engine. Diane Wallace was just climbing out of her battered VW Golf a few spaces along, her long dark hair blowing in the breeze. 'You're an early bird, Clare. How are you?'

Clare smiled, glad to see a friendly face. She and Diane had worked together on a few cases and Clare never ceased to be amazed by the information Diane could pull out of phones and laptops.

'Up against it, to be honest, Diane.'

'I heard about your murders. Needing some help from us?'

'Just a bit. You busy right now? I could do with a quick turnaround. We'd another attempted murder last night.

Same MO. But there's a news blackout until I find out if there's anything on this.'

She opened the boot and took out Nat Dryden's laptop.

'Bloody hell, Clare. It's non-stop laptops from you guys this week.'

'I know. Sorry.'

'Ach, no problem. Come away in and we'll get this one logged with the others. We've not had a chance to look at them yet but they're first on the list for this morning.'

'I've a dodgy website for you to look at as well, Diane. Top priority.'

'Is it ever anything else? Nice dog, by the way.'

Clare thought the Tech Support front office resembled the set from 'The IT Crowd' TV show. There were boxes of cables, assorted hard discs, computer towers and laptops sitting on every available surface. Diane saw her expression and laughed.

'We do know where everything is,' she said. 'Promise!'

Clare put Nat's laptop on the counter and waited while Diane took out a form to log it.

'Leave it with me, Clare. Once I've done this I'll fire it up and see what we can retrieve. I'll call you later today, if I can.'

'Any chance of a call by twelve? On this one at least?' Clare knew she was chancing her arm but she needed all the help she could get.

'Depends how easy it is to get into them,' Diane said. 'But I'll look at this one first and do what I can.'

'Thanks, Diane. Can you check this as well please?' Clare handed her the piece of paper on which she'd written the .onion web address.

Diane looked at it. 'Dark web.'

'It was found beside the third victim's laptop. This one here.' She tapped Nat's laptop.

'No problem. I'll be in touch.'

Clare and Benjy headed back to the station, arriving at ten to nine, just in time for the briefing. The DCI was in Clare's office tapping away at the computer so she decided to head straight to the incident room to gather her thoughts. By nine o'clock the room was packed, Benjy standing guard as usual on the station counter.

DCI Gibson entered last, just after nine, and seated himself on a desk. He looked round the room. 'Edinburgh lads?'

Clare raised her hand. 'I told them not to come in until ten, boss. They were here late then had the drive back last night. We can sort out what's needed and set them to work when they arrive.'

He nodded. 'So, to business. Mr Dryden? Any update on his condition?'

Sara cleared her throat. 'He survived the operation but he's in an induced coma probably for the next forty-eight hours. Might be less. The doctors are reviewing his condition every few hours. If he's stable they might start reducing his sedation a bit sooner. But he's lost a leg and they may have to amputate the other one. They won't know for a couple of days.'

'So we'll not be interviewing him any time soon. I presume there's someone keeping an eye on him?'

'Yes, Teresa from the Cupar station's there now and they've someone relieving her when her shift finishes so we're fine for today at least.'

The DCI gave her a quick smile. 'Thanks, Constable. What about next of kin?'

'His sister. Cindy Dryden. She's been at his bedside since early morning. I can try and have a chat with her if you like?'

DCI Gibson frowned. 'Maybe give it a few hours. Give her time to get used to what's happened.' He turned to Clare. 'Update please, Inspector?'

Clare stood and walked to the front of the room.

'We believe the same vehicle was used in the murders of Andy Robb and Bruce Gilmartin, and in the attempted murder last night of Nat Dryden. At each murder site, a card was left with a number written on it. First five, then four. Last night, a rain-soaked card with a clear number three was found. I believe the driver left in a panic, possibly because of the timely arrival of a dog walker.

'SOCO are analysing a trace of paint from the damaged lamp post which we hope will help us identify the year the vehicle was manufactured. We believe that vehicle to be a Land Rover Defender, possibly an older model. We also have a witness to the attack, a Mrs Sally Knight, who was walking her dog further down the road. She remembered part of the number plate because it included two of her initials. So we are probably looking for a Land Rover Defender with a registration that includes the letters SJ and the number seven. So far this hasn't matched with any vehicles either owned or stolen locally, so I'm afraid the plates may be false.'

'What are you doing about finding the car, Inspector?' DCI Gibson asked.

'Chris will co-ordinate that with the guys from Edinburgh. We're checking Land Rover Defenders registered to addresses within fifty miles of St Andrews. We'll also check farms within a twenty-mile radius. The car is bound to be damaged at the front after last night so we'll put out a shout to garages and body shops for anyone bringing in an accident-damaged vehicle.'

'I think it's worth going public on the Land Rover,' DCI Gibson said. 'No need to mention last night. In connection with two recent accidents. That sort of thing.'

'I'll draft a statement for the press office.'

'If you would, Inspector.'

'Any update on the fingerprints?' Chris asked.

Clare shook her head. 'Not yet. SOCO said it would be hard to get prints from the card left last night because of the rain, but they'll let us know. Should hear early afternoon, hopefully. In the meantime, we have reason to believe that the person whose prints are on the number five card is missing the tip of the middle finger on one hand. So we need to check everyone's fingers. Connor and Steve were down at Swilcan Taxis last night. Didn't hear anything from them so I'm guessing the staff there all checked out. But we also need to see Vicky Gallagher and her colleagues at Jensen's Diner, Nat Dryden's colleagues at the pub he worked at…'

'The Harvest Moon. South Street,' Jim added.

'Thanks, Jim. Yep. Someone needs to get down there and interview the staff, as well as checking their fingers. Then…' She paused to think.

'What about the first victim's wife,' DCI Gibson asked, 'and her boyfriend?'

'I looked at their hands when I was over there and they both showed a full set. However, Angela Robb gave me a pile of broken laptops her husband had kept over the years.

Jim took them down to Tech Support to see if they can find anything. More significantly, Chris and I examined a laptop at Nat Dryden's house last night. Not only did it have Tor installed but there was a piece of paper beside the laptop with the address of a website on the dark net.'

'Which is what, exactly?' DCI Gibson wanted to know.

'I'm not sure to be honest, other than it's a website hidden from normal search engines. Weird address too – just a jumble of letters and characters. But apparently it leads to websites the general public wouldn't want to visit.'

'Illegal?'

'Possibly. I took his laptop and the dark web address down to Tech Support this morning. I'm hoping Diane Wallace will be able to shed some light on it. I've asked for a call back by twelve. Not sure what she'll be able to detect by then, but hopefully it's something we can work on.'

'Manpower?' asked DCI Gibson.

'We could always do with a few more bodies if you can manage them, sir.'

'I'll see what I can do. Now, I'm concerned about this news blackout.'

Clare nodded. 'Me too, frankly.'

'Tell me your thoughts.'

'Normally I'd want to go as public as soon as possible,' Clare said, 'with names, possible connections and so on, to alert what could be another two potential victims. But I'm concerned that all three victims – yes, even Mr Gilmartin – may be involved in some criminal activity. For that reason, I'd like to see if we can get anything off the laptops before going public. If there is evidence of crimes having been committed we could possibly identify and pick up the others before our killer gets to them. All three hits have been late at night so we should have a few hours.'

The DCI frowned. 'It's a hell of a risk. If our man gets to them first – they might even be entirely innocent.'

'I'm aware of that, sir.'

DCI Gibson thought for a minute. 'Okay, Inspector. Let's review this at three o'clock. Meantime get the team to work. And keep me informed.'

He headed back to Clare's office then stopped in his tracks. 'Jennifer Gilmartin. Can she go back to the house now?'

'We should be done by midday, sir.'

'Go gently there, Inspector. She's still pretty shaken.'

And without waiting for a response he went into Clare's office, closing the door behind him.

Clare turned back to the team. 'Okay… Jim, take one of the Edinburgh lads when they arrive and check fingers – Vicky and the staff at Jensen's, and Nat Dryden's pub. Make sure you get full staff lists too, including casuals. I don't want anyone slipping under the radar. Oh, and not a word to the staff at the pub. Just that Nat had an accident last night. Again, check rotas at the diner and the pub. We want anyone routinely off on Thursdays, full set of fingers or not. Take photos of the victims with you and see if anyone remembers seeing Andy Robb or Bruce Gilmartin regularly on Thursday nights. That okay?'

Jim was scribbling in his notebook and gave Clare a nod.

Clare continued. 'Chris, I want you and the other lads on vehicles and farms. I'll chase up SOCO for the paint and prints. Oh, and someone needs to have a last look round the Gilmartins' house so we can get Mrs G back home.'

She looked around. A couple of the uniform lads raised their hands and she nodded her thanks. Her eye fell on Sara. 'If you could take over checking casinos and betting shops for any of the three men visiting on Thursdays, particularly anyone spending, regularly?'

'Will do,' said Sara.

'And have a look at their CCTV for the last two Thursdays. You never know.' Clare looked round the room again. 'Anyone free to cross-check mobile phone records for all three men? We're looking for any numbers in common or evidence that they were in touch with each other.'

One of the uniformed cops raised a hand.

'Right,' Clare said. 'I think that's it. Let's meet back here at… say, one o'clock and pool information. Okay, thanks everyone.'

There was a bark from the front office and Clare went out to find Vicky Gallagher standing uncertainly just inside the front door. 'Vicky, what can I do for you?'

The girl hesitated. 'It's probably nothing…'

'Come with me.' Clare led her to an interview room and closed the door. The girl looked exhausted, dark circles round her eyes which were red-rimmed with crying. Her blonde hair that had looked so thick and glossy on Sunday now hung in lank strands. Clare thought how starkly she contrasted with Angela Robb, already busy clearing out Andy's things. She pulled a chair out towards Vicky. 'Sit down, please. You look…'

'I know.' Vicky attempted a smile. 'I must look a mess. I just can't believe what's happened.'

'You're off work, I hope?'

'Doctor signed me off for two weeks. Thing is, I've nothing to occupy me. I think I might go mad.'

'It takes time. Did the doctor give you anything to help you cope?'

'He did. But I don't like taking those pills. They make me feel woozy. And I want to understand. What happened to Andy, I mean. I've been going over it and over it. Then I remembered what you said about Thursdays…'

Clare was alert. 'Yes?'

'Well, there was this one night, about a month ago, Andy was going out as usual. I was working a split shift so I was at home, having some tea, you know. Anyway, he phoned me. His car had broken down. Alternator, I think it was. So, I said did he want a lift…'

Clare tried not to show her excitement. 'Go on, Vicky.'

'But he said no, he didn't want a lift because he knew I was working. He asked if he could borrow my car. I said I had plenty of time to drive him and get back for my shift but he said he didn't want me rushing. He was lovely like that.' She smiled at the memory.

Clare waited. An anxious feeling was developing in her stomach. Was this the break they so desperately needed?

Vicky went on. 'He said if I could drive to where he was he would have a taxi waiting to take me back to St Andrews. And I said, why not just take a taxi yourself and he said it was too far and he might be back late. So I drove over there and met him with my car.'

'Where was this? Where did he break down?'

'Just before St Mike's junction. Heading towards Dundee.'

Clare raised an eyebrow. 'St Mike's?'

'Oh sorry. It's a crossroads, five or six miles north of St Andrews. There's a pub there called St Michael's Inn. Everyone calls it St Mike's. It's on the road to Dundee, just after Leuchars.'

Clare took out her phone and opened up Google maps. She navigated to St Andrews then followed the road through Guardbridge, then Leuchars. She zoomed in then asked Vicky to point out where Andy had broken down. It was about a quarter of a mile before the junction where St Michael's Inn sat.

'Just next to the railway line and the golf course.' Vicky indicated the spot. 'He said he'd called a friend to tow his car to a garage and he would leave the keys on the front wheel. Anyway, when I got there, the taxi was waiting.'

'Swilcan's?'

She shook her head. 'No, he said it was his night off and he didn't want to see a Swilcan's Taxi. I think it was Castle Cabs.'

'Go on.'

'Well, that's it, really. I got in the taxi and went back for my evening shift.'

'And which way did Andy go? In your car, I mean?'

'I didn't see. He waited until I was away. Waved me off. And he asked me to text him to let him know I was back safely. He was so caring like that.'

Clare thought it more likely that he didn't want Vicky to see which way he was heading.

'Vicky, can you remember the date? Exactly?'

Vicky nodded. 'I thought you might want to know so I looked back in my diary. It was the 18th of April.'

Clare noted this down. 'And your car registration please, Vicky?'

'I'll write it down for you.'

Clare watched as Vicky wrote down the number on a Post-it note. Both her middle fingers were intact, which ruled her out of any involvement with the numbered cards. Clare thanked her for her help and urged her to think about taking the medication the doctor had provided. The girl nodded and left. Clare went to find Chris.

'Got a minute?'

He followed her into the incident room and Clare related Vicky's tale. 'He was clearly heading off to one of those Thursday night meetings, or whatever they are, and didn't want Vicky to know where he was going.'

'So, just before the junction? He could have been heading anywhere. Left to Balmullo, right to Tayport or pretty much anywhere if he went straight on.'

'At least we know it's not in St Andrews. And not south of the town.'

'I suppose it's a start. Not sure where it gets us, though.'

'Well…' Clare was thinking. 'If he went north into Dundee he'd have crossed the Tay Road Bridge and the car number would be caught on an ANPR camera. The bridge is covered, if I remember correctly.'

'True.'

'Can you give the Traffic Control Centre a buzz? See if he crossed the bridge that night. If not, we can still narrow down our search a fair bit.'

She stood and moved to a large map of north-east Fife on the wall. 'If he was heading for Cupar, or even further west, I think he'd have turned left at Guardbridge, before he reached St Mike's. So I reckon his destination would be no more than a radius of five or six miles from St Mike's.'

'If he didn't cross the bridge…'

'Yes, if he didn't cross the bridge. Let's hope not.'

'Still a pretty big area, boss.'

'Yeah, I know but we're chipping away at it.'

'You do know tomorrow's Thursday?'

It hadn't slipped Clare's mind. In fact, she was torn between wanting to apprehend the hit-and-run driver before he killed someone else and finding out what the other two possible targets were up to on Thursday nights. She checked her watch. It was almost ten o'clock. 'You get back to tracing the cars, Chris. I'm going to take a run out to Hepburn Gardens. Just in case we missed anything last night.'

—

Clare started the engine but didn't pull out straight away. She was trying to come to a decision. 'Oh, what the hell.' She pulled out of the car park and headed for the Kenlybank Hotel.

At the reception desk, Pawel Nowicki was again on duty. Clare wondered if he ever went home. She asked him to call Jennifer Gilmartin and, after a few minutes, he handed her the phone.

'Mrs Gilmartin? I wonder if you could spare me five minutes.'

Jennifer Gilmartin sounded tired. 'I suppose so, Inspector. You know my room?'

Clare thanked her and handed the phone back to Pawel.

Jennifer was waiting at the door when Clare emerged from the lift. She greeted Clare and led her into the room. The bed was unmade and bore witness to a sleepless night but otherwise the room was tidy. She had unpacked very little.

'Is my house ready? Can I go home?'

'Hopefully in an hour or two.'

'And Benjy?'

'Back at the station being fussed over. I thought you might appreciate a few hours on your own to unpack and so on, then we could bring him over a bit later.'

'That would be a help. Thank you. You're very kind, Inspector.'

Clare took a deep breath and ploughed on. 'I wanted to speak to you, just the two of us, to ask something.'

Jennifer raised an eyebrow. 'Yes?'

'Did Mr Gilmartin go out on Thursday evenings?'

'He did, yes. That was his charity night.'

'Would you happen to know which charity?'

She shook her head. 'He did a lot of charity work, but I didn't really know the details.'

'Was it every Thursday?'

'Pretty much. It suited us both. I often went out myself.'

'Mrs Gilmartin, I have a difficult question to put to you…'

Jennifer's lips tightened and she drew herself up. 'Difficult? How so, Inspector?'

'Forgive me, but did you ever have any concerns that your husband might be engaged in… activities which were not strictly legal?' Clare watched her carefully for any reaction.

'Not strictly legal?' Jennifer's tone was icy. 'I'm not sure what you mean, Inspector.'

Clare swallowed. 'Your husband's laptop had a piece of software installed to allow him to browse parts of the internet that are hidden from other web browsers.'

Jennifer Gilmartin folded her arms. 'You are speaking, no doubt, of Tor?'

Clare was surprised. 'You know it?'

'A perfectly legal piece of software, used by millions of people worldwide.'

'Indeed but—'

'But nothing. You think because my husband – a man with an extremely high profile in case you hadn't realised – because he uses an internet browser which maximises privacy, he must necessarily be engaged in nefarious activity?'

'Mrs Gilmartin, I have reason to believe the browser may be significant. I can't say more at this stage but it is something we have to look into. I'm sorry if I've offended you but I can't ignore it.'

Jennifer was striding about the room now. She turned to face Clare again. 'Offended, Inspector, doesn't begin to describe it. My husband has been killed by some mad driver, I'm kicked out of my house, and you come here accusing *him* of criminal activity? How dare you!' Her eyes flashed with anger. She moved to open the door. 'This interview is at an end. And if you wish to speak to me in the future, my solicitor will be present.'

Clare had no option but to leave. The door slammed behind her. Out in the corridor she leaned against the wall and closed her eyes. The only decision she now had to make was whether to tell the DCI of her visit or wait for Jennifer Gilmartin to do it. She decided she might as well wait. There was plenty to do in the meantime.

Chapter 14

Clare turned the car back towards town and made for Hepburn Gardens, the site of last night's hit-and-run. There was little evidence of the accident now, other than a dark stain on the pavement and the damaged lamp post. She stopped for a minute to see if it made any more sense in daylight than it had last night. Then she pulled away and continued along, passing the roundabout where she had turned off to Nat Dryden's house. She realised now that she had joined the same road Chris had taken on Monday on their way to Fergus Bain's cottage.

'I'll get the hang of this place yet,' she muttered, slowing down as she neared the cottages. There was no sign of life and she carried on, passing rich farmland peppered with areas dense with trees. It was an attractive road and, in spite of the horrors of the current investigation, she thought how lucky she was to have found this little corner of Fife. If only she knew what the Lord Advocate's decision would be, she could start to make plans. Find a house she could call home.

Further along the road she noticed a large marquee erected in a field just off the road. A billboard reminded her that the Fife Beer Bonanza was taking place this coming weekend.

'Not much chance of going to that, now,' she said. But, as she passed the end of the field, another sign caught her eye. It read:

24-hour security – Cameras in Use.

Clare glanced in the rear-view mirror. A car was on her tail and there was a bend up ahead, making it difficult for her to pull in. She decided to turn round at the first opportunity and go back to the Beer Bonanza field. And then, as she rounded the bend, she saw a For Sale sign. It had been erected at the roadside near a gap in the trees and, as she passed, she saw a short drive leading to a property. She was on a straight stretch of the road now. With a glance in the rear-view mirror, she indicated and pulled in, allowing the car behind to pass her. Then she reversed back along until she came to the estate agent's board and turned the car into the drive. There was no sign of life and she wondered if the house might be empty. She parked in front of the door which was sheltered by a pretty wooden portico painted in a soft green. The windows looked to be new but in sympathy with the 1930s red brick walls. Clare stepped out of the car and walked to a window. She peered in, trying to see if there was any furniture. It was a bright day which made it hard to see inside but she thought it looked empty. As her eyes adjusted to the light inside the cottage she saw a fireplace and French doors, leading into another room which she thought might be a dining room. The land fell as she walked round the house making it difficult to reach the other windows. A high wooden gate leading to the back garden was locked and she decided against trying to open it. A stone trough stood beside it, bearing some late-flowering tulips, their heads just beginning to droop. It seemed substantial enough so Clare hoisted herself up onto it, clinging to the side gate to help her balance. Over the top of the gate she saw a grass lawn, bordered on one side by mature shrubs. On the other side, a path of flagstones led to a garden shed, painted in the same soft green as the gate and the portico. Clare jumped down and walked back round, past the front door to the other side of the property where a single garage stood. It had also been built in red brick, but was clearly a newer addition.

She couldn't see much more than that but what she had seen intrigued her. The sun was glinting through nearby trees, warming the walls, and for a few moments she forgot about Andy Robb, Bruce Gilmartin and Nat Dryden. She forgot that Jennifer Gilmartin was probably on the phone to DCI Gibson right now, complaining about her; most of all, she forgot that the family of the late Francis Ritchie were attempting to pursue her through the courts with every ounce of strength they possessed.

'I want to see more of you,' she told the house and she took out her phone to photograph the estate agent's board.

She returned to the car and reversed out onto the road, turning back towards St Andrews. Up ahead, a lorry bearing the name Gilmartin's Brewery was easing its way into the field where the Beer Bonanza was to take place and Clare followed it in. She could see that McMillan's Brewery also had a lorry there, the driver busy unloading kegs and crates. A Portakabin sat off to the side. Clare parked the car and knocked on the door. It was opened by a tall man wearing a security uniform. He stooped under the doorway which had clearly not been built for someone his size. He scrutinised Clare. 'Aye?'

An ID badge swung from a clip on his shirt pocket. Clare read the name – Iain Beharrie. She introduced herself, showed him her warrant card and he ushered her in. He pulled out two grey plastic bucket chairs and invited Clare to sit.

'You here about Mr Gilmartin?' he asked. 'Terrible business.'

Clare ignored the question. 'I'm after some information, Mr Beharrie.'

'Aye?'

'Can I ask about your security? On the site here. Do you have camera footage from last night? Say between eleven and one in the morning?'

Iain Beharrie shook his head. 'Sorry, no. The stock only started arriving last night so we've not switched the cameras on yet.'

Clare tried not to let her disappointment show. She tried again. 'Would there have been anyone on duty last night?'

The man moved to a chart on the wall. He traced along the dates. 'That would be Ralph. Ralph Paterson.'

'Times?'

'Started at ten and finished at eight this morning. He'll be in again tonight, probably the back of nine.'

'I could do with speaking to him sooner, if possible.'

The man moved to the computer and tapped a few keys. 'Just along the road in Strathkinness. I'll write the address down. He'll be asleep, mind.'

Clare smiled. 'I'll leave him as long as I can. Thanks for your help.'

'No problem. I hope you catch the driver. Good man, Mr Gilmartin.'

Clare thanked him and headed back to the station where she found the DCI had left to escort Jennifer Gilmartin back to her house. She could just imagine a furious Jennifer telling him about Clare's visit but she put this to the back of her mind. Time enough for that when he came back. She ruffled Benjy's neck and was rewarded with a lick. Chris was making himself a mug of coffee.

'Good news on the card SOCO found last night. There's a thumb print on the underside and it matches with the number five card. Nothing on the top though – the card was starting to disintegrate with the rain.'

'That's something,' Clare said. 'Paint?'

'Still working on it. They think it'll be an older model but that's not confirmed.'

She nodded. 'Anyone with missing fingertips or likely Land Rover drivers?'

'Sorry, boss, nothing concrete.'

She pulled a chair over and sank down. 'I've upset Jennifer Gilmartin.'

Chris gave a low whistle and sat beside her. 'DCI's going to love you. What have you done?'

'I asked if her husband might be involved in criminal activity. She took exception to that.'

'Straight in with both feet, then?'

'Yeah. But I wanted to speak to her without him hovering. Gauge her reaction.'

'Maybe he'll see your point of view. He is a detective, after all.'

'Yeah and pigs might fly. Tell you what, Chris, I think we need to have a closer look at our victims' significant others. Could you check if any of them have any previous? Cautions, even? Close relatives too. You were checking on Billy Dodds, weren't you? Anything there?'

'Sorry – got distracted. But I'll get that done now.'

'Quick as you can.'

Chris got to his feet. 'Just previous? Or do you want background as well?'

Clare thought about this. 'Hmm. Depends what you turn up. Maybe see where they grew up, went to school, that sort of thing. I'm pretty sure they're all entirely innocent and that there's some other connection between these men but we do need to check everything.'

'So just Billy and the wives? Angela Robb and the lovely Jennifer?'

'Let's do Nat Dryden too. Does he have a girlfriend? Ex-wife?'

'Not sure. I'll phone Sara and get her to check with the sister. I'll do her, too, while I'm at it.'

Chris went off to the incident room to find a vacant desk. Clare took out her phone and dialled Tech Support.

Diane answered. 'Ah Clare. Not worked through all the old laptops yet but definitely some dodgy stuff on Mr Dryden's machine.'

'How dodgy?'

'Photos. And not the kind you share on Facebook either.'

'Criminal?'

'Definitely.'

Clare whispered 'Yes' under her breath. 'Diane, can you get them to me?'

'I'm doing it now, Clare. You'll find them in a folder with your name on the network. Password set to "patch-work", all lower case. Change it immediately. I've given you editing permissions.'

'Thanks Diane. I really appreciate it.'

'I have to say, Clare, it would be really nice if you could pick these people up.'

'That bad?'

'That bad.'

Clare felt mildly sick at the prospect of what she would find in the photos. 'I'll do my very best, Diane.' Then she remembered the website address. 'Any joy on that website?'

'Not yet, but I'm hopeful. It's a site called Playroom. Mr Dryden's username is his email address – the numpty – so that was easy enough; but we're still trying to crack his password. The software's running now. If that doesn't work I've another couple of tools I can try. There might be something else too, Clare, but I'll let you know when I'm sure.'

Clare thanked Diane and looked round to see if Chris was still on the phone.

'I'm on hold…' he mouthed then he began speaking, 'Yes, DS Chris West. Yes, it is a serious matter. It's a murder enquiry…'

Clare left him to it and went to log onto a nearby PC. She navigated her way to where Diane had said she would upload the photos. Nothing there. She refreshed the drive a few times until finally the folder with her name appeared. She glanced over to Chris. He was still talking. She nodded her head to indicate he should come over and she opened the folder. As she was changing the password, Chris walked over, a printout in his hand.

'Angela Robb,' he was saying, 'cautioned for a breach of the peace. Looks like a girls' night gone wrong. But I don't think...'

Clare could hear his voice in the background, as she entered the new password and set the photos to play as a slide show. And then she heard no more as the images moved across the screen. A wave of revulsion swept over her and she instinctively clasped her arms across her chest.

They were all young. Not just young, but children. Perhaps some of the girls looked older but not by much. Four men in varying stages of undress were seen in an assortment of positions and poses, their faces carefully turned away from the camera. Clare leaned forward to look more closely at the men but it was impossible to tell who they were. She looked at the background detail. Hard to see clearly, but she didn't think it looked like a hotel room. Or a normal room, come to that. She could see wood panelling in the background but mainly the photos were focused on the men and on what they were doing to the children. One girl who looked barely pubescent was caught between two men, one front, one back. A boy who looked no more than twelve or thirteen, was being pawed by three of the men. He wore an expression so haunting that Clare could hardly bear to look.

'Shit...' Chris muttered, putting down the printout. For a few minutes he said nothing, watching as one image followed another. When he found his voice, it sounded hoarse. 'Clare, we have to nail these bastards.'

Clare hadn't heard him. She was looking closely at the photos, zooming in on one of the men. 'Does that one look like Andy Robb to you?'

'Could be. Is there a way we could crop out everything else and see if his wife or girlfriend recognises him?'

'Worth a go.' She picked up her phone and scrolled to Diane's number. 'What about the others?'

Chris peered at the photos as they moved across the screen. It was hard to tell. No distinguishing features were on show. It was clear the participants had taken care not to be identified. 'Not sure.'

Clare dialled Diane's number and she answered straight away.

'Hi Clare, you got the photos okay?'

'Yes, thanks, although I kind of wish I hadn't seen them.'

'I know what you mean. Desperate stuff.'

'Yep. No argument there. Listen, Diane, would you have time to crop the kids out of the photos? If you can, we might be able to have the men identified. I think three of them could be our hit-and-run victims.'

'Sure. That's a quick job. Give me the new password and, let's say, half an hour or so and I'll add the best ones to the folder.'

As Clare hung up the phone it rang again. It was Raymond from SOCO. She switched on the speaker so Chris could hear the call. 'Hi Raymond. Got anything for us?'

'The paint from the lamp post,' he said. 'Definitely Land Rover Defender. Ten or eleven years old.'

'That's great. Thanks Raymond. I appreciate the quick turnaround.'

'I'll check through the lists,' Chris said.

'And there's something else too,' Raymond went on.

The station door opened and DCI Gibson strode in. From his expression, Clare knew Jennifer Gilmartin had been crying on his shoulder.

'A word, Inspector.'

Clare covered the phone with her other hand. 'I'm just speaking to…'

'I don't care who you're speaking to. Call them back!'

Clare made her apologies to Raymond and followed the DCI into her office. She had barely closed the door when he started.

'What part of *go gently* don't you understand? I've just left a devastated Jennifer Gilmartin. It's not enough that she's lost her husband in a deliberate hit-and-run. Then you go crashing in with your great size tens telling her that her husband's a criminal! What were you thinking?'

Clare swallowed. 'I'm thinking he *is* a criminal.'

'And I suppose you have evidence to that effect?'

'Possibly.'

'Possibly?'

'We've recovered evidence of what looks like a paedophile ring.'

'And you think Bruce Gilmartin's involved?' He was almost spluttering with rage. 'What evidence?'

'Photographs. Quite clear, sir. They're on my computer now.'

'Then you'd better show me, Inspector.'

They emerged from the office and Clare led the DCI to the computer she had been using. She clicked to restart the slide show. There was a pause while the DCI took in what he was seeing.

'Where did these come from?'

'Nat Dryden, last night's victim. They were on his laptop. Diane at Tech Support said he'd hidden the folder but obviously not very well.'

DCI Gibson watched the images wordlessly for a few minutes. 'You can't seriously think Bruce Gilmartin is involved in this? I don't think you can identify anyone from these photos. They're not clear enough.'

Clare clicked until she came to the photo that looked like Andy Robb. 'Chris and I think this could be the first victim. The shape of the head and the build are the same.'

'You could say that about a lot of big lads.'

'Yes, that's true. I've asked Diane to see what she can do with the photos. If she can make them presentable, head and shoulders, say, I'll show them to relatives.'

DCI Gibson looked at Clare. 'You are not – repeat, *not* – to show any of these to Jennifer. If anyone's going to speak to her about – this – it'll be me.'

'With respect, sir, are you not too close?'

'You're suggesting I can't be objective?'

'Only that your fondness for Mrs Gilmartin might make it difficult to ask the right questions.'

'I'll be the judge of that, Inspector.' He turned to walk back to Clare's office then stopped. 'In future, I want everything run past me first. And I'll be bringing in a separate team to handle' – he waved a finger at the computer – 'this business. You can't possibly run a murder investigation and crack a paedophile ring with the resources you have here.'

Clare stood her ground. 'I believe it's the same enquiry, sir. I think our victims are possibly the men in these photos and that they are being picked off by our Land Rover driver, one by one.'

The DCI glared at her. He seemed about to argue. Then he shook his head. 'I knew you weren't up to this, Inspector. I'll have another team up here tomorrow. Friday at the latest.'

He marched into Clare's office and slammed the door.

A few of the cops who had witnessed the exchange stood watching Clare. She looked round at them, her cheeks burning.

'Okay, guys. Show's over. Back to work.'

They drifted off and Clare resumed her seat at the computer.

Chris hovered for a moment then, seeing Clare glance up, said, 'So, we have until Friday.'

'At the most. Better get to it then.' Her eye fell on the printout Chris had been holding. 'Sorry, Chris – you were saying?'

He shook his head. 'It's hard to think when you've just seen...'

'Yeah, I know. But we have work to do.' She looked at his face. 'Look, go outside for five minutes. Get some air. Clear your head. Then I want you back to checking those wives and relatives. It's more important than ever. I'll call Raymond back.'

Raymond answered immediately and asked Clare to wait while he reopened the case file. 'Ah yes,' he said, after a minute or two. 'The footprint on the first victim's shirt – Andrew Robb.'

'Have you managed to narrow it down?' Clare asked.

'Not to the type of shoe, no. But I've blown it up and examined it on the big screen.'

'And?'

'Well now, I can't be certain. But it does look to me as if it's a woman's shoe.'

Clare frowned. 'Really?'

'Pretty sure. It's much narrower at the toes than a man's shoe would be. Bit of luck, really. It's like the driver pressed a foot down on him to see if he was dead.'

Clare thought it hadn't been so lucky for Andy Robb but she thanked Raymond and went to relay the conversation to Chris. 'Funny, though,' she said. 'I didn't associate this one with a woman.'

'No reason it wouldn't be,' said Chris. 'It's the car that did the damage, not the driver.'

'Yeah, I suppose so. But we have two sets of prints, remember.'

'Doesn't mean we have two drivers, though,' Chris said.

A bark from the counter reminded Clare that Benjy was still there.

'I'd better take him back to Mrs Gilmartin,' said Clare. 'Get it over with.'

'Good luck.'

Clare looked at Benjy and patted her leg. He hopped from the counter and she slipped the lead over his neck. 'Hopefully she'll be so glad to see you she'll have forgotten she's angry with me.'

Chapter 15

As she turned the car into the Gilmartin's drive, Clare couldn't help thinking back to the scene that had met her on Monday morning. There was no evidence of it now. SOCO had finished their work and the gravel had been neatly raked, no doubt at the DCI's behest. Benjy, sitting on the front seat, was wagging his tail furiously as they approached the house. Clare opened the car door and he ran ahead of her towards the house. Clare followed him and rang the doorbell. Jennifer Gilmartin opened the door, sandwich in hand, and Benjy rushed in, running round and round her legs. In spite of herself, Jennifer smiled down at the dog. Then she raised her face to meet Clare's.

'Thank you for bringing him round, Inspector. And for looking after him. I'm obliged to you.'

'It was a pleasure. He's a lovely dog. And, please, let me say I'm sorry if I upset you.'

There was a hint of a smile on Jennifer's face and she gave a slight nod. 'Al Gibson's had a go at you, no doubt.'

Clare shrugged but made no reply.

'I do realise you have your job to do. But my husband was a good man.' She hesitated, as though considering something then spoke again. 'Can I offer you a cup of tea? Or coffee? As a thank-you for taking care of Benjy?'

Clare had hoped to drop Benjy off and be out of Jennifer Gilmartin's company as quickly as possible. But she appreciated the gesture and thought she might even learn something.

'Coffee would be lovely, thank you.'

She followed Jennifer into the house and through to the sunny kitchen. She strolled across to the window. She hadn't noticed the view the last time she had been there.

'You have a marvellous view.'

'We do, yes. The benefit of being that bit out of town. We look down towards St Andrews and across to Guardbridge. On a good day you can see the Perthshire hills in the distance. It's lovely when the sun's shining and dramatic when there's a gale.'

Jennifer motioned to Clare to sit. 'Sandwich?'

Clare waved this away. 'Please don't go to any trouble.'

'No trouble.'

They chatted companionably enough but there was no mistaking the tension between the two.

'I wonder,' Jennifer said, at length, 'when I will be able to bury my husband, Inspector.' She sighed. 'I can't believe I'm saying that.'

Clare gave what she hoped was a sympathetic smile. 'Hopefully in a few days. But DCI Gibson will keep you updated, I'm sure.'

'Are you married, Inspector? I really can't go on calling you Inspector. It sounds too formal when we're sharing a pot of coffee.'

'It's Clare. Call me Clare. And, no. I'm not married.'

'Never fancied it?'

Clare considered. 'I'm not sure it's compatible with this job.'

Jennifer looked at her severely. 'Life's too short, Clare. Look at me. This time last week I was looking forward to a girls' weekend in Amsterdam, not a care in the world, and now look where I am. Sitting in my kitchen with a police inspector, wondering when I can bury my husband's body.'

Clare wasn't sure how to respond so she sipped her coffee.

'Take my word for it. If you find someone who makes you happy, put them before the job.'

Clare thought of Tom, back in Glasgow. Tom, who would marry her at the drop of a hat. But then, thinking of Tom also brought thoughts of Francis Ritchie and his family.

'I'd better get back to work,' she said.

Jennifer saw her to the door, Benjy at her heels. 'Goodbye, Clare,' she said. 'I don't expect we'll meet again.'

As she walked back to the car, Clare wondered about that last statement. Was Jennifer planning a new life somewhere? Already? Given what had happened, Clare had to admire her composure. She had seemed remarkably calm. Shock, maybe.

Or had she meant something else by it? Was she warning Clare off?

She drove back to the station, mulling over Jennifer's advice to find someone to make her happy. Would she ever meet someone and settle down? She'd had Tom and had made a mess of that. Maybe she wasn't meant to be part of a couple.

–

Chris had been busy. 'Okay, first of all, I've checked out the relatives, and the victims.'

'And?'

'Bits and pieces but I doubt any of it helps us.'

'Tell me anyway,' Clare said, hanging up her jacket.

'Right, so, Andy Robb, nothing. Angela Robb – cautioned for a breach of the peace, five years ago. No action taken.'

'That it?'

'Yeah, she's clean otherwise. Grew up on the Broughty Ferry Road in Dundee. You know, just the other side of the River Tay?'

'I know where Dundee is, thank you!'

'Just checking. Went to local schools, nothing else of note. Both parents dead now. One sister in Canada.'

'Checked?'

'Yeah, she's still there.'

'Okay,' Clare said. 'And Billy Dodds?'

'Ah well now – he's been a naughty boy. One conviction for receiving stolen goods, admittedly seven years ago, and an assault ten years ago.'

'Did he do time?'

Chris shook his head. 'Suspended sentence for the assault, probably because the other lad had previous. Fine for the other one.'

Clare nodded. 'Anything else of note?'

'Nah. He's clean, otherwise.'

'Okay. Next?'

'Nat Dryden has no pre-cons and he doesn't have a girlfriend. According to his sister Cindy, he's not had one recently, as far as she knows.'

Clare thought back to the clutter and mess in Nat's house. 'Yes, I can believe that. How about Cindy?'

'Nothing at all. She and Nat are both local to St Andrews and she's never been in bother.'

'Which leaves the Gilmartins. I'm guessing nothing there.'

'Nope. Both squeaky clean. In fact, she's about as clean as it gets. Her father was a high court judge.'

'Really? Who was he?'

'Alexander Russell. Now Lord Russell of Findale.'

'Crikey. No wonder the DCI's keeping in with her.'

'Yep. Our Jennifer went to private school in Perthshire then spent two years at Edinburgh University. Not sure what she studied but she left after that. Worked in Daddy's office for a few years, helping out, while playing tennis and hanging about with the county set. Married Bruce Gilmartin when she was twenty-four and hasn't worked since. I'm guessing she's a lady who lunches.' He shook his head. 'Nice work if you can get it.'

Clare sat mulling this over. 'On balance,' she said, 'I think I'd rather not be married to someone like Bruce Gilmartin, even if it does mean working all the hours God sends for very little thanks.'

'Suppose.'

Clare stretched out her legs, making circles with her ankles. She yawned. 'God I'm tired, Chris. So – anything else?'

Chris shuffled through the printouts until he found the one he needed. 'Land Rovers. I've a list of all vehicles first registered ten and eleven years ago. There are only two within fifty miles of here. Our stolen one – you know, Fergus Bain's – and one out at Cairnharrow Farm.'

Clare searched her memory. The name wasn't familiar. 'Where's that?'

'Over towards Cupar. I can go now and check it if you like?'

'See if there's anyone at Cupar who could look at it for us. Check for damage. Save us some time.' Clare checked her watch. 'Let's get some lunch. The rest of the team should be heading back soon.' Her phone buzzed with a message and she took it out to check it.

Tom.

> Sitting outside your station. Up here seeing a client. Fancy lunch on me?

She sighed and went to the door. A sleek, silver Audi sat in the car park and she could see the familiar outline of his head, his hair falling over his eyes as it did when it needed a cut. She walked over to the car. The window was down and she looked in. Despite her misgivings she felt a rush of pleasure at seeing him.

Tom's face lit up and Clare suddenly remembered how infectious his easy, familiar smile was. But there was no time for that now. She had to focus.

Tom reached out and took hold of her hand. 'Clare, you look great. How are you?'

Clare squeezed his hand then let it drop. 'Busy. I have a double murder that's just become complicated.'

'Too busy for lunch?'

'Sorry. Another time perhaps.'

'Thing is, I'm free for the rest of the day. And I'm here now. If you can't do lunch, could I take you out for dinner?' He saw her hesitate. 'Or I could cook? I'll buy a couple of steaks and make a salad. Warm up some ciabattas?'

In spite of herself, Clare was tempted. Tom was an excellent cook and the idea of coming home after a very long day to a home-cooked meal was appealing. Perhaps Jennifer Gilmartin had a point.

He saw his chance. 'Great. I'll buy the makings of dinner. Just text when you're on your way home and I'll open the wine.'

'Better not have wine. In case I'm called out.'

'Half a glass then. I'll buy something really lovely and you can just have a taste.'

'Oh, go on then. Actually, there's the remains of a bottle of Chianti I opened on Monday. Would that do?'

'Definitely not. But I'll use it to make a sauce. Keys?'

She took out her house keys. 'I'll be late though, Tom. You could be hanging about for ages.'

'No problem. Anything you want done in the house? Any shopping? Dry cleaning? Make use of me when you're obviously so busy. I'll only be kicking my heels around St Andrews until you finish.'

She shook her head. 'No, honestly, it's fine. But thanks for offering.'

'You're so stubborn. Let me help, for goodness' sake.'

She pondered this. 'If you really want to help the grass needs a cut, although you won't want to get your nice clothes messy.'

'It's okay – I have an overnight bag. Thought I might have to stay over if my appointment ran on.'

She looked at him. 'Oh, really?'

'Oh really!'

'All right, the mower's in the shed. And there's a few bags for the charity shop, if you don't mind wandering back into town. They're in the spare room. And the hall light blew the other night. Spare bulbs are in the hall cupboard.'

'Leave it to me.'

'And now, I must go. I have a briefing at one and the troops will be back any time.' She made to move away and he reached for her hand again.

'And Clare…'

She avoided his eye. 'Yes?'

'We should talk. Tonight.'

Clare sighed. 'Tom, I'm snowed under just now.'

'All right. Let's see how you feel later on. Love you…'

She didn't respond but walked back to the station door. Did she love him? She thought she had, once. But that was before the business with Francis Ritchie. The Inquiry that Tom said he couldn't attend – even to support her. And, sitting there in that airless room, while the bones of the shooting were picked over, Clare knew that something had gone from their relationship; and that it would never be quite the same again.

Chapter 16

They assembled in the room, just after one. Sara sat near the back of the room with Connor, Steve and Phil. Chris, who Clare noticed hadn't gelled with the lads from Edinburgh, perched on a desk in the corner. She saw that his eye kept straying across to Sara who was having an animated chat with the three lads. *He doesn't like them chatting her up*, Clare thought and she wondered whether it was a case of Chris resenting the incomers, or if there was more to it than that. Jim sat near the door, keeping an eye on the front desk and the others were scattered around the room, sitting or standing in any available space.

'Right,' Clare began. 'First of all, Chris has looked into our three victims and their relatives. A couple of them, Angela Robb and Billy Dodds have some previous but nothing I think that's relevant to our investigations. So, for now, I'm ruling out any family involvement.'

Phil raised his hand. 'Anything from SOCO that might help us?'

'Thanks, Phil. We might have something.'

They were all alert now, the room silent. Clare said, 'There was a partial shoe print on Andy Robb's shirt and SOCO think it's more than likely a woman's shoe.'

There was a low murmur round the room as they digested this.

'Now, there's no reason why it shouldn't be a woman,' Clare said. 'But remember we have two sets of fingerprints on those cards so let's keep our options open.'

There was no response to this and she pressed on. 'Fingertips. Anyone with a damaged middle finger?'

Heads shook.

'Okay. Anyone who doesn't work Thursday nights?'

Again, this was met with a negative response. 'They all seem to work a mix of shifts,' said Jim, 'although the manager at The Harvest Moon confirmed Nat Dryden always has a Thursday night off.'

'Thanks, Jim,' Clare said. 'So, cars,' she continued. 'Where are we with that?'

Chris rose. 'Cupar lads checked out the ten-year-old Land Rover at Cairnharrow Farm. No damage.'

'Thanks, Chris.' She looked round the room. 'We now know that the Land Rover used last night to injure Nat Dryden was a Defender, ten or eleven years old. Or at least the paint is. So far we've turned up only two. The one that Chris has had checked out and our accordion player's stolen car.'

'Are we sure it was stolen?' asked Jim.

'Good point, Jim. We only have Fergus Bain's word for it. He could be hiding it somewhere, although goodness knows where. It's not turned up on any ANPR cameras.'

'If he was being careful, he would avoid routes with cameras,' Chris said.

'True. If our killer is clever enough to lure the victims out into the open, he's probably savvy enough to avoid cameras too.'

'Are we treating Mr Bain as a suspect?' Steve asked.

'Not necessarily. If he has hidden the car, he could be after the insurance money or there might be another reason he doesn't want it found. Maybe he had an accident, driving over the limit. It's not impossible he's involved but he couldn't have killed Andy Robb. Also let's not forget: we do have two sets of prints.'

'I think it's worth bringing Bain in for an interview,' Chris said. 'Lean on him a bit. See how he reacts. He may know something about the car. Could be nothing to do with the murders. As you say, it may be an insurance job and now, with these killings, he's too scared to say anything.'

'I'm not so sure,' Clare said. 'We don't want to scare him off and we don't want to be bounced into arresting him. As soon as we do that, the clock starts ticking and we haven't nearly enough to charge him yet. I'm not even sure he's involved. I think we'll drop into the cottage again and chat to him there. See if we can get to the bottom of that Land Rover.'

Phil raised his hand. 'We've notified all the local garages and body shops from Dundee down to Kirkcaldy and over to Kinross. Anyone brings a Land Rover in, they'll give us a shout.'

'Thanks, Phil. What about farms? Any of them with damaged vehicles?'

'Sorry, boss, negative on that,' Phil said.

'Okay, thanks, Phil.' Clare looked at Sara. 'Any luck with betting shops or casinos?'

'Sorry, no positive IDs, boss.'

'Thanks, Sara. And, phone records for the victims? Any numbers in common?'

The uniformed cops who had been checking phone records shook their heads.

Clare looked round the room. 'Right. What I'm about to say does not go outside this room. Understood?'

There were nods and murmurs of agreement. All eyes were on Clare.

'It is possible that our victims were targeted because they were involved in a paedophile ring.'

A low hum went round the room. Clare waited for it to subside then went on.

'Now this is obviously a highly sensitive area, particularly because DCI Gibson is a personal friend of the Gilmartins, so choose your words carefully when you're speaking to him.'

'Can you tell us what the evidence is, Clare?' Jim asked.

Clare hesitated for a moment. 'We've recovered images from Nat Dryden's laptop that show men engaged in sexual activity with what look to be early to mid-teen boys and girls.'

Someone muttered 'dirty bastards.'

Clare pressed on. 'I've asked Tech Support to crop the photos so we can show only the men's head and shoulders to relatives of our three victims. The quality isn't great, but Chris and I think one looks very like Andy Robb.'

'And that web address, boss.'

'Thanks, Chris. I was coming to that. We also found a note beside Nat Dryden's laptop with the address of a website on the dark web. The website's called Playroom and Tech Support hope to crack Nat's password. If they do, we can log in and have a look. So, we now have two parallel investigations. The Land Rover attacks and the paedophile ring.'

'Any indication of where the ring is operating?'

'If Andy Robb is involved then it could either be west, towards Balmullo, east to Tayport or north to the Tay Coast or even Dundee and beyond.'

'Negative on the Tay Road Bridge,' Chris said. 'Sorry, boss, with these photos, I forgot to mention it.'

'No problem. That means it's definitely in north-east Fife.'

'There might be EXIF data on the photos,' Steve said.

'Which would tell us what?'

'Location, date, time, even the device used to take the photos.'

'Thanks, Steve,' Clare said. 'I'll ask Tech Support about that too. Finally, there's a night watchman over at the beer festival, on the road to Strathkinness. There's no CCTV footage from last night but he was on duty from ten until eight this morning. It's the same road our killer would have taken from Hepburn Gardens, assuming he isn't keeping the vehicle in town, which I doubt. I'll pop over to see the night watchman mid-afternoon. Maybe call in on Fergus Bain on the way back.'

Chris raised his hand. 'Boss, what if the men in the photo aren't our victims?'

'Then we have absolutely no bloody idea who our killer is. Come to that, even if the victims *are* the men in the photos we still don't know who the killer is. But at least we'd have an idea why they're being killed.'

The room fell silent.

'I know,' Clare said. 'It's a lot to take in.'

Jim was the first to find his voice. 'What would you like us to do this afternoon, Clare?'

'Start by checking known sex-offenders in the area. Pay them a visit. See if they go out on Thursday nights. Scare the shit out of them with talk of a murderer roaming around. No reference to the hit-and-runs. Just put the wind up them. See if any of them knows anything. Even if they aren't involved, they may know something. Bring them in, if necessary, and pop them in an interview room to stew for a bit. And get out and about, checking garages and lock-ups for green Land Rovers.' She turned to Chris. 'I'd like you to come out with me. See what the night watchman can tell us. Then we'll call in on Fergus on the way back. And if Diane can do something with the photos, we'll take them round to the relatives. Might need to choose a couple of discreet work colleagues for Mr Gilmartin. The DCI will knock me into the middle of next week if I go anywhere near the fragrant Jennifer.'

Chris nodded. 'Just let me know when. Meantime, I'll get onto checking sex-offenders.'

Clare went to update the DCI on the briefing. He listened, tapping his pen on the desk then spoke. 'I'm not prepared to continue the news blackout any longer, Inspector.'

She could see his point of view. Even if Diane was able to crop the photos quickly, they needed to show them to the relatives to see if they could identify any of the men. It would be dark in a few hours with the potential for another victim that night.

'Agreed, sir. But if you could keep the detail to a minimum, I'd be grateful.'

'Leave it with me.' He picked up the phone to dial the press office.

She left him to it. 'Let's go and speak to the night watchman,' she said to Chris.

He grabbed his jacket and followed her out to the car.

–

Strathkinness lay three miles to the west of St Andrews. It was a small village, built on a slope, the original sandstone dwellings joined in recent years by more modern housing. Ralph Paterson's house was near the top of the village, a small, single-storey, terraced cottage on Church Road. The curtains were drawn and there was no sign of life. Clare looked at her watch. It was past three o'clock. 'Let's knock him up. Can't afford to wait any longer.'

It took a good few minutes for Ralph Paterson to come to the door. He was wearing jogging bottoms and a T-shirt. He yawned widely. 'Yeah?'

Clare introduced herself and Chris, and he stood back to let them in. He moved a couple of car magazines from the sofa and invited them to sit.

'Mr Paterson, we're keen to trace a green Land Rover Defender that may have been driven along the road, outside the entrance to the Beer Bonanza last night. The road would have been quiet at the time and we're wondering if you might have seen it.'

Ralph rubbed his eyes. 'Last night, you say?'

'Yes. It would have been sometime between half-eleven and midnight.'

Ralph lapsed into thoughtful silence for a moment before he spoke. 'I started at ten and I always have a mug of tea. It's usually about half-ten before everyone leaves. Have to keep a careful eye on the gates then. Easy for someone to slip in or a couple of kegs to slip out, ye know.'

Clare smiled. 'Go on.'

'It was wet last night – with the haar. Drizzly, ye ken? First wet night for a while. And I remember because the grass at the gate was pretty churned up and then a lorry arrived late. Boy had a blow out on the M8 and sat for three hours waiting on a recovery vehicle. So, he turns up about the back of eleven. And then he gets the lorry stuck. Eight-wheeler, so pretty heavy. He had umpteen cuts at trying to get in. Thought we were gonnae have to take down a bit of fencing or even unload on the road. In the end, the boy helped me roll out a couple of lengths of rubber mesh and he finally got in.'

'So, the two of you were at the gate for quite a while then?'

'Aye.'

'Would you know what time you left the gate?'

'I made the lad a coffee and he finished it just as the news was ending on the radio so that would be a bit after midnight. I'm guessing we went into the cabin maybe ten to twelve.'

Clare leaned forward. 'Ralph, this is very important. Did any cars pass you as you were helping the lorry driver?'

'I doubt it. The lorry was blocking the road. It swung out to turn then the front wheels got stuck.'

'So you would have seen if a Land Rover had gone past, say, between half-eleven and ten to twelve?'

'Definitely. It wouldn't have got past.'

'And after ten to twelve?' It was a long shot but Clare thought it worth asking.

'Sorry, couldn't say. I directed the lorry in, saw him parked, then headed in here to make the lad a drink.'

Clare got to her feet. 'Thanks Ralph. Just one last thing. If you do see any Land Rovers going up or down the road would you let me know, please? Especially if they're damaged round the front.'

Ralph agreed he would and the pair left. Out in the car, Chris said, 'Fergus Bain, now?'

Clare looked at her watch. 'He might still be out on the farm.'

'Worth a try.'

'Yep, let's see if we can catch him.' Clare pulled away and drove on until she came to a wider part of the street. She executed a three-point turn and headed back towards the St Andrews road.

As luck would have it, Fergus Bain was just stepping out of a set of muddy overalls when they drew up outside his cottage. He looked surprised to see them. 'You've no' found the Land Rover, have you?'

'Sorry, no,' Clare said. 'Could we come in, Mr Bain? We have a few more questions, if you don't mind.'

Fergus shook the overalls out and carried them round the side of the house to a garage with an up-and-over door. A moped stood propped up next to the garage. He wrenched at the handle and the door slid up. The garage was empty, save for a few tools. He hung the overalls on a hook then wheeled the moped in and pulled the door back down. He turned to them, dark eyes staring out from under his fringe. 'I'm not sure what else I can tell you but come in anyway.'

They followed him into a small sitting room. It was furnished with an assortment of ill-matched chairs and other small bits of furniture but was relatively tidy and clutter-free. He motioned to them to sit and he perched on the arm of an easy chair. Clare asked him to go over the day the Land Rover was stolen once again, and he did so with barely concealed irritation.

'You must be missing it.' Chris's tone was light. 'Are you managing okay?'

'Got the moped. It'll do till the insurance coughs up.'

'Insurance companies,' Clare said. 'Don't get me started. They wrote off my car a few years ago and gave me next to nothing for it.'

'Aye, they're a right shower,' Fergus agreed. 'I'll no' get anywhere near replacement value. They're quite collectible now, Land Rovers. But they dinnae take that into account. They'll say it's old and only worth a few hundred.'

Chris smiled. 'I've just changed to Corcoran Insurance. You're not with them, are you? Seem to be pretty decent, so far.'

'Naw. I'm with Farm Collective Insurers. Supposed to be cheaper if you're in farming, but I dinnae see much difference.'

Clare made a mental note of his insurance company. 'It must be a struggle when you've a gig on, though,' she went on. 'Can't be easy carrying your accordion on a moped.'

'Hammy picks me up, brings me back.'

'Hammy?'

'Hamish Munro. Band leader. Plays the fiddle. He lives down near Ainster.'

'Anstruther,' Chris muttered for Clare's benefit and Fergus suppressed a smile.

Clare mentally calculated the distance to Anstruther, an attractive fishing village on the East Neuk of Fife. Twenty minutes, maybe. 'Could you give us his address?' she asked Fergus.

'Aye.' He reeled off the address which Chris wrote down.

Clare pressed on. 'When was your last gig?'

'Last night,' he said. 'Rugby club down Kirkcaldy way. Fundraiser.'

'I like a good ceilidh,' Chris put in. 'Can't beat an Eightsome Reel.'

Fergus's lip curled. 'If they ken what they're doing. Often as not they're drunk and make a right arse of it.'

'Was it a late one? Those rugby lads party hard.'

'Finished at midnight. But we werenae back till after one, by the time the boy paid us and we loaded up the van.'

'Hard getting up this morning then?'

'Aye,' he said. 'Early night the night.'

Clare took over again. 'That's a lot – two gigs in four days, when you're working on the farm as well. It was your band at the wedding last Saturday, wasn't it?'

'Sometimes it's like that. They all come together. 'Specially in the summer. Gotta take the work when it's going. Farm labouring doesnae pay too well.'

'Do you take Sunday gigs?'

'If we're asked. But most folk like a Friday or Saturday. Naebody wants to get up on Monday morning when they've been drinking and dancing till the wee small hours.'

'So you weren't working last Sunday?'

He shook his head. 'No, why?'

Clare smiled. 'No reason. Thanks for the chat, Mr Bain. We'll let you get on now.'

He watched them from the door as they walked to the car. Resisting the temptation to look back, Clare said, 'Notice his hands?'

'I did. Full set of fingertips, from what I could see. We could still take his prints though. His could be the other set.'

'I'm not sure,' Clare said. 'Prints alone might not be enough. And we don't want to scare him off.' They reached the car and Clare stopped, key in hand. 'Ainster?' she said. 'What's with that?'

Chris laughed. 'That's Fifers for you. Don't ask me why they say Ainster and not Anstruther. It's a mystery to me.'

'Thought you were a Fifer.'

'How dare you! I'm a Dundee lad. Born and bred.'

'Nobody's perfect.'

Clare started the engine and pulled away. As she drove, she talked through her thoughts.

'We need someone down Kirkcaldy way to check they were both at a ceilidh until midnight. Can you phone the station there, Chris? And we don't just take Hamish Munro's word for it. Check with someone at the rugby club.'

Chris nodded. 'I'll get onto his insurers too. See what the claim value's likely to be on the Defender. As for the murders, he could have done Bruce Gilmartin but if Hamish Munro confirms his alibi then he couldn't have done Nat Dryden. And we know he didn't do Andy Robb.'

'All the same, I'm sure he's hiding something.'

'I agree. The question is what?'

Chapter 17

Clare pulled the car into the station car park and came to an abrupt halt in front of a clutch of journalists.

'Looks like the statement's gone out.'

Chris jumped out and moved them back to let Clare draw into a vacant space. As soon as the engine died they were round the car again.

'Are you hunting a serial killer, Inspector?'

'Is St Andrews in the grip of a crime wave?'

'Should you be warning residents not to go out after dark, Inspector?'

Clare ignored the barrage of questions and pushed her way, with some difficulty, through the journalists towards the door. But before she could reach it, one of them called out, 'Inspector, any comment on the Ritchie family's private prosecution?'

It was like a hammer blow to the chest. She looked at him, opened her mouth to respond but the words would not come. Chris, seeing her confusion, advanced on the journalist.

'We have a press office, guys. Use it!'

Then he turned, propelling Clare into the station in front of him. He guided her over to a corner, his hand still at her back. 'You okay?' he said, keeping his voice low. 'I didn't realise...'

She didn't turn round. 'Yeah. Thanks Chris. I'm fine. Don't fuss.'

Sara was looking irritated. 'They still out there?'

Clare raised her face to meet Sara's. 'Yep. Hopefully they'll get bored soon. Any calls?'

Sara, seeing Clare's expression, hesitated. 'You've just missed Diane from Tech Support. I said you'd call her back.'

Clare nodded and moved away, leaving Chris and Sara to chat. She opened the door to one of the interview rooms, flicking the sign to show it was occupied.

She closed the door behind her and sank down on a chair, phone in hand, and sat for a few minutes, taking deep breaths in and out. They would all know, now. About the Ritchie family. If the Press knew, it would be everywhere. Probably splashed all over tomorrow's paper.

Killer Cop!

A lump formed in her throat and she put down her phone. Tears welled up in her eyes and began coursing down her cheeks. For the first time since that night – that dreadful night – Clare gave way to her emotions. She didn't do tears. Never had. After the shooting she had buttoned up her feelings and carried on.

'It's not natural,' the counsellor had said. Clare responded that it was in *her* nature so it must be natural.

But now, after all this time, with one casual remark from a reporter, the mask had slipped. She felt her throat tighten as she sobbed involuntarily. Her face was soaking now with hot tears, and she put a hand over her mouth to stifle the sound. Her shoulders began to shake and she could hold it back no longer. With an overwhelming sense of relief, Clare gave way, sobbing audibly, no longer caring if she was overheard.

She wept for the worry she had caused her family; for the pitying looks from her colleagues – relieved it hadn't been one of them. She wept for Tom and their lost future, the life in Glasgow she had given up to come here – to this strange town she didn't know – and most of all she wept because she could feel her life spiralling out of control. And there wasn't a damn thing she could do about it.

She had no idea how long she sat there in that room. Gradually the tears subsided and her breathing began to slow. She dried her cheeks and gave her nose a final blow. A tension headache was beginning at the back of her neck so she massaged her temples with her hand. Her heart rate was returning to normal and she moved to the water cooler to pour herself a cup. She drained this then, clearing her throat, picked up her phone and dialled.

'Diane? Clare here. Sorry to miss your call.'

'Oh no problem. Hope you're making progress.'

'Getting there. We're up against it, though.'

'Clare – are you okay? You sound a bit odd...'

'Yeah, fine, Diane. Think I've caught a bit of a cold,' she said, hoping she sounded convincing.

'Ach, poor you. Hope it doesn't come to much.'

'Thanks Diane. So – any progress?'

'Think so. I've done the photos and added them to your folder on the network. I've also recovered some more files from one of those broken laptops and added them too.'

'Sounds promising. Any that would help us identify the men?'

'Yeah, possibly. Some good shots. Also, I've taken the colour out of a couple. It's easier to see the background detail in black and white. Walls and so on. They look to be quite unusual so might help you pinpoint the location.'

'Any location data on the photos?'

'Sorry, no. Either the camera didn't have GPS enabled or someone's used software to remove it. Timestamps on some, though. Mostly in the last six months but I'm not sure that's any help.'

Clare thanked Diane and ended the call. Out in the front office a cup of coffee and two biscuits were waiting for her. Sara and Chris eyed her and she made an effort to smile.

'Thanks for this,' she said, raising the cup to her lips. 'Don't suppose either of you have any paracetamol?'

Sara nodded and went to find her bag.

Chris moved to stand next to her. 'You all right?' he asked.

'I will be. Thanks, Chris.' She took another draught of coffee. 'Come on. Diane's uploaded more photos. Let's see what she's got for us.'

They went through to the incident room and sat down at a vacant desk. Clare navigated once more to the folder on the network, Chris looking over her shoulder. She found the ones Diane had added and zoomed in on one particular shot.

'This, I think, is Andy Robb. See there… he has a scar on his left shoulder. If I remember correctly, there was something like that mentioned in the PM report. Let me see if I can call it up.'

Minutes later, they were looking at the post-mortem report on Andy Robb's body.

'Gotcha.' Clare was exultant. 'See that? Five-centimetre lateral scar on left shoulder. I think there are a couple of photos here we can show to... let's show them to Angela. She is his next of kin, after all.'

'And probably more up to looking at them than Vicky,' Chris agreed. 'What about the others?'

'Can you call up a photo of Bruce Gilmartin, maybe from the brewery website? The hair here looks pretty similar but it's hard to tell when you don't know him.'

Chris took out his phone and found his way to the brewery website. He clicked on a smiling photo of Bruce Gilmartin. They peered at it, comparing it with the photos Diane had sent. 'It *could* be him,' said Chris. 'We could always ask the boss.'

Clare sighed. She didn't relish upsetting the DCI any further by confronting him with evidence that his old friend was involved in a paedophile ring. But it was probably easier than asking the brewery employees. 'All right. Let's see what he says.'

Clare put her head round her office door. The DCI looked up. 'Yes?'

'Something I'd like you to see, sir.'

DCI Gibson followed Clare over to the computer and sat to look at the images. She pointed out the scar on the shoulder of the man they believed to be Andy Robb and he nodded but made no comment. Then he moved onto the photos of Bruce Gilmartin, examining each closely.

After a while, he relinquished the mouse and rose from the seat. 'I would be very much obliged if we could keep this from Mrs Gilmartin in the meantime.'

'You agree these are photos of Mr Gilmartin?' Clare asked.

He sighed. 'What do you want me to say, Inspector? You're right and I'm wrong?'

Clare sat down again and took up the mouse, moving on through the next set of photos. 'Could these be Nat Dryden?'

Chris peered at the images of a grey-haired man and shook his head. 'Dryden's too young.'

Clare moved on through the photos until she found a new subject. 'This?'

Chris nodded. 'Yeah, could be. Can we take these up to the hospital to show the sister?'

Clare checked her watch. 'Yes, we could do that now. Need to check with whoever's on duty at the hospital that she's still there, though.'

'Let's just stop a minute and go over what we have,' said DCI Gibson.

Clare sat down at the computer again, next to the DCI and pulled the mouse towards her. 'I'll separate them out into folders with possible names.' She went back to the first of the photos and selected the first six. 'I think these are all Andy Robb. Most of them show that scar. If we can show these to Angela Robb I think we'll have a positive ID.'

'Nothing about why we're asking,' the DCI reminded her.

'No, of course not.' She moved the photos into a folder named *AR*. 'Now the next few we'll assume are Bruce Gilmartin?' She looked to the DCI for confirmation and he gave a nod. She dragged these into a folder which she named *BG*. 'Then we have grey-haired man who could possibly be our next victim.' She moved these into another folder. 'I'll call this *UK1*.'

'As in Unknown?' Chris asked.

'Exactly.' Clare selected another six photos. 'Now, these could be Nat Dryden. If Chris and I nip over just now we can get the sister to confirm.'

'Okay,' said Chris. 'But there's someone we're forgetting.'

'Who?'

'Whoever's behind the camera. Remember we've had three victims already, with the grey-haired man a possible fourth. But someone must be taking these pictures. And that person could be our fifth victim if we don't get a move on.'

Clare turned to the DCI. 'Is there any way we can alert the public without causing a panic?'

DCI Gibson sat back and considered this. 'I don't think it's the public who are at risk. These attacks aren't random. They're clearly targeted at certain individuals. Presumably the men in these photos. If we let the public think there's a madman mowing down people at random, we'll have more than the press outside to worry about. Better to step up patrols and ask the public to let us know if they see a dark green Land Rover Defender. Do you have the number plate?'

'Only a few digits but it may be a false one anyway. The driver could even have access to more plates. But it wouldn't do any harm to give it out. Let's get it on the Facebook pages too. If we maximise the publicity we may even put the murderer off coming out tonight. Buy us some time.'

'It's a pity, Inspector, that you talked me into that news blackout. We might have struck lucky with the car if we'd gone public earlier.' He looked at his watch. 'Nearly five o'clock. It's late enough as it is.'

'It won't be dark for a good few hours yet, sir,' she pointed out.

'Better get a move on then.' He turned on his heel and walked away.

Clare rolled her eyes. 'That went well.'

'I reckon you got off lightly, seeing as you just proved his old school buddy's a paedo,' Chris said. 'Ninewells Hospital now?'

—

They arrived in Dundee at the back end of the rush hour and navigated their way through the teatime traffic jams. Ninewells was a sprawling teaching hospital in the west end of the city. Built in the 1970s, its medical school and research facilities drew specialists from all over the world. Clare managed to find a parking space in one of the closer car parks and they set off for the main concourse.

Nat Dryden's room was in the major trauma ward. They followed the signs, taking the stairs down to the lower levels, arriving at a security door. They were buzzed in by a nurse who led them to a large bay with four beds. Teresa, one of the uniformed cops from Cupar station, sat at the end of the bay, newspaper in hand. She rose to greet Clare and Chris.

'No change,' she said. 'Still unconscious.'

'Get yourself a coffee, or some fresh air,' Clare said. 'We'll be here for a bit.'

Teresa escaped and Clare turned to look round the bay. Nat Dryden's bed was at the window. It was one of only two which were occupied, the other by an elderly man with an oxygen mask covering his nose and mouth.

Nat lay surrounded by machines and monitors, an assortment of lights and digital displays flashing. The bedclothes were elevated by a cage, protecting what remained of his legs. Clare tried not to think about the damage he had sustained. A woman in faded jeans and a pink T-shirt stood at the window, her back to them, taking in the view down and across the River Tay to Fife.

'Cindy Dryden?' Clare asked and the woman turned to face them. She looked tired and Clare could see the remains of mascara on her cheeks. Chris fetched an extra chair and they sat down at the end of Nat's bed.

Cindy seemed quite happy to talk. 'To be honest, it's nice to have the company,' she said. 'I've been sitting here since three in the morning.'

'Is there anyone you would like us to call?' Clare asked. 'Someone who can be here with you?'

She shook her head. 'My boyfriend, Ronnie, he's staying with our little girl. Taken the day off to look after her. I'll be fine. They've said Nat's out of danger.'

Chris offered to fetch her a cup of coffee but she declined. 'Your guys have been really good. Keeping an eye on Nat while I go for a break.'

'Are you up to answering a few questions, Cindy?' Clare asked.

She yawned. 'Yeah, go for it. Anything that will help.'

Clare began by asking Cindy about Thursday nights but she was clueless.

'I didn't even know he went out on Thursdays. He works evenings a lot so I wouldn't have noticed if he was going out.'

'I think you told my colleague Nat didn't have a regular girlfriend.'

She shook her head. 'Not for a while now. He did have one but she moved away with work. Janey, she was called. She lost her job – end of last year – and I think she hoped Nat would propose but he's not the settling down kind. So, she found this job in Birmingham and told him she was going.'

'Was he upset?'

'Not really. Plenty more fish in the sea, he said.'

'And was she upset?'

'To start with, yes. But then when she saw he wasn't bothered I think she realised she'd be better off without him.'

'Are you still in touch with her?'

'Yes, on Facebook. Here, I'll show you.' She tapped at her phone then passed it to Clare. 'See? Janey Flynn.'

'Do you have an address? In Birmingham?'

'No but she went to work for the fire service down there so you should be able to find her through them.'

Clare noted this down. 'Can you think of anyone who might have wanted to harm Nat, Cindy?'

Cindy thought. 'The pub, you know, they don't always get on; but this is a bit extreme isn't it? I honestly can't see anyone there doing this to him.'

'Who didn't he get on with?'

'Oh, just the manager. But, honestly, he's fine. If he'd an issue with Nat he'd just have fired him. It was a casual contract.'

Chris cleared his throat. 'Erm, Cindy, we have some photos that we think might be of Nat. They're taken from the side and behind. But we're not sure if it is him. Would you feel up to looking at them?'

Cindy nodded and Clare withdrew a sheaf of photos from a brown envelope. She handed them to Cindy and she leafed through them. At length she raised her eyes.

'I'm pretty sure it's Nat.' She picked out one of the photos and held it for them to see. 'See there? That mole, with the smaller one to the side? That looks familiar. I mean, I wasn't in the habit of looking at his back without a shirt on but I'm guessing you can check. The nurse might let you turn him over.'

Chris pushed back his chair and went to the nurse's station. The duty nurse was on the phone and, when the call was finished, Chris asked if it would be possible to move Mr Dryden slightly to examine his back. The nurse looked doubtful and went to fetch a colleague. The charge nurse who came seemed unwilling.

'It's a question of privacy,' she told Chris.

'I appreciate that but Mr Dryden was the victim of an attempted murder and this may help us track down the culprit who, we believe, has killed twice already.'

'Does his sister agree?'

'She does. It was her suggestion.'

In the face of such an argument, the charge nurse relented. 'But I'll have to record it formally,' she told Chris.

Clare took out her phone and was ready with the camera when they raised the unconscious Nat onto his left shoulder. And there it was. The larger mole with the smaller one to the side. She took a couple of photos, checked the quality then nodded to the nurse who lowered Nat gently back down.

'Any idea when he might wake up?' Clare asked the charge nurse.

'The doctor said he'll review it in the morning. The plan was Friday but it's possible they might start to reduce sedation tomorrow. Depends how he is overnight but he's doing well, so far.'

'We need to speak to him as soon as possible,' Clare said. 'He may have vital evidence that will help us prevent another murder.'

The charge nurse said she would let the cop on duty know as soon as there was any change.

The nurses left and Clare thanked Cindy. 'You've been so helpful.'

'Wait...'

'Yes?'

'Those photos. Where did you get them? I mean, where were they taken? Why is his shirt off?'

Clare smiled. 'At the moment, Cindy, I can't say any more. But we will let you know, once things become clearer.'

She looked at them, her eyes brimming with tears. *She knows*, Clare thought, as they walked back down the corridor to the exit. She knows he's been up to something. And her heart went out to Cindy. To her, to Jennifer Gilmartin and to Vicky Gallagher. Losing a loved one would be the least of their problems when it all came out.

They were on their way back to St Andrews when Diane phoned. Clare was driving and Chris switched the speaker on.

'Diane?'

'Hi again, Clare. Another bit of information for you. It's not much but might help fill in some of the blanks.'

'Go on.'

'Nat Dryden's laptop has been hacked. There's a keylogger installed.'

'A keylogger?'

'It's a piece of software that records any keystrokes used when accessing websites; then it sends them back to whoever tricked the user into installing it.'

'Would that include passwords?'

'Oh yes. And it would tell the hacker which websites the passwords related to.'

'So the hacker would be able to use that info to log in as Nat?'

'Precisely.'

'But why? What would the hacker get out of it?'

'Sometimes it's money,' Diane said. 'They impersonate the person they've hacked to order stuff, or even access their bank account. But in this case, I'd say the hacker was after information.'

'Such as?'

'Okay – I'm not the detective, Clare. That's down to you. But, having looked at the laptops from Mr Robb and Mr Gilmartin, they were much more careful about their security. Mr Dryden, on the other hand, is the weak link. He didn't even have up-to-date security software installed. It was nearly two years out-of-date. So if the hacker was trawling the web for guys involved in porn and the like, Nat Dryden would be easy to find. Send him an email with some porno photos taken from the internet.'

'And the email has this keylogger attached?' Clare was starting to see what Diane meant.

'You've got it. Once the keylogger was on Nat's laptop, the hacker could see his usernames and passwords and,' crucially, all his email contacts, Facebook friends and so on.'

Clare was turning this over in her mind as she drove. 'But, if the other two – Andy Robb and Bruce Gilmartin – if their security software was better than Nat's, how could the keylogger get past that?'

'It depends on how sophisticated the keylogger is. A clever hacker can find ways. And I think you're dealing with a very clever hacker here. It only takes one innocent-looking email and the damage is done.

'So, our hacker – whoever he or she is – found Nat through his online browsing, sent him an email with the keylogger and was able to find the Playroom by stealing Nat's username and password?'

'You've got it.'

'And would that let the hacker find the other Playroom users?'

'Probably. Now, I'm guessing the other Playroom members use untraceable email addresses – if they're breaking the law, they'd be daft not to. But all our hacker needs is one weak link, one scrap of identifying information, and he's in. He could have been monitoring the Playroom for weeks, months even. A bit of patience on the hacker's part and one slip up by the others.'

'I don't suppose you can identify the hacker?'

'I wish. One day maybe but not at the moment.'

'Did you manage to log into Dryden's Playroom account?'

'I did. It looks like he downloaded the photos from the Playroom, but that's it. The members aren't identified by name, only by a number.'

'Let me guess,' Clare said, 'one to five?'

'You've got it.'

'Nothing about the location of the Playroom? God, what a name…'

'I know,' Diane said. 'But no, sorry, nothing like that. The only other thing is a list of dates – all Thursdays. But I'm guessing that's not a surprise.'

'It just confirms what we suspected,' Clare said. 'Listen, Diane, thanks so much for all this. I really appreciate it.'

'Just let me know if you need anything else. We'll keep trying the other laptops from Andy Robb but I'm not expecting to find much more now.'

Clare drove on, lost in thought. She knew now why the victims were being targeted and that another two men were in danger. But she hadn't a clue how to set about finding them. They had two sets of fingerprints, neither of them on the system, a woman's shoe print and a Land Rover no one could find. Was that it? Were they just going to have to wait until their murderer struck again? Was he or she planning another hit tonight? She felt sick at the thought of it. She really needed a break.

Chapter 18

DCI Gibson put out a further press statement just after six, asking the public to look out for a dark green Land Rover Defender, particularly one with damage at the front. He had also drafted in extra uniforms to patrol the town overnight. Visits had been paid to known sex-offenders living in the area and police were stationed near their homes. None of the garages visited had seen a damaged Land Rover and the Fire Service in Birmingham were able to confirm that Janey Flynn had been at work for the past few days, effectively ruling her out.

Clare and Chris had arrived back and confirmed Nat Dryden as one of the men in the photos.

'I'm pretty sure the man with the scar on his shoulder will turn out to be Andy Robb,' Clare told the DCI. 'Maybe a couple of the Edinburgh lads could go over to Angela's to have it confirmed?'

The DCI nodded. 'Anything else?'

'I'd like to have another look through the photos Diane's uploaded but, apart from that, I'm not sure what else we can do tonight,' Clare said.

'What about that accordion player?'

'Fergus Bain? Chris and I both think there's something funny about him. But I can't work out what it is. Chris is checking up on the insurance value of his stolen Land

Rover right now… if he ever gets through to them. It could be that it developed a fault too expensive to fix and he's after the insurance money. I'm just not sure.'

'Where was he last night?'

'Playing the accordion at a rugby club ceilidh in Kirkcaldy. The club secretary confirms he was there up to midnight and the band leader says he dropped him home just after one in the morning.'

'Want a watch put on his house?'

Clare ran a hand through her hair. 'I'm not sure we can spare the manpower, sir, to be honest. We've nothing to go on, really. Just a feeling.'

'I'd rather spend a few quid on it than end up with another corpse.'

'Fair enough,' she agreed. 'But it's not going to be easy. It's light until quite late just now.'

'You work it out and I'll provide the bodies.'

'Okay. Thank you, sir.'

Chris came off the phone. 'He wasn't miles out. Insurance company said he put a low value on the car, probably to keep the premiums down. Plus it had a few bumps and scrapes. They reckon they'll pay out around £1000. Certainly no more than that.'

'It's a tidy sum, depending on your lifestyle, but not enough to replace it, I'd have thought.'

'Not with another Land Rover. He'd have been far better off selling it privately. They reckon he'd get ten times the insurance value for it.'

'So maybe it's been stolen after all?'

'Yeah, maybe.'

'Fancy another run out to Strathkinness?'

'If you like.'

'We need to scope out a possible observation point. The DCI's authorised a watch on Bain's house tonight.'

'Seems a bit extravagant, given there's the whole of St Andrews to keep an eye on. And he does have an alibi for last night, remember.'

'Listen, if he's putting up the money, I'm not arguing. And there's something not quite right with our Mr Bain.'

In the car park, Clare said, 'We'll take my car. I don't want him seeing the car we were in this afternoon again.'

They drove out along the Strathkinness road, slowing down as much as Clare dared as they passed Fergus Bain's cottage. 'Keep your eyes peeled for likely observation points,' she said. Once they had passed the cottage and rounded a bend, out of sight, Clare pulled into the side of the road. 'Anything?'

'Yeah, I think so. Just beyond the cottage, on the other side of the road, there's a stretch of overgrown beech hedge more or less opposite him. I reckon if you went in a bit further along the road you could work your way back without being seen and have a pretty good view of his cottage.'

Clare pulled away again. 'I'll head back by the other road. If he's watching for any police activity he'll notice the same car going past. I think we should all go home for a couple of hours, then meet back at the station at about eight. Would you mind bringing a cop out here first, though, so we can keep an eye on Fergus before it gets dark? Oh, and tell him to keep his eyes peeled for Land Rovers too. Especially if they're heading for St Andrews.'

DCI Gibson agreed their plan and Chris drove one of the uniformed officers back along the road to keep an eye on Fergus Bain's cottage. Connor and Phil had taken photographs round to Angela Robb's but hadn't yet returned. Clare decided not to wait for them and sent a quick text to Tom to let him know she was on her way back. He replied with a smiley face.

The steaks were resting while Tom, now more comfortably dressed in stone-coloured chinos and a grey Henley, swilled Chianti and balsamic vinegar round the pan.

'That's a wonderful smell to come home to,' Clare said as she slipped off her jacket.

'Let me pour you a glass,' Tom said.

'Sorry, Tom, I have to go back tonight.'

'Half a glass?'

'Not even that.'

'Quarter? It's a good one.' He held up a bottle of Malbec.

'Oh, go on then. But no more than that. I have to drive later.'

He poured a small glass for her and turned back to his red wine reduction. 'Ciabatta's warming in the oven. Salad on the table. It's a lovely evening. Want to eat in the garden?'

Clare looked out of the window. Tom had unearthed a plastic table and chairs from the shed and put them where they would catch the evening sun. The grass had been cut and the edges neatly trimmed. It looked as if he'd weeded the borders too. It was a tempting sight. 'Why not?'

The meal was delicious, as she knew it would be, the steaks cooked to perfection. Clare wiped her plate clean with a strip of warm ciabatta, savouring the last of the sauce. She tried to put the investigation to the back of her mind, for a few hours at least. She kicked off her shoes and flexed her feet, wriggling her toes. Tom took his cue and lifted one foot to his knee. He began to massage it and Clare leaned back and closed her eyes. Blackbirds were chirping their dusk song and, every now and then, she caught a whiff of Tom's Douro cologne. For a few minutes, she was entirely content. 'Thanks for doing this, Tom. It's crazy at work just now. This is lovely to come home to.'

He beamed. 'I enjoy it. You deserve to be spoiled.' He stopped massaging and held her foot for a moment. 'But I do think we should talk.'

'Tom – I don't really see the point. Until I hear from the Lord Advocate's office I won't know if I have anything to worry about.'

'But it must be on your mind.'

'Of course it is. But work is so busy. It leaves me very little time to dwell on things.'

'At least get in touch with Gavin Maitland. He's the best defence advocate I know.'

'I will, if it comes to it. Otherwise I'd rather not discuss it if you don't mind.'

He sighed. 'Okay, I know when I'm licked. But can we at least talk about us?'

'Actually, yes. There's something I wanted to tell you.'

He waited.

'I'm thinking of buying a house. Here, I mean. In St Andrews.'

'Oh.'

'You did know I'd sold the flat in Glasgow?'

'Finally?'

'Yep. Had the confirmation the other day.'

Tom was silent for a minute. 'But I thought you might…'

'Might what?'

'Well, I thought you might come back to Glasgow and buy something else there. I mean, once you'd had enough of St Andrews.'

'That's not going to happen. I like it here.'

'Seriously? Is this really you, Clare? All that golf – and tourists? Is this really where you see your future? You're a Glasgow girl. You know you are.'

Clare shrugged. 'Doesn't mean I can't live somewhere else. And I needed to get out of Glasgow. I needed a complete change.'

'Okay. I see that. But what if the Lord Advocate throws out the Ritchie family's application? Hopefully he will. Then there would be no reason to stay away. You could come back, find another flat – a house, even. Your friends are all there, family too. And it's always been your home.'

'And now I would like to make my home here. St Andrews is lovely – murderous drivers excepted. The people are great, it's close to the sea and it rains a lot less than in Glasgow!'

There was a pause. Then Tom said, 'And what about me? Do I fit into your plans at all?'

Clare traced her finger round the rim of her glass. 'Let's see what happens, eh? I can't think too far ahead just now.' She rose. 'Listen, I'll wash up, then I must get back.'

In the end they washed up together, studiously avoiding any further talk of their future, together or otherwise. Clare told Tom about the murders, about the photos of the victims, and her suspicion that Fergus Bain was somehow involved. Tom listened, then told her about the defamation case he was defending. The kitchen was soon tidy and Clare glanced at the clock.

'I'll have to go,' she said.

'Will you be late?'

'Depends what happens. The other hit-and-runs have all been around midnight, we think, so if nothing's happened by the back of one, I may come home.'

'Okay. I'll head back to Glasgow in the morning. But I'll hang about until the shops open. I forgot your charity shop bags so I'll take them in on my way back.'

'Honestly, Tom, it's fine. I can do it when I'm not so busy.'

'It's no trouble. I'll be passing close to the shops anyway. Just leave them so I can't get out of the house without tripping over them.'

–

The station was buzzing with extra cops when Clare arrived back. She looked for Connor and Phil and found them chatting to Sara and a couple of other uniformed cops. 'Any luck with Angela Robb?' she asked.

'Yeah, positive ID,' Connor said. 'She wanted to know where the photos had come from but I didn't give any details.'

'Gave us a look, though,' Phil said. 'I reckon she won't be surprised when it all comes out.'

Clare thanked them and turned her thoughts to the night ahead. She took Chris into the incident room and looked at a map of the area. 'Is the cop in place opposite Fergus Bain's cottage?'

'Yeah, he's been there since you went home. He's been calling in every thirty minutes. All quiet at the moment. Bain's at home and no sign of him stirring.'

'You've not left a car there?'

'No. Too conspicuous. There's a plain-clothes guy on a motorbike two minutes away, tucked in behind a hedge. If Fergus makes a move the bike will follow him.'

Clare nodded. 'So, it's just a waiting game now.'

'Yep. I just hope we're watching the right guy.'

Clare didn't want to think what might happen if they were concentrating their resources on an innocent man while the real culprit was roaming free. 'You know what, Chris, I think I'll just take another run out to that road.'

'Are you not risking him seeing you?'

'Might not be a bad thing if he did. If he is involved, it could scare him off going out tonight. But I'll try and sneak under his radar.'

'Want me to come with you?'

'No, I'd rather you were here in case something happens. Let me know right away if there are any developments.'

'Right-o.'

Clare left the station and picked up a pool car. She decided to approach the road from the other end so she wouldn't be driving into the sun. Ten minutes along the A91 took her to the Strathkinness turn-off and she drove up a winding road until she crested the rise and the village came into view. Carrying straight on she headed down through the village and over the crossroads at the bottom. The trees lining this section of road were in full leaf now and, in parts, the overhang was sufficient for the automatic headlights to come on. Clare was not given to nerves but there was something about this road. She was only a mile or so from Strathkinness and close to the St Andrews road now, but there was a sense of isolation and she was relieved to see the trees clear and the signpost for St Andrews come into view.

She drove slowly, allowing a few cars to overtake, her eyes flicking from left to right. She wasn't sure what she was looking for, but she was glad of something to do while she waited for darkness to fall. Clare stopped briefly as she reached the cottage that was for sale, the red bricks warmed in the evening sun. It looked more appealing than ever and she determined to follow it up, just as soon as this investigation was out of the way. It occurred to her that, if Fergus Bain was innocent, or if they didn't find enough evidence to convict him, she could end up being his near neighbour. His cottage could be no more than a mile further up the road. It was an uncomfortable thought. She put it to the back of her mind and drew away again.

She passed the field where the Beer Bonanza was taking shape, scanning the makeshift car park for Land Rovers, more in hope than expectation. There were none of course. *As if the driver would park it in full view.*

The trees and fields were bathed in rich sunlight and, at that moment, it seemed impossible to Clare that they were hunting a killer, a deranged driver intent on picking off members of a paedophile ring, one by one. As she drove along this quiet country road, Clare thought the world was far too lovely for such horrors to be happening. But happening they were.

Something glinted, but she was past it before she had the chance to look. Glancing in her rear-view mirror, she signalled into the side, allowing the car behind to pass her, then reversed back a short distance and scanned the foliage.

Nothing.

She reversed again, further back until she found a suitable spot to park. Locking the car, Clare crossed the road and walked along the verge to the point where something had caught her eye; but still she couldn't see anything.

The trees at the roadside were overgrown with ivy which had almost bridged the gap from one tree to its neighbour. And then she saw it again.

The glint came from a stout padlock which secured the doors of a wooden garage, set back from the road and hooded by the ivy-clad trees on either side. Stepping in, under the ivy Clare could see that the garage was as old as the padlock was new.

Her heart was beating fast now. Someone had put a new, substantial padlock on an old, run-down garage, so well hidden that she and Chris had missed it every time they had driven past. She looked around and stood, listening. There was nothing to suggest that she might be in danger, but training and experience had taught her caution.

Picking her steps carefully, she walked noiselessly round the garage, squeezing past where trees were leaning into its walls, and stepping round a large water butt at the side. There was no window, but at the back there was a small hole where a knot in the wood had once been. Clare took out her phone and turned on the torch, but there wasn't enough room to shine the torch and peer inside. She stood back and looked at the garage again. There was a narrow gap between two of the vertical planks where the wood had started to shrink. She looked down at her feet until she found a twig and forced this in between the two planks. This gave her enough of a gap to shine the torch into the garage. She then pressed her eye to the knot hole.

There wasn't enough light to see the vehicle clearly or even to see the colour but the light fell on the square rear number plate which clearly showed the letters SJ on the top row and the number seven on the bottom.

She took out her mobile phone and checked for a signal. One bar. Better to get out on the road and call from there. And then she heard footsteps and metallic sounds. Someone was undoing the padlock. She hadn't heard anyone approaching but someone was there now. Clare cursed herself for coming out alone. If she had Chris with her or even a uniformed cop she could arrest the driver. She contemplated calling for backup and attempting an arrest herself, when she heard a dull thud from the grass in front of the garage. She stole a quick glance round the side and her heart began to thump in her chest. The dull thud had come from a shotgun that had fallen over. Clare's time in the Armed Response Unit told her the gun was a Remington. Probably an 870. She wouldn't stand much chance at close range. There was a rustling sound. The driver had picked the gun up and was back at the padlock now. She would have to sit it out.

As the lock sprang free, Clare felt a familiar buzzing and realised, to her horror, that a call was coming through on her mobile. She flicked frantically at the mute button but her hands were clammy and her fingers would not obey. Seconds later, the still evening air was cut by her ring tone. She didn't wait for the driver's reaction but turned and plunged into the trees behind the garage. As she ran, her training kicked in and she weaved left and right, mentally calculating the range of the gun. The noise made by her feet and the pulse beating in her head prevented her hearing if she was being followed but she knew not to stop and check. She could hear the sound of fast breathing, twigs cracking beneath feet but was it her breathing? Her feet? No time to check. She ran on, leaping over fallen branches, taking the less obvious path. Only when she could see a break in the trees ahead did she dare to stop. She found a gnarled oak among the larch and pine trees and hid behind the trunk. She listened and heard nothing. She waited for a minute then, when there was still no sound, she peeped out from behind the trunk. Nothing. She looked all around and, when she was sure she hadn't been followed, began walking steadily towards the gap in the trees. A road was up ahead and she could hear the sound of traffic. She picked up the pace, jogging gently towards the road and, when she was clear of the trees, took out her phone and dialled.

'Chris! I've found the garage. And the Land Rover.' Her breath was coming fast now as the tension was released from her body. 'Can you come and get me? Head for Fergus's cottage. Carry on past and I'll flag you down. Get the cop on the motorbike to check if he's still at home. If he's there then he's not our man. But if he's slipped out… oh and make sure everyone knows – our driver's armed.' She put the phone back in her pocket with shaking hands and leaned against a tree for support. The reality of what had just happened was dawning on her and she hugged her arms across her chest to try and control the shaking.

Chris wasted no time. Clare heard the car before she saw it and climbed in, thankfully. He threw the car into reverse, bumping up against the verge then took off again back towards St Andrews.

'My car's about half a mile along the road. If you drop me…'

'Forget the bloody car. You're driving nowhere. You've had a shock. I'll get a cop to pick it up later. Meantime, tell me.'

'In a minute. Slow down,' she said, as they neared the location of the garage. 'And stop! Stop here.'

Chris pulled up at the side of the road and looked across to where Clare had indicated. He could see nothing. Clare jumped out of the car, surprised at how weak her legs felt. Chris followed, his hand at her elbow. Clare ignored this and reached up to pull back the curtain of ivy.

'There,' she said.

The padlock was gone. She fished a glove out of her pocket and pulled it on then eased one of the wooden doors open. Empty.

'Shit.' Her mind whirled. 'Get on to the motorbike cop. See if a Land Rover or Fergus's moped has passed him in the last half hour.'

As Chris spoke into his radio, Clare stared at the garage, reliving the moment her phone had gone off. She looked down at where the Remington must have fallen and shivered.

'And get a SOCO team out here,' she added. 'Might be something that will help us.'

Chris's radio crackled and Clare's heart sank.

'Sorry, Chris,' Jim's voice said. 'No Land Rover's passed our bike man. No moped either.'

'Any news on Fergus?' Chris asked.

There was a crackle and then, 'Negative. House empty.'

Clare's phone began to ring again. She fished it out of her pocket.

'Inspector?' It was Ralph Paterson, the night watchman. 'You asked me to let you know if I saw a Land Rover… Well, I'm pretty sure one went past here a few minutes ago. Heading for the Strathkinness junction.'

'Did you see the driver, Ralph? Or any visible damage to the vehicle?'

'Sorry, no. It's almost dark now. And I was up at the cabin. Just saw the lights and noticed it. Going pretty fast.'

'Okay thanks, Ralph. Much appreciated.' She hung up. 'Bastard's gone the other way.' She looked along the road.

'Could he have gone through Strathkinness then headed for the main road, back to St Andrews?'

'I doubt it. He'd risk being caught on the ANPR cameras at that end of town. No, he must be headed away from St Andrews.' Clare clicked the map icon on her phone and zoomed out to widen the area. 'He could be going anywhere. So many villages dotted around this part of Fife. Chris, get a message out to all stations in north-east Fife and tell them to get out on patrol. Give them descriptions of Fergus and the vehicle, plus what we know of the registration and tell them it's a murder hunt.'

Back at the station, there seemed little for Clare to do. Every available cop was out on patrol, looking for the Land Rover. Raymond from SOCO had arrived at the garage with a team and they were combing it for anything that might help identify the driver.

The adrenaline that had kept her running through the woods, weaving away from the driver had all but gone, and she sat at her desk, cradling the cup of coffee Chris had insisted she drink, poring over a map of the area.

The call came in just after midnight. Chris put down the phone and Clare knew by his face. Victim number four.

'Where?'

'Dairsie. It's a little village on the way to Cupar. Six or seven miles from here. A man called Professor Harris, according to a neighbour. Lived up a dead end. Same MO. Card with a number two written on it, placed on top of the body. On the plus side, one more then we'll have the full set.'

She didn't smile. 'I'll have to call the DCI. Can you get onto Raymond and see if he can get another SOCO team out? Pathologist too. What about Fergus Bain? Any sign of him?'

'Nope.'

'Call the press office. Name and photograph. Wanted in connection with a murder investigation. Bring him in. We'll fingerprint him and take DNA.'

The DCI arrived at five to one and asked for an update.

'We have reason to believe Fergus Bain, the accordion player from the wedding, is involved,' said Clare. 'He lives out on the Strathkinness road. We were watching his house, but it seems he's slipped out.'

'How the hell did that happen?' DCI Gibson demanded.

'Sorry, sir. He must have slipped out the back door. Meanwhile, I located the vehicle in a garage.'

'So, we've got the car at least.'

'Actually, no. I found the garage, just off the Strathkinness road and was round the back looking through a hole in the wood when I heard someone approaching. I'd seen enough of the number plate to know it was the murder vehicle. But I wanted to wait until whoever it was unlocked the garage so I could prove he or she had the Land Rover all along. And then I saw the gun.'

The DCI swore under his breath. 'What kind of gun, Inspector?'

'A shotgun. Remington, I think. Looked like an 870.'

The DCI stared. 'An 870? A pump-action shotgun?'

'It was hard to see but I think so.'

'Christ Almighty! A nutter on the loose with one of those.' He shook his head. 'I take it you stayed quiet until he'd gone?'

'Not exactly. My mobile…'

'You hadn't switched it to silent?'

Clare shook her head. 'No time.'

'And?'

'I ran. Through the woods behind the garage.'

'Did he chase you?'

'Didn't stop to look, sir.'

'Are you hurt?'

'No, sir, I'm fine.' She glanced at Chris, daring him to contradict her.

DCI Gibson took a few moments to process this and then he spoke. 'So, you lost the man *and* you lost the car, despite having both under observation?'

'To be fair, sir, I had only just located the car and I was there on my own. There was no prospect of making an arrest without assistance. I thought about it but then I saw the gun.'

'At the risk of stating the bleedin' obvious, Inspector, why the hell didn't you cover the road from Bain's house in *both* directions?'

Clare hesitated. He had a point. But hindsight was a wonderful thing. 'The cop observing the cottage from across the road would have seen him if he'd gone off on his moped. And we had the road between his cottage and St Andrews covered in case he made a move. All the attacks have been in the town...'

'Until tonight.'

'Until tonight,' Clare admitted. 'But we couldn't have anticipated him slipping out the back and going over the fields to reach the garage. And there was no way we could know the vehicle was further along the same road, in the other direction.'

'And you think this Fergus Bain is our man?'

'It's starting to look that way. He does have alibis for two of the attacks but it's too much of a coincidence, him slipping out of his house and the Land Rover being driven away. And, as a farm worker, he would have a shotgun.'

'Not a bloody Remington 870, though, surely?'

'Depends, sir. If he was doing a bit of game-keeping...'

'And now we have another body, is that right?' the DCI went on. He slapped the desk with his hand. 'Jesus Christ, Inspector, did it not occur to you to fingerprint Fergus Bain when you interviewed him?'

'We had no grounds, sir. He had a cast iron alibi for the first murder and for the attempted murder of Nat Dryden.'

'So, he has an accomplice. It's not exactly difficult.'

'With respect, sir, if I had picked him up earlier we might have lost him for lack of evidence. If I could have arrested him at the garage I would have. But he was armed. Even if he hadn't been, if I'd arrested him before he got into the garage, he could have argued he was nosing around, trying to find his stolen Land Rover. Any DNA or prints on the car would simply be put down to him being the owner. I wanted to catch him red-handed.'

'You cost a man his life tonight.'

'I don't agree, sir. We couldn't possibly have known who his next victim was. And we have every available man out looking for Fergus Bain and the car.'

'Bit late for that now, isn't it?' He moved his face closer to Clare's. 'Have you been drinking?'

Clare silently cursed the small splash of wine Tom had poured her. 'I had a red wine sauce with my evening meal.'

'Don't give me that, Inspector. I know boozy breath when I smell it. You're drunk! You're drunk and you're not fit to be running this investigation. I said from the start you weren't up to it and I was right. You're way out of your depth, Inspector Mackay.'

Clare closed her eyes. Her heart was thumping, her mouth suddenly dry. She was tired and worried, and rapidly running out of patience. She opened her eyes and looked the DCI square in the eye. 'Then breathalyse me, sir. Let's *see* how drunk I am. Jim – get a kit from the cupboard.'

The room was deathly silent now. Jim looked at Clare then at the DCI.

DCI Gibson shot Jim a warning glance. 'That won't be necessary, Sergeant. In my professional judgement Inspector Mackay is unfit for duty this evening.' He turned to Clare, his lips tight. 'Go home and sober up.'

She stood her ground. 'Sir, I had a very small—'

'I don't give a toss what you had, Inspector Mackay. Go home, sober up and report to me in the morning. And when you do, I suggest you ask your federation rep to accompany you.'

Chapter 19

Breakfast was a morose affair. Clare sat chasing muesli around the bowl, while Tom who had sensibly slept in the spare room chattered away in a vain attempt to lighten her mood.

Her gaze fell on the remains of the bottle of red from the night before. 'Pour that down the sink. I don't want to see it again.'

Tom raised an eyebrow. It hadn't been cheap. 'I'll take it with me and have the rest tonight. Too good to waste.'

'Whatever.'

'Would you like me to come with you this morning? Play the legal card?'

'Nope.'

'Clare…'

She glared at him, her eyes flashing. 'If you hadn't badgered me – yes, Tom – badgered me to have that glass of wine, I wouldn't be facing a disciplinary meeting this morning.' She had the bit between her teeth now. 'You know something? Maybe my judgement *was* impaired. Maybe he's right. I shouldn't have been drinking on duty. End of.'

'Clare, you had a couple of mouthfuls, no more.' Tom sat back in his chair. 'You didn't even finish the glass. You certainly wouldn't have been over the limit.'

'A drink's a drink. And I'm supposed to be hunting a murderer. I shouldn't have done it. I should have said no. But because I didn't, because I chose to drink the wine you bought, a man died. I had alcohol in my system when I was on duty and a man is dead.'

'But that wasn't your fault, surely? This – this mad driver you're hunting – can you honestly say if you hadn't had a mouthful of wine that you'd have stopped him before he killed again? Honestly?'

'We'll never know, Tom, will we?'

Tom took her hand in his. 'I'm sorry.'

She withdrew her hand. 'I'm a big girl, now. My decision, my mistake.'

He gave what he hoped was a sympathetic smile but she didn't return it.

'I'd better get to work. Get it over with. You heading back to Glasgow?'

He nodded. 'I don't have any clients this morning but I need to do a few things before a meeting this afternoon.'

'Thanks for dinner.'

'My pleasure. Oh, and I'll take those bags to the charity shop.'

'No need.'

'I'd like to. If it helps you, it's easy enough.'

'Okay.'

'Any particular shop?'

'The homeless one's closest. Market Street.'

'I'll find it. And, if you do decide to look at houses here and you'd like a second opinion…'

'Yeah, maybe.' She gave him a wan smile. 'Sorry. I'm being a cow. I just don't need a sanctimonious DCI on top of a triple murder investigation.'

Tom took her hand again and squeezed it. This time she didn't withdraw her hand but squeezed his back. She thought about hugging him. But she didn't.

—

DCI Gibson would be in full official mode, she knew that, but as Clare drove to the station, she believed she was ready for him. She had spent a fitful night, rising at four in the morning, and had made notes of her actions over the past few days. Other than the ill-advised glass of wine, she doubted the DCI had much of a case against her. But she'd find out soon enough.

She pulled into the car park and sat, thinking for a minute. After the activity of the night before, the car park was quiet. An idea had come into her head and she weighed it up. Then, she took out her mobile phone and dialled.

Elaine Carter was delighted to hear from her. 'Clare, I'm so glad you've decided to call. You know I'm always here for any issues at all, particularly when we consider what you have been through over the past year.'

She closed her eyes and let Elaine drone on. When she finally paused for breath, Clare seized her chance. 'I could do with your advice, actually.'

'It's what I'm here for, Clare.' Her tone was syrupy sweet. 'How can I help? I'm guessing the Lord Advocate's office has been in touch about the prosecution.'

That again! Would they never shut up about it? She bit back the irritation she felt. 'No, it's not that. I've put that to the back of my mind for now. It's a possible discipline issue, actually.'

'Oh. Perhaps you'd better tell me.'

Clare summarised the investigation then came to the events of the previous evening.

Elaine listened. 'You were entirely alone at the garage?'

'Yes.'

'Why didn't you have another officer with you?'

'I wanted my DS to remain at the base so he could apprise me of any developments. And I didn't know the garage was there. It's impossible to see it from the road.'

'So, you went, let's say, on a hunch?'

'I had a feeling the answer might lie along that road, yes.'

'And, had you not investigated, the garage, and indeed the car, may have remained undiscovered?'

'Someone else could have found it.'

'But they didn't, Clare. And you did. Perhaps you could go through your actions at the garage for me. In detail, please.'

Clare explained that she was keen to establish whether the car was actually in the garage without letting the driver know it had been discovered. 'There was a stout padlock, much newer than the garage. I didn't want to break in. If it was the murder vehicle − and I'm confident now that it was − I needed to link it to the driver. Otherwise there would be no chance of a conviction.'

'And what happened when the driver approached?'

'I concealed myself while he undid the padlock. And then, I realised he had a gun.'

'Did he see you?'

'Not at that point. I had no backup so I stayed quiet. And then,' Clare hesitated, recalling the moment when her phone rang out, 'my mobile phone started to ring.'

'Oh, Clare!'

'I know. So, I ran. I weaved through the trees and I kept running; and when I thought I was safe, I stopped and called my sergeant.'

The syrupy sweet tone had gone. 'Were you hurt, Clare?'

'No, not at all. Bit of a shock, I'll admit, but I wasn't hurt.'

'You should have seen a doctor.'

'Honestly, Elaine, I was absolutely fine. My sergeant drove me back to the station.'

'And was the driver apprehended?'

'No. The car had gone by the time we reached the garage. Unfortunately, we believe the driver claimed another victim late last night.'

'And the suspect?'

'We think he's a farm worker. Name of Fergus Bain. We had his cottage under observation and a motorcycle stationed up the road to intercept him if he left the cottage, but it seems he managed to slip out the back and make his way to the garage. I think he then drove off in the other direction.'

'Should you have had someone stationed in the other direction?'

Clare weighed this up. 'All the attacks up to last night had taken place in or around St Andrews so it made sense to monitor the road in that direction. And there was no way of knowing the car was concealed on that stretch of road.

'So, to summarise, you had the suspect under observation, a motorcyclist a short distance away ready to tail him, and no reason to suspect the car was concealed close by?'

'That's about it.'

'It sounds to me, Clare, as if you acted quite properly and that your actions alone have resulted in the murder vehicle being discovered, albeit not apprehended. The only possible criticism I can see is that you went out on investigations, alone, thus placing yourself in real danger. Inadvisable but hardly a discipline issue.'

This was going well. She took a deep breath. 'There's something else, Elaine.'

'Yes?'

'I went home for a break, early evening. Most of the team did. We all needed to eat, recharge our batteries.'

'You had been on duty since...'

'Eight in the morning.'

'So, ten hours without a break?'

'Yes, I suppose so. Anyway, a friend cooked me a meal and poured me a small glass of wine, some of which I drank.'

'I see. How much would you say you drank?'

'I had two mouthfuls.'

'You are aware—'

'Yes, Elaine. I know. Serious misconduct. I regret it absolutely and it was strictly a one-off.'

'And I'm guessing you're phoning me because this has come to the attention of your DCI?'

'I'm afraid so. He gave me a round of the guns and sent me home. I'm facing a disciplinary meeting this morning.'

'Did he take steps to assess how much alcohol was in your system?'

'I asked to take a breathalyser test but he denied the request.'

'So he has no evidence, other than what he believes he smelled?'

'I did start to say I'd only had some of a small glass but he cut me off.'

'And your DCI is…?'

'DCI Gibson.'

'DCI Alastair Gibson?'

'Yes, that's him. You know him?'

'We have met, yes.' There was a short silence, then Elaine spoke again. 'Clare, I have to ask, are you a regular drinker?'

'On days off, I might have a glass of wine or a beer. But if you're asking if I'm drinking in order to cope with work and a possible private prosecution, then the answer is no.'

'And, being truthful, is this a one-off or have you drunk on duty before?'

'It's absolutely a one-off. I was tired last night, a bit worried about the investigation, and I was persuaded by a friend to have a couple of mouthfuls of wine with my meal.'

'Mm. Well, Clare, you know I can't condone taking alcohol on duty but, given that your actions in relation to the ongoing investigation have been largely positive, I think your error of judgement should be overlooked. I'll come up to see you and your DCI this morning. I'm in Kirkcaldy now, as it happens, so I'll be with you in an hour or so. In the meantime, I'll telephone your DCI and instruct him not to speak to you about this matter and that, in my view, the best thing for your personal welfare and for the investigation is that you carry on with your duties. Providing, of course, that there is no further drinking on duty.'

'And he'll listen to you?'

She could almost hear Elaine preening. 'In matters of officer welfare, Clare, I outrank him every time. He has no choice but to follow my advice. Now, I'll want to speak to you and your colleagues so don't stray too far, please.'

Clare ended the call and, for once in her life, thanked God and all his angels for Elaine Carter who had seemed unexpectedly keen to back Clare up. She sat for a while longer in the car, mulling this over, then punched in another number.

'Clare! Great to hear from you. How's tricks?'

'Good thanks, Jackie. Must catch up next time I'm back in Glasgow.'

'I'll hold you to it.'

'Jackie, your ear's closer to the ground than anyone I know…'

'You after gossip?'

'Information, really. I've just spoken to Elaine Carter.'

There was a groan from Jackie. 'God. What have you done?'

'Long story. I'll tell you when I see you. But I'm having a bit of an issue with my DCI – partly my fault – and she seems surprisingly keen to weigh in on my side.'

'That doesn't sound like her. Who's the DCI?'

'Al Gibson.'

'Ahh. Well now, there's a story.'

'Yeah?'

'Oh yes. You know Elaine has a son in the force?'

'DC down in Edinburgh, right?'

'That's him. Stuart. Nice lad and doing well. Should make DS soon. Anyway, when he first started his boss was Al Gibson. Al was a DI at that time. And, for some reason, he took against Stuart. The lad could do nothing right. Al was always careful not to bawl him out in front of anyone who mattered but he chipped away at his self-confidence.'

'Surely, knowing who his mother was…'

'Stuart wouldn't take it to his mum. Precisely because she was his mum. But one of the others did. I don't know if they ever found out who but Elaine put a spy in the camp and within a couple of weeks had enough to call Al in for a friendly chat.'

'Sheesh. Bet he loved that.'

'He did not! Poor Stuart thought it was the end of his career. But Al was forced to apologise to him in front of Elaine and the whole shift. That was the end of it. A few weeks after that Al asked to be transferred to another team. I don't think their paths have crossed since.'

'Bloody brilliant! Wish I'd been there.'

'Oh, me too. Apparently, his face was a study. Anyway, if Elaine's backing you against him, I'm not at all surprised. Make the most of it.'

'I will. Listen, Jackie, I'd better go and show my face. Thanks again. Catch up soon, yeah?'

'Sounds good.'

Clare waited in the car for a few more minutes to give Elaine time to phone the DCI, then she locked the car and went into the station. The noise of general chatter gradually subsided as the assembled cops eyed her warily.

'Morning, boss,' Chris said and she threw him a grateful look.

DCI Gibson emerged from Clare's office, phone in hand. He stopped when he saw her. 'So, you've called in the cavalry, Inspector?'

Clare smiled sweetly and, looking round the room, announced, 'Briefing in five minutes.'

A few pairs of eyes strayed to the DCI. He seemed about to speak then changed his mind and went back into Clare's office, slamming the door behind him.

They assembled in the incident room, a little puzzled at Clare's still being in charge but no one dared ask what was going on.

'For the avoidance of doubt,' Clare began, 'I remain in charge of this investigation until further notice. I expect a specialist vice team to appear tomorrow morning to deal with the activities in those photos and we'll do a handover to them as soon as possible. We continue with the murder investigation. You may also be interviewed by Elaine Carter, the force welfare officer, who is coming up this morning. I won't prejudge what she might say other than to urge you to be entirely truthful in responding to her questions.' She smiled at them. 'Okay?'

A few of the cops smiled and Clare pressed on.

'Right then, we have a new murder to deal with, the possibility of another one very soon, and a suspect who has disappeared. So, let's recap what we know. Any sightings of Fergus Bain yet?'

Heads shook.

'I've put a couple of uniforms on the house round the clock,' said Jim.

Clare nodded. 'We may have to do a full search of the house but for now their priority should be keeping a low profile and watching out for him in case he comes back. Remember he's armed now and he knows we're after him. He gave our man the slip last night. So, they'll need to keep their wits about them.'

Clare continued. 'Now, the DCI has issued the usual statement about Fergus Bain – he's wanted in connection with our enquiries, that sort of thing. So if we get any response, I want to know about it. Nothing so far, I take it?'

'Sorry, Clare,' Jim said. 'Nothing.'

'The car, then. We know it's a Land Rover Defender, with the traditional green paint. Must be quite bashed around by now – it's run over three victims and partly run over a fourth, colliding hard with a lamp post so there will be a dent in the front. Number plate is probably false, but does include the letters SJ on the top row and seven on the bottom. Who's watching the garage, Jim?'

'Traffic man with a motorbike. He's pulled off the road, out of sight but he can see the garage.'

'Right. When we're done here I want every available officer out hunting Mr Bain and his Land Rover. Okay – last night's victim, what do we know?'

Chris raised his hand. 'Seventy-one-year-old professor, retired, lived alone. Neighbours say he was a quiet man, kept himself to himself, liked his books, that sort of thing.'

'Cause of death?'

'The usual. Multiple trauma consistent with a motor vehicle accident.'

'No witnesses?'

'Woman next door heard the car and went to the window but didn't see anything. Her husband went out to check and found the professor.'

'Dead? Or did he live long enough to tell them anything?'

'Killed outright, unfortunately.'

'Next of kin?'

'Nothing so far.'

'Okay, let's have two of you suited up to go through his house. Look particularly for mobile phones, computers, tablets as well as any personal information that might help us find family members. We'll need someone to ID the body. Neighbours, probably.'

Connor raised a hand. 'Steve and I can do that, boss.'

'Ideally, we want two neighbours to ID him, since they aren't family. And can you take the photos of the unknown fourth man with you, please? The grey-haired one. Pound to a penny it's him. Show them to the neighbours – discreetly, mind. Pathologist too. Maybe you could take photos over to the Path lab, Phil?'

'On it, boss,' Phil said.

She looked around. 'We're up against it here, guys. I think we all know by now that there could be a fifth murder very soon. The professor was found with one of those cards bearing the number two. The killer is counting down to his final victim. We have to get there first.'

'What about Fergus Bain's employers?' asked Chris.

'Good point. I think we'll go over and speak to them. They might know where he's hiding out. Right. That's all. Keep your radios handy. You may need to come back to speak to Elaine. And I want you all to report in every hour. We must make progress before darkness.'

Connor, Steve and Phil left, photos in hand and Chris set about co-ordinating the search for Fergus and his vehicle. Jim was manning the desk and catching up on paperwork. It was quiet in the station and Clare sat down to sift through the evidence they had so far. She couldn't afford any more mistakes. She was lost in thought when the door opened and Elaine walked in.

'Clare.' She came towards her, smiling broadly. 'I'm very pleased to see you.' She unwound a Hermes scarf from her neck and shrugged off her coat. 'Now, where might I find DCI Gibson?'

Clare indicated the door to her office and moved towards it, but Elaine waved her back.

'I'll call you in when I'm ready.' She swept into Clare's office without knocking, closing the door behind her.

Ten minutes later the door opened and Elaine motioned to Clare to join them.

In the office, DCI Gibson's expression was mulish.

'Now, Clare,' Elaine began, 'DCI Gibson and I have discussed what happened yesterday and he has agreed there is no need to interview your colleagues. He accepts your actions were out of character and, providing you give your word there will be no further drinking on duty, he is prepared to let the matter rest.'

Clare glanced at the DCI and he nodded briefly.

'In return, I have said that you and I will meet again for a chat, either within two weeks or once the current investigation is concluded, whichever is sooner. We do, after all, owe a duty of care to you.'

Clare had to hand it to Elaine. Like the Mounties, she always got her man. On balance, having to meet with Elaine to discuss her welfare, was a small price to pay for remaining in charge of the investigation and avoiding a formal disciplinary. She reckoned she'd now made an enemy for life of DCI Gibson but, again, it was probably worth it.

'Thank you, Elaine and… thank you, sir.'

The DCI gave Clare a nod and she escaped, having promised to keep in touch with Elaine. She returned to scrutinising the evidence when Chris appeared.

Clare raised an eyebrow. 'Search all sorted?'

'Yeah. And I've just heard from Connor. He and Steve found the professor's correspondence, neatly filed, including letters to his solicitor. I'm on my way round to see the solicitor now. Office is on South Street.'

'Anything else of note at the cottage?'

'Steve has a computer in the boot of his car. And the professor's mobile phone. I'll try to get someone to rush them down to Tech Support this afternoon.'

'That's priority, Chris. See if Phil can do it when he's back from the Path lab.'

Clare's phone rang. It was Gillian, one of the uniformed officers stationed at Fergus's cottage.

'Boss, there's a secure cabinet upstairs at the cottage. It's unlocked and empty. Looks like a gun cabinet.'

'Okay, thanks Gillian. I was pretty sure he was armed but it's good to know.'

Clare hung up then turned to her computer screen to look up a phone number which she then punched into her phone. With her hand over the phone, she said, 'Hold on for a minute, Chris. I need to check something.'

When the call was answered she said, 'Can you check for a shotgun holder, please? It's DI Mackay at St Andrews.'

Chris raised an eyebrow.

'Name please?' the voice in Clare's ear said.

'Fergus Bain. Address is between St Andrews and Strathkinness. He's a worker on – hold on a sec...'

She put her hand over her phone again. 'Chris, what's the name of the farm Fergus works at?'

'Woodknowe Farm.'

'Woodknowe Farm,' Clare repeated into the phone.

'Hold on please.'

While she waited Clare told Chris about the empty gun cabinet. 'It more or less confirms my suspicions that it was Fergus at that garage last night.'

Chris looked doubtful. 'I get that, Clare, but what about the attacks on Andy Robb and Nat Dryden? Fergus couldn't have done them.'

'He must have an accomplice.'

The voice in her ear interrupted their conversation.

'Yes, I'm still here,' Clare said. 'Any luck?'

'Fergus Bain,' the voice began, 'Number One, Wood-knowe Cottages, Woodknowe Farm, St Andrews.'

'That's him,' Clare said. 'Is his licence current?'

There was a pause and then the voice spoke again. 'Expires at the end of next year.'

'And the gun?'

'Shotgun. Remington 870.'

Despite the seriousness of her situation, Clare allowed herself a smile. She had been right about the gun. 'Can you email me over a photo of Mr Bain please? And a copy of the licence?'

'Of course, Inspector. Is it urgent or can you wait?'

'Urgent, I'm afraid. He's a murder suspect.'

'In that case, I'll email it to you now. Give me ten minutes.'

Clare hung up the call. 'Change of plan, Chris. Get Phil to call in on the solicitor for you, then ask him to head down to Tech Support after that. You and I are going to Woodknowe Farm.'

She walked over to the desk where Jim's head was still bent over a pile of papers.

'Jim, can you alert all the cops out hunting Fergus that he is carrying a Remington 870 shotgun and should be treated as potentially dangerous? Update the DCI and make sure the message goes out to other stations too. At this stage, I'd say Fergus has nothing to lose.'

Chapter 20

Clare and Chris were met at the door of Woodknowe farmhouse by a large man dressed in a checked shirt, cargo trousers and stout boots. Clare introduced herself and Chris. The man held out a calloused hand.

'Sam Walker.'

They shook hands then followed him into the farmhouse kitchen. A kettle sat to the side of a range cooker. 'Cup of something?'

'No thanks,' Clare said. 'We won't keep you long.'

'Take a pew then.' Sam indicated a bench seat in front of a dressed-pine table. A cream metal jug with some cut lilacs stood in the centre of the table, their scent filing the room. To the side was a laptop, its cable trailing across the floor to a wall socket. Next to it stood a large wicker trug full of long stalks of rhubarb. Sam moved the laptop and the flowers to the side and put the trug down on the floor, sweeping the table beneath it with his hand. Clare's mouth began to water as she recalled her mother's rhubarb crumble.

They stepped over the bench and sat. 'We're hoping you might be able to give us a bit of background on Fergus Bain, Mr Walker. I understand he does some work for you?'

'Call me Sam, Inspector. He's not in trouble, is he, Fergus? He didn't turn up this morning. It's not like him. Matter of fact, he was going to look at this laptop for me. It's been playing up and I need to update the farm accounts. I hope there's nothing wrong.'

Clare didn't reply to this directly but said, 'We're keen to get in touch with him. Would you know if he has any friends or family he might be staying with?'

'Not really. He's always been a bit of a loner, Fergus. Brought up in a home, you know.'

'A care home?'

'Aye.'

'Don't suppose you know which one?'

'Somewhere down near Edinburgh I think. Not sure.'

'No matter. Are his parents still alive? Do you know why he was in the home?'

'He never said. There's an aunty, though. Well, I *say* aunty... more like one of those women you call aunty.'

'So not a relative?'

'I'm not sure, to be honest. Fergus used to say he was going to visit his aunty. Once I asked him was it on his mother or his father's side. He just said it wasn't like that. She wasn't a real aunty. Friend of his gran, I think.'

'So as far as you know, he doesn't have any real family? Just this woman he calls aunty?'

'Think so.'

'Would you know where she lives?'

'No, but it's local. One day he said he was nipping round to hers to have a look at her washing machine. Leaking, he said. He went in his lunch break so I know it wasn't far.'

'I don't suppose you remember which direction he went in? St Andrews or Strathkinness?'

'Sorry, no.'

'No problem. What about girlfriends? Or has he been married?'

'Not that I know of. I've not seen him with girls. He's out a lot, with the ceilidh band, you know. That tends to get in the way of a social life. Out most Saturday nights.'

'Or boyfriends?'

Sam spread his hands. 'I really have no idea. All I can say is I've never seen him with anyone of his own age, boy or girl.'

'What about his mobile? Do you have his number?'

'Aye, hold on…' He reeled off a number which Chris noted down.

'Thanks, Sam,' Clare said. 'And you will let us know immediately if Fergus gets in touch? No need to let him know you've called us, though.'

Sam looked worried. 'He's a good worker. I really do hope he's not in any bother…'

Clare smiled. 'Let's hope not.'

They walked back to the car and, when Clare was sure she wouldn't be overheard by Sam, she spoke. 'What do you think?'

Chris shook his head. 'I don't think he's hiding anything.'

'Me neither. Interesting about the laptop, though.'

'Yeah, I noticed that. Our Fergus is good with computers.'

'I'm starting to regret not fingerprinting him when we had him,' Clare said. 'Come on. Let's call into the cottage. Check on the cops.'

It was a short drive to Fergus Bain's cottage. Clare rapped on the door and announced herself. One of the cops came to the door.

'Turned up anything?' she asked.

'This.' The officer held up an evidence bag containing a laptop. 'And this.' He held up another bag which, to Clare's dismay, held a mobile phone.

Clare took out her own phone and punched in the number Sam Walker had given her. Seconds later the phone in the bag began to vibrate and ring.

'Dammit. Either he's out without a phone or he has another one. I bet it's a pay-as-you-go. Bang goes our chance of tracking him through his mobile.'

'We can still look at his call and text records,' Chris pointed out. 'It's a start.'

'Suppose so. Chris, can you get Phil on the phone, if he's not already left? Tell him there's something else for Tech Support. No sense in making two journeys. Tell him to ask for Diane, mention my name and say we need the whole lot turned round this afternoon, if possible.'

–

DCI Gibson phoned in a request for an Armed Response Unit and it arrived just after one thirty. As the ARU team were being briefed by Chris, the DCI took Clare into his office.

'I need to know, Inspector, if you're comfortable working with armed officers, given the incident with that lad Ritchie.'

Clare had been thinking the same thing. But she knew she couldn't go through the rest of her career avoiding firearms incidents; no way was she going to give the DCI an excuse to keep her in the office. And it wouldn't be her finger on the trigger, if it came to it. She would do this and she would get through it.

She looked him straight in the eye. 'Absolutely, sir.'

He raised an eyebrow but said no more on the subject. 'Right then, ask the ARU commander to join us.'

Inspector Drew Walsh entered the room and sat in the chair Clare offered. 'Good to see you again, Clare. You're looking well. How do you like it here?'

'It's a lovely place, Drew. It doesn't have the buzz you get in Glasgow but you can have enough buzz.'

'I'd say a serial killer armed with a shotgun's enough of a buzz for most folk.'

She smiled. 'Good point.'

'So, to business. If you could bring me up to speed?'

Clare ran through the events of the past week, from Andy Robb's murder up to the discovery that Fergus's shotgun cabinet was empty.

'And you've no idea where he is?'

'Unfortunately not,' Clare said. 'I've just spoken to his employer but he wasn't able to help.'

'I'm not keen to keep my officers hanging about on stand-by if he's gone into hiding.'

'We can be pretty sure that he has one more target in his sights. The men he's been picking off appear in photos showing paedophile activity, and we believe he has one more to go.'

'Do you have photos of his next target?'

'No. We think he was the one taking the photos.'

'EXIF data?'

'Nope. Either the location has been removed or the camera didn't have GPS. But we do know they were all taken on Thursday nights. From what we can gather, these men met and carried out their activities on Thursdays.'

'So, tonight,' Drew said.

'That's right. But as we believe all four men in the photos have now been killed, I'm not sure if anything will happen tonight. If I were the last man standing, I'd be keeping my head down.'

'How does our man – what's his name?'

'Fergus Bain. He's a farm worker and accordion player. Bit of a loner. Lives in a cottage out on the road to Strathkinness.'

'How does he know where to find them? Who they are?'

'We believe he hacked into a website on the dark web where these activities were arranged. We've recovered information from a couple of the victims' laptops. There's a search of Mr Bain's house going on now. So far, we've recovered a mobile and a laptop. Both should be down at Tech Support in the next hour or so.'

Drew Walsh rose. 'Right, then. We'll stick around here. I can put a few of my men out and about just now, keep an eye out, that sort of thing.'

Clare frowned. 'I'm not sure I want armed officers on the streets of a small town like St Andrews. It might cause unnecessary panic. I don't believe he's a threat to the general public.'

Drew turned to DCI Gibson. 'It's your call, then.'

The DCI looked at Drew. 'It's not ideal, either way.' He turned to Clare again. 'Am I right in thinking the doctors plan to try and wake Mr Dryden today?'

'I think so, depending on how he is,' Clare said.

'And we might get the chance to interview him?'

'Possibly, if we go in softly.'

'Right. Hold off your men in the meantime, Drew. Let's wait and see if the Inspector, here, can talk to Mr Dryden.'

Drew nodded. 'Fair enough. Could we meet again, say, at four o'clock? Five?'

Clare checked her watch. 'Let's say five. The hospital's forty minutes' drive away and we don't want to be rushed if they do allow us to speak to him.'

Clare sent Chris out in a car to help with the search for Fergus and his Land Rover. When he had gone she went into the incident room, strangely quiet with almost everyone out searching. She angled the window blinds to allow some natural light in and sat down at a desk, firing up the computer. She navigated her way to the file of photographs taken from Andy Robb and Nat Dryden's laptops and began swiping through them, moving to the folder she had called UK1 for the unknown man. From what she had seen last night, the hair was the same as Professor Harris's, and it seemed likely that he was the unidentified man from the photos. Clare found it hard to feel any sympathy for any of the four men, but she had to set that aside. There was a job to do and she would far rather the fifth man stayed alive long enough for them to prosecute him for his part in the paedophile ring.

She clicked aimlessly through the photos again. She knew the images off by heart now; they were hard to forget. But was there anything else they could tell her? She began looking at the background detail. The furnishings, the lights, the walls – some of the walls were panelled in ornately carved wood, quite distinct in places. There were garlands of leaves and flowers, more detailed than Clare could ever recall seeing anywhere. Could that help them identify the location of this so-called Playroom?

She began searching online for experts in historical wood panelling. The results were worldwide so she narrowed the search to Scotland and trawled through the pages which appeared.

The same name kept coming up, a man called Geoffrey Dark. Might he be able to help? Clare searched for his contact details and found his website. He was based near Perth, but it looked as if he was a guest lecturer in Fine Arts at various universities in Scotland, including Dundee, just eleven miles away.

She picked up the phone to call the university.

Geoffrey Dark was giving a lecture in Dundee that afternoon but he said that if Clare could get over before one thirty he would be happy to look at the photos. She checked her watch. It was midday.

She picked up the folder of photos and selected half a dozen with the youngsters cropped out.

'Back in an hour or two,' she called to Jim and emerged into the sunshine. It was warm now, a perfect spring day and she drove past verges planted with tulips and narcissi, incongruous with the grim events of the past few days. And the murders, of course, were only half the story. Who were the youngsters in the photos? How had they come to be there? And where were they now? Were they anticipating another Thursday night, somewhere in north-east Fife? Another night of being abused by men? But of course there was only one left now. One of the five. 'Where are you, number one?' she muttered to herself. 'Where?'

She drove on, joining the Tay Road Bridge which led into the centre of Dundee. The city, set on the slopes of an ancient volcano, loomed up as she neared the end of the bridge and took the left slip-road alongside the V&A Gallery and out towards the west end of the city, and the university.

Geoffrey Dark occupied a temporary office in the old Duncan of Jordanstone Art College, now part of the university. Clare gave her name at reception and was directed to his office on the second floor. She struggled to hide her surprise when he opened the door. Instead of the crusty academic she had expected, she was faced with a tall, lean man in his late thirties, casually dressed in black jeans and a blue Oxford shirt. She was momentarily disarmed and suddenly quite nervous.

He smiled. A warm smile that lit up his face. He extended his hand. 'Inspector Mackay?'

Clare smiled back. It was impossible not to. She cleared her throat. 'Call me Clare.'

'Clare, then,' he said, adding 'and you must call me Geoffrey.' He stood back to admit her to his office and she moved past him into the room. Looking round, she thought it lacked the personal touch. There was a small pile of books on the desk beside a computer. A china mug stood on a coaster and next to it a Moleskine note-book with two very sharp pencils. A rather worn-looking brown leather briefcase stood to the side of his desk. Geoffrey Dark indicated a chair and Clare sat, her eye immediately caught by a painting on the wall opposite.

'Morocco,' Geoffrey said, following her eye. 'He was Head of School here, you know.' He looked at it for a few moments. 'Wonderful use of colour, don't you think?'

Clare looked at it. 'I'm afraid I know nothing about art, Mr Dark – sorry Geoffrey.'

He laughed. 'But I'm sure you know what you like, and what you dislike. That's a good place to start. The reasons for what you feel can be taught. But your innate taste is part of you. Never apologise for that.'

Clare hadn't ever had a conversation like this. She recalled the artwork that had adorned the walls of her flat in Glasgow and blushed at the thought of them. Some were from IKEA, for God's sake. She looked again at the painting and thought she would like to know more about it.

'There's an exhibition on next month. In Edinburgh,' he said. 'If you wanted to see more...'

'Oh, I'm not sure,' Clare said, quickly. She immediately regretted it. She must remember now that she was no longer part of a couple. And there was something about this man, the warmth in his eyes, his easy manner. She tried to rescue the situation. 'Maybe, when work's a bit calmer.'

He laughed. 'I wasn't offering – but I would be happy to take you; if you'd like to go, that is. I'll give you my card.' He reached into the hip pocket of his jeans and withdrew a wallet. 'I must say, Inspector,' he said, fishing out a small business card and handing it to her, 'I am intrigued. I don't think I've met a real detective before.'

Clare was relieved at the change of topic. 'I don't think I've met a real art expert before,' she countered with a smile, taking the card and tucking it into her pocket. 'It's an unusual job, if you don't mind my saying so.'

'I was a cabinetmaker by trade, originally, then I took a degree in fine art and ended up specialising in sculpture which, of course, includes intricate woodwork,' he explained.

Clare thought that, in different circumstances, she would very much like to hear him lecture, and perhaps more. But time was against her so she withdrew the photographs from the document wallet and spread them out on the table in front of him.

He scanned each photo closely. Then he rose and indicated for her to follow him. He led Clare down a corridor and into a room where a large magnifying panel sat on a desk. He flicked a switch and the panel lit up. He took a pair of tortoiseshell spectacles from his shirt pocket and perched them on his nose, bending down to peer at the photos.

'It's old,' he said.

'How old?'

'Seventeenth or eighteenth century, I'd say. But I'll have to check to be sure.'

He continued looking at the images then moved closer to examine the corner of one. 'Aha!'

'What?'

He lifted a pencil from a nearby table and pointed. 'See this?'

Clare looked at part of an ornate wood panel. 'What am I looking at?'

'That little thing on the corner. It's a peapod carved into the wood. You see how the pod is open and the peas are inside?'

Clare moved closer. 'Oh yes. How clever. Is it unusual?'

'Oh yes. It's the trademark of a sculptor called Grinling Gibbons. He worked mainly in England. Windsor Castle, Hampton Court Palace. Now, it was his habit to include a carving of a peapod somewhere in his work. It was said that if the peapod was open, he'd been paid for the work and if it was closed he hadn't. It's quite clear here. There's an open peapod. This is almost certainly Gibbons' work.'

'Does that make it possible to identify the building? Or at least narrow it down?'

'It helps, yes. He died in 1721 so the building will pre-date that. There won't be many around here of that age. But I'll have to do a bit of research to find them.'

'Will it take long? I'm trying to catch a murderer who, I am sure, will strike again very soon, possibly tonight.'

He looked at his watch. 'I should be finished up here by four. I can do some reading then. Gibbons took only a few commissions in Scotland, so it should be possible to narrow it down to a small number of buildings. It would certainly be an old building and the owners at the time would have been wealthy. Gibbons' work was highly regarded, for obvious reasons.'

'Is there any chance of coming back to me by early evening?'

He removed his spectacles and smiled at her again. 'I'll do what I can.'

Having ascertained that he would lock the photos away securely, Clare took her leave of Geoffrey Dark, humming to herself as she left.

Outside she checked the map on her phone and saw she was only a couple of miles from Ninewells Hospital. She wondered if there was any sign of Nat Dryden waking up and called Sara who was stationed at the hospital, keeping an eye on him.

'His sedation's been reduced,' Sara told her. 'They're trying to take him off the ventilator now.'

'Is he responding?'

'Coming and going, in and out of consciousness.'

Clare sighed. 'No chance of interviewing him then?'

'It doesn't look like it.'

'Okay, thanks, Sara. You need someone to relieve you?'

'It's fine, boss. The staff have been really kind, making me tea and toast and I have some food in my bag. Teresa will be along to take over in a couple of hours. Soon as he's lucid one of us will be on the phone.'

Chapter 21

Half an hour later, Clare drew into the station car park. She was prepared for the press pack this time, pushing her way through them and into the station. Chris had also returned and was on the phone.

'Clare's just back, Diane. I'll fill her in and she'll call you if need be,' he was saying.

Clare waited until he had finished. 'So?'

'Not much, really. Diane's still looking at Fergus's laptop but she has managed to get into his mobile. Only one number on it, though, and it's untraceable. Probably a pay-as-you-go. He must have another mobile.'

'Hm. Just the one number.' Clare said. 'Have you tried calling it?'

'No. I wasn't sure how you wanted to play it.'

Clare took out her phone and dialled the number and put the call on loudspeaker so Chris could hear. It went straight to voicemail. Clare left a message saying she had found this phone and wondered if the person she was calling could help her return it to its owner. Then she ended the call.

'Not surprising, really,' she said. 'It looks as if Fergus has an accomplice.'

'The person with the missing fingertip?'

'Yes, I think so. Let's recap the murders. Come through to the board.'

Chris followed Clare into the incident room where she indicated the photo of the first victim, Andy Robb. 'Fergus has an alibi for Andy Robb's murder. But the tyre tracks do indicate a Land Rover.'

'And we have one set of prints on the number five card. The prints with the missing finger.'

'Don't forget the footprint on his shirt. SOCO thought it was a woman's shoe.'

Chris frowned. 'And while the accomplice is running Andy Robb down, Fergus is safely in the hotel with a hundred wedding guests for an alibi.'

'Exactly. Now, let's assume for the moment that he has a female accomplice.'

'I'm not sure where that gets us, though,' Chris said.

'Nor me, but let's go with it. Then we have Bruce Gilmartin. Now Fergus *could* have committed that murder, and that would make sense because the number four card showed a different set of prints.'

'Fergus's?'

'Could be.'

'Want his laptop sent to SOCO? Bound to be prints on that.'

Clare considered. 'On balance, I'd rather see what Diane can find, first. I'm pretty sure he is involved. Prints can be done once we have him in custody.'

'Yeah, fair point. So, we have two killers and they're taking it in turns?'

'I think so. And I'm betting whoever isn't driving the Land Rover makes damn sure they have an alibi for the time of the murder.'

'Right then. We have the female — if it is a female — doing the first murder and Fergus the second. What about Nat Dryden?'

'Fergus has an alibi for that, so we're back to the female. And last night, of course, Fergus went AWOL.'

'By that reckoning, it's the female's turn for the next one,' Chris suggested.

'I'm not so sure. Things have gone a bit wrong for them, with Nat surviving the accident. Fergus went out the back, remember, so he must have known his house was being watched. I don't know how much he saw at the garage last night but he might have recognised me. If he did, he'll know we're on to him. Things are starting to go wrong and that's when mistakes are made. Also, we have no idea who this female accomplice might be.'

'What about the ceilidh band? They might know.'

'Good thinking. I have the number of the band leader. Hamish. If I dig it out, would you mind giving him a call? See what he knows?'

'Yep, no problem.'

Left alone in the incident room, Clare took out her own mobile phone to check for messages. Her sister had sent a video of baby James and she was smiling over this when the door opened and Drew Walsh came in.

'Hi, Clare. Taking five?'

'Yes, just a wee lull in proceedings. I'm waiting for a call back that might help place the building where the photos were taken. Sorry to keep your guys hanging around.'

He smiled. 'It's fine. Nice to have a bit of a breather.' He hesitated, as though he was going to speak.

Clare fixed him with her eye. 'Something on your mind, Drew?'

'Aye.' He paced up and down then took a seat next to Clare. 'Obviously, I've heard, you know, about the Ritchie family wanting a private prosecution.'

'Yes, so?'

'Well, hopefully it won't come to anything. And if it does, then I just wanted you to know that I'll be in that witness box, backing you to the hilt.'

She looked at him. 'Why do I feel a *but* hanging in the air?'

'Thing is, there's one of the squad who was there that day... The Ritchies are saying they're going to call her as a witness for the prosecution. I just thought you should know.' He struggled to meet Clare's eye.

She was silent for a moment. 'For the prosecution? Who? Who is it?'

'It's Pam.'

'Pam Cassidy?'

'Yes.'

'But Pam and I started together. We were at police college at the same time. We've been pals for years. Why would she testify against me?'

He spread his hands. 'It makes no sense to me. Something about you and her being torch bearers for armed female officers, and you shooting that lad has set the cause back years. I think she wants to show that females can be trusted with guns.'

'She's not here? Not in your team today?'

He hesitated. 'Sorry, Clare. I'd no choice. I've three off sick and two abroad on holiday. But I'll keep her out of your way. She's in the van just now.'

Clare's knuckles were white. She tried to remember her counselling sessions and relaxed her hands, taking a breath or two before she spoke. 'So, a colleague – an officer I worked closely with, someone I thought of as a friend – she's saying now that I can't be trusted with a gun.'

'I think that's what she means, yes.'

'And what about you? Were you relieved when I resigned from armed duties?'

'Absolutely not. Had that lad Ritchie's gun been real he could have killed us all. And there was no way of knowing. I'd have done the same as you.'

She looked at him. 'Would you, though, Drew? Would you really?'

He couldn't meet her eye. 'Clare, you have to know I'm one hundred per cent behind you.'

'That's not what I asked.' She scraped back her chair noisily and walked from the room.

Chris was bent over his desk as Clare approached. She felt her face burning. She stopped at the water cooler and poured herself a cup of cold water which she gulped down.

Chris looked up. 'Boss, are you all right?'

'Absolutely fine. Just finding out who my real friends are.' She took a couple of deep breaths and went on. 'Any luck with that ceilidh band leader?'

'Well, yes and no. I managed to get hold of him but he didn't have much to offer. He's never known Fergus to have a girlfriend or any other kind of friend for that matter. Says he's more likely to spend his nights playing computer games. To be honest, he seemed more bothered because he can't get a hold of him and they have a gig on Saturday night. He muttered something about finding another accordion player, permanently.'

Clare's phone rang and she snatched it up.

It was Diane Wallace. 'Hi, Clare. Not good news, I'm afraid. Fergus Bain's laptop – the hard disc is encrypted.'

'Oh. Does that mean it'll take longer to get into it?'

'Till the end of time, I'm afraid. Unless someone builds a quantum computer in the meantime.'

'So, we can't get anything off it?'

'Afraid not.'

Clare swore under her breath. 'No matter, Diane. We'll get him somehow. Thanks for trying.' She hung up. 'No go with Fergus Bain's laptop. Diane can't get into it.'

'Not surprising, really,' Chris said. 'If he's managed to find these men on the dark web then he clearly knows his way round a computer.'

'Suppose.' Clare fell silent. She was running out of options. At this rate, the killer would claim victim number five and then disappear from trace. Her phone began to ring again.

'Clare? It's Geoffrey Dark. I managed to wrap my lecture up early, as you said it was urgent.'

'I appreciate that, Geoffrey. Any luck identifying the building in the photos?'

'I've managed to narrow it down. There are three buildings within a forty-mile radius of St Andrews. One south, towards the East Neuk, one to the west, and the other to the north. There are others in Edinburgh of course, but I had the impression that would be too far for your purposes.'

'I think so,' Clare said, motioning to Chris to pass her a pen. 'But I may come back to you on that. If you could just give me the details…' She began scribbling down the names of the three properties on her notepad.

'And…'

'Yes?'

'That Morocco exhibition. If you do fancy it – well, I'd love to take you.'

Clare took a breath. 'I'd like that very much.'

'Good,' he said, easily. 'It's a date. And now, I'll leave you to your enquiries. It's been a real pleasure, Clare. Hope to hear from you soon.'

She clicked to end the call, suppressing a smile. Chris raised an eyebrow.

'Geoffrey, is it?'

'Shut up, you. Get hold of Drew. We need to see the DCI now.'

The four of them squeezed into Clare's office and she began to explain. 'The photos of the so-called Playroom show intricately carved wood panelling. I've spoken to an expert in sculpture who has identified the carving as the work of a late seventeenth-century woodcarver called Grinling Gibbons.'

'How sure is he?' asked DCI Gibson.

'Very. Apparently, Gibbons always carved a little peapod somewhere in his work and, as luck would have it, the photos show a peapod carved into the wood panelling in the room. Now Gibbons worked mainly in England and took on only a few commissions in Scotland. Long story short, he's given me the names of three properties within forty miles of here that Gibbons worked on.'

'Three?'

'Yes, but I think we can discount one of them. It's eight miles south of St Andrews. If you remember, Vicky Gallagher told us Andy broke down one Thursday night and wanted her car. She met him near a crossroads north of the town So, I'm pretty sure it won't be that one.'

'And the other two?'

'The first is Gundor Lodge. I think that's the one to the west.'

DCI Gibson typed the name into the search engine and a map appeared. 'It's near Newburgh.'

'Would Andy Robb go to that crossroads if he was heading for Newburgh?' Chris asked.

'He might, if he was trying to avoid ANPR cameras,' Clare said. 'But it's certainly not the quickest way.'

'And the second one?' DCI Gibson asked.

'Mortaine Castle. That's T-A-I-N-E, sir.'

The DCI typed this into the search engine. 'Out towards Tentsmuir Forest,' he said.

'Which is close to the crossroads at St Mike's, I think,' Chris said. 'I'd say that one was more likely.'

'Possibly,' Clare said, 'but we can't take a chance on it.'

'Can you divide your men between the two?' the DCI asked Drew.

'Not really. We'd end up not covering either location adequately. Better if we can find out which it is.'

Clare took out her phone. 'I'll try Sara at the hospital again.'

Sara answered on the second ring. 'I was just about to call you, boss.'

'What's happened?'

'Dryden's awake. I'm heading back to St Andrews now.'

'Who's with him? Teresa?'

'Yeah.'

'Good. Come straight to the station. ASAP, Sara. We need every officer we can get at the moment.'

'On my way.'

Clare hung up.

'Good news?' Chris asked.

'I hope so. Come on – we're heading to Ninewells. Dryden's awake.'

Chapter 22

'Only a few minutes and I don't want him upset,' the doctor warned.

'We won't be long,' Clare assured him.

They entered the bay. Clare couldn't help noticing that the elderly man who had occupied the other bed on her last visit was gone now, his bed stripped bare. She hoped it was because he had recovered.

Nat Dryden was propped up in bed, surrounded by pillows. His head was bandaged, battered and bruised and the cage over his remaining leg was still in place beneath the bedclothes. There was stubble round his face and Clare marvelled that the body, even in the face of such trauma, carried on with its normal functions. Looking at him now, helpless and exhausted, Clare found it hard to believe he was capable of such depravity. Then she remembered the images taken from his laptop and her heart hardened.

Chris put down two chairs and they sat, one on either side of him.

'Mr Dryden, my name is Detective Inspector Clare Mackay and this is Detective Sergeant Chris West. We'd like to ask you a few questions, if you feel up to it.'

Nat raised his hand slightly.

'Mr Dryden, before we proceed, I must caution you that you do not have to say anything and that any statement you give will be noted and may be used in evidence.'

Nat's eyes flicked from Clare to Chris and back to Clare again.

'Do you understand the caution?'

He gave the merest nod.

'We need your help urgently to prevent another murder and, if you do assist us, I will make sure that it is noted if you are subsequently charged with other offences.'

She paused to let this sink in and, again, he raised his hand a little.

'We want to ask you about Thursday nights. You go out on Thursdays, don't you?'

He closed his eyes. Exhaled through his nose.

'We need to know where.'

Nat licked his lips and his eyes moved to a side table where there was a water bottle with a straw. Chris stepped round the bed, picked up the bottle and held the straw to Nat's lips. He sucked and a little water dribbled down his chin. Chris dabbed him gently with a tissue.

'Mr Dryden, was the house you visited near Newburgh?'

Nat frowned and he took a shallow breath in. He shook his head.

'Not Newburgh then? Was it Gundor Lodge?'

He moved his head slightly to the side.

'Is that a no, Mr Dryden?'

A nurse approached. 'I think, officers, that's long enough for now. Mr Dryden's looking tired.'

Clare turned to her. 'Just a couple more questions. A man's life may depend on it.'

The nurse's eyes widened. 'Only if I can stay and see he's not upset by your questions.'

'Of course.' Clare turned back to Nat. 'Was the house near Tentsmuir, Mr Dryden?'

Again, he licked his lips and this time the nurse picked up the bottle and held the straw to his lips.

'Mr Dryden.'

There was no response. His eyes were closed now.

'He's very tired,' the nurse said. 'I really do think—'

'Please,' Clare said, 'let me ask him just once more.'

'Muh,' said Dryden. 'Mor—'

'Mortaine?'

A slight nod.

'You went to Mortaine Castle on Thursday evenings?'

He closed his eyes and gave another nod. Clare rose from her seat. 'Thank you, Mr Dryden. That'll be all for now.'

As she turned to leave, he raised his hand again.

'Yes? Was there something else?'

He swallowed, with some difficulty, then whispered, 'Sorry.'

–

In the car park, Clare threw the keys to Chris. 'You drive, I'll phone the DCI.'

DCI Gibson answered immediately. 'What did you get?'

'It's Mortaine Castle. Out towards Tentsmuir Forest. But, sir, I don't want us going in mob-handed. We need Fergus alive.'

264

'I don't want another death, Inspector. We've dallied long enough on this one.'

'Please, sir, it won't be dark for another couple of hours. Can you at least wait till I get back and we can look at the area together?'

'I'll speak to Drew, Inspector, but he's keen to have his men in place well before dark. However, if you can get back here in the next half hour, we'll hold off.'

'Any chance you could look into who lives there while we're driving?'

'I'll get one of the lads to do that. Just get yourself back here.'

They reached the car and Clare jumped in. 'Foot to the floor,' she told Chris. 'We need to get back there before the ARU set off for Mortaine Castle.'

—

'We're potentially looking at making three arrests, for very different reasons,' Clare said to Drew Walsh and DCI Gibson. 'Fergus Bain for some of the hit-and-runs, an unknown female for the other attacks and the owner, or occupant, of Mortaine Castle for sexual offences. Who lives there? Do we know?'

The DCI lowered his specs and looked at his notepad. 'Edward Collinson. Made his money in property, sold the business and bought Mortaine Castle ten years ago. We've got the landline number for the castle but nothing so far for Mr Collinson.'

'Anyone else live there with him?'

'Not that I can see. He divorced before he bought the place. Wife got a big payout, as I recall. Read about it in the papers at the time.'

Clare sat back and thought for a minute. None of this was going to be easy. 'We need Fergus alive and well, if we're to stand a chance of convicting Edward Collinson. He's been clever enough not to appear in any of the photos. The only direct evidence is the photographs of the wood panelling in the house and he could argue he was away on Thursdays and unaware of the activities.'

'I doubt a jury would believe that,' DCI Gibson said.

'I'd rather not take the risk, sir. We need to take Fergus Bain alive.'

'Armed men don't tend to give themselves up.'

'I know, sir. But I don't want Collinson slipping through the net for lack of evidence. Nat Dryden's not out of the woods yet. If anything happens to him, Fergus might be our only hope of convicting Collinson.'

Drew checked his watch. 'I'd like to get my team in place as soon as possible. That lad's running round with a shotgun. For all we know he could be there now, watching the property. I won't have the team put at risk.'

'Anything more on Fergus Bain's background?' the DCI wanted to know.

'Not much. No girlfriend, a sort-of aunt in the town somewhere. We don't have a name for her yet.'

'He was brought up in a children's home,' said Chris.

'Interesting. Any idea where?'

Chris looked at his notebook and leafed back through a few pages. 'The ceilidh band leader mentioned it. Here it is – Garthley House.'

DCI Gibson sat forward. 'Garthley House?'

Chris nodded. 'Is there something we should know?'

The DCI seemed to be choosing his words carefully. 'It was hushed up at the time. No charges were brought in the end. But there were rumours…'

'Abuse?' Clare asked.

'Yes. But nothing could be proved so the investigation was closed.'

Clare sat back, processing this. 'So now we know why he's doing it,' she said. 'He's been a victim himself.'

'But surely, I mean, I know for a fact that Bruce Gilmartin had nothing to do with social work. And he wasn't old enough to have abused someone of Fergus Bain's age.'

'I'm guessing it didn't matter to Fergus,' Clare said. 'If he couldn't find his own abusers, then he'd go after men who were abusing other youngsters. I'd say he's been trawling the dark web to find local paedophile rings and exacting his own form of justice. For all we know, these five men could just be the start of it.'

'If you're correct, Inspector,' the DCI said, 'then Edward Collinson is the last member of the paedophile ring. The Thursday night group.'

'I agree. The one behind the camera and Fergus's final target.'

'We could go now,' Drew said. 'Pick him up before it gets dark.'

'The evidence against him is flimsy, at best,' DCI Gibson said.

Clare was frowning. 'If we arrest Collinson now, and Fergus Bain is watching the house, we'll lose him. But, if we leave Collinson in situ, as bait…'

'That's a dangerous game, Inspector. If Bain is successful then we have another death to explain. One we could conceivably have prevented.'

'Surely,' said Chris, 'this Edward Collinson must know the others have been killed and he'll be staying safely indoors? He can't be run over in his front room.'

'But Fergus Bain has a gun now,' DCI Gibson said. 'What do you think, Drew?'

Drew considered for a few moments then said, 'I'd like to recce the area. We can use thermal imaging. If Bain is hiding in the bushes we'll find him. If there's no sign of him and we can escort Mr Collinson out safely, I think we should do it.'

Clare looked at him. 'If you can do that, I'll sit in the house, put the lights on, that sort of thing. Let Fergus think there's still someone there.'

'Absolutely not, Inspector,' DCI Gibson said. 'I won't take a risk with your life.'

'I'll wear a vest, sir. And if it makes you happy I'll have a couple of Drew's guys with me. I don't want to lose him at this stage. Drew will tell you how resourceful I can be.' She looked right at him, daring him to contradict her.

Drew looked directly at the DCI. 'Clare was one of my finest officers and I was sorry to lose her. I'd have her back in a heartbeat.'

Clare, too, looked at the DCI. He was silent, weighing it up.

'Let's wait and see if we can pick up Edward Collinson first,' he said. 'Then we'll decide.'

Clare rose to leave but Chris put a hand on her arm. 'Hold on,' he said.

They turned to look at him.

'There's someone we're forgetting – the other driver. The one we think is a woman. She could be someone from his past. A fellow victim from Garthley House.'

'Good point, Sergeant,' the DCI said. 'Get someone looking into that, please.'

Drew rose. 'Right. We'll get down there now. I'll take the long way round and have the team in place before darkness. Radio silence from ten o'clock.'

Out in the main office, Clare took Chris aside. 'How's your acting, Chris?'

'Non-existent. Why?'

'Fancy making a call to Mortaine Castle to see if he's in?'

'Saying what?'

'The usual sales rubbish. PPI or something.'

'Why can't you do it?'

'I'm crap at stuff like that.'

'You think I'm any better?'

'Go on. And use the desk phone, not your mobile.'

Chris went to the phone behind the counter and dialled the number for Mortaine Castle. After a few minutes he hung up.

'Just ringing out,' he said.

'Doesn't mean he's not at home. He might be holed up, scared.'

'Or he might have legged it.'

'True. Check DVLA for cars registered to him or to that address. If he's gone we can maybe check ANPR camera records to find out where he's heading.'

Chris went off to check this, returning a few minutes later. 'He has an old Jaguar and an Audi Q5. I've written down the registration numbers. Want me to ask Traffic Control to check?'

'Yes, please. Go back to last Friday. Before the killings started.'

'He could be taking back roads, of course.'

'I'd rather not think about that, Chris.' She looked at her watch. 'We're in for a long night. I'm going to pop home to grab some food and I'll be back in an hour. Phone me if anything turns up.'

'Stay off the vino, now.'

'Not funny, DS West.'

–

'Neither car has passed any ANPR cameras in the past five days,' Chris told her as she arrived back. 'The Jag showed up going to Edinburgh a week last Tuesday but it also showed up coming back again. If he's legged it, he's gone by the back roads.'

Clare saw Drew signalling to her from the incident room and she went to find him holding a Kevlar vest. She looked at it. 'I'd forgotten how cumbersome these are.'

'Take it or leave it, Clare. But you're not coming along without one.'

Clare went to put the vest on. When she came back, Drew and the DCI had the whole team assembled in the incident room. She saw Pam Cassidy standing in the corner. Clare eyed her and then looked away, avoiding further eye contact.

When the room had quietened down, Drew stood to address them.

'Right,' he said. 'The primary purpose of tonight's job is to arrest this man.' He indicated a recently procured photo of Edward Collinson which had been added to the whiteboard. He looked to be in his fifties, balding, running to fat. He wore a dinner jacket in the photo and was smiling broadly. Clare thought she would enjoy arresting him very much.

'This is Edward Collinson,' Drew went on. 'We believe he's the leader of a paedophile ring. He's also the owner of Mortaine Castle, out towards Tentsmuir Forest. I have two men out there now. They've had a look round and it seems that no one is at home. He has two cars – a Jag and an Audi and the Audi isn't there, as far as we can see. Our lads have gained entry through a cellar door and there's no sign of anyone in the house so I think we can assume he's gone driving in the Audi. The number plate has been lodged with the ANPR database and they'll contact us immediately if it passes one of their cameras. As soon as Edward Collinson is spotted, he should be advised to come into protective custody for his own safety. We want him voluntarily if possible. If he refuses then he should be detained in connection with enquiries into the sexual abuse of minors. Make absolutely sure he is cautioned properly. He's not daft and we don't want him wriggling out of any possible charges. A vice team will be here tomorrow to take over questioning him, but we need to get him first. Clear, so far?'

Heads nodded and Drew went on.

'Okay. Our second target is one Fergus Bain.' Again, he tapped a photo of Fergus up on the board. 'We believe him to be armed with a Remington pump-action shotgun and, as such, he is considered highly dangerous. He is also the driver of a Land Rover Defender, currently with false plates which include the letters SJ and the number seven. It will have substantial damage to the front, where it hit a lamp post, but we know it's still drivable. We believe Fergus and an accomplice are responsible for four hit-and-runs, three of which resulted in the death of the victims. We also believe these victims are members of Edward Collinson's paedophile ring.'

'Sounds like he's doing a bang-up job, this Fergus Bain,' one of the armed response team said. This drew a sharp look from Drew but no comment.

'We believe Fergus Bain will try to finish what he started, by attempting to kill Edward Collinson, possibly tonight. So, as I have said, Mr Bain should be regarded as highly dangerous. I don't want any of you taking chances. That said, we need him alive if at all possible. Without his evidence the Vice cops may not be able to secure a conviction against Collinson.'

'Are we authorised to shoot, sir?' one of the ARU team asked.

'If you believe it's the only way to stop him, yes. If you or your colleagues' lives are threatened then shoot to kill. If he's escaping, then shoot to wound.'

Drew paused to let that sink in. 'Now we know Bain has an accomplice, a female, but we know absolutely nothing about her, other than she possibly has one finger shorter than the others. So you should also be on the lookout for any females around the area. Anyone found in the grounds of Mortaine Castle – male or female – should be detained.'

Drew looked across at Clare then back round the room. 'Finally,' he said, 'DI Mackay here is going to sit in the property, along with two armed officers. She has met Bain and may be able to talk him out of doing anything silly, if he does manage to get into the house. DI Mackay has a vest on but I don't need to tell you that her protection is your top priority.'

Clare and Chris drove in silence, taking the right fork for Tayport at St Michael's junction. As they drove along the road, they passed fields, punctuated by dense pine woods.

Chris glanced at the satnav. 'It's just round the next bend, I think. There's a drive through the trees and the house is in a clearing.'

They rounded the bend and saw the stout stone pillars flanking the entrance to the drive. Clare turned the car in. There was no sign of any police activity at all. Drew's team were well concealed.

The trees gave way to a circular drive of pea-gravel, beyond which sat an imposing sandstone dwelling. To call it a castle was perhaps a bit of an exaggeration, but it was an impressive house, all the same. It had been built in the Scottish Baronial style, with a round tower at one end and crow-stepped gables. As they drove round towards the front entrance they were flagged down by a member of Drew's team.

'Car over here, please, Inspector,' he said, indicating a small offshoot which curved round behind a thicket of trees. Following the track, Clare came across several police vehicles hidden from the main drive and house. She parked where the officer pointed and stepped out of the car.

As she did so, Drew appeared out of the trees. 'We'll need it to be dark to be absolutely sure but I don't think there's anyone concealed in the grounds. But once we use the thermal imaging we'll have a better idea.'

Clare looked towards the house. 'Who's inside?'

'Two of my team. Ronnie and Eva. Both experienced. They'll look after you.'

'I have done armed response before, Drew. Remember?'

'Yeah, okay.' He glanced up at the sky. 'Sun's low now. Better get yourself in there. The constable here will show you where to go. The rest of us will get out of sight now.'

'The DCI?'

'Back at the station. We don't want him cluttering things up.'

Chris slapped Clare on the back and gave her a cheery smile but his eyes told a different story. 'You take care in there, boss.'

She nodded, then turned away. She couldn't think about Chris – or her family. There was a job to be done. Clare followed the constable through the trees and round to the back of the castle. A small flight of steps led down to a dark green, wooden basement door. It opened noiselessly and Clare found herself in a room that smelled faintly of damp. She blinked, trying to accustom her eyes to the near dark, following the constable to another door, which in turn opened onto a flight of stairs.

'This takes you up to the main hallway,' said the constable. 'Ronnie and Eva are in the front room, just off the hall.'

Clare thanked him and made her way up the stairs, emerging through a worn, velvet curtain into a tiled hallway with a broad staircase to the left and the front entrance to the right. All round her was the Grinling Gibbons wood panelling and she knew she was in the right house. Across the hall, light poured out from an open door. She went to join the two officers. Although it was not quite dark they had drawn the curtains and lit some lamps around the room.

'Makes it look lived-in,' Ronnie said.

'Could be a long night,' Eva added. 'Make yourself at home, Inspector.'

Clare took out her mobile phone to text Chris her location but there was no signal.

'Walls two feet thick,' Eva said. 'There's probably radio reception somewhere in the house.'

Clare shook her head. 'It's fine. Not a problem.' And she settled herself in an easy chair with a clear view of the door.

Chapter 23

Clare was bored out of her skull. She had walked round the room, admiring the ornate wood panels, trying unsuccessfully to find the carved peapod. This wasn't the room where the photos had been taken but there was no doubting the similarities in style. She wandered round the edge of the room, looking at the books in the bookcase, flicking through a few, and marvelled at the plasterwork on the ceiling but still there was no sign of Edward Collinson.

'Anything happening outside?' she asked Ronnie and Eva.

They shook their heads. 'I'll head upstairs in a bit to see if I can pick up a signal,' Eva said.

Clare moved to the door. 'Fancy a coffee?'

'Please,' Eva said. 'Both milk, no sugar.'

'Nice and easy, then.' Clare went back out to the hall and looked round. The kitchen would be to the rear of the house, she supposed. She walked along the hall, passing the main staircase on her left and found a door tucked in behind it. She opened this and felt in the dark for a light switch. Her fingers found it and the room was bathed in light. Despite the age of the building the kitchen was modern. It was fitted out with a cream Aga, the walls lined with light oak units. The floor was covered with large black and white tiles arranged diagonally and a substantial waxed refectory table stood in the centre of the room.

A lot of kitchen for one man.

She moved to the sink to fill the kettle. The water pressure took her by surprise and she overfilled it, spilling some water as she carried the kettle over to the plug next to the Aga. As she waited for it to boil she looked round at the kitchen. It was a lovely room, no expense spared. But it was lacking something. She thought Edward Collinson probably didn't do much beyond heating ready meals in the microwave. Suddenly her phone buzzed as she picked up a signal. She took it out of her pocket and saw the voicemail icon flashing. Chris. She put it to her ear and listened.

'Clare, it's Chris. We think Fergus might be in the house. The Land Rover's hidden in trees, further down the road. The engine's cold and there's no sign of him in the grounds. Stick to those ARU guys like glue. Drew's sending the team in.'

Clare's heart was beating fast now. Fergus in the house. She had a vest on but no weapon. The sensible thing would be to get herself back to Ronnie and Eva. If they had no radio signal they wouldn't know either. But, if Fergus was in the house, somewhere, was it possible he might trust her? He would see she was unarmed. The kettle came to the boil with a rush of steam and a click. A second, softer click came from the kitchen door being closed very gently.

'Hands where I can see them,' Fergus said. 'Then turn round.'

'I'm unarmed,' she said, turning slowly.

He smiled. 'I know.'

Clare thought Fergus Bain looked leaner, more haunted, than when they had interviewed him – was it only yesterday? It seemed a lifetime ago. The thick fringe made his eyes look darker than ever. He stood now, back against the kitchen door, shotgun trained on Clare. He nudged a chair towards her.

'Sit.'

'I'd be a lot happier if you would lower your gun, Fergus.'

He responded by lowering the gun slightly so it was aimed closer to her feet. She fought back the nerves she felt, trying to ignore the memory of the last time she was facing what she thought was a gun. But this time it *was* the real thing. The Remington 870. She wouldn't stand much of a chance if this one went off.

Clare forced a smile. 'I'd like it if you and I could go into the station and have a proper chat. Without all the other cops outside. You do know there are armed police outside, Fergus?'

'Out and in. They'll no' let me out of here alive. But as long as I have you—'

'I won't be your hostage.'

He raised the gun again.

'You'll have to shoot me right here. And then they'll shoot you.' She looked at the gun again and he lowered it slightly. 'And we want you to live, Fergus. We want you to help us nail the man who lives here.'

Fergus said something that sounded like 'sick bastard', but Clare wasn't completely sure.

'Is this how it was for you? At Garthley House? Is that why you set out on this vendetta?'

Clare watched him carefully. Was there a flicker of something in those dark eyes? She tried again. 'We know it went on. Back then, at Garthley. They just couldn't prove it at the time. But then you know all about that, don't you Fergus?'

The flicker again. Was she getting somewhere with him? Starting to reach him?

'It never leaves you, does it?' Clare went on. 'Something like that. Scars you for life.'

He ran a tongue round his lips. 'You must have seen the photos.' His voice was flat. 'If I could get into their laptops, your lot certainly could. The men who did those things to me...' He broke off.

Clare waited.

Then he began again. 'They're long gone,' he said. 'Some dead, some – dinnae ken. But it still goes on. You've seen it.' He raised his eyes to meet hers and she saw they were bright with tears.

'I have, Fergus. And I can assure you that the man who's in hospital and the owner of this house will feel the full force of the law. I promise you that.'

'Hospital?'

Clare nodded. 'Your third victim didn't die. Life-changing injuries, but he'll live.'

'She said it hadn't gone to plan.'

She. It had been a woman.

'Who said that, Fergus? Your accomplice? Someone who's been helping you with these killings?'

Suddenly he seemed to recall himself. 'I'm saying nothing more. Now let's you and I get out of here.'

It was the softest creak. Clare only just heard it. She didn't think Fergus had but perhaps her face gave it away.

Fergus whirled round to face the kitchen door and raised the gun.

Clare saw her chance and leapt from her chair, aiming low.

As his finger crooked round the trigger she rugby tackled his legs, wrapping her arms tightly around them, pulling him down and away from the door. His head collided with one of the stout oak cupboards. The gun went off with an ear-splitting boom. The recoil caused Fergus to lurch backward, away from Clare, and he lost his grip on the gun. The slug blasted straight through the cupboard door, shattering china as it went, lodging in the thick stone wall behind. Dazed as he was, Fergus reached out for the gun, but Clare was quicker. She jumped forward and shoved the gun across the floor. Then, grabbing his arm, she forced it up his back. The training from her days in the armed response team kicked in and she remembered the protocol.

'Hold fire! Weapon secure. Room clear,' she shouted, her ears still buzzing from the blast.

The armed officers entered and one immediately sprang to Clare's side. Another took up position, a few feet from Fergus, weapon trained on him. Clare, with an eye on Fergus, got unsteadily to her feet.

'I'm fine,' she said, 'or I will be once my ears stop ringing.' She looked at one of the masked officers, gun trained on Fergus. The head was obscured by a balaclava but something about the eyes seemed familiar and Clare stared, trying to remember.

'It's Pam,' the officer said. 'Pam Cassidy.' Pam's eyes fell on the shotgun and the hole in the oak cabinet. 'That's one hell of a hole. What's he used?'

'Certainly not pellets,' Clare said. 'Pretty big slug by the looks of it.'

Pam looked at the kitchen door. It wasn't original, but a newer design and panelled. Thin, compared to the solid oak cupboard doors. Had Clare not brought Fergus down, the slug would have gone straight through the kitchen door and through the person on the other side of it. Pam. She looked at it and Clare followed her gaze.

'Pam,' Clare said, her voice soft, cutting through her colleague's thoughts. 'Let's get him cuffed and in the van. And no rough stuff. He has valuable information.'

–

'You're going to hospital,' DCI Gibson insisted.

'With respect, sir, I'm bloody not.'

'Don't make me order you, Inspector.'

'Sir, I am absolutely fine. I banged my elbow, but that's about it.'

'Oh you're a doctor now, are you Inspector? You probably have a perforated eardrum from the blast, for starters. You could even be suffering from shock.'

'Do I look like I'm in shock? Remember I used to do this sort of thing, day in, day out.'

Chris weighed in. 'How about I take you, get them to give you a quick once-over then I'll run you home?'

'We have witnesses to interview.'

'Not tonight, we don't, Inspector. We have two suspects, both on their way to the station now and we're doing nothing until we've had Drew's debrief which will be at least another hour. I want a doctor to look you over, then you can join us for the interviews tomorrow, *if* the doc says you're okay. We'll meet at nine and sort out who's seeing who.'

'Two suspects?' Clare said, alert again. 'The other driver?'

The DCI shook his head. 'No. Collinson. DS West can fill you in on your way to hospital.'

Clare shook her head. 'Nope. Not going.'

'Then you'll not be back to work tomorrow,' the DCI said. 'And even Saint Elaine of Carter will back me up on this one.'

Clare had to smile at that.

Chris saw his chance. 'Come on, Detective Inspector. Let's get you seen to then we can all get home to bed.' He checked his watch. 'We might just make the community hospital before it shuts,' he said. 'Save a trip to Dundee...'

'Oh for goodness sake! Come on then – let's get it over with.' And she began walking towards Chris's car.

'Phone me, DS West, once the doctor has seen the Inspector,' DCI Gibson called after them.

'Will do, sir.'

–

In the car, Chris filled Clare in with the events of the evening.

'Collinson's Audi flashed up on a camera, north-west of Dundee. The traffic lads picked him up at the Tay Road Bridge.'

'What's he saying?'

'Livid. Demanding to be allowed to go home, threatening to call the Chief Constable. Usual wanker stuff.'

'Is he an influential wanker though?'

'Not sure. But the DCI's happy to have him arrested if he becomes difficult. At the moment he's been persuaded to attend on a voluntary basis. But the boss says to detain him if necessary.'

'But, if Nat Dryden positively identifies him...'

'Let's hope so.'

They reached the community hospital half an hour before it was due to shut for the night. After Chris explained the situation, Clare was seen straight away. The doctor examined her ears and found both eardrums perforated.

'No treatment, I'm afraid,' she said, 'just avoid blowing your nose, swimming, flying and keep them clean. No dusting or digging the garden.'

Clare took the proffered painkillers and swallowed a couple. The doctor wanted to give her a sedative and recommended forty-eight hours rest, away from work. Clare took the sedative, tucked it in her pocket and promised she would follow the doctor's instructions. Outside, a wind had blown up and she was suddenly cold.

'It's the shock,' Chris said. 'Come on – I'm driving you home and you are not to come in before nine tomorrow morning.'

'Yes, Sergeant.'

'That's a good Inspector.'

Chapter 24

Friday, 24th May

Clare was surprised when she turned over in bed and squinted at her bedside clock. Ten past eight! After the events of the previous night, she hadn't expected to sleep at all. But tiredness had overtaken her and, apart from the ringing in her ears which had now given way to a muffled buzzing, she felt rested. She also felt completely empty. When had she last eaten?

She padded downstairs, pulling her dressing gown round her and filled the kettle. Rooting around in the freezer she found a bag of ready-to-bake croissants and put two of these in the oven. She felt a strange sense of calm, at odds with the experience of staring down the barrel of a Remington 870. Fergus and Collinson had both been detained and she was hopeful that Fergus and Nat Dryden would talk, giving them enough to charge Collinson. It wasn't the best result with three men dead and one seriously wounded but, with luck, they could find the children in the photos and save them from any further abuse.

In the bathroom she turned on the shower. Recalling the doctor's instructions the night before, she plugged her ears with cotton wool then stepped under the stream of water, her face turned up. As she stood, she reflected on the events of the past week. It hadn't even been a week. Barely six days. And they weren't done yet. There was still an unknown, female driver to find – Fergus's accomplice.

Despite her uninterrupted sleep, she yawned. 'You need a holiday, Clare,' she told herself turning off the stream of water and reaching for a towel. Her thoughts turned to the cottage she had seen. With Fergus in custody she need have no more fears about a house so close to his. Maybe if they charged both men – and found the accomplice – she could think about viewing the house. But there was still the prospect of the private prosecution hanging over her. Until that was resolved there could be no plans.

She heard a beeping from the kitchen and ran back downstairs, towel on her head, to take the croissants out of the oven.

–

By the time Clare arrived at the station Edward Collinson's solicitor had been there for forty minutes. He was minded to be awkward. 'My client agreed to attend for interview, voluntarily last night at – what was it, eleven o'clock? And you have not yet questioned him?' He looked at his watch. 'I believe you have trespassed on his good nature long enough, officers. Mr Collinson is leaving.'

DCI Gibson was ready for this. 'Our enquiries were delayed, sir, until your own arrival. We can begin the interview now, though.'

'And if he declines?'

DCI Gibson smiled. 'I hope, sir, that won't be an issue. I might add that we advised your client to accompany us to the station, initially for his own safety. We had reason to believe that his life was in imminent danger.'

'Perhaps you would clarify that,' the solicitor said.

'We'll discuss that during the interview,' the DCI said.

'If that was indeed the case,' Edward Collinson piped up, 'I'd have thought a hotel with a policeman in attendance would have been more appropriate.'

Jesus, Clare thought, *where do these people get their ideas from?* Instead, she pushed a form across the table towards him and began her formal preamble.

'Mr Collinson, this is a form which you have signed confirming you are attending the station voluntarily to assist us with enquiries. Are you still happy to be interviewed on that basis?'

Edward Collinson pushed back his chair and got to his feet. 'I rather think not, Inspector. It's been a long night and I would like to return home now.'

'I'm afraid that won't be possible, sir. Your house is currently a crime scene.'

'Then, as I said, perhaps a hotel...'

Clare took a deep breath. 'Very well, sir. Edward Collinson, I am detaining you formally in connection with offences against minors which we believe to have taken place at your home, Mortaine Castle. You are not obliged to say anything but anything you do say will be noted and may be used in evidence. Do you understand?'

Edward Collinson looked at his solicitor. The solicitor raised an eyebrow at Clare who put her hand out, indicating the seat Collinson had just vacated. He took the hint and sat down again.

Clare went on. 'Can you please tell us what you know about these activities?'

The solicitor spoke for his client. 'Mr Collinson has no knowledge of any such alleged offences and denies any involvement absolutely.'

'Perhaps Mr Collinson could speak for himself?'

The solicitor looked at Edward Collinson who sighed heavily. 'As my legal representative has already said, I cannot help you, officers. I know nothing of any events of this nature which may have taken place in my house during my frequent absences. I deny any wrongdoing absolutely. And I may say I am utterly shocked at having my house taken over by armed police with neither my knowledge nor my consent.'

Clare was not put off by this. 'Do you know a man by the name of Andrew Robb? He was a driver for Swilcan Taxis.'

He smiled. 'Not as far as I am aware. I do, however, take taxis from time to time so I may have met him without knowing it.'

'Bruce Gilmartin?'

'The brewery chap? I read about his death. Hmm... possibly at charity functions? I like to do my bit.'

'Nat Dryden?'

He shook his head.

'Professor Bertram Harris?'

'I think not.'

Clare looked steadily at him but he returned her gaze. 'Perhaps you recognise this photograph?' She pushed the photograph of the wood panelling with the peapod carving across the table. He removed a pair of reading glasses from his jacket pocket and put them on.

He peered at the photo. 'It's a rather beautiful piece of wood carving.'

'From Mortaine Castle.'

'I can't say. It's possible but then there are other examples of this type of work found in properties of a similar age. It's not unique by any standards.'

'But unusual?'

'Indeed.'

She pushed another three photos across the table. 'Are these photographs of furnishings in Mortaine Castle?'

He looked at them and smiled again, removing his glasses. 'They could be from any country house, Inspector.'

'How many people have keys to your property?'

He sat back and clasped his hands together, making a pretence of thinking about this. 'Let's see, now: myself of course, then there is the woman who comes in twice a week, the letting agent who handles lets when I'm away from home… I think that's all.'

The solicitor leaned forward. 'So you see, Inspector, my client's trusting nature means his home could have been used for other purposes, without his knowledge or permission. I really think you have little on which to hold him any further.'

Outside the room, DCI Gibson said, 'He's right, you know, Inspector. We don't have anything concrete.'

'It's possible Nat Dryden will be well enough to give a statement. But I'd have to make sure he has a solicitor present. Leave it with me, sir. I'll find something on the weasely bastard if it kills me.'

—

The DCI was happy for Clare and Chris to interview Fergus and they made their way to the interview room where he was waiting. Fergus was subdued, mostly staring down at the table in front of him. He had declined a solicitor. Clare cautioned him and he acknowledged the caution. She started the recording and, after a long continuous beep, the interview began.

'Fergus,' she said, 'you will shortly be charged with the murders of Bruce Gilmartin and Professor Bertram Harris, and with conspiracy to murder Edward Collinson. You will also be charged as a co-conspirator in the murder of Andy Robb and the attempted murder of Nat Dryden; finally you will be charged with abduction and with the attempted murder of a police officer last night. But before we proceed with charges, I would like to ask about your accomplice. Because you did have an accomplice, didn't you, Fergus?'

He continued staring at the table.

'We fully expect to find your DNA and fingerprints on the numbered cards found at the murder scene. It's highly likely you'll be convicted, even if you deny the charges. But someone else must have carried out at least two of the attacks; and we need to bring that person to justice.'

Still nothing.

'Last night, in the kitchen at Mortaine Castle,' Clare went on, 'you stated *she said it hadn't gone according to plan.* Who did you mean? Was that your accomplice? A woman friend? Someone from Garthley House, perhaps?'

His eyes flicked a glance at her then away again. Was that the way in, Clare wondered? She decided to carry on.

'Okay, Fergus. I'll tell you what I think and maybe you can agree if I'm right.' She glanced at him and he gave a slight shrug of his shoulders. She went on.

'Fergus, I think you were the victim of abuse, when you were living at Garthley House. I think you were abused by people you should have been able to trust. And experiences like that, well, they never leave you, do they?'

Clare paused but Fergus's head was still bent.

'I think that you're pretty good with computers, and that you were able to find people online who were also abusers. Perhaps not the men who abused you but abusers all the same. I believe you wanted to stop the abuse and to stop the men, and that's why you embarked on these killings. Fergus,' Clare softened her tone, 'if I'm right then you are as much a victim as the men you killed.'

Fergus's face was growing red and he drew a hand across his eyes. Clare pushed a box of tissues across the desk but he ignored this.

Clare went on. 'I can't do much about the charges that will be preferred. We have enough evidence for a conviction; but we would like your help to bring the two men who remain alive to justice. There are specialist crime officers in the station who would like to interview you in connection with that. And, while I can't promise anything, if you help us with this, I will make sure it's mentioned in court.'

He raised his gaze to meet Clare's. For a moment, she was transported back to the kitchen of Mortaine Castle the previous night and she shivered involuntarily.

'They give you stuff,' he said suddenly, his voice gruff. 'Fags, chocolate, vodka. Stuff to keep you sweet. But they'd do it anyway, even if you dinnae take the stuff so you're as well taking it. The older lads – the ones who'd been there a while – they told us what to expect, like. What they'd do – what we had to do.' He cleared his throat and paused.

Clare rose from the table and went to the water cooler, pouring him a cup of water. He drank from this, pushed his fringe back over his head, then went on.

'Couldnae take it in at first. What the lads said they'd do. But they said you get used to it. After the first couple of times. Doesnae hurt after a while.' He raised his eyes. Clare noticed for the first time that they weren't dark at all. They were a piercing blue. It was his thick lashes, hooded by the fringe that made them seem dark. She pictured him as a dark-haired, blue-eyed boy and thought it was no wonder the abusers had picked him. He must have been so appealing and she felt sick, imagining what he had endured.

'They were right,' he said, 'sort of. It was okay. Got used to it. Knew what they wanted, even learned how to get them to slip me a few extra quid. But then they got wise to that, the folk at the home. Took it off me.'

Clare glanced at Chris and he took the cue.

'Was there no one you could tell?'

Fergus shook his head. 'They warned us about that, the older lads. Tell, and you get beaten. One lad had his ribs broken.' He glanced up at Chris. 'They told us it was a privilege. That we were special for being chosen.' He took another drink then went on. Now he had started, he seemed almost relieved to talk. 'I said to one of them that I liked computers. Next week we got a new laptop and every few weeks they'd give us games and that.'

'You had no family?' Chris asked.

Fergus shook his head. 'Never kent ma dad. Then ma mum died. Some sort of cancer. They never told me. Next thing, they're taking me off to this place. Garthley. Never heard of it and suddenly it was ma home.'

Clare said, 'Your employer, Fergus…'

'Sam?' He seemed surprised. 'What about him?'

'When we spoke to him he mentioned you had an aunt – somewhere in St Andrews. Could you not…'

'No!'

They were surprised by his sharp tone.

'No?'

He shook his head. 'No. She wasn't a real aunty. Friend of ma gran's. One of those family friends. Didnae have anyone herself.'

'Could she not have taken you in?'

'Naw. Too old and not a blood relative. She came to see me a few times. For a visit, like.'

'And you couldn't tell her – what was happening?'

He shrugged. 'No point. They wouldnae believe me; wouldnae let her take me home with her and I've have got a walloping for speaking out. She was nice, though. Still see her now and then.'

Clare wondered at a system that wouldn't allow a kind elderly lady to look after a young lad she knew, preferring to put him in a home where he was at the mercy of those in charge. She wondered if things had improved since Fergus's time.

Cutting across her thoughts, Chris asked, 'How long did it carry on for, Fergus?'

He shrugged. 'Dunno. Pretty much all the time I was there. A good few years. Thing is,' he said, meeting their eyes, 'after a while, you forget. Forget what's wrong and what's right. It's just what you do. And then suddenly, you're sixteen and you're out in the world. And it stops. They only want the young ones anyway. All those lads I left behind.' He looked at them. 'Day I left, there was a young lad brought in. Wee red-head. Cute wee thing. I wanted to tell him, but what would be the point? I couldnae have saved him.'

Clare closed her eyes for a moment. It was almost more than she could bear, the thought of all these young boys. Girls too, probably. Then she gave herself a shake.

'What happened when you left the home, Fergus?'

'I walked around. Walked anywhere and everywhere. You can't imagine the feeling of freedom, knowing I didnae have to go back. They gave me a few quid to get started and the address of a hostel. But I didnae fancy that. Had enough of being in institutions. So I walked to the edge of town and I came to a farm. Offered to work, for ma keep, like. Farmer's wife was good to me. Paid me a bit and gave me a caravan to sleep in. First time I'd ever had somewhere that was mine. Oh, it was draughty, leaked at one end, but it was mine.' He paused then shook his head. 'You never lose the fear of someone coming into your bed at night. I used to barricade the door. Still put a chair under ma bedroom door handle at the cottage.' He took another drink of water, draining the cup and sat back, his story told.

'Do you know what happened to the men who abused you, Fergus?' Chris asked.

Fergus flicked a glance at Chris then away again. 'Naw. To be honest, I never knew who they were. Some of them seemed old to me. Probably dead now.'

Clare said, 'Fergus?' and waited until he met her eye. 'You know we have to question you now about criminal charges. I can't stop that happening. But what I can do is to ask for you to be seen by a psychologist. They can recommend help – treatment. To help you deal with what's happened.'

Fergus simply shrugged. Clare said, 'I think we'll take a short break just now, Fergus. Get us all a coffee. And when we come back I'd like to ask you about the attacks on the four men.'

They left the room, closing the door behind them. Clare exhaled and leaned against the wall. 'Jesus, Chris. How do Vice do this, day in, day out?'

He shook his head. 'Poor bastard. No wonder he's gone off the rails.'

DCI Gibson approached. 'How's it going?'

Clare sighed. 'Pretty awful, sir, to be honest. He's just taken us through the abuse he suffered as a kid.'

DCI Gibson nodded. 'Doesn't change what we have to do, though. We still need to question him about the attacks.'

'Yes, I know. Chris, could you do three coffees then we'll carry on. Sooner we get it done, the better.'

'Remember we still have Collinson in the other room,' the DCI reminded her. 'You need to get up to Ninewells to see if Dryden will implicate him.'

'Okay, sir. Soon as Chris does the coffees we'll resume questioning Fergus.'

When they re-entered the room, Clare thought Fergus looked different. Lighter. As if unburdening himself had somehow lifted years of tension from his body.

'Fergus,' she began, 'I would remind you that you're still under caution. I must also tell you that you are likely to be convicted of the attempted murder of a police officer at Mortaine Castle last night, an offence which carries a custodial sentence.'

Fergus nodded. 'Aye, I ken that.'

'So, with that knowledge,' Clare went on, 'would you tell us please about the attacks with your vehicle? Any co-operation you give will be taken into account when you are sentenced.'

He looked at Clare, as though weighing his options. Then, finally, he said, 'Aye okay. I'll tell you.' He took a couple of breaths in and out then began. 'I did the brewery lad and that professor over in Dairsie. I hit them both with my Land Rover. Hit them and killed them.'

Clare looked back at him. 'Just to be clear, you are confessing to killing Bruce Gilmartin and Bertram Harris.'

Fergus nodded.

'For the tape please?'

He cleared his throat then said. 'Aye, that's right. I killed them both.'

Clare glanced at Chris. They had done it. They had him in the station and he had confessed. To two of the killings at least.

Chris took over. 'Fergus, can we ask you now about the other two attacks? Andy Robb was killed while you were playing accordion at his sister's wedding. And Nat Dryden was almost killed while you were playing at a rugby club ceilidh in Kirkcaldy. So who was responsible for these killings?'

The shutters came down again. Fergus allowed his fringe to fall over his eyes and he sat back, folding his arms. 'No comment.'

'But surely you must know?' Chris went on. 'We know it was your vehicle and we also have reason to believe the driver was a woman.'

Fergus closed his eyes but said nothing. Clare and Chris made a few more attempts to draw him back into the conversation but he sat mutely. Finally, Clare said, 'All right, Fergus. We'll leave the other two attacks for now. But there is something else you could do for us.'

His eyes widened a little but he said nothing.

'Fergus, we believe you hacked into at least one of the victims' laptops. Nat Dryden. Is that correct?'

Fergus laughed. 'Muppet. He didnae even have basic security software. A twelve-year-old could've done it.'

'And that led you to a site on the dark web?'

'Yeah. That and plenty of others.'

Clare swallowed. Had he just said *plenty of others*?

'We have colleagues from the specialist crime division in the station today. They specialise in breaking paedophile rings. Fergus – would you help them? Help them find any others who are out there?'

'Ma laptop. I'll need ma laptop,' he said.

Clare rose from her seat. 'I'll arrange for that,' she said. 'And I'm terminating this interview now.'

Chris leaned forward. 'Inspector, before you do, I'd like to ask Fergus one more question.'

Clare sat down again and looked at Chris. He glanced at her, then said, 'Fergus, I have to ask, we had men all round the grounds of Mortaine Castle last night and we searched the house. How did you get into the kitchen?'

A ghost of a smile crept across his face. 'I got you there, didn't I?'

Chris nodded. 'You did. So?'

'The Jag. I was in the Jag. Your lads checked the garage. I heard them open the doors, had a quick look round but they didnae think of opening up the car boot. Soon as they'd gone I was out and up the back stairs to the passage behind the kitchen. Kids' play.'

Chris sat back in his seat. He had to hand it to Fergus. He'd worked it all out.

Clare rose again. 'I'm terminating this interview now, Fergus. I'll let you speak to my colleagues then we will charge you and you will be remanded in custody. Maybe you should think about that solicitor now.'

Out in the main office, Clare telephoned Tech Support and asked them to find a local officer to bring Fergus's laptop up to St Andrews without delay. Then she called the specialist crime officers into the DCI's office to update them all together.

'Fergus Bain has agreed to talk to the Vice cops. But he wants his laptop, lads. So you'll have to wait for that to arrive. Tech Support are sending a cop up with it now.'

'What about the murders?' the DCI asked.

'He's coughed to Bruce Gilmartin and Professor Harris. But he won't say anything about the other two or who his accomplice is.'

'Have you charged him?'

'Not yet. I'll wait to see what else he comes up with once he has his laptop. But I'll be charging him with two murders and the attempted murder at Mortaine last night. We'll take his prints and hopefully match them to a couple of the white cards. But it looks as if he's staying quiet about his accomplice.'

'What about the home? Garthley House,' the DCI suggested. 'Could it be someone from back then?'

'Yes, good point, sir, but it might be a needle in a haystack, given the number of kids who pass through a place like that.'

'Worth looking into, though, Inspector. Given how few friends he seems to have it's a strong possibility.'

'I'll get some of the cops onto it, sir.'

They began to file out of Clare's office and the DCI called Clare back. When the Vice cops had left, he said, 'How are you today anyway, Inspector?'

'I'm fine, thanks, sir.'

'Ears okay?'

Clare's hand went involuntarily to her right ear. 'Buzzing a bit, I must admit, but the doc says they should mend.'

'Try and get home early tonight then,' he said and he gave her a rare smile.

—

Clare nipped out to buy a sandwich. When she returned, Jim was manning the desk.

'What's happening, Jim?' she asked.

'Not much. Fergus Bain's laptop has arrived. I've given it to one of the Vice lads. Bain's with his solicitor just now. And that Inspector from Vice…'

'Kate?'

'Aye, that's her. She and one of the other lads have interviewed Edward Collinson but he's denying any involvement. Some story about being away from the

298

house a lot, and anyone could have been using it. Is he not in the photos from Nat Dryden's computer?'

Clare shook her head. 'Nope. He's been too clever for that.' She stood lost in thought for a minute then spoke again. 'Is Kate still around?'

'In the incident room.'

Clare went through to the room and saw Kate's unruly mass of red curls bent over a laptop. She was scrolling and pointing while her colleague took notes. They looked up when Clare entered and Kate rose to greet her.

'Clare – good to see you. Doing okay? Heard you had a bit of excitement last night.'

'Yeah I'm fine, thanks.' She rubbed her ear again. 'Ears are a bit annoying but I'm told it'll pass. How are things with you?'

'Can't complain. This is Brian. My DS.'

Clare smiled at Brian then looked back at Kate.

'I know that look, Clare. What are you after?'

'Kate, I hear you're the go-to person for paedophile victims.'

Kate laughed. 'Yeah, unfortunately I do have that honour. What you after?'

'Any chance you could look at some photos? We've a suspected paedophile with an arsey solicitor champing at the bit to have him released; and I don't want to lose him.'

'Of course. Anything to put another one of them out of circulation.'

Kate stood aside to let Clare use the laptop. She navigated her way to the folder on the network where the photos were stored. 'If you recognised any of the kids here there's a chance they could identify our Mr Collinson.'

Kate nodded, took the mouse and began flicking through the photos.

'Stop,' Brian said. 'Go back one. Yes, that one.'

Kate looked more closely. 'Jasmine Greene?'

'That's what I thought.'

'You know her?' Clare asked.

'Yeah, quite well. I'll check, but I think she's in a residential home the other side of Cupar.'

'Could we interview her? It could give us the evidence we need to put Collinson away.'

'Let me make some calls.'

Kate started phoning round to track down Jasmine Greene while Brian and another officer from Vice went to see Fergus. Clare sought out Chris. He looked up and she hesitated.

'Oh, God. What?' he said.

'Job for you.'

'One I'm not going to like, judging by your face.'

She sat down. 'Sorry but it's important. The DCI thinks Fergus's accomplice might be someone he knew from his time at Garthley House. Probably a fellow abuse victim. Maybe a girl he kept in touch with.'

'And you want me to track her down?'

''Fraid so.'

'How long ago did he leave?'

'About twelve years ago. Social Work will know.'

'And he was there how long?'

'I think about four years but, again, get Social Work to check it out. See if any of the staff remember Fergus, and whether he was pally with any girls while he was there. Or if he wasn't, do they remember a girl with the tip of her middle finger missing. Might save you some time.'

Chris sat back in his chair and exhaled. 'Four years? Clare, have you any idea how big a job that is? Kids come and go at these places all the time.'

'I know. But it's important. There's a woman out there who's committed one murder and damn near a second and, unless Fergus gives her up, we haven't a clue who she is. And for all we know, she could have more targets in her sights. Get Connor, Steve and Phil on the phone and bring them in.'

Chris threw her a *You Owe Me* glance and lifted the phone.

Clare went to let the DCI know she was heading over to Cupar to interview one of the possible abuse victims.

'I'll take a laptop with the photos and see if we can get Collinson identified. Kate from Vice knows her and will smooth the way.'

'Make sure you mix the photos up, Inspector. Throw in a few rogue ones so we're not accused of leading the witness.'

'Already done, sir. And a social worker will be present when we interview her. I'm not losing Collinson at this stage.'

As they were talking, Brian, the DS from Vice, poked his head round the door.

'Fergus Bain,' he began, 'we need to put him on the staff, never mind charging him.'

'He's come up with the goods?'

'Yep. By the time he's done I reckon we'll have a handle on at least another three paedophile rings in Fife alone. The guy's a bloody genius with the dark web.'

'He's also a murderer,' Clare reminded him.

'Well, don't go upsetting him before he's given us all the info.'

She saw Brian's point. 'Get what you can from him then I'll have him charged. That'll let us hold him while we track down his accomplice.' She checked her watch. 'I'm all set to head over to Cupar now, if Kate's free. I'm just sorting out photos of the men on a laptop.'

'I'd suggest taking printed copies,' Brian said. 'It'll be easier for Jasmine to leaf through them.'

'Good point. I'll set the printer going now.'

While the photos were printing, Clare's mobile buzzed in her pocket. Tom. She let it go to voicemail. Too busy just now. The last photo dropped out of the printer and Clare scooped them up and headed out to the car with Kate.

Chapter 25

Kate drove while Clare called the officer on duty at Nat Dryden's bedside. 'Advise him to have a solicitor there this afternoon. Let's say two o'clock? He'll be questioned in connection with possible criminal charges.'

The call made, she sat back and chatted to Kate. 'Tell me about the girl we're going to see.'

'Jasmine Greene. She must be nearly fifteen now,' Kate said. 'In and out of care most of her life. Fostered a couple of times but mostly in residential care. She can be a bit of a handful. Not surprising, really. Mother died of a heroin overdose when she was five or six. Jasmine was found alone with the mother's body. Needles all over the place.'

Clare shook her head at this grim picture. 'Is she likely to co-operate?'

'Yeah, I think so. She's a nice kid, once you scrape away the tough veneer.'

They drove on in silence past fields, slowing down as they entered Cupar. The town was bustling with cars and shoppers but soon the narrow street broadened out and they drove past school and college buildings before reaching farmland again. A few miles on, a flat-roofed modern building in honey-coloured brick appeared. Kate pulled off the road and into a car park. They were buzzed in by a young woman in a Laura Ashley-type dress who Clare thought was probably in her late twenties.

She introduced herself as Miranda. 'Jasmine knows you're coming but I've not explained why.'

Clare thanked her. A young girl with pierced eyebrows was hanging about, twisting a strand of hair in her fingers.

Miranda called her over. 'Can you ask Jasmine to come to my office?'

The girl eyed Clare and Kate, then turned without response and disappeared. Miranda led them into a small office. It was sparsely furnished with a desk, a stack of bucket chairs and a grey metal filing cabinet. The desk was an old L-shaped one with a trio of filing trays at one end and the obligatory computer in the centre. Miranda moved the monitor to the side and set out the chairs. A few minutes later the door opened and a girl in her mid-teens came in, her eyes flicking between the three women. Clare recognised her from the photographs and she felt a lump in her throat. This wasn't just a sulky-faced teenager. This was a girl who was suffering systematic abuse. Right now in 2019. Why the hell was this still happening? She smiled at the girl but the smile wasn't returned.

'Jas,' Miranda began, 'these officers are from St Andrews and would like to ask you some questions. Now, you're not in any trouble and nothing you say will result in anything happening to you. So please be truthful and tell them everything you know.'

Jasmine said nothing but eyed Clare with suspicion. Kate gave her a friendly smile.

'Remember me, Jas?'

Jasmine nodded.

'This is Clare,' Kate went on. 'She's the DI at St Andrews and you can trust her.'

Clare took over. 'Jasmine, we believe you might have been forced into some sexual activity with older men. Now, if that's true then you won't be in any trouble at all. Quite the reverse. We'll give you all the help and support you need. But those men... well, they'll be in a lot of trouble. Do you understand?'

Jasmine eyed Miranda who gave her an encouraging smile.

Jasmine turned back to Clare. 'Yeah.'

'Can I ask if you go out regularly? In the evenings?'

Jasmine looked at Miranda who smiled. 'Go on, Jas.'

'Can I have a fag?'

Miranda laughed. 'Not indoors. You know the rules. Maybe after.'

Jasmine looked back at Clare. 'Thursdays. We go out on Thursdays.'

Miranda frowned. 'But surely that's your gym night, Jas?'

Jasmine wouldn't look at her. 'It was to start with. Then *she* said did we fancy a bit of extra cash. Good money, yeah?'

'She?' Miranda was dumbfounded. 'You don't mean Mrs...'

'Yeah, her. That Jennifer woman.'

Clare looked at Miranda. 'Jennifer?'

'Gilmartin. Jennifer Gilmartin. She takes an interest in the youngsters. She's been so kind. Organising a minibus to take them swimming, to the gym.' She put her hand to her mouth. 'Oh my God. What have we done?'

Clare took out her phone and opened Google. She typed 'Jennifer Gilmartin' into the image search. The first result was a photo of Jennifer and Bruce at a brewers' dinner.

She showed the photo to Jasmine. 'Is that the lady, Jasmine?'

'Yeah. And him. She took us in the minibus and he was there. We did stuff with him. Sex and that.'

The colour drained from Miranda's face. 'Jas, why did you do it? Did you not feel you could come and tell me?'

Jasmine shrugged. 'Dunno. We got money, nice food and that. I've had worse.'

Miranda sank back in her seat, lost for words.

Clare asked Kate to take Jasmine through the photographs and excused herself to call Chris.

'Get over to Jennifer Gilmartin's house and bring her in,' she said. 'Tell her nothing. Just that we need to speak to her in connection with enquiries. She's up to her neck in it.'

When Clare returned to the room Kate had the photographs divided into two piles.

'These are the men Jasmine has identified as taking part in the Thursday evening *parties*, as they were called.'

Clare leafed through them. They were all there, including Edward Collinson. 'Yes,' she said under her breath. 'Jasmine, you are absolutely sure about these photos?'

'Yeah. Been there loads of times.'

'And Jennifer Gilmartin took you in a minibus?'

'Yeah. It's in the countryside so she drove us.'

'Did you notice where you were going?'

'Uh-huh. That castle on the Tayport Road. Mort something. Take you there if you like.'

'You're very observant, Jasmine. Are you sure that's where it was?'

'Oh yeah. I was fostered in Tayport for a bit. Used to pass it in the car. Always wondered what it was like. Dead fancy inside.' She jabbed a finger at the photo of Edward Collinson. 'It's his place. He's loaded!'

Clare tried not to let her excitement show. 'We may need you to give evidence, Jasmine. But it would be by video-link. You wouldn't have to see anyone.' She decided not to tell Jasmine that only two of the men were still alive at this stage.

'Yeah, fine. Can I have that fag now?'

'Just one more thing, Jasmine. Can you tell us who the others were?'

'The other kids?'

'Yes.'

'Yeah. Miranda knows. All of us who went with Jennifer.'

Miranda looked shocked. 'All of you? The boys as well?'

Jasmine shrugged. 'Yeah,' then she said, 'fag?'

Miranda reached into her desk drawer and took out a packet of cigarettes. She took one out and handed it to Jasmine. The girl rose to leave.

'Jasmine, just one thing,' Clare said, 'Please don't mention this to anyone. It's very important this doesn't leak out to the press. If that happened these men could claim they wouldn't have a fair trial. We need to play this by the book, yeah?'

Jasmine nodded and left the room. Miranda looked close to tears.

'She's such a nice lady, Jennifer. I really trusted her...'

—

Clare called DCI Gibson while Kate prepared a statement for Jasmine to sign. 'Just taking a statement, sir,' she said. 'Should be back within the hour. But there's something I need to tell you.'

'Yes?'

Clare told him about Jennifer Gilmartin. 'Chris should be bringing her in any time now. I thought you should know.'

There was an uncomfortable pause before the DCI replied. 'You're sure about this, Inspector?' His voice was hoarse.

'Afraid so, sir. One of the youngsters named her, and the duty officer at the home confirmed Mrs Gilmartin takes a minibus of youngsters out every Thursday. She thought they were being taken to the gym.'

The DCI was about to reply when Clare heard a volley of barking over the phone.

'Is that Chris back with Mrs Gilmartin?' she asked the DCI.

'Hold on,' he said.

Clare waited and a few minutes later she heard his voice again. 'She's gone, dammit. Must have been tipped off. Car gone and a note for the cleaning lady saying she'd be gone for a few weeks and to feed and walk the dog. DS West has brought the dog back.'

'Can I speak to Chris, sir?'

'Just a minute...'

When she heard Chris's voice she spoke quickly. 'Get her car registration to the ANPR database. I want her flagged up as soon as she passes a camera. Who the hell tipped her off?'

'Already done, boss. No idea how she knew, though.'

'Leave it with me.'

Clare rang off and glared at Miranda. 'Is there any way you or anyone else here could have alerted Mrs Gilmartin that we were on our way here?'

'Definitely not. There's only me here today and I didn't tell anyone why you were coming.'

'Any of the kids around when you took Kate's call?'

Miranda shook her head. 'I'm fairly sure they weren't. They would only have heard my side of the conversation anyway.'

Clare's mind was in a whirl. 'What about Jasmine? Could she have phoned her? Misplaced loyalty?'

'I doubt it but I'll give her a shout.'

Jasmine denied it. 'I don't care if she goes to jail. Serves her right. Perv.'

'Phone please, Jas.' Miranda held out her hand.

Jasmine scowled but handed the phone over. 'I didn't call her. You'll see.'

Miranda scrolled to Jasmine's call record. 'Nothing here, although you could have deleted it.'

Clare interrupted. 'Jasmine, we can check your call records with the phone company so, if you did phone Mrs Gilmartin, you might as well tell us now. You won't be in trouble. I just need to know.'

'I didn't call her!' Jasmine stuck her chin out. 'Check all you like.'

Clare nodded. 'Okay. Thanks, Jasmine. We'll be in touch.' She looked at Kate. 'Better get back.'

Kate rose, thanked Miranda and the pair left. As they drove back, Clare ran over the events of the past twelve hours in her head. Who could have alerted Jennifer Gilmartin?

She took out her phone again. 'Chris? Can you get a hold of Jennifer Gilmartin's mobile number please? The boss should have it. I need her call records from the phone company. The last twenty-four hours. Then get phone numbers for Fergus, Nat Dryden and Edward Collinson. Compare them to see if there were any calls or texts between them since Collinson was stopped last night. Top priority. Get the Vice guys to help if there are any spare.'

'Will do. Anything else?'

'Not that I can think of, just now at least. I need to order my thoughts. Any sign of her car?'

'Not yet. But it should turn up.'

'Okay, thanks. With you in twenty minutes.'

As Clare entered the station, Benjy, who had taken up residence in his usual spot on the front desk, leapt off and bounded towards her. She scooped him up, grateful for the welcome, then returned him to his perch on the counter.

'No sign of Jennifer Gilmartin yet, boss,' Chris said. 'The Vice guys are working their way through the phone numbers for us.'

At that, one of them shouted. 'Got a match. Text message just before nine this morning.'

'From?'

'Mobile registered to a Mr Edward Collinson.'

Clare thumped the counter, making Benjy growl. 'Got you, you bastard. Can you print those records out for me, please?'

Five minutes later, Clare was seated in the interview room again with Edward Collinson and his solicitor. She put the sheaf of phone records out on the desk in front of them.

'This document,' she began, indicating the top sheet, 'shows the record of calls and text messages sent from your mobile phone in the last twenty-four hours. You'll see I've highlighted one of the entries.'

Edward Collinson glanced down and feigned an air of disinterest.

Clare moved the page to the side and indicated the next sheet. 'And this one indicates messages received by a mobile phone registered to Mrs Jennifer Gilmartin. Jennifer Gilmartin is married to Bruce Gilmartin, who you said you may have met but did not know.'

The solicitor was looking at his client, a hint of concern on his face. 'May I ask, Inspector, where this is leading?'

'These records show that your client sent a text message to Jennifer Gilmartin this morning just before nine o'clock. If you recall, at nine this morning your client was here on a voluntary basis and would still have had possession of his mobile phone.'

'And?'

'And he sent a text message to a person he is on record as saying he does not know.'

'I'm sure my client must have made an error, Inspector. It's easy to type the wrong number isn't it?'

'Perhaps then Mr Collinson would let us know who he meant to text? Then we can check the number.'

Edward Collinson waved this away. 'With everything that's going on, Inspector, I can't possibly remember. Have you any idea how distressing this whole business has been for me?'

Clare ignored this. She stacked the sheets of paper neatly and put them to one side. Then she looked levelly at Edward Collinson. 'We believe Mrs Gilmartin is involved in procuring youngsters for the purposes of sexual exploitation. We also have a witness who will positively identify you as participating in sexual activities with minors. Repeatedly.'

He snorted. 'Some girl who'd say anything for a packet of fags?'

'What makes you think it's a girl, sir?'

He saw his mistake and tried to rescue the situation. 'Well, it was you who mentioned minors. I just assumed you meant girls…'

Clare rose. 'I can assure you, sir, that the witness was interviewed correctly, in the presence of two police officers and an independent third person, and that your photograph was positively identified from a selection of more than twenty photos. A statement has been taken and we *will* be charging you with offences in relation to that statement. And now, *sir*, perhaps you would like to speak with your solicitor alone.'

–

DCI Gibson was relieved to hear they had enough to charge Edward Collinson. 'He'd have made one hell of a stink if we'd had to let him go.'

'He's as guilty as sin, sir,' said Clare. 'If Nat Dryden also identifies him then we're home and dry. I'll see to it that he goes away for a good long stretch.'

'And Fergus Bain?'

'Struggling with him, to be honest, sir. He's confessed to the murders of Bruce Gilmartin and the professor and the attempted murder of Pam last night. But I doubt we'll get him on conspiracy to murder the other two unless we can find the accomplice. We could try, but I'm not convinced the fiscal would take it to court. Even then we might not get a conviction. Might be the best we can do.'

'What about the accomplice? Any luck with Garthley House?'

'Chris was working on it but he left off to go over to the Gilmartins'. Connor, Steve and Phil are here now, though, and in touch with Social Work. It won't be a quick job but they'll keep at it till we get a result. Or not...'

'And Mr Dryden?'

'I've sent a message to him to have a solicitor there at two this afternoon so we can take a formal statement. Chris will come with me.'

'Okay, Inspector. Let me know if you have any problems.'

Clare hesitated. 'You know, sir, speaking to Fergus about his own experiences at the home – I kind of understand his actions. It's pretty desperate stuff. He must be so damaged.'

'We can't think like that, Inspector. We're here to prosecute where we see illegality. The rest is up to the courts.'

'I suppose.' Clare left his office went to the incident room. It was empty and she sat down for a minute. She was bone tired and her ears hurt. She longed for this investigation to be over.

'Not there yet, though,' she said to herself.

Chris poked his head round the door.

'We're due up at Ninewells in just over an hour to see Nat Dryden. Fancy a quick bite of lunch first?'

'That's an excellent idea, DS West.'

'I've been known to have them.'

–

Nat Dryden was sitting up in a chair when Clare and Chris entered. Clare tried to avoid looking at the space where his leg would have been, smiling instead at a smart woman in a dark suit.

'My solicitor,' said Nat. 'Valerie Grimmond.'

Clare shook hands with the solicitor then sat down beside the bed. She looked at Nat and her mind involuntarily flicked back to the photos he had appeared in. She thought of Jasmine, stony-faced, apparently immune to her experiences. Only concerned about getting a fag from Miranda. And this shadow of a man sitting before her, one leg missing, bruised, battered and hooked up to monitors – this man was one of Jasmine's abusers. *Remember that, Clare. Remember what he's done.* And then she thought of Fergus. His life in ruins. Ruined from the day he first entered Garthley House. And these men – men like Nat with their perverse appetites – these men were ruining more lives every single day; boys like Fergus, girls like Jasmine. She looked at him and fought back the contempt she felt. This interview was vital. She mustn't blow it.

'Nat,' she began, 'I'm going to caution and charge you formally today. I'll be taping this interview. If, at any time,

314

you feel unwell or need to take a break we'll be happy to do so. I would also say that any assistance you can give us will be noted, should you be sentenced in court.'

Nat glanced at his solicitor, who said, 'That's fine, Inspector. Please go ahead.'

The interview was as short as Clare could make it. Nat understood the charges relating to sexual conduct with a minor and, on the advice of his solicitor, made no response. But when Clare asked him to identify the other men present at the parties, he said he couldn't help.

'We were all known by numbers. The idea was the less we knew about each other the safer the whole thing would be. I was number three. Maybe the others knew names but I didn't.'

Clare removed a sheaf of photos from her bag and asked if Nat could identify any of the men in them. He quickly identified Bruce Gilmartin.

'He was number four,' he said, handing back the photo.

And when he was shown the photo of Andy Robb he identified him as number five. Predictably, the professor was number two. Clare then handed him the photo of Edward Collinson. Her palms were damp. So much was riding on this. They had Jasmine's evidence but there was no way of telling how she might react to questions from a skilled defence advocate.

Nat looked long and hard at the photo.

He doesn't know him. Of all the photos we needed a positive ID on, he doesn't know this one.

After some moments, he handed back the photo and met her gaze. He didn't speak for a few seconds then he cleared his throat and began. 'He was the one who worried me. I mean, *really* worried me. The rest of us, we

315

were all up for a bit of sex with the girls. I mean, they were under age, but not by so much. Hard to tell these days with some of them. I didn't want the really young ones. Fourteen, fifteen – that was okay. But him... He liked them *really* young. Boys and girls.'

Clare looked levelly at him. 'Nat, for the tape, can you please say if you can identify the man in this photo? I am showing Mr Dryden photo number forty-five.'

'Absolutely. This man owned the house where we met. The house was between Tayport and St Mike's junction. He was at all the parties, took photos and he engaged fully in sex with minors. The younger the better.'

Nat's hands were shaking. Clare looked at his solicitor. The colour had drained from her face.

The solicitor cleared her throat. 'Perhaps, Inspector, you have all you need? I think my client should rest now.'

Clare nodded. 'Thank you, Mr Dryden. You have helped us a great deal.'

Nat looked away, drawing a hand across his eyes. Clare rose from her seat and nodded at Chris to follow her. He was staring at Nat and she tugged his sleeve. 'Come on, Chris. Let's get out of here. Let's get some fresh air.'

–

They drove back to St Andrews in silence. At length, Chris said, 'Do you think you ever get used to that? Dealing with folk like him?'

'Probably not.'

They lapsed into silence again.

Then Clare said, 'We need to get statements from the other girls over at the home.' She glanced at Chris. 'I'll get Vice to do it. Think we've both had enough for one day.'

Her phone rang.

'See who that is, would you?' she said to Chris.

'Don't recognise the number.'

'Let it go to voicemail. Whatever it is, it'll keep.'

They were driving over the Tay Road Bridge when the phone rang again.

'It's Jim,' Chris said.

'Take it, would you?'

Chris answered the call and after a few minutes hung up.

'Jennifer Gilmartin's car popped up on the M90 heading for the Queensferry Crossing.'

'Airport?'

'Possibly. We'll know soon. She'll be pinging every ANPR on the motorway.'

'Notify traffic in Edinburgh. We want her stopped. Also, get on to the airport. Glasgow airport too. If she tries to get through passport control they can pick her up. And notify car hire companies at both airports. She's not daft so let's try to cover all possible options.'

Chapter 26

Jennifer Gilmartin's car was found an hour later at Ingliston Park and Ride, a mile or so from the airport.

'It's possible she's taken a taxi into town,' Jim told Clare and Chris, 'but we reckon she's probably taken the tram to the airport. If we're right, she'll turn up at a check-in desk before long.'

'Or car hire,' Clare said.

'That too. They've all been notified. Name and photo.'

They didn't have long to wait.

'She's checked in for a flight to the Dominican Republic,' Jim advised. 'Leaves in an hour. The Edinburgh lads are on their way to pick her up. They'll call when they have her in custody.'

'Make sure they caution her. We don't want any slip-ups.'

'Will do, Clare.'

And suddenly there was nothing to do.

Fergus Bain had been charged with murder, attempted murder and with Clare's abduction. Edward Collinson had been charged with sexually assaulting Jasmine Greene, with other charges to follow once the statements had come back from the Vice cops. It was likely that Jennifer Gilmartin would be charged with causing children to participate in sexual activity and Clare felt confident that none of them would see the outside of a cell any time soon. There was a lot of paperwork ahead but somehow she felt disinclined to make a start.

'Think I'll take Benjy for a walk,' she said. Chris nodded in response and she lifted her jacket and Benjy's lead from the coat stand in the corner. The dog, seeing his familiar red lead, leapt off the counter and sat down at her feet, waiting for the lead to be attached.

It was a lovely May afternoon. Mild and sunny with just a bit of a breeze. She headed out of the station and began walking along Tom Morris Drive. Whether by design or accident, she found herself walking up the curiously named Shoolbraids in the direction of Scooniehill Road. She wondered idly if Angela Robb would be at home. She would have to be told about the arrests. Billy Dodds' Qashqai was parked outside. Clare rang the bell. Angela's face fell when she saw it was Clare, but then she spotted Benjy and bent to welcome him. Amazing what the sight of a dog could do to people's moods.

'You'd better come in,' she said, stepping back to admit Clare and Benjy.

Billy Dodds was watching *Countdown* and he pressed the mute button when Clare entered. Benjy leapt up on the settee and Clare tugged at his lead to pull him off.

'Leave him,' Angela said. 'He's fine. Sit yourself down. Want a coffee?'

Clare shook her head and sat beside Benjy. 'I won't keep you. I just wanted you to know that we've made some arrests in connection with Andy's death.'

'Oh aye?' Billy responded. Angela said nothing.

'I'm afraid we can't give you any details at the moment. They'll be up in court on Monday and there will be a statement for the press, but I thought you'd like to know before it's made public.'

'Thanks. Appreciate it.'

'And perhaps you could let the family know? Andy's sister and so on.'

'Yeah. I'll tell them.'

'There's something else I have to tell you.'

'Aye?'

'We believe Andy was targeted, among others, because he was engaged in… sexual activity with minors. Under sixteens, I mean.'

Billy was shaking his head. Angela said nothing.

'We'll try to keep the detail to the minimum. For the press, I mean. But it's bound to come out. It always does.'

Angela found her voice. 'He always was one for the girls, ye know. But I didn't think…'

'I know. It's hard to fathom,' Clare said. 'I'm sorry to bring you such awful news.'

She rose and Benjy leapt off the settee after her. 'I'll leave you now. If there's anything else, I'll be back in touch.'

Billy showed Clare to the door. 'I'll look after her, Inspector. Dinnae worry.'

She smiled and left them to digest the news. She stood outside, trying to work out which way to go. Vicky Gallagher deserved to be told as well, but Clare couldn't face it. Not after the day she'd had, to say nothing of the events of the previous night. The lack of sleep, the constant buzzing in her ears – it was all catching her up. Angela had shown little emotion but Clare knew Vicky's reaction would be a whole lot different. She might even send Chris and Sara to break the news.

'Come on,' she said to Benjy. 'Back to the station. We have Jennifer Gilmartin to interview.'

—

Clare's phone was ringing as she pulled into the station car park. 'Just coming,' she said, jumping out and locking the car. She walked into the station and then she saw Chris's face.

'What?'

'Jennifer. She's given them the slip. Never went through airport security. She checked in a suitcase but we don't know where she went after that.'

'And?'

'Flight's gone. The case was taken off the plane when she didn't board.'

'Did they open it?'

'Yeah. Wasn't even locked. Full of men's clothes. Looks like we've lost her.'

Clare swore under her breath. She saw they were waiting for her to speak. 'Right,' she said. 'Get onto the press office. I want her photo on the news, on our Facebook page, alert all railway stations, wanted in connection with serious crimes. No details, mind.'

Chris went off to call the press office and Clare sought out the DCI.

'Have you any idea where she might have gone, sir?' she asked.

He shook his head. 'Not that I can think. No family round here that I can recall, and I don't really know who her friends are.'

'Can you authorise a trace of her mobile phone?' Clare asked. 'Might help us pin down where she's heading.'

'You set it up and I'll authorise it.'

Chris met her at the office door. 'Press office are on it. What else?'

'I need her mobile phone tracked. See which masts she's pinging. The DCI will authorise it.'

'Okay, Clare. Anything else?'

'No, do that and I'll phone Glasgow airport. She might have taken a taxi or even a train.'

–

Chris put the phone down. 'Looks like you're right. She's picking up all the phone masts along the M8 towards Glasgow airport.'

'Must be in a taxi,' Clare surmised. 'Right, I want plain-clothes officers at the airport. Hanging round the taxi ranks. If she sees uniforms she might tell the driver to carry on. Make sure every check-in desk and security guard has her photo. I don't want her getting away a second time.'

As Clare had suspected, the phone was tracked to Glasgow airport but, half an hour after she pinged the closest mast there was still no sign of her.

'So she's still in or around the airport,' Clare said. 'Why haven't they spotted her?'

'Must have slipped past our guys,' Chris said.

'How the hell?'

'Clare, it's easily done. Wait for a bus coming in from the long-stay parking and mingle with the passengers. Engage one of them in conversation as you go through the door.'

'Yeah, I suppose. Passport Control alerted?'

'Yeah. Should get her okay this time. They know to delay her at the check-in desk.'

Clare's brow creased. 'Thing is, Chris, if she takes a domestic flight...'

'She doesn't need a passport. Dammit.'

'Right. Get back onto the airport and ask them for passenger lists for all domestic flights going out for the rest of today. If that turns up nothing we'll try tomorrow morning. Let's hope she's booked onto one of them.'

—

It took the airport half an hour to find her.

'Booked on the five thirty flight to Luton,' Chris said. 'And this time she's gone through security.'

'Please tell me they're picking her up?'

'Should be doing that right now,' Chris said. 'Just waiting to hear.'

They sat round the station, waiting anxiously. No one could settle to anything so Clare phoned for a pizza delivery. As the delivery man struggled through the door with half a dozen boxes the phone rang. Chris snatched it up, listened for a few minutes then gave them the thumbs up.

'Got her?' Clare asked when he had finished the call.

'Yup.'

A cheer went up around the room and the pizza man took a bow. Clare handed him her credit card and he produced his card reader. She tapped in her number then checked her watch. 'I doubt they'll be here much before half seven,' she said. 'Let's eat and relax for a bit. We'll need our wits about us when she arrives.'

The atmosphere in the station had lifted. Chris sat, chatting to Sara, doubtless enjoying the fact that Clare had sent the Edinburgh lads home. Clare watched them for a few minutes. Chris was laying the charm on thickly and Sara didn't seem to mind. She wondered if she was watching the start of something. Benjy had been driven crazy by the aroma of pizza. Clare asked Gillian to go out and buy him some dried dog food while she gathered her thoughts. It was going to be a long night.

She carried the remains of her pizza into one of the interview rooms and closed the door. She'd have to be well prepared for Jennifer Gilmartin's interview. Clare knew now that she had the DCI's full backing but she was still oddly nervous about it. Perhaps it was the closeness they had shared in Jennifer's kitchen. That time when she had said to Clare she doubted they would meet again. Had she been planning to do a runner, even then? Realising what was happening to the five men, she must have known the police would find their way back to her door, eventually. Or was it the text message from Edward Collinson that had tipped her off? It didn't much matter now but Clare knew she'd have to have her wits about her.

–

Jennifer Gilmartin arrived at the station shortly after her solicitor. From the set of her jaw, Clare could see that Jennifer had no intention of co-operating. She showed the pair into an interview room and left them to speak for a few minutes. The DCI, she noticed, was keeping well out of the way and she had asked him to keep Benjy in her office.

'I don't want any distractions,' she said, handing over the lead and he agreed. After consulting with Jennifer, the solicitor told Clare her client would exercise her right to silence. Clare nodded at this and began by cautioning Jennifer under the Sexual Offences Act.

Jennifer made no reply, staring at the wall above Clare's head. Clare went on.

'I understand you have been involved with children in residential homes,' she said, 'and that you've taken them on outings. In a minibus.'

Jennifer said nothing.

'Mrs Gilmartin, we have a witness who will testify that you took ten children out in a minibus each Thursday evening. Initially, these outings were to gyms and swimming pools. Is that correct?'

Jennifer shrugged and began examining her manicured nails. Clare carried on.

'We have another witness who has given us a signed statement asserting that these outings changed at some point; that, instead of visiting sports centres, you drove the children to Mortaine Castle, near Tayport. Is that correct?'

'A witness?' Jennifer said, suddenly, her eyes burning. 'You mean one of those kids? You've dragged me here, all the way from Glasgow airport on the word of some kids from a sink-estate?' She laughed, and leaned across the table, her face close to Clare's. 'Oh Clare – you'll have to do an awful lot better than that.'

Clare caught a whiff of her perfume. Not one she recognised. She held Jennifer's gaze. 'Do you deny it?'

'Absolutely. If you think for one minute a court would believe the likes of Jasmine Greene...'

'You admit you know Jasmine, then?'

Jennifer sat back in her seat. 'Of course I know her. And I know what she is. What they all are. Little whores. Do anything for a packet of fags, that lot. Well, whatever they've told you, it's a pack of lies.'

Jennifer's solicitor laid a hand on her arm and she sat back again.

'What sort of thing might they do for a packet of fags?' Clare asked.

Jennifer shrugged.

'You called them,' Clare hesitated, 'little whores.' She looked directly at Jennifer. 'Why did you use that term?'

'What would you call them?' she snapped.

'I'd call them children.'

'That just shows how little you know,' she said. 'My father, in case you are unaware, was a high court judge. Saw all sorts. Many a good man brought down by lying, scheming little tarts. Boys and girls. Do you think for a minute I had to force any of these kids? That they didn't do it willingly?'

Again the solicitor put his hand on Jennifer's arm but she shrugged it off. Something had snapped within her and she was past reason now.

Clare said, 'Mrs Gilmartin, what would you say if I told you that the man who murdered your husband had himself been systematically abused as a child? That he lived daily with the physical and psychological consequences of what he had endured? What is your reaction to that?'

Jennifer's eyes narrowed. 'I'd say, Clare, that it was a trendy excuse these days. All this bloody *Me Too*, crap. It's complete rubbish. Face it. Everyone likes sex. You like it – I like it! If we didn't, mankind would have died out long ago.'

Clare shook her head. 'This wasn't sex. It was abuse. How could you allow your husband – your own husband – to participate in these acts? How could you share your life – share your bed – with a man like that? Dammit, you drove the children there yourself!'

Jennifer laughed. 'Oh Clare. Don't be so high-minded. Bruce had his appetites. I had mine.'

'You had affairs?'

Jennifer sat back and crossed her legs. 'Of course. Mine happened to be with consenting adults. But Bruce – well his tastes were different, shall we say.'

'And you didn't mind? You didn't mind helping him to abuse minors?'

'My goodness, Clare. You've a lot to learn about men.'

Clare made an effort to control her voice. 'Why don't you educate me.'

In a further attempt to quiet his client the solicitor interjected 'Mrs Gilmartin, I must advise—'

Jennifer's hand came up to silence him and a smile crossed her face. 'Clare, It's like this. Bruce, you know, was a good businessman. He knew about brewing and he knew how to make it pay. That meant we had a nice life.' She fingered a diamond engagement ring, as if to prove the point. 'You've seen the house. Holidays too. Money for the finer things, you know.' She brushed a speck of dust from her jacket. 'We had standing. When we went places. On Bruce's arm, I was someone.'

'And?'

'And – he liked young girls.' She stopped for a moment, then went on. 'He was rather stupid about it. There was an incident, you see. In a public lavatory.' She shook her head.

'You didn't think of leaving him?' Clare asked.

Jennifer looked surprised. 'Certainly not. I had far too much invested in my marriage. I wasn't about to throw it all away because Bruce couldn't keep his hands off a few young girls.'

'And so?'

Jennifer met Clare's eyes. 'And so, I decided to manage it for him.'

Clare stared. 'Manage it?'

'Indeed. I knew about the place in Cupar. I started taking the youngsters out on Thursdays. The gym, swimming, bowling sometimes.'

'A hell of a risk, surely,' Chris said. 'What if one of them had told the staff?'

Jennifer laughed. 'Oh sergeant. Have you forgotten what it's like to be a teenager? Kids love the idea of sex. Talking about it, boasting about it, even if they've no experience. I just casually mentioned STDs one night and that got them talking. Full of it, they were. Once I dangled the idea they didn't take much persuading. Amazing what they'll do for a pizza and a few quid.'

Clare shook her head. 'So, you are saying that you arranged these evenings to satisfy your husband's appetite for sex with minors? To keep him from being caught elsewhere?'

Jennifer shrugged. 'That's about the size of it.'

'And the other men?'

'That was Bruce's idea. It made sense too. They paid. I gave the kids a few quid to keep them quiet and tucked the rest away for a rainy day.' She smiled again. 'Win win, really.'

Clare could feel anger rising and she fought to control her voice. 'And that website – the Playroom?'

'Oh it's good, isn't it? I was so pleased with how it turned out. Amazing what you can learn online.'

Clare could hold back no longer. 'You're – despicable. Utterly contemptible.'

Jennifer's face darkened and she leaned across the table. 'Well, at least I haven't shot anyone, Clare!'

Clare started towards her but Chris held her back. 'She's not worth it, boss.'

Clare scraped back her chair, her face scarlet. 'Interview terminated at—' she glanced at the wall clock, '—eight thirty pm.' She switched off the machine and turned to leave, Chris at her back.

As they reached the door, Jennifer called, 'I suppose a decent cup of tea's out of the question? This stuff's like dishwater.'

—

'She's been charged and she'll be up in court on Monday, along with the others,' Clare told the DCI after Jennifer had left the station.

'How was she?'

Clare's jaw was clenched. 'If you'll pardon me, sir, she's a fucking psycho. All grace and charm on the surface but she's organised a paedophile ring to keep her marriage together. To begin with she wasn't even going to say anything. Then she completely flipped. Went off on a rant about these kids being whores and how the *Me Too* movement was a lot of crap. It's the most bizarre interview I've ever done.'

'Think she should see a psychologist?' the DCI asked.

Clare spread her hands. 'I'm no expert. But if I was her defence solicitor I'd probably have her examined. She sounded quite unbalanced in there.'

'I agree,' Chris said. 'But I think she's more than aware of what she's done. She's just not sorry.'

The DCI sat back in his seat. 'You think you know someone...'

Clare didn't know how to respond to that. Instead, she said, 'We'll have to go through the charges with a fine-toothed comb. I'd bet both Collinson and Jennifer Gilmartin will hire the best legal teams money can buy.'

The DCI nodded. 'Any news on Fergus Bain's accomplice?'

'Not so far. Connor, Steve and Phil were chasing up all the girls who were at Garthley House at the same time as Fergus, even for a few weeks, but it's a long job. I've sent them home now anyway. Get a fresh start in the morning.'

The DCI looked at Chris. 'You get off home too, son. I just need a word with the Inspector.'

Chris smiled. 'Thanks, sir. Just a couple of things to finish up then I'll get away. See you in the morning, Clare.'

When he had closed the door, the DCI said, 'You look tired, Clare. Last night catching up with you?'

He had called her Clare. Miracles did happen.

'I'm okay, sir. Just been a busy few days. And, to be honest, I'm angry with myself. Angry that I didn't suss Jennifer out when I spoke to her before. I've always trusted my instincts but they let me down this time. Maybe I'm losing my touch...'

DCI Gibson shook his head. 'Clare, she pulled the wool over everyone's eyes. The social worker, me – for

God's sake! I've known the woman twenty years and I had no idea.'

'Suppose. I'm just annoyed with myself.'

'Stop that now,' he said. 'You've done a bloody good job here. I admit I had my doubts but you've proved me wrong. I'd be happy to work with you any time.'

It really was Miracle Season, Clare thought. 'Thanks, sir.'

'Ach, call me Al. Everyone else does. Anyway, you've broken the back of this case,' he went on. 'And a paedophile ring, to boot. It's getting late now. I think you should go home and get some sleep. We'll sort the paperwork out tomorrow, Sunday at worst. And, after Sunday, I'll be back in Edinburgh. Give you your office back.'

This was possibly the best news she'd heard all day. She headed for the door, stopping only to pick up Benjy's lead.

'Night all,' she called and stepped out into cool May evening. The sun had gone behind clouds and it looked as if there might be rain overnight. She smiled at an elderly woman making her way across the car park as she unlocked her car.

She opened the door for Benjy. He climbed in and onto the passenger seat where he sat looking out of the window. And she very nearly made it. She nearly managed to drive out of the car park and go home for a relaxing evening. But, as she inserted the key and started the engine, the door of the station opened and Chris motioned to her to come back inside.

Chapter 27

'I've put her in Interview Room Two,' Chris said. 'The DCI wants to sit in.'

Clare waved Benjy back towards the counter and he jumped up, taking his usual place. 'Do we know who she is?' she asked Chris.

'Name's Rena Bishop. Says she's Fergus Bain's aunt.'

'The friend of his gran's? The one who isn't a real aunt?'

'Think so.'

'Then I'd better see her.'

Chris put a hand on her arm, to stop her. 'There's something else though.'

'What?'

'She's missing the tip of the middle finger on one hand.'

Clare, DCI Gibson and Chris squeezed into the interview room and sat in front of the desk. On the other side sat the elderly woman Clare had seen crossing the car park as she left the station a few minutes earlier. Clare glanced at the woman's short, middle finger. After all their legwork, Chris, the Edinburgh lads – even some of the Vice cops – poring over Social Work records for hours, all that work, then this. The owner of the fingerprints simply walks into the station and presents herself. It beggared belief.

Clare regarded her with some interest. She looked to be in her seventies and had the bearing of an elderly schoolmistress. Her silver hair was lightly permed and her face, while lined with age, was alert. She was spare, as if her bones would snap with the slightest touch. She sat, ramrod-straight in her chair, her hands folded in front of her.

Clare cleared her throat and began.

'Mrs Bishop, I am Detective Inspector Clare Mackay. This is Detective Chief Inspector Gibson and this gentleman is Detective Sergeant Chris West. I understand you wish to make a statement.'

'First of all, Inspector, it is Miss Bishop. Miss Rena Bishop.'

'My apologies, Miss Bishop. Perhaps you could tell us what you would like to say?'

'I wish to confess to three murders and to one attempted murder.'

Clare looked at Chris and the DCI but before she could speak Miss Bishop spoke again.

'I killed all of them,' she went on. 'The chap at the wedding, then that brewery man...'

Clare interrupted her. 'Miss Bishop, before we go any further, I need to caution you formally and I strongly suggest you have a solicitor present.'

'I assure you, Detective Inspector, I have no need of a solicitor.'

'Nevertheless, I would like you to have the duty solicitor at least, if you don't have one of your own.'

She unfolded her hands and began twisting a ring on her finger. 'Very well. If you insist, I'll write down my solicitor's details. But please note I do not intend to contradict anything I have just said.'

Rena Bishop's solicitor arrived half an hour later. Clare asked Chris and DCI Gibson to stay and emphasised that if Rena felt unwell at any time the interview could be suspended.

'I am perfectly well, Detective Inspector,' she snapped. 'I simply wish to have this over and done with.'

Clare nodded. She went through the usual preamble for the tape, then cautioned Rena who replied that she understood the caution. Clare then asked what she was confessing to and Rena reeled off the murders of Andy Robb, Bruce Gilmartin, Bertram Harris and the attempted murder of Nat Dryden. She was precise about dates and times, locations, the numbered cards placed on the victims' chests; in fact, she was accurate in everything she said.

'Miss Bishop,' Chris began with a smile, 'we found some footprints at the murder sites. Would I be correct in guessing you take a size four or five in a shoe? You have quite a slim foot, I think.'

The first flicker of doubt passed across her eyes. Brief and then it was gone. But it didn't escape their notice.

'Sometimes it gets muddy,' she said, 'and I have larger boots you see. Men's boots. Keep them in the Land Rover.'

'And did you use these boots at any of the crime scenes?'

Her gaze was once again steely. 'I may have done.'

'Can you recall which?' Chris persisted.

'The brewery one. The chap Gilmartin.'

'So, after running Mr Gilmartin over, you climbed down from the vehicle, wearing the larger boots.'

'That is correct.'

Chris paused for a moment. 'The thing is, Miss Bishop, that the Gilmartins' drive was gravel. And there was no rain the night Mr Gilmartin was run over, or the day before. So, the drive would not have been muddy and there would have been no need for the large boots. We didn't actually find any footprints that night. Furthermore, we already have a suspect in custody who has confessed to the murders of Bruce Gilmartin and Bertram Harris. So I'm afraid your statement is untrue.'

'Fergus did none of them,' she said. 'He's trying to protect me.'

'I didn't mention any names,' Clare said, watching Rena carefully.

They waited for a response. Rena Bishop pursed her lips and her solicitor leaned forward. 'I think, officers, I should like to consult privately with my client.'

The three of them rose and left Rena and her solicitor to speak.

'What do you make of that?' Clare asked the DCI.

'At a rough guess I'd say she wants to spare Fergus prison. She knows what he's been through and wants to take the blame.'

'But she must know he wouldn't let her do that. He wouldn't tell us anything about his accomplice. I'm not even sure I believe her.'

The DCI looked across the room. Rena Bishop's solicitor was hovering. 'See what he says and let me know if there are any problems. I'll leave you to it.'

The solicitor seemed hesitant then spoke. 'It's an… unusual situation, Inspector. Normally I wouldn't be speaking to you like this but…'

'You don't believe her either?'

He shook his head. 'But she insists on signing a confession to three murders and to one attempted murder.'

'Any idea why?'

'Not really, other than…' he seemed reluctant to continue.

'Could she be protecting someone?'

'I think so. I really should not be telling you this but I'm concerned if I don't that a miscarriage of justice may occur.'

'Go on,' Clare said.

'Miss Bishop – she's very fond of the grandson of a close friend. Her friend died some years ago and Miss Bishop has taken an interest in the lad. It seems that he had a difficult time when he was in a children's home. She harbours some regrets that she wasn't able to help him. I think this is her way of making it up to him.'

Clare considered. 'You do know that we can't allow that to happen? We have to prosecute those we believe are guilty. It's up to the courts after that to decide what happens to them.'

'Of course,' the solicitor said. 'I just thought you should know. I'm as keen as you that my client shouldn't confess to a crime she has not committed.'

Clare stood thinking for a minute then said, 'I'd like to have her examined by a doctor. To assess her capacity to plead.'

'She won't like it.'

'No, she won't.'

336

Rena Bishop was indeed outraged at the idea of being examined by a doctor. 'I am in no need of a psychiatrist, I assure you, Detective Inspector. I am fully in charge of my faculties.'

'Miss Bishop, you have voluntarily walked into a police station and confessed to the most serious of crimes. I would be failing in my duty of care to you if I didn't ascertain that you are competent to make such a statement.'

She made no reply to this.

It was growing late now but the doctor agreed to come out. He arrived shortly afterwards and Clare left him to his patient.

Twenty-five minutes later the doctor emerged. Clare called the DCI and Chris to hear his thoughts.

'A tough cookie,' he observed. 'She only agreed to co-operate when I hinted at the possibility of her being detained under the Mental Health Act.'

'And what's your view, doctor?'

'Mentally, she's as sound as a bell. If you want a specialist to look at her it'll take longer but I very much doubt she'll be found unfit to plead.'

The DCI nodded. 'Anything else?'

The doctor hesitated. 'If what she says is true then she won't be with us very much longer.'

'Meaning?'

'After I concluded the examination of her mental capacity I asked a few questions about her general health and she came right out with it. She has an inoperable tumour and expects to live no longer than six months.'

The DCI stared. 'Do you believe her?'

'Frankly, yes. She doesn't look well and, given her age, it's not particularly surprising. But you'll be able to confirm this with her GP. She's given me the details.'

Clare took the note with Rena's GP's details and thanked the doctor. When he had left the station, she turned to Chris and the DCI. 'Chris, get on to her GP and find out if she's telling the truth about having six months to live. Then we'll get her fingerprints done and see if she matches the white cards. We'll remand her in custody while we wait for the results of the prints. If they match the white cards, I'll charge her with the murder of Andy Robb and the attempted murder of Nat Dryden.'

The DCI frowned. 'Do you still think she's lying, Inspector? About carrying out all the attacks?'

'I'm sure of it, sir. I think she probably did the two that Fergus has alibis for – Andy Robb and Nat Dryden. But I reckon Fergus did the others – Bruce Gilmartin and Professor Harris and we have his signed confession.' Clare put a hand to her ear which was now buzzing loudly, a gesture that didn't go unnoticed.

'You get away,' the DCI said to her. 'Young Chris and I will sort out Rena Bishop.'

A sharp bark alerted Clare to the fact that Benjy was still there. She eyed him and Benjy eyed her back.

'Go on,' Chris said. 'Sounds like the pair of you need to get home.'

Clare smiled at Chris and the DCI. 'Thanks guys. I appreciate it.' She turned to Benjy again who cocked an ear. 'Okay,' she said, and he leapt off the counter and ran towards her.

'I'll take this young man home,' she said. 'And, unless anything desperately urgent comes up, I'm taking tomorrow off to go and see my sister and my nephew.'

DCI Gibson flashed a rare smile. 'Sounds like a good idea, Clare. You too, DS West. We'll sort everything out on Sunday morning. Let's say ten o'clock.'

–

This time, Clare made it home without being called back. Benjy trotted round her feet and she realised he was probably hungry. Fortunately, she still had some of the dog food left and she poured a generous helping and some water into the ice cream tubs. Benjy gobbled the food up greedily and Clare's thoughts turned to her own evening meal. The pizza was a distant memory now but it was late and she was too damned tired to cook. She went to the fridge and took out a bottle of rosé wine and a tub of humous, which she carried to the front room. There, she flopped onto the settee.

She looked around the room. It had been an easy house to move into a couple of months ago when she'd upped sticks from Glasgow, but it wasn't really for her. A bit too modern and soulless. Her mind wandered to that cottage along the road from Fergus. She vaguely recalled seeing a sign at the entrance. Daisy Cottage, or something like that. She would really like to have a proper look round. She checked her watch. The estate agents had closed hours ago but perhaps she would call them in the morning and arrange a viewing for next week. In fact, if she called them now and left a voicemail – then she remembered the phone call she had ignored.

She fished her mobile phone out of her bag and saw that she had four voicemail messages. She switched her phone to speaker, clicked to start playing the messages and uncorked the wine, pouring herself a glass.

The first was from Tom. Asking her to call him. Hoping she was okay and not too busy with the investigation. She smiled. If only he knew what had happened in the past twenty-four hours. He'd be flapping round her like a mother hen. 'Thank the Lord he doesn't know,' she muttered, taking a glug of wine.

The next message was from her sister Judith asking if she was free at the weekend.

'Baby James would love to see his Aunty Clare,' her sister's voice said.

'And Aunty Clare would love that too,' Clare said to her phone.

Realising she had brought nothing to dip in the humous, and that she was too tired to go and fetch some tortilla chips, she stuck a finger in the tub and scooped as much as she could with her fingertip.

'And I don't even care,' she told Benjy, as the next message clicked on.

'Oh hello, Inspector. Geoffrey Dark here. Just to say it was nice to meet you and I hope I was able to help. And – well – I'm back in Dundee next week, lecturing. Evening this time. Perhaps if you're free, you'd like to come along? We could meet first for a drink and I could explain a bit about it. You have my number so, it would be lovely to hear from you. Bye, then.'

Clare thought back to the tall figure in dark jeans and the blue Oxford shirt. The cabinetmaker turned sculpture expert. She thought his lecture might very well turn out to be her thing. And maybe – just maybe – he would turn out to be her thing too. Perhaps she could ask him to look round Daisy Cottage with her. An expert eye, so to speak. A smile played on her lips and she clicked to save the message.

And then the final message began to play.

'Clare? It's Drew Walsh here. I was hoping to speak to you, but you're probably still tied up with this investigation. Anyway, I just wanted to let you know about Pam Cassidy. Spoke to her this morning and the upshot is she's withdrawing the statement she gave to the Ritchies' solicitor. She won't be testifying against you if their private prosecution comes to court, which it probably won't now. I think she was their only witness. Anyway, I thought you'd like to know. That's all. Good work last night. Remember, if you ever want to come back to armed response, just let me know. Okay – well, bye for now, Clare. Take care.'

Clare let her phone fall to the floor. Suddenly, she was outstandingly tired. The events of the previous night flashed before her eyes. Fergus in that kitchen. His gun inches from her. The split-second decision to tackle him to the floor and the gun going off. The armed officer's eyes beneath the balaclava. The eyes that became Pam's face. Pam, whose life she had probably saved by flooring Fergus before he could fire through the door. And now Pam was returning the favour.

It changed nothing. Yes, the private prosecution against her would probably be abandoned now. But she had still shot and killed Francis Ritchie, mistaking his replica for a real gun. A mistake she would have to live with.

That would never go away.

She reached down for her phone and dialled her sister's number. 'Jude? Hiya. I'd love to come to see my nephew tomorrow if that's okay. I could do with a day off.'

Her sister was delighted. 'Oh, Clare. That would be lovely. Will you stay?'

'Not this time, Jude. I've to be in work on Sunday. But maybe I could bring my new lodger? He's called Benjy...'

Acknowledgements

The crime-writing community is endlessly kind and supportive and I must thank Claire MacLeary, Dawn Geddes and the remarkable Ray Banks for their help and encouragement in the early days of this book. Thanks also to my dear friends David Murtagh and Ruth Darbyshire who ploughed manfully through the early drafts.

For technical information I cannot thank my brothers, Iain, Stuart and Kenneth and good friends Alan Rankin and Richard Renwick enough. They fielded endless questions from me with seemingly inexhaustible patience. Any errors and inaccuracies in these matters are entirely mine.

I was so lucky that Diane Banks at Northbank Talent Management liked the manuscript for *See Them Run* and that she placed me with my incredible agent Hannah Weatherill who has made this whole process such a thrill. I'm also so grateful to my amazing editor Louise Cullen whose insight and skill has helped me craft a better book.

I must apologise to the good folk of St Andrews, Strathkinness and the surrounding area for taking some liberties with this most beautiful part of Scotland. I hope they will forgive the occasional geographical inaccuracy and the worrying body count! Likewise, to Police Scotland whose procedures I have tweaked for literary convenience.

Finally, to my wonderful children, Ally, Euan and Alicia, and to Peter, my long-suffering other half: thank you for bearing with me and for believing in me. Without your love and patience, DI Clare Mackay would still be a vague idea.

Do you love crime fiction and are always on the lookout for brilliant authors?

Canelo Crime is home to some of the most exciting novels around. Thousands of readers are already enjoying our compulsive stories. Are you ready to find your new favourite writer?

Find out more and sign up to our newsletter at
canelocrime.com